*To the memory of the late Vera Grace Clarke (née Taverner)*
*A lovely person and a wonderful mum*

# IRREFUTABLE EVIDENCE

A Cotton & Silk Thriller

---

DAVID GEORGE CLARKE

Gupole Publications

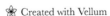 Created with Vellum

# Books by David George Clarke

## The RareTraits Trilogy

Rare Traits

Delusional Traits

Murderous Traits

---

## The Cotton & Silk Thrillers

Irrefutable Evidence

Remorseless

---

## Non-Fiction

Hong Kong Under the Microscope

*A History of the Hong Kong Government Laboratory 1879–2004*

# IRREFUTABLE EVIDENCE

# Chapter One

Giacomo Riley squeezed on the brakes of his gleaming new tandem, gently bringing it to a halt by one of the many paths that led into Harlow Wood.

"This is the place, Nore," he called over his shoulder. "Off you get."

"But the barrier's down, Jackie."

"It's only a wooden pole. We'll just duck under it and head along the path. There'll be no one around, not at nine o'clock on a Saturday night. They'll all be in the pub or watching the telly."

Noreen clambered from the tandem's rear saddle and nudged him with her elbow, her eyes roaming his sleek Lycra-encased body. "As long as they're not hiding behind the trees watching us."

Two hundred yards into the wood, Giacomo propped the tandem against a tree and turned expectantly to his girlfriend. Catching the fire in his eyes, she let her face register a look of mock horror.

"Not here, Jackie, it's much too open. Let's get a bit further into the woods."

She turned around and pointed over her shoulder at her backpack. "And get that bedroll out of me bag. I haven't carried it all this way to leave it rolled up. I don't want this fancy kit you bought me all snagged and covered in mud and leaves."

Giacomo grinned. "You won't be wearing it for much longer, Noreen Smart. I can hardly wait."

"Well all the more reason to spread out the bedroll. I don't want no twigs sticking in me bum. And anyway, before you get your hands on me super stretchy shorts, you'll have to catch me."

She giggled and ran off, leaving Giacomo holding the bedroll.

"Wahey!" he whooped and sprinted after her, grinning in anticipation as he dodged from the path around a thick stand of trees before jumping out in front of her.

"Jackie!" she squealed.

"Got you!" he cried, grabbing her arms.

As she wriggled playfully from his grasp, Noreen's eyes were busy scanning the area around them. "That looks like a good spot," she said, pointing through the trees to a relatively flat patch of grass in a small clearing.

They bent under some low branches to enter the clearing and Giacomo laid out the bedroll. He had hardly flattened the ends before Noreen was lying on it, looking up at him with an attempted air of mystery.

"Come on then, my Latin lover boy, what are you waiting for? You're half Italian, aren't you? Surely all the biking hasn't worn you out."

She stretched out her body and wiggled her bottom, reaching her arms behind her to grab hold of a branch from a bush near her head.

Giacomo gulped as he knelt down and reached for the waistband of her shorts, his eyes exploring her body. Noreen pulled on the branch. "P'raps you should tie my wrists to this, like they do in them movies. Put a mask on me." She looked out provocatively from under her eyelids. "Enslave me!" she panted, dragging her tongue over the words.

Giacomo tugged on her shorts and she giggled again as he tickled the bare skin he'd exposed. Bending over, he ran his tongue over her belly button and the small gold star dangling from her navel ring.

"Ooo, that's more like it, my Jackimo," moaned Noreen thickly as she arched her back and reached farther into the bush, searching for a stronger branch to grasp.

Giacomo suddenly ducked his head in alarm as a piercing scream pounded his eardrums.

"Jackie!"

"Christ, Nore, what's the matter? I hardly touched you; I can't possibly have hurt you."

He looked up to see Noreen's arms thrashing wildly as her whole body became a shuddering, quivering jelly.

"Jackie!" she screamed again.

From nowhere, she was on her feet, tugging at her shorts. She hopped away from the bedroll. "Th … there!" she jabbered, pointing a shaking finger. "In the bushes. It felt like … There's a foot in the bushes!"

"Don't be daft, Nore, it—"

"There is!" she insisted. "I felt the toes. They were all cold and clammy."

Giacomo laughed nervously. "It'll be nothing, Nore, just some branch. Probably got moss or lichen all over it."

He leaned forward from where he was still kneeling and reached out to pull the nearest branch aside. He peered into the space behind and froze.

"Nore."

"What?"

"It's not just a foot, it's a body. A dead body, Nore. Hidden in the bushes."

He turned his head to his girlfriend to see her desperately wiping her hands down her shorts, trying to remove all traces of the feel of cold, lifeless flesh.

Suddenly her knees buckled. She clamped her arms around her shuddering body, her jaw trembling. "What are we going to do, Jackie?"

Giacomo pulled her to him. "We'll have to call the police. We can't just leave her there."

"Her?"

"It's a woman. At least, I think so. She's wearing a short skirt."

"We can't do that!"

"Why not?"

"Me dad! He'll kill me if he finds out what we've been up to. He'll kill you too."

"We'll tell him we were going for a walk and I saw the foot sticking out of the bushes. Nothing wrong with that, Nore. Anyway, we didn't do anything."

He wrinkled his nose dolefully. "Didn't get a chance."

## Chapter Two

Jennifer Cotton felt a pulse of excitement as she stopped her car behind the untidy group of vehicles blocking the narrow track on the south side of Harlow Wood — an ambulance, patrol cars with their lights flashing and several unmarked cars.

Her passenger Detective Sergeant Neil Bottomley looked up and grunted.

"Looks like the guv beat us to it, Cotton. That's his Sierra. He won't be chuffed to be here on a Saturday night."

He looked around. "No sign of Justin's little red devil, of course."

Jennifer laughed. "He's bound to be along in a mo, Sarge. Got to live up to his name."

Like Jennifer, Derek 'Justin' Thyme was a bright young detective constable with the newly created Nottingham City and County Serious Crime Formation, but unlike Jennifer, his personal organisation was chaotic and he was famous for arriving everywhere at the last moment in his scarlet Mini Cooper.

Bottomley released his door and swung his substantial bulk onto his left leg as he hauled himself out of the car. "Better be, or the guv'll be kicking his arse. Come on, Cotton, let's see what's what."

He waved at a young uniformed constable who was keeping a

log of the vehicles. The constable pointed to a path disappearing into the trees. "Everyone's down there, sir."

They made their way towards a floodlit area about fifty yards along the path. Even though it was now approaching eleven p.m., the late May evening was still not completely dark. Nevertheless, Jennifer shone a torch onto the path ahead of the sergeant. She didn't fancy having to help him up if he tripped.

As they neared the small clearing, Jennifer could see a number of people dressed in white disposable coveralls moving quietly about their business, making notes and taking photographs. These were the SOCOs, the scene-of-crime officers whose job it was to protect the scene from any further contamination after the point of discovery, and then to make a painstaking search of the area. Having already established the likely limits of the overall scene and protected any obvious evidential material, they were now working outwards from the body, recording, collecting and bagging anything that was likely to be of significance.

The entire clearing was cordoned off with blue and white crime scene tape, so those not occupied with protecting and preserving the evidence were crammed onto two of three narrow paths leading into it. The third path was part of the crime scene, the tape disappearing along both sides into the woods.

Detective Inspector Rob McPherson turned his head from where he was standing watching the SOCOs' every move, his hands thrust deep in his pockets, his face grim.

"Ah, Neil, and DC Cotton."

"Guv," nodded Jennifer, her eyes roaming the scene and taking in as much as she could. McPherson could see the enthusiasm written on her face.

"First murder, Cotton?"

"Yes, guv. Or at least the first one I can get close to. I attended a couple in Newark when I was in uniform, but I was only really taking particulars of attending personnel. A bit like the lad by the cars. What do you want me to do?"

The DI looked around. "Where's Thyme? Why is he always the last one to arrive anywhere?"

On cue, there was a rustling from the path and a breathless

DC Thyme emerged from the trees, ducking his powerful six-foot-two West Indian frame to avoid banging his head on any low branches.

"Sorry, guv," he panted.

"Maintaining your reputation, Justin?"

"No, guv. I mean—"

McPherson held up a hand to silence him and turned to address his team.

"Right, let's get you up to speed. We have the body of a young woman lying in those bushes over there. She's around twenty, fully clothed and there's a wound to the back of her head, but not much in the way of blood. However, it looks as if we might be in luck. The SOCOs have found what is most likely the route the killer used to bring the girl here."

He pointed to the crime scene tape across the clearing.

"That path there goes to one of several tracks that lead into these woods. Our vehicles are on another. The track is for forestry vehicles and barred at both ends, although there was no sign of a padlock.

"The SOCOs found a fresh tyre mark in some soft ground at the end of the path. They reckon it's from a largish vehicle, a four-by-four or something like that, but the tyre isn't the rugged deep-profile-tread sort used by the forestry people. So we're thinking that was the spot where the killer drove to with the girl and the tyre mark could be from the killer's vehicle."

Jennifer had taken out her notebook and was scribbling furiously. "Presumably that wasn't the path used by the couple who found the body, guv?"

"No, Cotton, it wasn't. They entered the woods from the main road on a different path."

Bottomley frowned. "Where's their car?"

"They weren't in a car, Neil, they arrived on a tandem."

"A what?"

"A tandem. You know, a two-person bicycle."

"I know what it is," snapped the sergeant, not even attempting to hide his indignation, "but I don't think I've seen one since I was a lad."

"Well, they must be making a comeback," said McPherson. "You should see theirs; very hi-tech."

Jennifer looked up from her notebook. "So this couple were cycling past here and just happened to notice a body?"

McPherson's eyes registered his amusement. "I think, DC Cotton, they had finished their cycling for the day, or at least they were taking a break. They were involved in other activities."

Jennifer flushed, feeling stupid. "Ah," she said, looking down at her notes. "Do we know anything about the dead girl?"

"Nothing at the moment, except that she's dressed like a hooker. Fred White, the head of the SOCO unit, is searching through her clothing right now.

"Meanwhile, we want to learn all we can from the couple that found her. The stories they told the WPC who spoke to them earlier are rather garbled, particularly the one from the lass, who was very upset. We need to be clear on exactly what happened. No need for a statement at the moment, just a chat."

He looked past Jennifer to where Derek was standing behind her. "Thyme, for some reason I can't fathom, you seem to appeal to young women of the lass's age. Talk to her while Sergeant Bottomley takes the lad into another car. Nice and gentle — they've done nothing wrong — but we do need to know how much they disturbed the scene."

He shifted his attention to Jennifer. "Cotton, get me some coveralls and a set for yourself. I want you to watch what the SOCOs are doing, and get a look at the dead girl."

The pulse of excitement she had felt earlier buzzed again in Jennifer's head. The guv was giving her an opportunity.

As Bottomley and Thyme were about to make their way back to the patrol cars and the young couple, Fred White emerged from the bushes by the dead woman and called out to McPherson.

"Got the contents of the girl's purse from the inside pocket of her jacket here, Rob."

He walked over to where they were all standing.

"It doesn't look as if it's been disturbed, but we won't know for sure until we've examined it thoroughly in the lab. All the contents have now been sealed separately. Of interest right now are this medical card and there's a letter from an employer, although judging from the card and the girl's clothing, I doubt she was employed as a nanny like the letter says."

"Go on, Fred," said McPherson.

The SOCO read from the medical card. "According to this, the girl's name is Miruna Peptanariu. She's Romanian. The medical card is from an STD clinic."

"Anything else?" grunted McPherson.

"Well, we're still waiting for the pathologist, but it doesn't look as if her clothing has been disturbed — there's a small amount of blood in the hair on the back of her head and some marks on the neck, but not really what you'd expect from strangulation. So no, nothing positive. There are no drag marks anywhere, so I'd guess the girl was carried, possibly all the way from the car. We will, of course, be searching along the path for any signs that her clothing or the clothing of the killer snagged on anything as she was brought here, but that'll be best done in daylight."

"How long do you think she's been here?" asked McPherson.

White shrugged. "It's not really my call, but there's still some rigor, not much in the way of flies, no animal bites, so at a guess, I'd say probably no more than twenty-four hours. Don't tell the pathologist I said so though, will you?"

McPherson nodded. "Last night then, possibly the early hours of this morning. Makes sense. Anything on the tyre mark?"

"It's been photographed, measured and cast. I can get someone to run it against the tyre print collection on the computer first thing, so we should able to narrow it down a little."

"Good," said McPherson, looking up as he heard someone coming along the path. "I think I recognise that heavy breathing; here comes Horace. We should have some more answers about the girl soon. Meanwhile, off you go, you two, and see what you can get from the couple."

Bottomley and Thyme stood back to make room for Dr Horace Lawson, pathologist-on-call, to pass them.

"Evening, Doc." Rob McPherson was suddenly all smiles.

"I suppose it is," said Lawson ambiguously.

"OK if we gown up and follow you in?" said McPherson.

"It's your party," grunted the pathologist. "Just don't get in my way."

Derek caught Jennifer's eye and winked at her. She grinned at him, motioning with her hand that he should hurry after the sergeant.

# Chapter Three

Amelia Taverner studied the poster outside the Theatre Royal in Nottingham's city centre.

### The Ripper Returns.

*A twenty-first century Victorian crime thriller from award-winning playwright Tobias Monkton. Starring Henry Silk of TV's Runway Two-Seven*

She ran her eye down the rest of the cast. It was quite a gathering of TV celebs drawn from a number of soaps, guaranteed to pull in the punters, put bums on seats. She took her stalls ticket from her pocket and walked towards the entrance. She doubted she was going to enjoy the play, it wasn't really her thing, but she wanted to see her man in action, get a feel for him, learn how he moved his arms and body, watch how he walked.

Three hours later, she felt well rewarded. To her surprise, she had enjoyed the play and been drawn into the plot. More importantly, Henry Silk's character had appeared in many of the scenes, giving her plenty of opportunity to study him. Although Silk was acting a part, the character he was playing didn't have any peculiarities — he didn't limp or have strange twitches — so there was probably a lot of the real man on stage. She'd learn more when she followed him back to his hotel.

As the applause died down and the audience stood to leave, Amelia took another look at her programme, turning to the page devoted to Henry Silk. He was a good-looking man of around fifty with close-cropped salt-and-pepper hair and far softer features than the unsmiling brute he played in the TV soap. He was a good actor, far better than she'd realised, but that didn't lessen her resolve. She'd chosen him, researched him; he was on her list. She already knew much about him from articles in the gossip magazines. He was higher profile than the others had been, but that was good; it was time she upped her game, took a few more risks. The rewards in terms of self-satisfaction would be that much greater, and the abyss that much deeper for a man like Silk.

After zipping up her cheap tracksuit top, she adjusted the plain, forgettable frames of her oversized tinted spectacles and tied her headscarf over her shoulder-length mouse-brown wig. No one would give her a second glance, which was the way she wanted it. She didn't hurry leaving the theatre; it would be a while until Silk appeared from the stage door.

From her research on the actor, she knew that he was something of a loner, a man whose intellect outshone many, but who had a limited number of friends. He had a reputation for being distant, wary of others in his profession.

It all seemed rather unfair. He had blotted his copybook many years before, having been blamed for the death of Dirk Sanderley, a young up-and-coming hero of the stage and screen — Britain's James Dean, they had described him — a potential colossus in the making robbed of his place in history. The country had mourned the young actor and as far as the country was concerned, it was Henry Silk's fault.

Perversely, while the country had now largely forgiven him, the profession had not. Directors and producers used him grudgingly, forced by their bean counters to cast him if it was thought he would add to revenue. Which he did. In his role in Runway Two-Seven as a misogynistic brute, he was the character the fans loved to hate.

Half an hour after the performance ended, the 'Ripper' cast, minus Henry Silk, appeared at the stage door in a guffawing, self-aware fluttering mass. Several autographs were signed, petulant tosses of the head thrown by those who hadn't had programmes thrust at them, after which they all floated away, heading for the nearest pub.

When Henry Silk emerged alone. Amelia shrank into the shadows as she watched him politely sign the programmes of several women who had waited excitedly for him, smiling at their thanks and regally offering a few words to the eldest and youngest of them. Then, with a wave, he was gone, striding up the street in the direction of Standard Hill and the Old Nottingham Hotel.

Amelia fell in behind him at a distance of about fifty yards. She wasn't worried about losing him since she knew exactly where he was going, but she didn't want him to disappear once he entered the hotel. As she studied his walk, she thought about his height. She estimated he was about six foot tall, some two inches more than she was, but lifts in her shoes would deal with that.

She was pretty sure he would head for the bar — his after-performance drink something of a ritual according to some airheaded journalist in one of the glossies who had been granted a rare interview with him. Amelia remembered the article read as if the girl had spent more time telling Henry about herself than getting him to talk. But that was the egocentric way of the young, she thought. She smiled to herself; she sounded like someone's grandmother.

As she pushed open the hotel's main door, Amelia was in time to see Henry wave to the receptionist as he turned left into the bar. The receptionist, who at this late hour doubled as barman, scuttled after him.

"Evening, Mr Silk, sir. How was the show tonight?"

"Excellent, thank you, Michael, an appreciative audience. They always are in this great town."

His empty smile was lost on the barman, as was the oft-repeated platitude. By using the phrase 'this great town', Henry didn't even have to remember where he was.

"Vodka, sir?"

"Yes please, Michael. Would you like one yourself? I'm sure you've got a long night ahead of you."

"Thank you, sir, that's very kind. A small one, if I may."

Amelia slipped out of line of sight of the bar. She had visited twice before in the past two months and she knew exactly where the CCTV cameras were. She wanted to check once again that there were no new ones and that none of the existing ones had been moved. She glanced around and was pleased to find everything was the same and that standing where she was, her presence was not being recorded. The only camera aimed in her general direction was focussed on the main door, and Amelia had been careful to keep her head down as she passed through its field of view.

She strolled over to a table on which a dozen tour brochures were laid out. 'City Walks', 'The Castle', 'The Old Markets', and one that caught her eye, 'Visit Sherwood Forest'. All in good time, she thought.

"Can I help you, madam?" said Michael on his way back to the desk.

"I'm fine, thank you," said Amelia, using a soft Edinburgh accent. "I'm waiting for a friend."

Michael turned away, his duty done, and immediately forgot her.

Amelia looked back to the brochures.

A few moments later another voice sounded behind her.

"Goodnight, Michael."

Henry was heading for the lift.

"Goodnight, sir, and thank you."

Once the doors had closed, Amelia turned to watch the lift's progress on the indicator. It stopped at the second of the four floors before returning empty to the ground floor.

One more task for the evening, then home. She walked to the rear of the lobby where a door next to the washroom doors led onto stairs that would not only take her up to the guest rooms, but also down to the guest car park, a gated, open area behind the hotel. She knew that while there was a CCTV camera aimed at the lift doors at the car park level, the door from the stairs fifteen feet away was not in its field of view. She would still have to be careful but she didn't need to move far from the door since she was merely checking that Henry Silk's car was there.

She opened the door from the stairs. and glanced into the car park. The lights only triggered with movement so she waited while her eyes adjusted before looking around. There it was: a dark green Nissan X-Trail. She smiled, having ticked the final box, and climbed the stairs back to the lobby.

Slipping quietly through the door, she was ready with an excuse that she'd lost her way to the loo, but Michael was engrossed in a card game on his computer screen and didn't even register her presence. She crossed the reception and left through the main door, walking across town to where she had left her white van on a meter in a street with no cameras.

# Chapter Four

For her final checks the following evening, Amelia swapped her drab, shoulder-length wig for something darker, the hair shorter but with strong waves set in it, the style old-fashioned. Her shapeless pleated skirt, full cotton blouse buttoned up to the neck and slightly too large navy-blue acrylic jacket labelled her 'holy roller' to anyone whose glance lingered on her for more than a moment. She had fattened her face with cotton pads in her mouth, removed all make-up and scrubbed her cheeks. To reduce the visual impact of her face even more, she had put on the plainest spectacles in her collection, their bottle-bottom lenses making her eyes water.

She was sitting in the lobby of the Old Nottingham, seemingly engrossed in a copy of Christianity Digest but actually looking over the rims of the spectacles to watch Michael's movements and checking yet again on the locations of the CCTV cameras. She was also waiting for Henry Silk to return following his performance. If he was true to form, he should stride through the main door in the next five minutes or so and head to the bar for his nightly glass of vodka.

Exactly six minutes later, she heard brisk footsteps approaching the hotel. As the door opened and Henry walked through, Amelia reached down to her bag on the floor as if to retrieve something, turning her head away from Henry's line of sight as she did. But he didn't even notice her, his attention taken by Michael who had looked up as the door opened and called a greeting across the lobby.

"Good evening, sir, I'll be with you once I've finished logging this booking. It'll only take a jiffy."

"Take your time, Michael. There's no rush."

In anticipation of Henry Silk's nightly generosity, Michael's tapping on his keyboard became more urgent, reaching a crescendo with a noisy stab at the return key and an eager glance in the direction of the bar. As he stood, he looked around the lobby in case there were any guests requiring attention, but there was only the drably dressed, God-bothering type sitting sideways to him in the far corner. Michael half-squinted his eyes as they settled on her, imagining an assignation with a local high-up from the church. Good luck to him, he thought. I reckon her knees are probably glued together.

As she heard Michael walk from the reception desk, Amelia turned her head. In the reflection from one of a pair of open glass doors separating the lobby from the bar, she could see Henry sitting on a bar stool. He appeared to be looking at something above eye level. Then she remembered; there was a television on the wall.

"One of yours, sir?" she heard Michael ask as he glanced at the movie playing on the screen.

There was a dismissive bark from Henry. "Well, as it happens, I *am* actually in it, but I don't think I could call it one of mine. In a few moments you'll see me step forward from that line of centurions and utter the immortal words, 'Immediately, commander,' with all the thespian talent I could muster."

He gave a wry smile as he glanced at the barman.

"I was only nineteen and I was keen to do anything. Burton was rumoured to be taking the lead, but he upped and died, so the part went to someone else. I was on set for all of two days, so it was hardly the big time I imagined it would be. We were all decked out in thermals for that shot. It was freezing and those uniforms were not made for warmth."

He took his drink, waving a hand at the bottle to indicate that Michael should pour himself one.

"Happy days," he said, emptying his glass. "I'm off, Michael. Enjoy the movie."

Michael's 'goodnight, sir' followed Henry out of the bar as he walked towards the lift, his back to Amelia who was waiting to double-check the floor where Henry was staying.

Satisfied, Amelia picked up her bag and headed for the door.

Three hundred yards along the main road from Standard Hill, she stopped by a telephone booth she had earlier confirmed was unvandalised. She opened her bag, found the card she'd picked up at the Old Nottingham and dialled the number. It took a few rings to answer since Michael was away from the desk in the bar watching the movie.

"Old Nottingham Hotel. Good evening, Michael speaking. How may I help you?"

"Hello. Yes, I'd like to book a room for tomorrow evening."

Amelia had shed the Scottish accent and was now slightly strident Home Counties.

"Certainly, madam. May I take your name?"

"Taverner. Mrs Amelia Taverner."

"Thank you, Mrs Taverner. Could I possibly have a credit card number to guarantee the booking?"

Amelia read out a number and followed by asking if she could have a room on the second floor. "I stayed at your hotel a couple of years ago. Like to be on the same floor, if I may."

"Absolutely, madam, that's no problem at all," replied Michael, wondering what could be so special about the second floor. The views were pretty ordinary on all the floors.

Amelia put down the receiver and stared across Maid Marion Way towards the lights of the city. She smiled to herself. Everything was falling perfectly into place.

# Chapter Five

Jennifer Cotton ran up the stairs to the first floor of the old police station that was now the Nottingham City and County Serious Crime Formation HQ, the handbag bouncing on her hip in danger of knocking her phone and coffee cup from her hand.

Before pushing open the door to the incident room, she peered through its scratched plastic window to see if the meeting had started. To her relief, she saw her team's boss, Detective Chief Inspector Mike Hurst, walking slowly to the front of the room while deep in conversation with the 'guv', DI Rob McPherson.

Jennifer shuffled past several rows of seats to a vacant spot Derek Thyme had kept for her. He grinned at her triumphantly as she sat down.

"Don't look so smug, Derek. Arriving before me once in a lifetime doesn't wipe out your reputation."

"Perhaps I've changed my ways."

"Perhaps that bright yellow sun out there is about to reverse direction and set."

Derek wasn't about to throw away his brief advantage. "Not like you to be late, Jen."

"Sodding alarm didn't go off and then the cat I'm looking after for a neighbour threw up over my shoes."

Derek wrinkled his nose in distaste. "Can't expect anything else from a cat; they're all the same: parasites. No time for them, me."

"It's just as well your mother didn't take that attitude when you were decorating her blouse as a babe in arms."

Derek grunted. On the athletics track, his sprinting was world class and he was currently shortlisted with the Olympic squad for the one hundred and two hundred metres. However, in the game of last words with Jennifer, he always came a poor second.

DCI Hurst reached the front of the room and looked around, making sure he had everyone's attention before he started. The group was a mixture of detectives, some old school, some not, and the increasing number of civilian officers recruited to take on many of the office-bound and routine investigative tasks previously carried out by police officers. For Hurst, it was a strange new world, completely different from the police force he had joined thirty-four years before, and one he wasn't fully sure he liked. But at approaching fifty-five and three months from retirement, he no longer found the machinations of the senior command to be of much interest to him. This was likely to be his last big case and he wanted to leave on a high.

"Morning everyone; sorry to ruin your Sunday but we need to get moving. Just to ensure we're all on the same page, last night at around nine thirty, the body of a young woman was found by a courting couple in Harlow Wood, a part of Sherwood Forest three miles south of Mansfield. Unfortunately, I was a hundred miles away visiting my wife's relatives, so I couldn't attend the scene. However, as DCI, I shall be leading the investigation as required by the SCF protocol.

"At first sight, it looked as if the young woman had been killed by blows to the back of the head, but the pathologist reckons she died of suffocation, probably from having a polythene bag pulled over her head. He'll be confirming that at the pm tomorrow.

"Documentation from a purse in the inside pocket of her jacket has identified the woman as Miruna Peptanariu, a 19-year-old Romanian working as a prostitute in the Forest Road West area here in the city, although according to the anti-prostitution squad, to whom she was known, she had also been seen working in Mapperley. So she might have been treading on toes and killed to set an example, depending on who's running her. That's our first line to look into. To this end, DI McPherson will allocate duties at the end of the meeting.

"We've had uniforms talk to a couple of her night shift companions and it seems she was last seen late on Friday night, shortly after midnight. She told one of them that she had a client picking her up. No name as yet but we have her mobile number from the women the uniforms spoke to and we're in the process of tracking calls and messages.

"The timing ties in well with the pathologist's initial findings at the scene. He estimated that she had been dead between fourteen and twenty hours, which puts the time of the murder in the early hours of Saturday morning."

He turned and pointed to a large-scale map of Harlow Wood.

"SOCOs found a fresh tyre print here at the edge of an unpaved forest track, which as you can see is about fifty yards from where the body was found. Could be from a four by four, but not one of the forestry vehicles.

"From the general lack of disturbance at the scene, apart from that definitely from the courting couple who found her, the SOCOs' initial thoughts are that Miruna's body was carried to where she was found rather than dragged — there're what appear to be some fibres of the same colour as the fluffy collar of her jacket caught on a couple of the bushes along the path — so it could be she was killed in the car.

"As we speak, traffic are looking at CCTV footage from the early hours of Saturday morning from cameras covering Forest Road West and adjacent streets. With luck, we'll see Miruna being picked up and maybe we'll get a number plate. The killer's probably using a stolen vehicle, but information on the location of the owner could help."

He paused and waited for the group to catch up with their notes. Jennifer raised her hand.

"Yes, Cotton?"

"Did the pathologist say any more about the blows to the head, boss? How hard they were?"

Hurst nodded. "He reckons they were hard enough to knock her out but not intended to kill. However, the skin was broken and there was minor bleeding."

Still scribbling on her pad, Jennifer called out another question.

"What about the weapon? Could the pathologist say what it might be?"

"Up to a point, yes. It had a rounded end, probably a cosh of some sort. Maybe hard rubber rather than metal. We'll get more on that from the pm."

"So we could be looking at premeditation as opposed to, say, an argument that escalated," persisted Jennifer.

"What makes you think that?"

"Well, boss, not many people drive around with coshes in their cars. It could have been brought along for the purpose of killing her or knocking her out."

"Good point, Cotton."

Hurst noticed Derek Thyme's hand hovering in a tentative wave.

"Something to add, Thyme?"

"Was there any sign of the polythene bag at the scene, boss?"

"No," said Hurst, shaking his head. "But of course the killer could have shoved it in his pocket."

He turned to a whiteboard behind him covered in photographs and notes in felt-tip pen.

"Now, the other thing that's important is the girl's clothing. As you can see from the photos, she was wearing a short denim skirt, a red sleeveless top and a thin shiny black plastic jacket with a fluffy fake fur collar. Her underwear appeared to be in place so it seems that if there was any sexual activity, it could have been oral. The mouth swabs should confirm that.

"However, we only found one shoe, which she was wearing on her right foot." He pointed to a photo. "As you can see, it's quite dressy with a high heel and a pointed toe. So far, there's no sign of the other one. The SOCOs conducted as thorough a search as they could last night and they'll be back about now to check the whole area again in daylight."

A hand went up at the back of the group, one of the civilian intelligence officers.

"What about the couple who found the girl? Can they be ruled out of any involvement?"

Hurst turned to Rob McPherson to answer the question.

"Totally," said the DI. "Firstly, Miruna had been dead for over half a day when she was found so they would've had to murder her somewhere else and then take her to the scene. Secondly, they arrived on a tandem, not in a car, and thirdly, they are, in my opinion, genuinely spooked by the whole incident, the girl especially. No, we can rule them out."

Mike Hurst checked his watch. "Right, if there's nothing else, I've got to brief Superintendent Freneton. The pm's set for tomorrow morning at ten. Horace Lawson has kindly agreed not to start until after the morning briefing. DI McPherson and I will attend. Thyme, you will be coming with us. You'll be exhibits officer so you can bag and label the girl's clothing for submission to the lab. Meanwhile, go and join in with checking out the CCTV recordings. The more eyes we get on those, the better."

Jennifer felt Derek shrink into his seat beside her.

"Christ, what did I do to win that one? I hate post mortems and the boss knows it."

"Stand at the back and close your eyes if it all gets too much," said Jennifer as she caught Hurst's eye, wondering what he had for her.

She soon knew. "Cotton, we have the address where Miruna was staying. Go with Sergeant Bottomley and see what you can find out about her. There are a couple of uniforms already there to stop the two other women she apparently shares with from disturbing her things."

"Lucky sod," muttered Derek.

# Chapter Six

Still wearing her holy-roller outfit and wig, with a headscarf to hide much of her face from the high-angle side-view shot she knew the CCTV camera would record, Amelia Taverner checked in to the Old Nottingham Hotel at two in the afternoon.

She leaned over the desk, speaking quietly to the receptionist. "Hello. I called last night to make a reservation. My name is Taverner."

The receptionist hit a few keys on her keyboard.

"Mrs Amelia Taverner?" she said, without looking up.

"Yes. I asked for a second floor room."

"That's right, Mrs Taverner. We've put you in room two zero eight. It's a nice room with a view over The Park."

"Sounds perfect, thank you."

Amelia took the form the receptionist had pushed towards her, filled it in and slid it back across the counter top.

"Thank you," said the receptionist, finally looking up from her monitor. "If I could just take a credit card number as a guarantee. It won't be charged at this stage and you don't have to pay with it when you check out, if you'd prefer not to."

No, thought Amelia, but even if it's not charged, the number will still be in the system, so I might as well use it. Using cash is unusual and might raise a flag in the receptionist's memory. Use a card and the girl will have forgotten me before I reach the lift.

The receptionist handed Amelia a folded card containing her magnetic room key.

"Do you have a car, Mrs Taverner? The keycard opens the gate to the car park, but I'll need to take the number."

"No, I don't. I came up by train."

"No problem," assured the receptionist irrelevantly. "I hope you enjoy your stay with us."

Amelia remained in her room only long enough to deposit her padlocked holdall, after which she headed back out of the hotel to the nearby multi-storey car park where she'd left her white transit van. She needed to change out of her disguise and get back to work before she was missed.


By six p.m., she was back in the hotel, dressed once again in her forgettable clothes and wig. She knew that Henry would leave for the theatre by half past the hour at the latest, but she needed to be sure. There was no point in putting all her plans into place if Henry had suddenly reported sick and let his understudy play the role that evening.

She needn't have worried. At six fifteen, from her spot in the corner of the lobby, Amelia heard the lift roll into action as it was called from the second floor. It returned carrying Henry Silk who strode through the lobby and out of the main door, dressed as usual in jeans, cream linen jacket over a thin brown woollen pullover, multicoloured woollen scarf and what Amelia was beginning to regard as his trademark dark blue baseball cap pulled firmly down over his head.

Keeping a distance of about fifty yards, Amelia followed Henry to the Theatre Royal and watched him disappear through the stage door. She allowed herself a slight smile. All systems go.

Back at the hotel, she checked the car park once again to make sure Henry's car was still in its usual place and then returned to her room. She hung a 'do not disturb' sign on the door and set about unpacking the holdall she had brought with her earlier and a second one she'd arrived with at six o'clock. She checked and rechecked that she had everything she needed. Satisfied, she sat back on the bed to relax until it was time.

At ten o'clock, the alarm on Amelia's smartphone pinged. She always set it in case she dozed off, although she never had. She picked up the ancient Nokia lying next to it, one with an unattributable prepaid SIM card, and punched in a number. The call was answered after two rings, the voice on the line heavily accented even when it had only said 'Hello'.

Amelia put her hand over her mouth and dropped her chin. She had practised this accent many times, but she could never be complacent; it had to sound authentic, especially since she wanted to sound like a man.

"Zis is Klaus. I called you yesterday. You can be ready for me at one o'clock?"

"I had other calls for tonight, good clients," lied Miruna Peptanariu. "I don't know if I come."

Amelia sighed. This wasn't the first time this had happened. The girls were greedy and so unsubtle.

"Forget ze other customers. I have booking with you. I make it worth your time." She paused to ensure she had the girl's attention. "Double what we agreed."

"Double?"

Amelia could hear the change of heart in the girl's voice.

"Yes, and more if you really please me."

"I be there. Call ten minutes before so I can get straight into car."

"I'll call at one."

Amelia ended the call and swung her legs from the bed.

The woman who left Amelia's room bore little resemblance to the one who had checked in several hours earlier. She was dressed in a smart, mid-grey business suit, the skirt's hemline two inches above her knee, an expensive, pure silk, cream blouse under the perfectly fitting jacket. The luxuriant hair of her blond wig fell effortlessly onto her shoulders, its style assisting her carefully applied make-up to lengthen her face, while rimless, slightly tinted spectacles spoke of a senior, decision-making position in a boardroom. A Prada handbag and matching pair of black Manolo Blahnik shoes completed the picture, the shoes lifting Amelia's already tall frame to six feet.

Carrying a large ring file crammed with totally fictitious papers, she walked to the lift, careful to keep her face down to avoid the Cyclopean gaze of the camera above the door.

Michael was still young enough to regard any woman of more than late twenties as a mother figure, especially one who was elegantly dressed. Hence his attention hardly drifted from the card game on his computer screen as Amelia glided gracefully from the lift to the bar and settled herself at a table by the far wall, one from where she had a good view of the lobby.

She opened her file and unclipped some papers, spreading them over the table. Removing a Cartier fountain pen from her handbag, she settled to the pretence of reading through her papers and making notes in the margins. Constantly aware of all movement in the lobby, she saw Michael suddenly look up and notice her. He hurried over, full of apologies.

"I'm sorry, madam, I was busy with late bookings and I didn't see you here. Can I get you anything?"

"An orange juice," replied Amelia dismissively.

He brought the drink along with a bowl of unwanted peanuts and left her to it. Miserable cow, he thought.

At eleven fifteen, Amelia heard the hotel's main door open followed by the now familiar sound of Henry Silk's stride as he made his way to the bar. Unlike Michael, Henry was old enough to regard an elegantly dressed woman of around forty as anything but a mother figure, and he settled on a bar stool to enjoy the view while Michael poured his vodka and tonic.

"Help yourself to one," said Henry as he took the glass. Michael thanked him, and, catching Henry's eye, he nodded towards Amelia, flicking a finger under his nose.

Henry smiled to himself. Someone dressed like the woman

sitting across the room from him exuding an air of total confidence was on another planet from Michael; she would make mincemeat of him in seconds.

Amelia let Henry enjoy his drink for a few minutes, and then, when she gauged he had more or less finished, she gathered her papers together, stacked them in the file and stood to walk towards the lobby. She allowed herself to catch Henry's eye for the first time and as she did, she stumbled on the carpet and dropped the file, the papers scattering across the floor.

"Damn it!" she spat, "I've just sorted them all out."

"Oh dear," sympathised Henry as he jumped from his stool. "May I help you?"

"That's so kind, thank you," replied Amelia through an embarrassed giggle. "What an idiot. Think I've had one vodka too many."

"And there I was about to offer you another," said Henry as he knelt on the floor gathering the papers.

"Thank you, but I don't think I should."

She took the sheaf of papers from him and tapped its edge on the counter top. "I knew I should have clipped them in; serves me right for being lazy."

"It could happen to anyone," said Henry. Then he laughed. "Well, anyone in three inch heels on an uneven carpet. Are you sure you won't have another drink?"

"Quite sure, thanks."

She held out her hand. "Thanks for coming to my rescue; this skirt is hardly suitable for scrabbling across the floor picking up papers. Jane Brown. Boring, isn't it, but there we are."

"A name's only a name, unless you think that it influences your character. Henry Silk at your service, Ms Brown."

Amelia frowned. "That sounds familiar."

"Bit like Jane Brown," shrugged Henry with a smile. "Loads of them around."

She narrowed her eyes. "I don't think so. Henry Silk? Of course, I'm sorry, I should have recognised you. I saw your photo on a hoarding outside the Theatre Royal. Aren't you starring in the whodunnit that's playing there?"

"Guilty as charged, m'lady," said Henry, touching his brow with a forefinger.

"How interesting," gushed Amelia. "Much more exciting than my line of business."

"Which is …"

"Hedge funds."

"I'm sure it has its moments," replied Henry, not sounding convinced.

"Well, on payday it certainly does. But tell me, why the baseball cap?" She pointed to the cap Henry had placed on the bar.

He smiled. "You probably don't have much time to watch TV if you're tripping around the country funding hedges, but for my sins I appear in a soap that grips the nation's couch potato classes four nights a week. The character I play is not particularly nice, you know, aggressive, always looking for a fight. I suppose I must be doing something right since many people assume that I'm really like that. Couldn't be further from the truth, actually. But the upshot is that I've had more than a few likely lads picking fights with me.

"Fortunately, one of the plus sides of acting is that in order to look convincing in certain movies or TV parts, you get to learn a few basic survival skills, like horse riding, fencing and in my case, boxing. So I can look after myself. But I still try to avoid unnecessary confrontations and the best way is to remain incognito. Hence the cap when I'm walking around a city like this."

He paused and turned his head towards the bottles behind the bar.

"Look, I'm thirsty after spouting my lines all evening. I'm going to have another. Surely you'll join me."

Amelia smiled. "You're a persuasive man, Mr Silk, but I think we might have a problem."

Henry looked puzzled. "Really?"

"Yes," she said, nodding towards the lobby. "Our young barman is rather occupied."

Henry followed her eyes and saw that Michael was attempting to field a crowd of Korean businessmen trying to check in, several of them gazing hopefully at the bar.

"Mmm," muttered Henry. "This place is going to degenerate into a noisy pit of boozing, toasting and drinking competitions within minutes. Look, don't take this the wrong way, but I'm in the habit of following my drink down here with some far classier vodka I keep up in my room. I always have a bottle of Belvedere with me, and this week's no exception."

"That's the Polish one, isn't it? Very fashionable."

"I believe so, but I don't let fashion dictate what I drink; I leave it to my taste buds."

"Well, I don't know, Mr Silk, I hardly know you and you're inviting me to your room. My mother told me about actors."

Henry laughed and held his hands up defensively. "Drinks only, Scout's honour."

"I'm not sure that Scouts are allowed to drink vodka, Mr Silk. It was certainly frowned upon in the Girl Guides. But that was a while ago so I don't think the pledges still hold. And it's not often I get the offer to share an expensive vodka with a famous actor."

"More like infamous," said Henry, as he picked up his baseball cap.


Michael was so flustered dealing with the Korean businessmen that Henry chose not to disturb his train of thought by calling good-night. Amelia smiled to herself — an added bonus: Michael would have no idea whether Henry left the bar with her or not. As they approached the lift, Amelia opened her handbag and peered inside.

"Damn. I've left my phone in my car. I'm expecting a text from my boss."

She pointed to the door leading to the stairs. "I'll run down and get it. What's your room number?"

"Two zero two. But I can wait, if you like."

"I should take the lift while you can."

She nodded towards three of the group at reception that Michael had managed to process and who were now walking towards them.

"I'll be there in a moment."

Amelia headed off in the direction of the stairs while listening for the lift doors to close. She walked down as far as the door to the car park where she waited for a minute before climbing back up to the second floor.

Henry answered the gentle tap on the door almost immediately and stood aside to let Amelia in. She held up her phone and smiled.

"That's good," said Henry. "Can't be without the things these days. Did you get your text?"

Amelia shook her head. "Not yet. The old soak's probably in a bar somewhere."

He ushered her towards two armchairs by the window.

"Here we are," he said, retrieving a black bottle with elegant gold lettering and motif from the fridge. "Belvedere Unfiltered. My particular favourite. Make yourself comfortable and I'll pour. You'll take it on the rocks, I assume?"

She shook her head. "Actually, as it's already cold, I'd prefer it with just a twist of lemon."

Henry shrugged. "As you wish, but I can assure you that the ice adds to the experience."

She raised her eyebrows in amusement. "You sound like an advertisement."

Henry poured the drinks and brought them to the small table by the armchairs.

"I do, don't I? It must come from doing so much voice-over work. A jobbing actor's bread and butter, you know."

"I can see that you would be good at it. You have the right sort of voice."

"Thanks, but it's mainly training the vocal cords to do the right thing at the right time."

He raised a quizzical eyebrow, closed his eyes slightly and let his voice fall to a lower register. "Cue mellifluous, add a drop of honey and even a credit card can sound exciting."

Amelia tossed back her head and laughed. "Bravo! You know, I think I'd like some ice after all. Would you mind?"

"Not at all. I know you won't regret it."

He stood, picked up her drink and turned to walk over to the fridge.

Amelia was ready. Her hand flashed inside her handbag to retrieve a syringe. In one rapid action she uncapped the end, squirted the contents into Henry's glass and returned it to the depths of the bag, the whole process taking less than two seconds. In case Henry had registered any movement, she picked up her phone and was staring at the screen when he turned back with her drink.

"My boss at last," she said, holding up the phone. "I've told him I'm busy and that I'll check in with him in the morning. That's bound to keep him up all night fretting about the Asian markets."

Henry placed Amelia's glass next to her and sat down.

"Is it true what they say about hedge fund trading?"

"What do they say?"

"That it's gambling with other people's money."

She laughed. "That's a rather cynical view."

"So how would you describe it?"

She paused to think, half-closing her eyes in amusement.

"Gambling with other people's money. But to be fair, most of the financial world can be described in that way, it's merely a question of degree."

Henry raised his glass. "Here's to gambling. Cin cin!"

Amelia leaned forward and clinked his glass.

"Happy days," she said as she took a sip and watched in delight as Henry downed half his vodka.

Henry sat back and sighed. "Ah, exquisite. There are so many subtle flavours. What do you think?"

"I think you're in advertising mode again, Mr Silk, but I agree, it's delicious."

Amelia continued with the small talk, asking Henry questions about the theatre and acting. He was more than happy to entertain her with several amusing tales.

After ten minutes, Henry's glass was empty while the level in Amelia's had hardly changed, despite her appearing to take several sips.

"You're lagging behind, Jane," said Henry. "Can I top you up?"

She heard the slur in his voice and saw the change in his eyes. As he stood, she saw him rock on his feet. She had used a strong dose since she wanted to be sure he remained asleep. It was taking effect even more quickly than she had anticipated.

Henry paused and looked back down towards Amelia. Her face was beginning to blur and there was a strange whirring noise in his head. He took a deep breath and forced his eyes to focus.

"Don't know what happened there," he said, unaware that the entire sentence came out as one word. He took a step and then stopped. "You know, I'm feeling a little odd. Might need … to lie down for a moment."

His arms dropped to his side. Amelia jumped to her feet and took the empty glass from his hand. "Let me help you," she said, as she touched the base of the glass onto the small of his back and nudged him gently towards the bed. Until she gloved her hands, she didn't want to touch him.

Henry tried to say that that would be nice, but what came out of his mouth was incomprehensible. He wasn't even aware of lying down and by the time his head settled on the pillow, he was unconscious.

Amelia opened her handbag to retrieve a pair of surgical gloves. After snapping them on, she lifted Henry's feet onto the bed, untied his shoelaces and removed his shoes. She checked the sole pattern. It was nothing special, but the stick-on repair soles were quite worn, which might help the forensic scientists link them if they found any shoeprints. She waited for two minutes before prodding Henry hard in the ribs, but there was no response.

She now moved with total purpose. Picking up Henry's key card, her file of papers and her handbag, she quietly opened the door, listening carefully for anyone in the corridor.

Back in her room, she dropped the file and handbag on the bed, picked up the two holdalls with her equipment and went straight back to Henry's room three doors away. Once inside, she put the holdalls on the floor, unlocked them and spread their contents neatly in front of her.

There was a checklist in her head that she was about to tick off.

But before paying attention to it, she stood to one side, pulled off her shoes and removed her own clothes down to her plain white cotton bra and pants, and sheer tights. She'd be undressing Henry in a moment and she didn't want his clothing fibres on her suit nor her fibres on him. She carefully folded the jacket and skirt along with her blouse and placed them in a plastic suit bag from one of the holdalls. The shoes went into another plastic bag.

First on her mental list were the drinks glasses. She took them to the bathroom and washed them thoroughly, dried them and put one back on the shelf next to two other larger tumblers. She then poured a shot of vodka from the Belvedere bottle into the second glass and put the bottle back in the fridge. She tossed a couple of ice cubes and a slice of lemon into the glass and put it back on the small table. Finally, she pushed the chair where she had been sitting back against the wall. Now, for all intents and purposes, even if Henry had a vague memory of her in the room, which was unlikely, the single glass and chair would contradict that memory. He had been drinking alone.

The next task was Henry's clothes. She peeled off his trousers, and, with a little more difficulty, his pullover. Henry had already removed his linen jacket and scarf and hung them on the back of a desk chair, while he'd tossed his baseball cap onto the desk. Amelia made Henry comfortable and looked briefly at his body, now wearing only boxers, a T-shirt and socks. Although she had little physical interest in men, she still appreciated his physique; he was clearly a man who looked after himself.

From her stock of items on the floor, she took a new plastic comb, removed its wrapper and combed it through Henry's hair, making sure that there were some of his hairs trapped in it. Henry's hair was fashionably short, but nevertheless, a few hairs settled in the teeth of the comb, quite sufficient for her purposes. If she planted too many it would raise suspicion; too few and they might not be found. It was a tricky balance but she would rather risk their not being found than overdo it. She placed the comb in a ziplock bag and sealed it.

The next part needed great care and of all her preparations, was the one most likely to wake Henry, which was one further reason she had given him a generous dose. From a large plastic bag on the floor, she took out a mannequin's forearm and right hand, the fingers complete with a set of false fingernails that she had glued on earlier. She walked over to the bed where Henry was stretched out on his back, snoring gently. Pushing his head to his right, she took the mannequin hand by the wrist and pulled the fingernails slowly but firmly down Henry's neck, making sure that the scratches she made were deep enough to bleed — she wanted both skin cells and blood to be transferred. Before returning the hand and arm to the bag, she inspected the nails closely to make sure she could see sufficient material trapped under them.

Another large plastic bag contained a side-handle baton, an excellent two-handed weapon for delivering powerful and accurate blows at close quarters. Specifically chosen from the range of options available, this model had an extendable grip that slid from inside the baton's main shaft. She pulled out the grip extension and walked back to the bed. Taking Henry's right hand, she folded his fingers round the extended grip, after which she folded the fingers of his left hand around the baton's side handle — she knew from watching Henry on stage that he was right-handed. Placing her own gloved hands over Henry's, she squeezed his fingers tightly, making sure they made good, firm contact. She then pushed the grip extension back inside the body of the baton and returned the baton to its bag.

Now all that remained were Henry's clothes, which she had left folded on the end of the bed. Henry had been carefully chosen for a number of reasons, one important one being that since he was only a little taller than Amelia and was slim with well-toned muscles, his clothes would fit her reasonably well.

Before putting them on, she removed her bra and replaced it with a tightly fitting sports bra. Her breasts weren't large and the elasticated cotton made a good job of flattening her. Under Henry's pullover and jacket, there would be nothing to be seen.

She pulled on his jeans, tightening the belt to compensate for Henry's larger waist size, and then the pullover. Checking her reflection in the wall mirror by the desk, she wound the hair from the blond wig onto the top of her head, pinned it in place and pulled Henry's baseball cap down over the top, the piled-up hair helping to pad out the cap. Under the wig, she was wearing a tightly fitting skullcap to minimise the chance of any of her own hair ending up on Henry's clothing or at the crime scene she was about to create.

Before slipping on Henry's shoes, she popped in some heel lifts, which made them surprisingly snug, but then, she had large feet. Finally she put on the linen jacket and scarf and looked at herself again in the mirror. Adjusting the cap so that it covered more of her face, she shuffled around in the clothes until she was comfortable before packing all her gear back into the holdalls. Last on her list were Henry's car keys and phone: both were lying on the desk.

Back in her room, she dropped the unwanted holdall and looked at her watch. Twelve fifty; time to move. Using Henry's phone, she dialled Miruna's number. It answered almost immediately.

"Yes?"

"Zis is Klaus. I—"

"This is not same phone."

Amelia nodded in approval; the girl was sharp. To reassure her, she gave the number of the Nokia she'd called from earlier, adding, "That one is out of credit."

There was a brief pause as the girl decided.

"OK." Her tone was businesslike. "Sometimes police try to trick us."

"Don't worry, I have no love of the police. I am slightly early. Are you ready?"

"Yes."

"Good. I'll be at the spot we arranged on Forest Road in about ten minutes. The car is a dark green four by four. I'll flash the lights once as I approach."

"OK, when I see car, I come onto street. Stop in darker place between street lights."

Amelia ended the call and pocketed the phone. She took a deep breath. Now for the fun part.

## Chapter Seven

To make sure that she wasn't the last to arrive for the briefing on Monday morning, Jennifer set three alarms, but unlike the previous day, she had been awake and up making tea before any of them sounded.

She was amazed to find that Derek Thyme was once again in the incident room before her. A reformed character? — she doubted it. She was about to ask him about what progress he had made when DCI Hurst marched in followed as usual by Rob McPherson.

Hurst cut straight to the chase.

"Morning everyone. As some of you will know, we made a certain amount of progress yesterday, and once the pm's done this morning, I'm expecting a lot more.

"As far as background on Miruna Peptanariu is concerned, the girls either living with her or working the same patch that she did have been tight-lipped, which would indicate that they are scared — we've no information yet as to who her pimp is. They've told us conflicting stories — some say Miruna was a popular girl with a number of regulars; others say she didn't have any. They are probably all lying and competing against each other for the favours of any of Miruna's more lucrative clients.

"The search of her room has given us some background about

her, but little about her professional life. She obviously played it carefully; she must have been quite streetwise for her age.

"There was an ageing laptop on which there were several emails to and from her family back in Romania. We've had a uniform who is half-Romanian translate them for us and it would appear that the family is under the impression she works as a model for the Hyson Modelling Agency. The company is real — DC Cotton managed to raise them even though it was Sunday afternoon — but they have never heard of her. She must have got the name from the Internet. Apart from her clothes, which were cheap, and her laptop, she had few possessions of any significance. The laptop has been seized for examination. Yes, Cotton."

Jennifer had put up her hand. "What about her mobile, boss?"

"Not yet been found. However, we have the number so the techies should still be able to link calls and texts from the records of the service provider."

He turned to the many photos attached to the whiteboards.

"Where we have made good progress is with the street cameras. A quick run through yesterday afternoon showed what appeared to be Miruna getting into a vehicle, a dark Nissan X-Trail, on Forest Road West at three minutes past one on Saturday morning. The lighting wasn't so good and the plate was partly obscured, but we got a partial number to run. Other cameras picked up the vehicle with what looks like Miruna in the front passenger seat leaving the city and heading north. One shot gave us more on the number plate, enough in fact to give us a full number: LJ11TTV. The vehicle is registered to a Henry Silk who lives in Hampstead, London. This information only came in a few minutes ago so we haven't yet tried to contact Mr Silk."

Jennifer raised her hand again.

Hurst cocked his head to one side, the look in his eyes telling her that the interruption had better be worth it.

"Is that the same Henry Silk who's an actor on the TV soap Runway Two-Seven, boss?"

A mutter of amusement went around the room as Hurst voiced what they were all thinking.

"I'm surprised you've even heard of Runway Two-Seven, Cotton. Not your normal cup of tea, from what I've been told."

Jennifer blushed. In the short time she had been in the SCF, she had gained a reputation as the group's intellectual, preferring to read the classics on her Kindle and talk about arty, foreign films. She was also known to be fluent in French and Italian.

"I do allow myself a couple of vices," she said defensively, "and Runway Two-Seven's one of them. Henry Silk has quite a reputation for his bad boy character but," — she paused as the ribbing got louder, and then raised her voice — "if it is him, the fact that he was appearing here at the Theatre Royal all last week could be significant."

The ribbing suddenly stopped as the group realised that the case might well have just moved significantly forward. Jennifer raised her chin towards them and continued.

"There was an advert in the Post for the play he was in, and then when I passed the theatre a few days ago, I saw a large poster with Silk's photo and name on it."

She paused again; she could see the DCI's mind was in overdrive. But before he could speak, one of the civilian intelligence officers put his hand up and launched into his own question.

"You said that the girl's face was visible on the CCTV footage, sir. Was the driver's face also shown?"

All eyes turned to Hurst, who put up his hands.

"Hold on a minute. We haven't yet confirmed whether the Henry Silk who owns the Nissan is Henry Silk the actor, but, to answer your question, the driver's face was obscured. He had the visor down, which must have been deliberate since it's not the sort of thing you'd normally do at night."

Another of the civilian intelligence officers had been tapping furiously on his mobile phone. He raised his hand and waited until Hurst saw him.

"Yes … Pete, isn't it?"

"Yes, sir. I've checked the Theatre Royal's website and it says that the play that Henry Silk was in finished on Saturday night, so he has presumably left the city. However, he's in another play here in July."

Hurst thanked him. "That's interesting. What we need to know now is whether the Nissan owner from Hampstead is the same Silk and whether his vehicle has been reported stolen. Could someone get onto that immediately, Rob?"

"Certainly," answered McPherson. He nodded to Derek Thyme who got up and headed to his computer in the adjacent main operations office.

"I also think it would be useful if, Cotton, you called the Theatre Royal to find out where Silk was staying and what they can tell us about him," added McPherson.

Jennifer followed Derek out of the room and sat at her computer. She entered her password, called up the Theatre Royal's number and punched it into her desk's landline. While the number was ringing, she heard Derek exclaim, 'Got it!' as he rushed over to a printer and waited impatiently for a sheet of information to emerge.

"Is this him?" he said, brandishing a copy of Henry Silk's driving licence under Jennifer's nose.

Jennifer nodded. "That's him, yes. Is it the same address?"

"Checking now," said Derek as he tapped some keys. Jennifer saw his eyes scanning the information on the screen.

"Yes," he said, "It's him all right. Any answer from the Theatre Royal?"

"No, probably too early for them; it's not yet eight thirty. I'll try the various hotels within walking distance of the theatre. I reckon the actors will have their favourites that are not far from the theatre so they can have a few post-performance drinks and not worry about driving."


Jennifer walked back into the main incident room to find it buzzing with activity. With the confirmation of Henry Silk as the owner of the vehicle and the information that he had been in Nottingham, Hurst and McPherson were busy allocating more tasks. One intelligence officer had already confirmed that there was no record of the Nissan being reported stolen, another had somehow obtained the name of Silk's insurance company and discovered that his vehicle insurance named him as his car's only driver.

Jennifer caught Hurst's eye. "Boss, he was staying at the Old Nottingham Hotel on Standard Hill. According to the receptionist I spoke to, it's his regular haunt when he's in a play here."

"OK, Cotton, get over there now with Thyme and talk to the staff. See what CCTV coverage they've got."

He turned to McPherson. "Right, Rob, let's get as many people as we can checking through every frame of the footage from traffic. There has to be one shot with Silk's face in it. Put him in the car and we've got him. Game over."

# Chapter Eight

Shortly before one in the morning, Amelia left her room carrying a single holdall. Dressed in Henry Silk's clothing and now wearing a pair of thin leather gloves over the disposable gloves, she walked down the corridor to the lift, altering her stance and stride to match Henry's. She pressed the call button and waited, her head down. Once inside the lift, she continued looking down at her feet so that all the CCTV camera could really see clearly was the top of Henry's baseball cap.

To her surprise, the doors opened at the reception level and four tipsy Korean businessmen started to bustle their way into the lift. On seeing her, they immediately backed away with a chorus of "Oh, solly, solly," together with much bowing. She graciously bowed her head in return while glancing at the desk where, as the lift doors closed, she was relieved to see Michael engrossed in his usual on-screen card game.

As she walked through the car park towards Henry's car, she once again made sure she was in the field of view of the CCTV behind her — it was show time and she wanted to tease her future viewers. Before starting the car, she removed the side-handle baton from the holdall and stowed it in the netting pouch attached to the rear of the front passenger seat, angling the handle so that she would be able to reach round the headrest to grasp it.

Four minutes later she turned into Forest Road West, having taken main roads from the city centre to ensure that the car would be recorded on several traffic cameras. Two hundred yards along the road, she slowed the car, her eyes scanning the parked cars, the pavement, the road and the side roads. She knew the anti-prostitution squad would be active on a Friday evening but fortunately, at this moment, there were no obvious patrols. She lowered the passenger window, flashed the headlights once and immediately saw a movement from the shadows on her left. The girl walked purposefully towards the car, although her eyes were quite deliberately looking elsewhere. As the car slowed to a halt by her, the girl bent towards the window.

"Klaus," said Amelia, and the girl slid into the car.

The Nissan sped off to where the road became Forest Road East, continuing on to the end where it turned left into Mansfield Road, the A60 that headed north out of the city towards the town of Mansfield some fifteen miles away.

The traffic was light but Amelia remained vigilant. She didn't want to be stopped for any reason with an obvious hooker in the car.

"Where we go?" said the girl, her voice harsh, suspicious.

Amelia glanced at her. "Fasten your seat belt," she instructed.

Miruna's head shot round. "You a woman, stop car now! You cop?"

Amelia forced a smile. "Hey, cool it. I'm not a cop. I'm just a girl looking for some fun, that's all. Is that a problem? Surely you're not fussy?"

"Cost more. I don't usually go with women."

"Not usually, perhaps, but you have done."

"Of course."

"Well then, it's not a problem."

"OK, but pay more."

"Naturally, but I want a good time."

She reached over and lightly brushed a hand over Miruna's right breast. "Nice," she said.

"Hey, stop that. No touching yet."

"Relax. And remember, I'm paying you well."

"Why you dressed as man?"

"I should have thought that was obvious. If you'd seen a woman driving the car, you wouldn't even have got in."

"Where we go?"

Amelia smiled. "Somewhere quiet and private out in the countryside. It's a great evening. I thought we could have some fun under the stars."

"You crazy."

"Have you ever been out to the woods with your clients?"

"You joking. All they want is quickie in dark alley. Ten quid for blow job, twenty for screw up against wall. Finish in few minutes."

"Well, I'm going to be paying you more than you normally earn in a week for a relaxing night you'll remember. And if you're clever, you won't have to give it all to your pimp."

She put a hand on the girl's knee.

"The question is, Miruna, are you up to it? I hope you're not going to disappoint me."

The girl threw her head back and gave a haughty flick of her hair.

"I'm the best. Look at me, young, slim, good tits — real, not silicon like most of those tarts — no disease. You'll have your fun."

She paused, looking sideways at Amelia. "You give me money first?"

Amelia laughed. "I wondered how long it would take you to demand that. Look in the glove box, there's a couple of hundred. You'll get the rest later."

Miruna snapped open the box and took out ten folded twenty-pound notes that Amelia had put there when she got in the car. She counted them and stuffed them in the inside pocket of her jacket. She wasn't carrying a bag.

As they approached Harlow Wood on the right of the A60, Amelia slowed the car at a spot where an unsurfaced track led into the trees. A barrier barred the way, but there was no padlock and even if there had been, the bolt croppers in one of the holdalls would have made light work of it. She told Miruna to get out and lift the barrier.

"Close it again once I've driven through," she added.

When the girl looked up moodily, Amelia thought the extra work might be accompanied by a demand for even more money, but Miruna got out of the car and did what she was asked.

Once the girl had settled back in the car, Amelia drove about three hundred yards along the winding track, stopping at a point where it widened slightly. She switched off the engine and clicked on the interior light.

Turning towards the passenger seat, she reached out a hand, stroking her fingers through Miruna's hair.

"You're a pretty girl. If I like you, this could become a regular meeting," she promised. "Now, it's a nice night, but we don't want to get chilly. I've got several blankets in the boot, along with some wine, beer, whatever you like, and a selection of tabs that I think you'll enjoy."

The girl suddenly registered interest at the mention of drugs.

"What you got?"

"All in good time. Before we do that, I can't wait for you for much longer. I've been thinking about this all day. Could you push your seat back as far as it will go? Good, that's it. Now hop out of the car while I climb into your seat and recline it. OK, now get back in. We'll close the door and you can kneel down in front of me."

Miruna did as she was told. "There's not much room," she complained.

"You're not very big," said Amelia, smiling at her. "We'll be fine."

She reclined her seat a little more and pulled up Henry's pullover to reveal the belt holding Henry's jeans.

Miruna understood. She undid the belt buckle, unfastened the jeans and lowered the zip. Amelia lifted her bottom for the girl to pull down the jeans, pants and tights until they were below her knees.

Putting her left hand between Amelia's thighs, the girl looked up into her client's eyes.

Amelia smiled encouragingly. "That feels good," she whispered.

She took Miruna's head in both hands and gently turned it so that the girl's focus was entirely between her legs. Without looking up, the girl reached out her right hand to steady herself, gently grasping Amelia's shoulder through the pullover. Amelia arched her back slowly and reached out her right arm over the side of the reclined seat, feeling for the baton.

In a movement she had practised a hundred times in her own car, she freed the baton from the netting and lifted it into the restricted space over her head. The swing would be impeded by the lack of room; she knew this and would allow for it. Practice makes perfect. In a flash, her left hand shot up to grab the side handle and with both hands she whipped the baton down onto Miruna's head, using just enough force to knock her out.

Miruna grunted, her nails digging reflexively into Amelia's shoulder as she collapsed. Amelia hardly noticed, all her concentration focussed on the slumped body. Was there some movement? Maybe. She lifted the baton and delivered a second blow to the same spot on the back of the girl's head. Now she was definitely out cold.

Amelia shoved the girl's body away from her and pulled herself back into her clothing. Now she was ready. She sat up and grabbed the holdall from the back seat, dropped it onto the driver's seat next to her and unzipped it. She peeled off the leather gloves and, after a glance to check the disposable gloves still on her hands hadn't torn, she reached into the holdall to pull out a heavy-duty polythene bag from an inside pocket.

She leaned forward and pulled the bag over Miruna's head, wrapping the opening around her neck and holding it firmly to cut off the air supply. In two breaths, the bag was tight against the girl's mouth and nose. She could feel some automatic resistance as Miruna's lungs fought for air, her arms and torso twitching and writhing, but the resistance quickly faded and she was soon still. Amelia knew that death would take far longer than the few seconds normally shown in the movies. That was fine; she had both the time and the patience to sit there for as long as it took. She kept her hands firmly around Miruna's neck, holding the bag in place for several minutes before releasing it and checking the girl's pulse. Satisfied she was dead, she removed the polythene bag and put it back into the holdall.

Amelia released the door next to her, swung her feet over the slumped body and climbed out of the car. Reaching back in, she pushed her forearms under Miruna's armpits, lifting her out and carrying her to a firm but grassy patch of ground about four feet away.

Reaching inside the girl's jacket, Amelia retrieved the banknotes, after which she stood back to assess her next move. Her intention was to leave evidence of contact. There had already been some while lifting Miruna out of the car, but she wanted more. She'd originally planned to lie down on the body, but again she was wary of overdoing it. And having now seen Henry's clothing and the girl's, Amelia knew there would be enough contact carrying the body along the path to the spot in the woods she had already chosen. Fibres from Henry's pullover and scarf would definitely be left on Miruna's clothing, while a few of the mix of long pink and white polyester fibres from the faux fur of her jacket collar should end up on Henry's pullover.

But before carrying the body into the trees, there was more work to be done and for that she needed better light. She reached into the holdall to find a powerful LED head torch and slipped it on over the baseball cap. Angling the beam towards her hands, she retrieved the polythene bag with the comb containing Henry's hair from the holdall, pulled a few single strands from the teeth and rubbed them into Miruna's clothing at breast level.

Now for the delicate part. She bagged the comb and put it back in the holdall before pulling out the larger bag containing the mannequin hand. Kneeling down, she picked up Miruna's hands and examined the fingernails. There would definitely be fibres from Henry's pullover under the nails, maybe even some from the scarf. However, there was a problem: Miruna had touched Amelia's legs and groin area and although she hadn't penetrated her, there was a possibility of secretions containing Amelia's DNA being present on her hands. To remove these, Amelia retrieved a packet of surgical wipes from the holdall and used several to thoroughly clean the girl's hands, fingers and nails. After making sure the hands were dry, she began the process of transferring more fibres to Miruna's nails. The first part was easy — she took each hand in turn and rubbed the nails down Henry's pullover and scarf — but for the second part, which involved only the right hand, she took a plain wooden toothpick from a packet in her kit and carefully rubbed the tip under the nail glued to the index finger of the mannequin's hand, removing skin and dried blood from where she had scratched the nails along the unconscious Henry's neck. This debris she carefully wiped along the inside of the nail of Miruna's right index finger. Satisfied with her efforts, Amelia repeated the process for the other fingernails, matching like with like.

As she stood and looked down at the body, she wondered about the dyed orange hair, but caution again told her that there would almost definitely be one or two hairs in the car from when Miruna had slumped against the glove box. Why not let the techies earn their money and find them? The girl's fingerprints would also be in the car along with plenty of other evidence to link her with the car and with Henry.

All that remained now was to hide the girl's body. Fortunately Miruna was short and light, so carrying her into the woods would not be difficult. Amelia bent down to pick her up, one hand round her back under her arms and the other under her knees. The spot she'd chosen was a small clearing about fifty yards into the wood with some large bushes to one side that would screen the body from view. She wondered how long it would be before a passer-by or a dog discovered it. She guessed it would almost definitely be within the next forty-eight hours.

The path through the trees to the clearing was narrow, which guaranteed that both Henry's clothing and Miruna's would snag against the branches and twigs that reached across the path. All the scientists had to do was find fibres and work out the scenario, all of which would add to the convincing case against Henry.

Satisfied that Miruna's body was well hidden in the bushes, Amelia returned to the car to tidy up and the first thing she saw was Miruna's left shoe lying in the front footwell. Slightly cross with herself for not noticing that the girl was missing a shoe, she considered putting it back on the body. But as she reached for the shoe, she realised what a great piece of evidence it would make. However, she couldn't simply leave it there; Henry would see it the following day. She picked up the shoe and glanced around the car interior, finally deciding to stow it out of sight under the front passenger seat where there were enough obstructions to prevent it rolling forward. It would remain in place until some sharp-eyed person found it.

The remaining tasks were straightforward. She picked up the side-handle baton from the driver's seat where she'd dropped it and pulled out the main grip extension — the part bearing Henry's fingerprints — letting it click into place. Shining the torch briefly onto the surrounding trees to find the best direction, she threw the baton hard and high, away from the path to the clearing where Miruna's body now lay. If it were found, all well and good; if not, there was plenty of other evidence. The prints on the baton grip extension would be icing on the cake, and no one would expect that someone planting evidence would be so cavalier as to risk it not being found.

She finished her tidying by putting the reclined passenger seat back in an upright position and sliding the seat forward, checking as she did that the girl's shoe was still well hidden. Finally, she took the girl's phone from her pocket — she had removed it from the girl's jacket when she left her in the bushes. She had no use for it so she switched it off and threw it into the woods.

Every box now ticked, she climbed into the car and headed back to Nottingham, keeping the sun visor pulled down as she had on the outward trip, her leather gloves now back on her hands over the surgical gloves as she gripped the wheel.

It was twenty minutes to three by the time she parked Henry's car at the back of the Old Nottingham. This time she took the stairs all the way to the second floor — she didn't want to risk a chance meeting with Michael. However, as she walked past the lift door on the second floor lobby, she deliberately came close enough to make sure that the CCTV camera would capture a fleeting glimpse of her.

Back in her room, she took off the baseball cap and carefully searched it for blond hairs from the wig. If the forensic scientists were later to find blond hairs in it, their presence would strengthen the case for Henry not being the murderer, that someone had dressed up in his clothes, someone wearing a wig. Finding one or two elsewhere on his clothes or on the dead girl didn't matter: without a source they were of little value, but it was important that any in the cap were removed. Her diligence was worth it: her search produced a solitary hair that she lifted out and dropped into the holdall for later disposal.

Another box ticked, she walked back to Henry's room carrying the baseball cap in her gloved hand. The click of the magnetic lock sounded brutally loud in the silence of the hotel but it made no difference: Henry hadn't moved.

After carefully taking off Henry's clothes, she left them on the end of the bed. She had no plans to try to dress him again — dressing an unconscious man was considerably more difficult than undressing him and there was always a risk that he might rouse from his slumbers. When he found his clothes, Henry would assume that he'd been compos mentis enough to undress.

She had none of her own clothing with her since she was confident from the lack of any noise from other rooms that even the Korean businessmen were asleep, so there was little risk in skipping down the corridor to her own room in her underwear. If she did happen to bump into one of them, she'd wink at him and disappear into her room, leaving him with a tale to tell that would most likely be put down to a vivid, booze-induced imagination.

After one final check around the room, Amelia put Henry's key card on the desk and opened the door. Once she'd shut it, there was no returning.


Half an hour soaking in a steaming bath left Amelia feeling relaxed and delighted with her night's work. One hooker fewer on the streets of Nottingham — the girl was scum to her, not worth another thought — and one public figure about to fall spectacularly from grace. She lay in the water, luxuriating in its heat as she ran through everything in her mind. It had been a truly professional job. Henry Silk would soon have the full force of the law bearing down on him, and with no alibi and a mountain of evidence to implicate him, there was little chance of anything he said being believed. She had set up his destruction, as she had with others previously, but this fish was bigger. All she had to do now was sit back and watch him being reeled in, twitching and jerking like a man on the end of a noose. But unlike a man in his death throes, Henry Silk would suffer the degradation she had created for him for as long as she chose, after which she might consider mercy. That his life would become a living nightmare gave her a sense of satisfaction like no other.

# Chapter Nine

The receptionist at the Old Nottingham Hotel was the same bored twenty-year-old who had checked in the mousey Amelia Taverner the previous Friday. However, after a weekend experimenting with some new tablets her boyfriend had bought, she would have found it difficult to describe Amelia even if her life depended on it.

Jennifer walked round the reception desk to the girl's side and gave her a reassuring smile — the girl had looked immediately furtive when she and Derek Thyme had announced they were police officers. "Was it you I spoke to earlier on the phone, Sheryl?" she asked, reading the receptionist's name badge.

"No," said the girl, "I was a bit late this morning." She glanced sheepishly in the direction of what Jennifer assumed was the manager's office. "It would have been Denise you spoke to. She covered for me till I got here."

"Hectic weekend?" asked Jennifer, noting a residual glassiness in the girl's pupils.

"Yeah, I—" Sheryl stopped as she remembered who Jennifer was. "Yeah," she repeated less enthusiastically, and looked down.

"Don't worry, Sheryl, I won't let on," said Jennifer.

Sheryl was suddenly defensive. "Let on what?"

Jennifer waited a beat before continuing.

"I can see it in your eyes. Whatever it was you were taking, it was strong, and having seen a lot of users, I can assure you it will be addling your brain."

"Don't know what you mean. I've not done nothing."

"As I said, Sheryl, I'm not here to find out about your weekend. I need some info about one of your guests. His name is Henry Silk. A regular, I think."

Suddenly Sheryl was only too pleased to help. She needed to keep this cop onside, but she was also concerned that the police were interested in Henry Silk.

"You're right, he is a regular. Right gorgeous, he is, even though he's old enough to be me dad. A real gentleman, completely different to the bloke he plays on the telly. That Jake Morrison in Runway is a right sod. Mr Silk's nothing like that."

She was starting to warm to her theme. "I went to see him last week in the play — I was working days, same as this week, so I could. He was brilliant. Really evil. Dunno how he does it."

"When did he check out, Sheryl? Sunday, after the final performance on Saturday night?"

"No, it was Saturday lunchtime, although he left his car here until Saturday night. Told me he was driving straight down to London after the play finished. I bet he's got a penthouse or something; somewhere really smart."

"So you spoke to him on Saturday? What time was that?"

"It was around lunchtime, which is unusual for him. I mean, he's never down early for his breakfast, but he's always there. But Saturday, he missed it."

"How did he seem?"

"What's he done? I don't want to get him into no trouble."

"You won't, Sheryl, you'll be helping him and helping us as well. So, how was he?"

"Well, he looked right dreadful, all bleary like. Sort of puzzled."

"Puzzled?"

"Yeah, like he didn't know where he was."

"Did he say where he'd been?"

"He'd been in his room. He told me. Overslept, he said. Said he thought that the play had been harder work than he thought. So

I got him a cup of coffee — strong, black, like he always takes it — and sat him in the restaurant with it. I think he might've had a sandwich. Do you want me to check?"

"No, it's OK, we can talk to the kitchen staff later if we need to."

Derek looked towards the bar. "Does Mr Silk have a drink at all when he comes back after a performance?"

Sheryl nodded as she looked Derek up and down. The female cop had been so pushy that she'd hardly noticed him. Quite good looking, for a cop. Tall too. And black. Her boyfriend Wes was black.

She gave him what was meant to be a coy smile. "Every night, like clockwork. Marches in, all theatrical, and has his vodka and tonic." She looked around before leaning towards Derek and dropping her voice. "Normally buys whoever's on duty one too. Such a gentleman."

"Just the one?" asked Derek.

"Always," nodded Sheryl. "But I happen to know that he keeps a smart bottle or two in his room. The maid what does his room just loves him. Told me that she's cleared more than one empty bottle from his bin. Fancy stuff too, she reckons. Wouldn't know, myself, don't really drink much."

She glanced at Jennifer in time to catch her knowing look and suddenly stared at her feet.

Derek felt he'd got the receptionist's confidence.

"Didn't happen to say where he's gone this week, did he, Sheryl? Another town with the play?"

"No, the play's finished. He told me later what he was doing. Once he'd had a bite to eat and more coffee, he seemed OK. That was when he checked out and told me about his car."

"What about his car?"

"That he was driving down to London, like I said."

"Yes, of course. So he's in London."

"Yes, but he said he was going to be filming for the telly. Outside stuff, he said. They do it all at Luton airport, you know. I knew that coz it was in Celeb magazine."

She smiled as she remembered something.

"He was really sweet. I gave him a photo of the actress who plays the airport manager's secretary, the dizzy one, Beryline Hertford. Me dad thinks she's wonderful. Mr Silk said he'd get her to autograph the photo. Bring it me in a couple of weeks when he's back."

"Sounds like he's quite a guy," interrupted Jennifer. She wanted to move on. "The other thing we'd like to know about is the CCTV that you've got here. I've been looking around but I can only see a couple of cameras. Are there more?"

"There's not many, no," said Sheryl, shaking her head.

She pointed around the lobby. "There's that one looking at the door, there's one up there, above us, looking at where we are, and there's one in the bar, but that's aimed at the till."

"Aren't there others?" prompted Jennifer. "There must be one in the lift, surely."

"Yeah, and outside the lift on each floor, except here in the lobby. There's one in the car park too."

Jennifer looked up at Derek. She could see he was thinking the same thing that she was. If there was footage of Henry leaving the car park late on Friday evening and then coming back in the early hours of Saturday morning, that would more or less clinch the case.

She turned her attention back to the receptionist.

"Right, Sheryl, we're going to need to look at the recordings from each of the cameras starting from the middle of last week until Saturday afternoon."

Sheryl shook her head. "I can't give you those, they're nothing to do with me. You'll have to talk to the manager. Hey, what's this all about? Is Mr Silk in some sort of trouble?"

Jennifer ignored the question.

"Where's the manager's office?" she said.

"I'll call him for you," said Sheryl as she pressed a button on the phone in front of her and lifted the receiver.

"Hi, Mr Jackson, it's Sheryl on reception. There's a couple of police officers here who want to talk to you. Shall I send them through? Oh, OK."

She put the receiver back on the cradle. "He says — Oh, here he is now."

Jennifer turned and saw the concerned-looking manager as he hurried from his office. She walked towards him, wanting to avoid Sheryl's interruptions and get the CCTV recordings as soon as possible. She looked back and was pleased to see that Derek had got the message and was distracting Sheryl by asking her more questions.

The manager blanched when Jennifer mentioned a murder inquiry and, concerned for the reputation of his hotel, he willingly handed over the discs once he realised that stalling for a warrant would gain him no favours.

As they hurried out of the hotel with the discs and signed paperwork releasing them into their custody, Jennifer tossed Derek her keys. "You drive, I've got to make a couple of calls and I don't want to waste time."


Back in the SCF, they headed for Mike Hurst's office where they found the DCI talking to Rob McPherson.

Hurst held up a hand as Jennifer was about to launch forth with what they'd discovered.

"From the look on your face Cotton, I'd say you've made some progress. Am I right?"

"Yes, boss, I—"

"Well, to save time, let's get Bottomley in here too."

He shifted his eyes to Derek. "Thyme."

Derek scuttled out of the office and was back within thirty seconds followed by the detective sergeant.

Hurst sat back in his chair. "Right, Cotton, let's hear it."

"Well, boss, from what the receptionist at the Old Nottingham has told us, it would appear that Henry Silk could be very involved."

She went through everything from the hotel, holding up the bag of CCTV discs as she explained the manager's cooperation.

"You've got them all signed for I hope, Cotton. We don't want to bugger up the chain of evidence."

"All sorted, boss. Boss, on the way back, I called Luton airport security and they confirmed that the TV company that makes Runway Two-Seven is filming outside shots there for the next three days. In fact they're already there; something to do with the light. Apparently they have a spot on the airport perimeter they use that gives them background of planes taking off and landing during whatever action is being filmed. That ties in with what Silk told the hotel receptionist, but just to be sure, I asked the security guy to quietly check if Silk's car is there, and it is."

"Good work, Cotton. Both of you, in fact," said Hurst.

He turned to McPherson. "Rob, I think you and Neil should head for Luton airport and have a chat with Mr Silk. If his car matches the one in traffic's CCTV, we need to seize it and get it back here. Sounds to me like Mr Silk has a lot of explaining to do."

McPherson and Bottomley made for the door, but Jennifer hovered where she was. Hurst looked up suspiciously.

"What's the matter, Cotton? You look like someone stole your pet rabbit."

"Well, I was thinking, boss, that having a female go along too might distract Silk a bit, perhaps loosen his tongue."

"He's probably murdered a prostitute, Cotton. Do we really need to distract him?"

"He's got something of a reputation as a ladies' man. It might help."

Hurst kept a deadpan expression.

"You're right. Who do you suggest we send along?"

Jennifer caught the tone in his voice.

"I think perhaps someone who's a big fan of the series, knows about the cast and who would love to have the opportunity to see it being filmed. No, forget that last bit. I meant, someone professional enough not to be overawed by the whole TV razzmatazz."

"OK, Cotton, you can go, but don't forget that Mr Henry Smooth-as-Silk is a killer."

Jennifer raised her eyebrows a fraction, but said nothing more. She was shocked that Hurst's position on Silk had gone from victim of car theft to murderer in the space of a few hours. Old-school thinking or instinct that comes with years of experience? She wasn't sure.

## Chapter Ten

The drive from Nottingham to Luton took them a little over two hours. Longer than it should but, as ever, there were sections of the M1 motorway under repair. An hour into the journey, McPherson took a call from Derek Thyme about the post mortem findings.

"OK, Thyme, I'm putting the call on speaker so that all three of us can hear it."

"Right-o guv. First up, as well as confirming the cause of death as being asphyxiation with a plastic bag, Dr Lawson has also confirmed that there was no evidence of any sexual activity immediately prior to death. Nothing on any of the swabs."

McPherson grunted. "They probably had an argument that got out of hand before they got around to anything. She was probably demanding too much money. Greedy lot, the girls on Forest Road."

Sitting in the back of the car and listening intently to the conversation, Jennifer wondered how he knew.

"What about the injuries to the head?" continued McPherson.

"The Doc also confirmed that they were from a blunt, rounded object and by themselves wouldn't have been life threatening."

"So, nothing new, Justin."

"No, guv. The clothing has been sent to the lab and samples from the girl to toxicology."

"Right. Let's hope that new lab we're using — what's it called?"

"Forefront Forensics."

"Yes, well, let's hope they're keen enough to get the results out quickly. What are you doing now, Justin?"

There was a pause and Jennifer smiled to herself; she could imagine the look of confusion on Derek's face.

McPherson sighed. "Apart from talking to me, I mean."

"Oh, right, guv. I'm about to start looking at the CCTV footage from the hotel."

"Keep me posted on anything you find." McPherson ended the call and turned to Jennifer. "What else do you know about Henry Silk, given that you're such a fan, Cotton?"

Jennifer ignored the sarcastic tone.

"From what I've read, guv, he's something of a loner. He's got a reputation of being a talented actor, particularly in character parts. Apparently he can put on all sorts of regional and foreign accents."

Neil Bottomley, who was driving, chimed in.

"Funny how some actors can do that and others can't. You'd think it would be part of their training."

McPherson grunted his lack of interest in accents.

"So why do you say he's a loner?"

"It's what the magazines say, guv, I don't know the man. It seems there was an incident many years ago. In the late eighties, I think. He was blamed for the death of that actor they called the British James Dean."

"Dirk Sanderley?" suggested Bottomley.

"Yes, that's the one. I don't know much about the incident except that it was a car crash and Silk was driving. It put a blight on Silk's career. Even after all these years, he can't get work with any of the big studios in Hollywood, all of whom were raving about Sanderley at the time. Seems very unfair to me. Several other actors from Runway have got good parts in Hollywood films or TV series and they're not a patch on Silk."

Another grunt from McPherson. "I shouldn't feel too sorry for him, Cotton. After our visit today, Silk might well be putting his acting career on permanent hold. Unless they do Christmas panto where he's going."

"Guv, we haven't …" started Jennifer, but then thought better of it.

"Haven't what?"

"Doesn't matter," replied Jennifer quietly. She wanted to talk about the criminal justice system being based on the premise that a person was innocent until proven guilty, but she knew what the response would be: that was the job of the courts — judge and jury. The job of the police was to catch the criminals and to present the facts to the CPS, the Crown Prosecution Service, for consideration. What concerned her was that they hadn't even spoken to Henry Silk and yet her bosses were already thinking the case was done and dusted. She hoped that the passing years would not make her so blinkered, that she would always be able to keep an open mind.

Rob McPherson had called ahead to the local police in Luton who had in turn asked the airport division to send two patrol cars in case support was needed. They waited half a mile down the road for the unmarked CID car and the three cars swept into the filming location together, causing immediate consternation to the director, who yelled at his harassed assistant.

"Anthony! What are they doing there? We haven't ordered any police cars for today or even for this week. And they are right in the way just as we're ready to start."

He paused, his weekend hangover threatening to return.

"Why is nothing ever easy?" he whined. "You arrange for the plods to be here and they're late; you don't arrange it and they're in your face. Get on over there and politely but firmly tell them to shift their uniformed backsides."

He pivoted on his foot and marched off in the direction of a group of actors standing by an airport vehicle being used as a prop on the tarmac.

"Sorry," he said, reaching for a cigarette before jamming the packet back in his pocket in frustration as he remembered the smoking restrictions on or near the runway. "Those boys in blue are in the way. We'll get them shifted, pronto. Jesus!"

Henry Silk cast a wary eye to the clouds scudding across the sky.

"I'd suggest sooner rather than later, Jonty. This weather doesn't look like it's going to hold. If we're not careful, we'll have to reshoot the whole lot in rain gear."

The director slapped the palm of a hand to his forehead.

"I can't bear to even think that might happen; I'll sue the buggers. Don't they know how much delays like this cost?"

He turned to look for his assistant.

"What's taking Anthony so long? Oh, God, what are they doing?"

He could see that despite his assistant's protestations, none of the police cars had moved and now three people — two men and a young woman — were marching towards him with Anthony half-running along behind them.

The director had had enough. He thrust his clipboard into the nearest pair of hands and stormed off towards the approaching group, booming at them from a distance of twenty yards.

"Listen, I don't know who you are but I need those police cars and that other car out of here now. Not in a minute. Now!"

Jonty Peters was an imposing figure. At six foot four, with a shock of wild grey hair and matching bushy eyebrows, vivid blue eyes and a florid complexion from over-frequent sampling of his extensive collection of single malts, he was used to getting his own way. At five foot six but built like a bulldog, McPherson was having none of it. He pulled his warrant card from his pocket and held it up.

"Detective Inspector Robert McPherson of Nottingham City and County Serious Crime Formation. These are my colleagues Detective Sergeant Neil Bottomley and Detective Constable Jennifer Cotton."

"And that interests me because …"

McPherson narrowed his eyes, but bit his tongue.

"We need to talk urgently to a Mr Henry Silk of Lambton

Court Gardens, Hampstead. We have reason to believe that he is working on your set."

"Working on my set!" yelled Peters. "He's more than working on my bloody set. He's the lead actor in today's filming. Filming that costs a lot of money and which you are interrupting. Tell me, Inspector, to whom do I send the bill for this unacceptable delay?"

"If you'd calm down, sir, we can probably get this sorted out very quickly," lied McPherson, knowing full well that it would be anything but quick. "Now, perhaps you could point out Mr Silk."

"God! What planet do you live on, Inspector? I can only assume from that request you're not one of the legions, millions should I say, of fans who are riveted nightly to this programme. Fans who will be extremely unimpressed by police harassment on the set of their favourite show."

McPherson had had enough. "If you want to make a complaint sir, I suggest you go through the normal channels. Now—"

He stopped as Jennifer tapped him on the shoulder.

"He's over there, guv, the one dressed in the black uniform trousers and white shirt."

"Fetch him, Cotton, will you?"

"Now look here!" protested the director as Jennifer walked off. He reached out to stop her but McPherson blocked him.

"I didn't get your name, sir."

"Jonty Peters. I'm the director and I shall indeed be making a formal complaint."

"Well, Mr Peters, I should advise you that obstructing the police in the commission of their duty is a serious offence, as is assaulting a police officer, which you just came very close to doing. I'd also advise you to back off or this might well take all day."

Peters had met his match. "Look, I'm sorry, Inspector," he said, wilting. "You must understand that I'm under a lot of pressure here. If we don't move forward with the filming, the whole schedule is stuffed. Already the weather is not playing ball and now …"

Arsehole, thought McPherson.

"We'll be as quick as we can, sir," he said, walking away, followed closely by Bottomley.

Jennifer walked over to the group of actors. The women glanced at her, logging in microseconds her trim, well-toned figure, her pretty, open features, her short but stylish dark brown hair and her no-nonsense, well-cut pants suit. The men merely registered a good-looking twenty-five-year-old as their eyes roamed her figure.

Henry Silk was talking quietly to one of the younger actresses and had his back to her as she approached.

Jennifer coughed. "Mr Silk?"

Henry turned and let his eyes stay on hers, the corners of his mouth lifting in a slight smile. She was an attractive young woman, to be sure, but there was something else about her, something vaguely familiar. But then again, he'd met so many women of that age, and the older he got, the more they seemed to come out of a mould.

Jennifer felt rather intimidated to be face to face with not only Henry Silk, but also with a number of other familiar faces from the soap she regularly watched. She took a breath and held up her warrant card.

"Detective Constable Jennifer Cotton of the Nottingham City and County Serious Crime Formation. Would you mind coming with me, sir? My colleague, Detective Inspector McPherson, would like a word."

Henry shrugged his shoulders and grinned at the rest of the bemused cast. "Lead on, Detective Constable, lead on."

Meanwhile, Jonty Peters had recovered his equilibrium and was now pacing after McPherson. Bottomley heard him and leaned forward to the DI.

"Rob," he said, nodding his head in Peters' direction.

McPherson growled and turned to the director. "I'll give you a shout if I need you, Mr Peters. In the meantime, we must talk to Mr Silk on his own."

Peters started to protest but then thought better of it. He stopped and stood where he was, looking like a lost child.

Henry Silk walked up to McPherson and held out his hand.

"Henry Silk, Inspector. How may I help you?"

The DI ignored the outstretched hand and got straight to the point.

"Could you please confirm, sir, that you are Henry Silk of number thirteen Lambton Court Gardens, Hampstead?"

"I am, Inspector, yes."

"And are you the owner of a dark green Nissan X-Trail registration number LJ11TTV?"

"Yes."

"Could you also confirm that you were in Nottingham last week from Sunday until Saturday?"

"I was, yes. I was appearing in a production of 'The Ripper Returns' at the Theatre Royal. Perhaps you saw it."

"No, sir, I didn't. And where—"

He was interrupted by a pointed cough from Jennifer, to whom the line of questioning sounded like an interview, and under the rules, all interviews had to be recorded using audio and video. Also, if the questions were deemed to be an interview, the clock would immediately start ticking on how long they could hold Silk. It would be better to take him to Nottingham and start the whole process there.

McPherson got the message and scowled.

"Actually, sir, it's your car we're interested in at the moment. Do you have it with you today, the Nissan X-Trail?"

Henry frowned. "I do, yes. Why?"

"We have reason to believe that your car was used in the commission of a crime in the early hours of last Saturday morning. Could you show us where it's parked?"

"That's crazy, Inspector. My car was parked at my hotel the whole of Friday night and Saturday. It can't possibly have been used in a crime. If it had been stolen, I should have known. After all, car thieves don't normally return cars to where they stole them from, do they? Especially a secure car park. What sort of crime do you think it was used in?"

"A murder."

"A murder? Inspector, you can't think … look, there's obviously been some enormous mistake. I was asleep in my room on Friday night. All night. And my car keys were in the room with me."

He tried to picture being in his room on Friday night, but all he could remember after leaving the theatre was waking up late the next morning with what felt like a giant hangover. There was a vague, fleeting fragment of memory, way in the back of his mind, of raising a glass and toasting 'cin cin!' with someone, but he also remembered that when he put away his Belvedere vodka bottle on Saturday morning, a more seriously depleted bottle than he expected, there was only one glass next to it.

McPherson was watching Henry intently, trying to read his reaction.

"Your car, sir?" he said.

Henry sighed in frustration. "Follow me, it's over there."

They reached the cars and Henry pointed. "There, Inspector, that's the one."

"Thank you, sir. Could you please stay here for a moment with Sergeant Bottomley?"

Without waiting for a response, McPherson moved to the rear of the car. Jennifer followed, pulling a file from her bag. Inside were several images from the CCTV showing the front and rear of the Nissan together with the registration plates. She handed them to him and looked over his shoulder as he compared the shot of the car's rear end with the car itself. He gave a non-committal grunt and walked to the front. He grunted again.

"No outstanding features, but nothing that's obviously different."

Jennifer reached into her bag for her notebook and pen, as ever wanting to log everything.

"You're thinking that perhaps the car shown in the CCTV footage had false plates, guv?"

"Got to be considered, Cotton."

"Yes, guv. Well, the vehicle licence disc's in the same place on the car and in the photo, and there's a vignette for Switzerland below it. Look, you can just see it in the photo too. I hadn't noticed it before."

"A what?"

"This sticker," she said, pointing to the place on the photo. "It's called a vignette. It shows the road tax for using the motorways in Switzerland has been paid for this year. He's obviously driven in or through the country in the last few months. It's a one-off payment you make at the border."

"Well spotted, Cotton. Of course, you'd know about driving in Europe, being Italian. I'd forgotten that."

"I'm not Italian, guv, I just grew up in Italy."

"Same thing. OK, let's get his keys. I want you to have a look inside, without touching anything, of course. This is looking more promising by the minute."

Jennifer took a pair of disposable gloves from her bag and pulled them on as she walked back over to Henry.

"Mr Silk, may I have the keys to your vehicle please? I need to take a look inside. When I do, I'd be grateful if you could stand a few feet behind me so you can see clearly what I'm doing."

Henry fished in a pocket. "Here we are, Constable, fill your boots," he said, tossing the keys to Jennifer. "They'd normally be in my jacket in the trailer, but I needed to fetch my newspaper from the car — I like to do the crossword in between takes. It can get quite boring being on set, you know. I popped them in my trouser pocket rather than go back to the trailer. Jonty wouldn't like it, but what the hell."

"Thank you, sir," said Jennifer as she caught them. "I'll open the driver's door first."

She pressed a button on the fob and after carefully opening the door, she scanned the driver's seat and footwell but could see nothing out of the ordinary.

She pointed to a newspaper in the door pocket. "Not that paper, then?"

"No, that's yesterday's," replied Henry. "I forgot to throw it away."

"Let's take a look at the passenger side," said Jennifer. The three men followed her around the car.

Opening the front passenger door, she glanced around before bending down to peer under the seat, taking care not to touch anything. Suddenly she let out a gasp. "Guv, I think you should see this."

McPherson moved forward and bent down to look where she was pointing.

"Christ!" he said. "Got your phone, Cotton, we'll record it as it is. Can you see any size markings?"

Jennifer peered closer. Looks like thirty-seven."

"In English, Cotton."

"A UK size four, guv. I'll get a shot and contact Derek."

She took several photos and then moved out of earshot to make the call.

"What is it, Inspector?" asked Henry starting to walk towards the car.

McPherson turned round and stopped him with an upturned hand.

"There's a high-heeled shoe under the passenger seat, Mr Silk. Could you tell me anything about it?"

"A what!" cried Henry as he peered over the inspector's shoulder. "That's ridiculous. May I take a look?"

McPherson studied the look of incredulity on Henry's face for a few moments, his own jaw set. Then he pointed to a spot on the tarmac. "If you squat down here, sir, clear of the car, you should be able to see what I'm talking about. Please don't touch anything."

Henry went down on his haunches and, supporting himself further with his hands on the ground, he looked under the seat. He turned to McPherson, shaking his head in disbelief.

"I've never seen it before in my life, Inspector."

McPherson scanned the parking area, suddenly worried that Henry might claim the shoe had been planted.

"Could anyone have taken your keys this morning, or at any other time, and accessed your car?"

"As you saw, Inspector, I had the keys with me. So, no, they couldn't."

Jennifer finished the call and walked over to McPherson.

"Guv," she said, drawing him away from Henry.

"I've checked with DC Thyme and the shoe is the same size. I also sent the images and he reckons that the style is the same. The girl was still wearing a right shoe — scarlet, high-heeled, pointed toe with a worn leather sole — and this is its partner. DNA testing of sweat on the insole should confirm it."

McPherson smiled. "I think we've got enough to arrest him now, Cotton, don't you?"

Jennifer wasn't certain. "It's still circumstantial, guv. Despite what he says, if Silk suddenly remembers that he lent his car to a friend after all, we'd be in trouble. Wouldn't it be better to wait until Thyme's finished looking through the CCTV from the hotel? If Silk's shown on that, we'll have more to throw at him."

"How's Thyme getting on with that?"

"He's only just started. There was some problem with the compatibility of the files. The techies have it sorted now."

"OK, let's get Silk back to the station."

They walked over to Henry and the sergeant.

"Mr Silk. In the early hours of Saturday morning, a young woman was murdered and her body dumped in a wood north of Nottingham."

Henry nodded. "I know, Inspector, it made the late editions of the Sunday papers."

"Exactly, sir. We have reason to believe that your car, the Nissan here, was involved in transporting the girl and the presence in your car of a shoe matching one found on the dead girl reinforces that belief. We'd like you to accompany us back to Nottingham where we can interview you using the proper procedures."

"What, now? Are you arresting me?"

"No, sir, not at the moment. Although if you refuse to come voluntarily I am of the opinion that I have enough to do so."

Henry ran a hand through his hair.

"Inspector, I've got an incredibly hectic schedule over the next three days. If we lose a day's filming, it will not only cause chaos, it'll cost the production company a fortune."

"We're investigating a murder, sir, I'm afraid that must come first."

Henry gave a resigned sigh. "Whatever you say, Inspector. Are you going to break it to Jonty or shall I?"

He pointed towards the director who had been quietly inching his way towards them in the hope of finding out what was going on. At the raising of McPherson's arm to beckon him, he came rushing over.

"All sorted out, Inspector?" he beamed, although his eyes were full of doubt.

"Jonty, I've got to go with these police officers," said Henry, before McPherson had a chance to answer. "Perhaps you can rearrange the schedule to do the shots that don't involve me today. It's all one huge mistake, which I'm sure we'll sort out in no time. I'll be back first thing in the morning."

"What! Are you arresting him, Inspector? What's Henry supposed to have done?"

"I'm not at liberty to discuss the case, sir."

Peters launched back into ballistic missile mode.

"Not at liberty? This is totally outrageous, Inspector. Well, I *am* at liberty to discuss the case and I'll tell you with whom I'll discuss it. I'll have you know that the chief constable is a personal friend. He has visited the set on a number of occasions."

"I'm pleased to hear it, sir. Now, I'll get these police cars shifted out of your way, although one of them will remain here in the car park until the loader arrives to take Mr Silk's car back to Nottingham."

Henry pointed to his clothing.

"May I change, Inspector? These are not my clothes and they really should remain here."

"I'd rather you kept them on for now, sir. Perhaps you could go with Sergeant Bottomley to get the clothing you wore to come here this morning. Oh, and we'd like to look at your phone."

Jonty Peters pulled out his own phone, threw his arms in the air in frustration and turned to walk away.

"You haven't heard the last of this, Inspector, I can assure you."

## Chapter Eleven

There was no conversation in the car on the drive to Nottingham. Henry Silk was sitting in the back alongside Rob McPherson, who was staring pointedly out of the window, while in the front passenger seat Jennifer was tapping furiously on her phone. Neil Bottomley was driving.

Henry's head was reeling with the events that had unfolded at Luton Airport, but he was trying to retain an outward appearance of calm. After two failed attempts at asking for more information, he gave up, realising that he would get nothing until they reached Nottingham — the police officers were all studiously ignoring him. However, when, half an hour into the journey, he asked McPherson if he could call his solicitor, the response was immediate.

"As I said at the airport, Mr Silk, you are not under arrest so you are free to call whoever you please."

"Thank you, Inspector. I think in view of what you've told me so far, it would be prudent if my solicitor were present from the outset. He's got to drive up from London, so I apologise that there will be something of a delay."

"Then I suggest you call him straightaway, sir."

Five minutes later, Henry informed them that his solicitor

would be leaving late afternoon and that he had told Henry not to answer any questions until he arrived.

"As I expected, sir," sighed McPherson, not even trying to hide his irritation.

Henry sat back and passed the time by staring at the back of Jennifer's not unattractive head and, when he could see it, her even more attractive profile. He was trying desperately to recall the events of Friday evening, but there were only fragments, a blur of disconnected half images from the time he left the theatre until he woke up feeling dreadful late on Saturday morning.

Whatever had caused the loss of memory had affected his performance on Saturday evening. He had forgotten his lines on three occasions — something he prided himself on never doing — and jumped a passage in act two. His cast were professional enough to handle it and it was unlikely anyone in the audience noticed a thing, but he had to fend off some serious ribbing after the performance. Contrary to his normal practice, he treated the whole cast to drinks in their local to thank them, although since he was driving down to London afterwards, he stuck to sparkling water.

Henry's solicitor, Charles Keithley, arrived at six thirty p.m. and, having established that Henry hadn't eaten, insisted that he be allowed to fetch some sandwiches and a drink before they got started.

A few minutes before seven, McPherson left his office to head for the interview room. He called out to Jennifer, who was busy at her computer.

"Cotton, the boss wants you to sit in on the initial chat with Silk. We both reckon that given the man's reputation with women, a female officer might distract him and keep him off his guard. You've been with him for over three hours today and in the car he couldn't keep his eyes off you, so it's down to you. Sorry to spring it on you and sorry if it offends any sexist sensibilities, but we've got to play our cards right, especially since his solicitor's present."

"Not a problem, guv," said Jennifer, as she closed her computer and grabbed a notepad.

She hurried after the DI, pleased to be sitting in on the interview, although she knew her bosses' reasoning was unsound: from her background reading on Silk in the more responsible magazines, his reputation as a lady's man was unfounded.

McPherson entered the interview room followed by Jennifer. He started by systematically going through the initial formalities for interviewing a suspect as required by PACE: the Police and Criminal Evidence Act. Once he had set up the tape recorder and video camera and announced who was in the room, he asked Henry to state his name, address and date of birth.

Satisfied that everything was being done by the book, McPherson proceeded with his interview plan.

"I should like to remind you, Mr Silk, that you are not under arrest and that you are free to leave at any time. Do you agree that you have come voluntarily to the Nottingham City and County Serious Crime Formation to answer questions?"

"You hardly gave me much option, Inspector, but yes, I agree."

McPherson nodded. "Now, before we go any further, I should like to ask you to give a buccal swab for DNA profiling and your fingerprints. Since we are examining your car, we will need both for elimination purposes."

Henry turned to Charles Keithley who signalled his agreement.

The DI continued. "As you may be aware, if we are later satisfied that you have nothing to do with the case under investigation, both your DNA profile and your fingerprints will be removed from the databases and destroyed."

"I wasn't aware of that, Inspector, but thank you for pointing it out."

Jennifer stood and picked up a bag from a table behind her. She put on a pair of disposable gloves, swabbed Henry's mouth and took his prints.

Although he wasn't trying to unnerve her, Henry found himself staring into her eyes, carefully watching every expression, every flicker of her eyelids. He was impressed that she ignored him until she had finished, when she thanked him and gave him a brief smile before leaving the room to hand the samples to Derek Thyme, who was waiting for her in the corridor outside.

Once Jennifer had settled back in her chair, McPherson continued by explaining once again to Henry about the discovery of Miruna Peptanariu's body.

"What can you tell us about that, Henry?"

Henry immediately bristled. "Inspector, you have a first name, I seem to remember?"

McPherson frowned. "Yes."

"Do you expect me to use it? Are we going to be chummy-chummy? Shall I also call the detective constable here Jennifer?"

"I expect you to address us by our ranks."

"Then I expect the same level of respect, Inspector. It's Mr Silk."

McPherson's expression darkened.

"I'll repeat the question, Mr Silk. What can you tell us about Miruna Peptanariu and the fact that her body was discovered in Harlow Wood?"

"I can tell you nothing, Inspector. I've never heard that name before today and I've never been to Harlow Wood. I don't even know where it is."

McPherson checked his list of points.

"Mr Silk, could you tell us where you were last Friday evening, the 30th of May?"

Henry outlined his movements from early Friday afternoon, his leaving the Old Nottingham Hotel, his performance in the play at the Theatre Royal and his return to the hotel. At this point he faltered.

"Inspector, I'm not trying to be evasive, but I'm afraid I'm having a hard time remembering much between leaving the theatre and waking up rather late on Saturday morning. My usual practice, both last week and always when I'm in rep, is that when I return to my hotel after a performance, I have a drink at the bar to unwind, normally a brief chat with the barman and then I go to my room where I have another drink, a vodka on the rocks, before showering and going to bed."

"Are you saying that you did or did not do this on Friday night, Mr Silk?"

"I'm saying that I don't remember. I suppose you could ask the barman at the Old Nottingham. His name's Michael; he should be able to tell you."

"Do you remember adopting this procedure on other nights last week?"

"Very clearly, yes."

"Then can you give any reason why you can't remember what you did on Friday evening?"

"No, Inspector, I can't."

McPherson checked his list again.

"Mr Silk. What would your reaction be to my telling you that we have CCTV footage of your car in various locations in the city and on roads north of the city between the hours of about one and three o'clock last Saturday morning, the thirty-first of May? By your car, I mean a Nissan X-Trail registration number LJ11TTV. Do you agree that you are the registered owner of that car?"

"I am, Inspector, yes. As to my reaction, as you describe it, to its being in those locations at that time, I should say you are somehow mistaken. To my knowledge, my car was parked in the car park of the Old Nottingham from when I parked it there after using it last Wednesday until I drove down to London in it late on Saturday night after the final performance of the play."

"Did you lend your car keys to anyone or give permission to anyone to use your car on Friday night?"

"No, to both questions, Inspector. I left my car keys on the desk in my room, and that's where they were on Saturday before I checked out."

McPherson opened a file in front of him and pulled out three photos. He placed them on the desk in front of Henry.

"For the recording, I am now showing Mr Silk three prints taken from the Nottingham Traffic Office's CCTV cameras. The date and time of the photos is shown on the prints. Mr Silk, I'd like you to look at these photographs. Do you agree that they are of your car?"

Henry studied each one closely and showed them to Charles Keithley.

"They show a Nissan X-Trail with the same registration number as my vehicle. Whether it is actually my vehicle, I can't say."

"What were you wearing on Friday evening, Mr Silk?"

Henry scratched his head. "As I recall, jeans, a brownish pullover, cream linen jacket and a woollen scarf. Oh, and a dark blue baseball cap."

"Could you describe what the person shown in the photo timed at zero two thirty-three is wearing?"

Henry peered at the photo. "I can't see clearly, but I should say it's a pale jacket, there might be a scarf and under a dark T-shirt or … pullover." He faltered. "Are you trying to say that that's me?"

"I'm asking you if it is you, Mr Silk."

"It can't possibly be."

"Please look closely at the windscreen of the vehicle in the same photograph. Could you please describe what is visible imme-diately below the vehicle licence disc?"

"It looks like a motorway sticker for Switzerland. I can see the number fourteen on it, so it's for this year."

McPherson pulled another photograph from the folder.

"For the tape, I am now showing Mr Silk a photograph of his car taken this afternoon at the Nottingham Police Traffic Pound. Could you please describe what is shown on the windscreen of the vehicle in this photograph, Mr Silk? Your vehicle, as you've already agreed."

Henry nodded. "It's a Swiss tax disc for motorways. I had to buy it when I drove through Switzerland on my way to Rome two months ago."

"So, getting back to the vehicle shown in the CCTV footage, would you now agree that it appears to be your vehicle?"

Henry's reply was barely audible. "It would seem so, yes."

"Could you speak more loudly please, Mr Silk?"

"I said that it would seem so."

"And do you agree that the person shown driving the vehicle appears to be you?"

Charles Keithley made to interrupt but Henry stopped him.

"I would agree only that the person driving the car seems to be wearing clothing that is similar to mine, Inspector."

A knock on the door broke the tension in the room. Derek Thyme walked in, which McPherson announced for the recording. Derek leaned over and spoke quietly into the DI's ear and handed him a printed sheet of notes. McPherson scanned them before saying anything else.

He looked up.

"DC Thyme is now leaving the room. Mr Silk, despite what you've told us about having no memory of events on Friday night after your performance, I should like you to explain the following. We have now examined CCTV recordings from various cameras positioned around the Old Nottingham Hotel which show you leaving the hotel at twelve fifty-five a.m. — and by leaving I mean standing by the lift on the second floor, entering the lift, leaving the lift at the car park level, getting into your car and driving away — following which we now have enhanced shots from the traffic cameras that show your car picking up Miruna Peptanariu on Forest Road West at one ten a.m. and shots of her in your car with you at various locations in and beyond the city. Further, at various times between two ten and two forty a.m. there are images of you driving your car alone back in the direction of Nottingham. At two forty-two a.m., the hotel's cameras again show you parking your car in the hotel car park and walking through the car park towards the stairs. You are then shown briefly passing the lift door on the second floor, so presumably you took the stairs all the way to the second floor. What would your reaction be to this sequence of events I have just described?"

Henry was silent. His eyes wandered in disbelief from the photographs in front of him to McPherson and then to Jennifer, who was scribbling notes. He sighed. "My reaction, Inspector, is one of incredulity. I simply cannot explain it."

"OK, Mr Silk, further to everything I've described, as you know from the preliminary examination of your car by DC Cotton this morning, a red, high-heeled left shoe was found under the front passenger seat. That shoe has been compared with a right shoe worn by Miruna Peptanariu when her body was found and the two make a perfect pair in brand, style, size, colour, wear pattern and general condition. We shall be conducting DNA tests on the shoe insoles, but there seems little doubt that the shoe found in your car belonged to the victim. Can you tell us anything about the shoes, Mr Silk?"

Henry raised his arms, palms outstretched. "I am at a total loss, Inspector."

"Mr Silk, we have examined the mobile phone you voluntarily passed over to us."

Henry turned and nodded to Charles Keithley to agree that this had happened.

McPherson continued. "Amongst the calls made on the phone, there is a record of a call made at twelve fifty a.m. last Saturday, the thirty-first of May, to a prepaid phone account that we know was used by Miruna Peptanariu. This call was made a few minutes before the Old Nottingham Hotel's CCTV footage shows you leaving the hotel. Could you tell us anything about that?"

Henry felt as if he were at the losing end of a twelve-round boxing match. His head was dizzy, his mouth horribly dry. He had protested his complete ignorance of everything that had been thrown at him and yet the blows kept coming.

McPherson waited, knowing that often at this stage, silence was the best strategy. His suspect was buckling; he could feel it. He turned his head a fraction in order to see Jennifer out of the corner of his eye. She had finished scribbling notes and was staring intently at Henry Silk, her face expressionless, but McPherson could feel her tension.

Henry's eyes slowly focussed on the table top in front of him.

"I can tell you nothing about any phone call made at that time. I can tell you nothing about any of this."

He turned and leaned over to talk in Charles Keithley's ear. McPherson could sense a confession coming, but Jennifer was still puzzled. She had been trying to come to terms with how someone so apparently pleasant, intelligent and open as Henry Silk appeared to be could also be a cold, calculating killer. It was the first time she had been in such close proximity to someone like him and she was trying to analyse every movement of his face, every shrug, every crossing and uncrossing of his arms. She felt that he was using his acting abilities to their fullest, drawing on everything he'd ever learned to portray an innocent victim of circumstance while really being as guilty as hell. At least she had reached that conclusion based on more evidence than her bosses had used. But then again, perhaps their years of experience had given them insight into the man's character that she was still too inexperienced to notice.

Then suddenly she saw them. The scratches. She stifled a gasp.

She leaned to whisper to McPherson. "May I ask him a question, please, guv?"

"What about?"

"The scratches."

"What scratches?"

"May I please ask?"

"Go ahead."

Jennifer coughed and Henry looked around at her.

"Mr Silk," she began. "There appear to be several scratches on your neck. On the left side. I could see them as you leaned over to talk to Mr Keithley. Could you please tell us how they came about? How you got them?"

Henry raised his left hand to the marks and felt them, a frown on his face as if he'd not previously noticed them.

"I ... I don't know, Constable Cotton. I first noticed them on Saturday afternoon when I had a shower. The hot water stung them slightly. Since then they've healed over and I've not felt them. I'd forgotten they were there. I have no idea how I got them."

He glanced nervously at Charles Keithley who was trying desperately to hide being horrorstruck by this new development.

Jennifer leaned over to McPherson, speaking quietly. "Shall I get DC Thyme to call the pathologist to look at them?"

"I'll do it, Cotton. Horace won't want to come out to do what he'll regard as a duty doctor's job, but I'd rather he did it. He and I go way back. He'll come tonight if I speak to him."

He looked across at the pair opposite him.

"I am terminating this interview at," — he looked at his watch — "seven fifty-six p.m. pending the arrival of a doctor to examine the scratches on Mr Silk's neck."

He leaned forward and stopped the tape.

"Mr Silk. I shall have to ask you to remain here for the pathologist to arrive."

Henry hardly heard him. He had genuinely forgotten about the scratches. He had felt so wretched on Saturday that they hadn't really figured in his consciousness. After glancing at them, he had paid no further attention to them. Like everything else that had surfaced on this nightmare of a day, he had no idea about them, no memory. But what concerned him more was the awful realisation that there appeared to be a considerable and ever-increasing body of evidence to connect him with the death of a prostitute he had never met or heard of in a wood he'd also never heard of or even been near. Had his car really been used? Perhaps there was something the police had overlooked and, ridiculous coincidence that it was, a set of plates the same as his had been attached to a stolen X-Trail, an X-Trail that went to and from ... the hotel? And then there was CCTV of him. He looked down at his hands.

"How did she die?" he asked quietly.

McPherson was making for the door. He turned. "What?"

"How did she die, Inspector? The girl."

"Suffocation with a plastic bag. She was beaten unconscious with a blunt object and then a bag pulled over her head. But I suspect you knew that already."

He spun on his heel and marched out of the room.


"Consistent with having been made by four fingernails," announced a characteristically impatient Horace Lawson almost before he was through the door of the DCI's office where Hurst and McPherson were waiting for him. Having severely bent McPherson's ear about being inconvenienced, he had arrived to examine and photograph the scratches soon after ten p.m.

"Given there wasn't any sexual activity or any other signs of intimacy, I'd say that while he was in the process of suffocating her, she reached out in a desperate bid to stop him."

"So after he clobbered her, she wasn't unconscious like you thought," said Hurst.

Lawson pulled a face. "It would seem not."

"Poor bitch," replied Hurst. "She was fighting for her young life."

"Bastard," added McPherson.

Hurst turned to him.

"Rob, we've got more than enough. Arrest him."

## Chapter Twelve

The elation shared by the whole team in the briefing room on Tuesday morning was attenuated by the presence of their squad commander, Detective Superintendent Olivia Freneton. Stony-faced, she was sitting to the right of Mike Hurst, her eyes slowly moving from one member of the team to the next. For the few who looked closely, her unsmiling features appeared slightly more relaxed than normal, an encouraging sign. However, most of the team avoided looking her way, preferring to keep their attention firmly on Hurst, who for his part was determined not to let the presence of the woman known universally as the Ice Queen dampen his spirits.

Hurst stood.

"Morning, everyone," he said, before turning to Olivia Freneton. "Thanks for joining us this morning ma'am. I'm sure you'll have something to say to the team in a moment."

Freneton gave the slightest of nods as her eyes continued their review of the room.

"But first," continued Hurst, "let me say, well done, all of you. We've knocked this case on the head in record time thanks to all your efforts. As you know, the devil is in the detail and you've all dug out plenty of that in the last forty-eight hours, and every bit has been another nail in Silk's coffin.

"As you know, Silk hasn't confessed yet, but I can't help feeling that he soon will, since frankly, he hasn't got a leg to stand on. We've still got many of the forensic results to come, DNA in particular and of course, neither the plastic bag he used to kill Miruna nor the weapon he hit her with first have yet been found. We have a team of SOCOs and a squad of uniforms courtesy of Mansfield nick going back to the scene in Harlow Wood this morning to conduct a wider search.

"And as soon as this meeting's over, DS Bottomley and DCs Cotton and Thyme are heading off to London to search Silk's house in Hampstead. Also, this afternoon, the night shift receptionist from the Old Nottingham, who doubled as barman last Friday night, has agreed to come in and make a statement about Silk's movements on Friday.

"So, there's still plenty to do. Until we get the forensic results back for correlation, I want the rest of you here to learn as much as possible about Silk's background. We know that he's a loner, and we know that many in the acting world don't like him, so much in fact that many directors shun him. Has this caused frustration on Silk's part that has driven him to violence, so much so that he wants to take it out on defenceless victims? Is there any indication that Silk has been involved with other unsolved deaths of prostitutes in the city in the past? — you'll remember there were three last year and two the year before which are now regarded as cold cases. Maybe we have the answers in Silk. His DNA will, of course, be compared with profiles found in those cases and all other cases on the outstanding crime database, but I also want anything else there is to be had. I want a full life history of the man. He said he isn't married. Has he been in the past? We'll be interviewing him further on this, but his solicitor might object to questions that aren't immediately relevant to the present case, so we'll have to do our own digging."

He turned to Freneton. "Ma'am?"

As the detective superintendent stood, Jennifer made the normal assessment of a fellow female. She was tall — about five nine or ten, Jennifer estimated — and there was clearly no waste on her. Her obsession with physical training was well known, as were her unarmed-combat skills — her tendency not to pull her punches in training had left more than one of her trainers with a reason to dislike her.

Jennifer herself was no slouch when it came to personal defence. She had passed all the police training with the highest marks and she had dabbled in karate, but had never really had the time to take it to a serious level. She noted the fluidity of Freneton's movements under her handmade, dark grey cashmere suit trousers and jacket, and reckoned that although the woman was around fifteen years her senior, her extra height and reach, combined with an uncompromising ruthlessness, would make her a difficult opponent. Not that Jennifer had any thoughts of taking her on. It wasn't wise to engage in a fistfight with your senior officers.

Jennifer's eyes moved to the superintendent's face and hair. Her close-cropped but expensively cut dark brown hair showed no sign of help with its colour that she could see — everything looked real all the way to the roots. But it was her eyes that really caught Jennifer's attention. Pale blue, they were cold and humourless as she continued to look slowly around the team before speaking. No wonder she's known as the Ice Queen, thought Jennifer. The sarge reckons she lowers the temperature of any room by ten degrees, minimum.

Olivia Freneton didn't have to wait for silence as she stood; everyone was motionless, any thoughts of comments to neighbours after the DCI's speech abandoned.

"I want to add to what DCI Hurst has said by congratulating you all on your work so far in this case," she began, her voice without accent; flat and emotionless. "To have an arrest this quickly is not only good for the reputation of the force, it will reassure the public that we will not tolerate vicious criminals on our streets.

"As you know, I am new to this city, still learning the ropes, but the reputation for results you as a squad have achieved in the short time you have been together is clearly well deserved. I am impressed with your teamwork and I feel confident that you will only build on the already strong foundation of the case against this man Silk in the coming days. I understand that as a public figure in the entertainment world, despite his reputation within the industry, he still has a strong fan following. It's important that there be no sympathy vote for him, that the press don't suddenly want to fight his corner. We need to show the world what a cold, calculating killer Silk is, so the more you find, the better.

"To that end, I should like to underline the need for the three of you heading for Silk's house to be as thorough as possible in your search. As DCI Hurst said, the weapon initially used on Miruna Peptanariu has yet to be found. At present, all we know is that it had a rounded end. It's unlikely to be as large as a baseball bat, but it could be similar. Or it could be one of the many types of truncheon available online. Look for anything similar in his house; he might have more than one, and check any computers for a history of searching for them, or online purchases. You never know, he might have slipped up; he's certainly shown himself to be rather sloppy so far. Also look for any heavy-duty plastic bags. I spoke to the pathologist and he reckons that something fairly thick would be a better choice when suffocating someone that way; less chance of it being bitten through.

"More generally, I should add that the senior command are delighted with progress so far and they have indicated to me that you have their full support. We'll devote whatever time and resources are necessary to completing the case against this man so that we, and the public, can rest assured that he will pay for his crime."

She turned and nodded to Hurst before marching out of the room.

Sergeant Bottomley broke into Jennifer's thoughts. "Come on, Cotton, now we've had the benefit of advice from on high, you're going to show me your driving skills, and if you're lucky, I'll stand lunch once we're done at Silk's place."

Jennifer grinned at him. "Lead on, Sarge."

She liked Bottomley; he was old school, a career sergeant, not a go-getter, but a solid workhorse who recognised talent when he saw it and who was willing to share his extensive experience with his juniors. Freneton could learn a thing or two from him, she thought. You'd think that with all the courses she'd been on, one of them would have covered basic smiling.

The next two days were taken up with legwork, searching, collating, endless phone calls and trawling through public and restricted databases. The Thursday morning briefing was delayed by two hours after Hurst was advised that a raft of forensic results would be ready that morning. He wanted the team to enjoy them all.

Finally, at eleven thirty, everyone was gathered in the briefing room. The mood was even more positive than it had been two days before, unconstrained this time owing to the absence of Superintendent Freneton who was attending a meeting of a Home Office committee on which she sat.

Hurst marched in armed with a burgeoning file that he banged down on the desk alongside him.

"Right," he said, rubbing his hands together. "Rob, perhaps you'd like to start with what's been found about Silk's background."

McPherson stood. "There's nothing particularly profound in Silk's recent history, and I should say here that any thoughts of linking him with other prostitute murders in the city can be forgotten — he wasn't here when they happened and he has solid alibis for all of them. In fact, when two of them occurred, he wasn't even in the country.

"However, there's something in his history that might be significant. We've discovered that he was married for three years back in the eighties to an Antonia Frances Caldmore. They were divorced in 1988, a month after the car crash in which Silk was driving that killed the actor Dirk Sanderley. It was this accident that buggered Silk's career. Up until then, he had been a rising star.

"Because he was driving and under the influence of drugs and alcohol, he was blamed. Sanderley was also stoked with booze and drugs, but that seems to have added fuel to the anti-Silk lobby — they blamed him for Sanderley's habit. Lucky for him, he's a good actor and through persistence over the years, he has made a living in the profession, but there are plenty of people who would rather not see his face on the TV or in films, especially directors.

"Getting back to his marriage, what's interesting is that we've tried to find Ms Caldmore, but she seems to have disappeared off the face of the earth. There's no one with that name matching her age and description living in the UK, her passport expired in the early nineties and wasn't renewed, and there are no credit cards or bank accounts that we can find. Nothing. There was a driving licence issued back in the late seventies to someone of that name, but it was the old booklet type that's never been renewed and the address never updated.

"We've tried seeing if she changed her name, but Deed Poll records can be difficult, and back then, when they were far less computerised, records remained in local offices. It would be a huge job to follow it up."

Hurst interrupted. "What does Silk say, Rob?"

"He says that he has no idea where she is. According to him she went abroad after the divorce, although she hardly spoke to Silk at all after the car crash. It seems she hated her ex and wanted nothing more to do with him."

Hurst frowned. "Seems odd that his ex-wife could disappear so completely from his life. Were there any kids?"

McPherson shook his head. "None that we know of."

"Wonder if he did for her as well," piped up Bottomley. "Maybe he was responsible for the death of the other actor like the acting community thinks. If Sanderley was doing better than he was, perhaps he was jealous. Perhaps Sanderley was banging his ex-wife."

McPherson sighed. "Ifs and buts and maybes, Neil, and it all happened over twenty-five years ago. His ex-wife's disappearance wasn't regarded as suspicious at the time; certainly there was no investigation."

Hurst nodded his agreement. "Exactly, Rob. It's not relevant to the present case and we don't want to get distracted trying to dig up stuff from the dark ages. We'll keep a note in the file and move on."

Jennifer Cotton raised her hand from the notepad on which she'd been scribbling.

"May I add to that, boss, that we found nothing at Silk's house regarding his ex-wife — no papers, letters, no old photos stuffed away in a box, nothing."

"Looks like he blotted her out of his memory too," grunted Hurst. "OK, Neil, let's hear the good news about Silk's house."

The sergeant opened his notebook, although he knew it by heart.

"Basically, we found clothing that matched that shown in the various CCTV footage. By found, I mean there was no attempt to hide it and it hadn't been washed.

"There was a pair of jeans, a pullover and T-shirt all lying on a chair in Silk's bedroom, and a cream linen jacket hung over the back of the chair along with a woollen scarf. There was a dark blue baseball cap on a chest of drawers in the same room. They've all been bagged and seized, along with other items that are similar from Silk's wardrobe and chest of drawers. But I reckon the stuff lying over the chairs is what we were after, and I've flagged it for priority processing by the lab."

"Excellent," said Hurst. "Anything else?"

"Nothing of interest on his computer, and no stash of baseball bats, if that's what you mean."

A mild titter of amusement floated around the room.

Hurst silenced them by raising a palm.

"Well, as you know, I like to leave the best bit to last. The new lab on the ring road is proving very efficient. What they've found so far is absolutely clinching the case.

"We've got what appears to be Silk's hair on Miruna's clothing — it's the right colour and length, although without roots they can't of course do the DNA; there are traces of theatrical make-up on the faux fur collar of Miruna's jacket that match make-up found on Silk's pullover; there are synthetic fibres from that collar in the car; there was one of Miruna's dyed orange hairs in the car too and there are fibres on the knees of Miruna's jeans that match the carpet in the X-Trail's footwell. In addition, there is DNA matching Miruna's on the shoe found in the X-Trail and last but not least, Miruna's fingerprints in the car.

"So, we are now in absolutely no doubt that Miruna was in Silk's car, that is, we're not dealing with a stolen X-Trail that someone had stuck Silk's number plates on. It's definitely Silk's car. What that means is that the images of the driver shown on the CCTV footage that look like Silk must be him."

He paused, letting his team absorb the information. Then he continued, his voice triumphant.

"You might say that all that only points to the car and since the CCTV footage of the driver doesn't show Silk's face, there's an outside chance it could be someone else. Well, there's also the debris under Miruna's fingernails. And what that contains, as well as fibres that we'll be comparing with Silk's pullover and scarf, is skin debris that is bloodstained. The lab has profiled the DNA and it's Silk's. No question; a perfect match."

There was a collective 'Yes!' around the room as the team members all grinned at each other in delight. Hurst held up his hands again to quieten them.

"And thanks to DC Cotton's eagle eyes," he continued over the hubbub, "we have the source of the skin and blood — the scratches on Silk's neck that he conveniently cannot explain."

Jennifer was blushing at the mention of her name, but there was something else she wanted to know. She put her hand up.

"Yes, Cotton."

"Did the barman from the Old Nottingham have anything useful to add, boss?"

Hurst pulled a face. "Unfortunately, not much. He normally shares a drink with Silk when he gets back from the theatre — Silk's treat, apparently — which he did on Friday night as usual. According to him, Silk seemed perfectly normal, not pissed or anything. After he'd had his drink, he was busy checking in a busload of Korean businessmen for about an hour so he didn't notice when Silk left the bar.

"The only thing he did say was that there was a woman in the bar when Silk arrived, a businesswoman in a smart business suit, is how he described her. Said she was middle-aged, but he couldn't remember anything about her, like her height or hairstyle and colour. He doesn't know if she spoke to Silk or when she left.

"However, we've checked the hotel CCTV and there's footage of Silk going up in the lift alone at eleven forty-one. No sign of a business type then or at any time later."

"Did we get a name?" asked Jennifer.

"No, the barman had never seen her before. She didn't go up in the lift, so she probably took the stairs. But since the CCTV doesn't cover the corridors, we don't know which floor or which room she went to. However, given the chain of events, I don't think she's of any significance."

"But we have a list of guests from the hotel on Friday night?" persisted Jennifer.

"Yes, Cotton … that is, I think we do."

Hurst looked to McPherson for the answer.

"I've got it here, boss," called out Derek Thyme.

"Is there a reason you think it's important, Cotton?" asked Hurst.

"It's only that Silk is adamant that he can't remember anything from the time he left the theatre until late the following morning. But we now have the barman saying that he saw Silk returning, and there's no indication from him that Silk is either drunk or the worse for wear in any way, which kind of contradicts what Silk says. I was thinking that if it became necessary, we could probably identify the woman from the guest list and ask her if she noticed Silk in the bar, spoke to him perhaps, and whether he was out of it or perfectly rational."

"Good thought, Cotton," said Hurst, once again impressed with Jennifer's attention to detail. "However, given the barman says he was fine, I think for the time being we don't need to go to the time, effort and cost of locating her. I'll put a note in the file and we'll follow it up later if necessary."

# Chapter Thirteen

The following Friday, Jennifer was again asked to sit in with Rob McPherson for another interview with Henry Silk, now under arrest on suspicion of murdering Miruna Peptanariu. The entire team was hoping that with the huge amount of evidence they now had against Silk, he would capitulate and confess.

McPherson carefully went through all the formalities before reading out a detailed summary of the results they had gained so far. After each result on the list, he stopped to ask Henry if he could explain the findings. To McPherson's irritation, the answer in each case was that he couldn't.

By now, Henry had got over the initial shock of the weight of evidence against him and was starting to think more clearly. He knew full well that he wasn't guilty of killing the girl. Apart from anything else, he didn't use prostitutes, he never had, and he had no strong feelings about them or their trade. Everyone has to earn a crust.

The main thing that worried him was his lack of recall for many hours from late on Friday through to the middle of Saturday. Apart from the odd flashes in his mind of unconnected images that made no sense, he didn't remember talking to anyone in the bar apart from Michael, and that was only briefly. However, he decided that he must in some way have been drugged and then a series of events set in place that involved killing the prostitute and framing him for the crime.

What he couldn't understand was who and why. Yes, he had plenty of enemies in the industry, people who would rather he wasn't around. But would they go to this extent, with all the inherent risks involved? If they hated him that much, why didn't they simply have him killed? It would ultimately be less risky, although of course he would just be dead, whereas now he was likely to be spending many years in prison, his name and reputation ruined. That thought was both frightening and depressing. Perhaps that was what whoever had done this was trying to achieve. But why?

He had talked it through with Charles Keithley, who was not only his solicitor but also a good friend of many years. Together they had drawn up a list of everyone they could think of in Henry's world — fellow actors, directors, producers, agents, distributors, film crew in general — who would have the means, opportunity, motive and intelligence to carry this out. Most failed the intelligence test while those remaining failed the rest.

"Quite frankly, Henry, there's no one," said Charles Keithley sitting back in the uncomfortable upright chair in the legal interview room at the prison where Henry was now being held. "There's not a single soul on this list who has the wit to go through with it, let alone the opportunity and so on."

He leaned forward and put his hand on Henry's arm. "I know it wasn't you, Henry. That's not from some ill-considered faith in you. I know. I know you as a person and a friend. I know what you're capable of and what you would and wouldn't do. I knew you in your younger, wilder days, and I've seen how you have coped with adversity in the form of rejection by narrow-minded morons in your industry. I'll help you as your solicitor in any way I can, but at the moment, like you, I'm totally at a loss. The police seem to have a cast-iron case with evidence that I agree must have been planted, but in such a clever way that it's beyond my comprehension."

"Thank you, Charles," said Henry. "I appreciate that more than I can say. I know you will do all you can, that you will scrutinise everything the police have. And if you do clear my name, I want it to be because you've found out the truth, not because the police have made some procedural cockup, which frankly must be incredibly hard not to do with all the hoops they have to jump through. That wouldn't be enough; it would in many ways be worse since I'd be free but guilty in the eyes of the world. Certainly still ruined, never able to hold my head up wherever I went. No, we have to find the truth."

The interview with Henry progressed to the increasing frustration of McPherson and the puzzlement of Jennifer. She could hardly call herself experienced in dealing with murderers, and the fact that this one was an actor was ever-present in her thoughts. But there was something about him, something that seemed fundamentally honest, that raised questions in her mind that she'd rather not hear.

She found it odd that he'd never once suggested in interview that he'd been framed, even though it was the only alternative explanation for the mountain of evidence against him. Jennifer thought the suggestion was nonsense; no one, surely, could have carried out such a complicated sequence of events and not made a mistake, not left something of themselves behind. No, this man was not only guilty, but also, she supposed, totally insane.

Despite the new evidence, it was becoming clear that Henry was never going to confess. After they had finished, Charles Keithley took the unusual step of asking to see Mike Hurst.

"Detective Chief Inspector," he said, as he accepted Hurst's invitation to sit in the quiet of his office. "I know this is unusual, so I want to emphasise that I'm not here to ask for anything more than a few minutes of your time."

He went over his conversations with Henry, explaining his own conviction of Henry's innocence and all the reasons why. To his surprise, Hurst was sympathetic.

"This is off the record, Mr Keithley, since I know that you don't want it to be known that we've been discussing this any more than I do. However, I trust you as an honourable man not to try to use this conversation to your advantage in court."

"I'm not a barrister, Chief Inspector, so I won't be standing up in court, and I can assure you that this conversation will remain between ourselves."

"Good. Mr Keithley, I've been a police officer for more than thirty years and I'm soon to retire. I've seen every type of scumbag criminal that exists out there and I've seen many sophisticated men and women who thought they were above the law. Regardless of who they were or their background, they all had one thing in common. It's more of an attitude than anything else, a way of speaking, holding themselves, the way they look at you. All I can say is that Henry Silk doesn't have that, which is a surprise to me, because as I said, I thought I'd seen it all.

"My job, Mr Keithley, is to collect the evidence, process it and act on it. That's what I do. Silk's demeanour surprises me but I can't get it out of my head that he is an actor, and a good one. The only explanation I can come up with is that somehow, for some reason, he's playing the part of his life. I don't know what the motive is and his plans may have gone astray. But he's got you totally on his side, and I know that he's caused a number of us to question everything in great detail.

"However, the simple fact of the matter is that we have a huge amount of irrefutable evidence against him. You have suggested to me that it could have been planted; you're not the only one. I've thought that one through too. You see, we're not all blinkered, lock-'em-up-at-the-first-opportunity types. But I've seen planted before, on more than one occasion, and if there's one thing that people who plant evidence do, it's that they leave too much. So much normally that it's sitting there waving at you.

"Now, this case isn't like that. Yes, there's a lot of evidence, and it's strong, but it's also quality evidence, not over the top. Take the girl's hair in the car. The two hairs found by the forensic people might easily have been missed. And then there's the weapon used to knock her unconscious. We still haven't found it. You'd imagine someone planting evidence would make sure it was found.

"So, Mr Keithley, I don't think this evidence is planted, it's too subtle for that. Therefore the only other conclusion I can come to is that your man is guilty."

## Chapter Fourteen

Henry Silk may not have confessed, but that didn't dampen the team's mood for celebration. Friday evening saw Jennifer join Derek Thyme, Neil Bottomley and Rob McPherson in the Horse and Hounds pub a few steps from the SCF HQ. It was a regular watering hole for the men — Jennifer normally found an excuse not to join them — somewhere they felt they could relax.

Even the normally dour McPherson was smiling. "It must be something of a record for a crime where the culprit has no known connection with the victim," he crowed, echoing the DCI's words. "A couple of days like that. Magic."

He downed his pint and headed for the bar for another round.

Putting the drinks on the table, he noticed that Jennifer had hardly touched her first glass of red wine.

"Sup up, lass, this is a special night. You won't get many cases like this in your career, so you want to remember it, enjoy it."

Bottomley was less gung-ho.

"What's up, Jennifer, is something wrong? You of all of us should be celebrating. You've done very well, come up with some really good points that pushed the investigation along nicely. And you stopped Rob here dropping himself in the poo down in Luton."

McPherson grunted while Jennifer averted her eyes. She knew she had been pushing it by stopping her senior officer in full flood, but rules were rules.

"She was right, Neil," growled McPherson, to everyone's surprise. "I would've got a right bollocking from the Ice Queen."

He shuddered theatrically and grinned. "Probably be on parking meters by now."

Bottomley wanted to pursue it. "Come on Jennifer, out with it, unless it's personal — I don't want to pry."

Jennifer laughed. "You mean you want me to come clean about my affair with the chief constable."

"No, we all know about that; we've seen the photos," said Bottomley, deadpan.

"I don't get why you're down either, Jen," chimed in Derek. "After all, you got special mention from Hurst, and even the Ice Queen was seen to smile in the briefing."

"She was?" they all said together.

Derek was amused by their response.

"Well, what she thinks is a smile. It's a microscopic twitch, just here," he said, pointing to the corner of his mouth.

"I didn't see it," said McPherson, half believing him.

"You must have blinked, guv," countered Derek.

"We all must've," said Jennifer, finally taking another sip from her wine.

The men fell silent and waited. They weren't going to let it drop. Jennifer knew what they were doing and finally sighed.

"OK, I give in. It's probably my inexperience showing but I reckon that although Henry Silk might be a lot of things, he's certainly not stupid. In all the interviews, he's come across as an articulate, sensible, informed and polite man. In fact, given the circumstances, I'd say he was remarkably relaxed, and really quite persuasive."

"Classic traits of a psycho," shrugged McPherson, taking a large swig from his pint.

"Maybe," nodded Jennifer, "but one of the things that bothers me is that he's clever and he knows about forensic evidence — we know that since he's been in a few TV things other than Runway that involve forensic—"

"He was a pathologist in one I saw," said Derek.

"Exactly. So why on earth didn't he do more to cover his tracks. It's almost as if he wanted to get caught."

"Totally arrogant." McPherson was dismissive. "I've seen his sort before. They think they are so clever that they'll taunt us, play games. Perhaps he didn't originally intend to kill her, perhaps he was disturbed by someone who hasn't come forward."

Jennifer shook her head. "No, I don't agree. It was premeditated enough. There were no signs of a struggle in the car. Anything but, in fact. I think he had every intention of catching her totally by surprise."

Bottomley was shaking his head. "Me, I reckon he knew her, or had some connection with her. We'll probably never find out what it was."

Jennifer frowned. "You mean you don't think he killed her at random, Sarge?"

"Hard to say, but he has no history of aggression towards prostitutes, in fact to anyone. He's been on the receiving end of a few punches, fights in pubs and so on, which weren't his fault, by all accounts. There's no indication that he goes around picking fights."

"Whether he knew her or not," continued Jennifer, "don't you think it's odd that he made no attempt to clean out his car? I saw his face when we found the shoe — it was a complete surprise to him."

"Of course it was," snorted McPherson. "If he'd known it was there, he'd hardly have left it, would he?"

"No, but I don't mean that. I mean that his face didn't register an oh-shit-I-missed-it kind of look; it was total incredulity. What I'm saying is why didn't he clean out the car? If he'd killed her there, he must have known there'd be fingerprints from her, hairs, fibres and so on."

"Perhaps he did and that's what was left," said Neil through his pint.

"No," insisted Jennifer. "If he'd cleaned it, he might have left a few traces since as we know, it's difficult to remove everything, but not that much. And although it's yet to be confirmed, the lab said there's a load of foreign fibres on the tapings from the girl. Brown wool, which I'd bet a pay cheque are from him. The scientist I spoke to said there are tons; they're just waiting for the controls from the pullover we seized to compare them."

"He could hardly have removed all those," said Derek, not understanding where her argument was going.

"What I mean is, why are there so many? There was no sexual assault or even consensual sex."

"Easy," said McPherson. "He carried her from the car to where she was dumped. Bound to end up with a load of his fibres on her."

"So why didn't he dump the pullover and the rest of his clothes?" argued Jennifer. "He hasn't even washed them."

McPherson raised his eyebrows at her. "Sounds like the smooth-talking Mr Silk has cast a spell on you, Cotton."

"Rubbish," harrumphed Jennifer. "Not at all. But surely you'd agree that his apparent total lack of awareness is almost perverse."

Bottomley rubbed the stubble on his chin. "So, do you think he's innocent? How do you explain all the evidence?"

"Planted?" Jennifer's question was hesitant, knowing the reaction she'd get.

They all laughed.

"Who by and how?" chortled McPherson. "Come on, Jennifer, get real. Think of the planning. Perhaps it was the invisible man."

"Perhaps he was drugged." Jennifer knew she was getting nowhere, but she felt she had to continue.

McPherson was enjoying himself, showing off his experience to a novice.

"You mean like a date-rape victim. That would take some doing, especially since there's no indication that he was with anyone.

"Look, sometimes you have to accept that there's no rhyme nor reason to why someone's done something like this, especially when it seems to be out of character. You can't put yourself inside the head of a culprit like that because his head is a mess. There'll be no rational or sensible explanation. People who do this sort of thing are either dense low life or calculating psychopaths. Cold-hearted killers when you're dealing with murder."

Jennifer stared at her wine, not feeling like drinking any more.

"I know all that, guv. I'm just not convinced he's either."

## Chapter Fifteen

Despite the promise in her pep talk of providing whatever resources were necessary, Detective Superintendent Freneton was keeping a keen eye on expenditure. In her role of resources manager, the buck stopped with her for the entire SCF. If they went over budget, it was her head on the block with the high command.

One of the cost-cutting initiatives she had introduced almost before her coat had settled on its hook on the day she assumed office as squad commander was to cut overtime payments. The measure was not well received: detectives supplemented their salaries with overtime, especially when there was a big case on. Freneton knew that, but costs were escalating and needed to be reduced. She instructed that once a certain number of hours of overtime had been worked, the officer would take time off in lieu for any more clocked up, or work for nothing. Mike Hurst knew it wouldn't work; it had been tried before, but Freneton insisted.

For this reason, the following Monday morning, Jennifer was at home in her apartment in Nottingham's Park district, a private estate of large Victorian houses a stone's throw from the city centre, taking time off in lieu. Her stepfather, the Milan-based and internationally renowned fashion designer Pietro Fabrelli, had bought her the apartment as a present when he heard she was moving to the Nottingham area as a police officer. He thought her career choice was crazy — he would have far preferred to use her intelligence in his business and for her to help him deal with the wreck that her mother had become — but he knew better than to resist, so he decided to help her in any way he could.

"It's going to be a hard life, carissima, long hours and much pressure," he had told her in a phone call from his baroque-inspired office in the Via Monte Napoleone, his liquid tones attempting to perform their persuasive magic. Jennifer always imagined him sitting there in a brocade silk jacket and powdered wig.

"You've got to have somewhere private where you can relax, somewhere quiet and comfortable, away from all the madness. I've seen the cop shows; I worry about you."

Jennifer's apartment was one of four in the expensively restored Lincoln View House that in the eighteen hundreds had been one of the grander of The Park's exclusive residences. Occupying half of the first floor, the apartment had a fine view over the adjacent Lincoln Circus, a large, tree-fringed circular garden popular with dog walkers. Originally, Jennifer had found the ground floor apartment, which came with its own private garden, a tempting proposition, but even though the plot was walled and protected with a high, electronic gate, Pietro was still worried about security, preferring the extra barrier against intruders that living one floor up would bring.

The spacious living room had once been a master bedroom with its own balcony. In summer, nearby trees filtered the light flooding through the south-facing French doors, filling the space with a brilliant softness that was hardly ever too hot; in winter the unfiltered rays were guaranteed to boost the temperature on the coldest days. Jennifer had fallen in love with it as soon as she walked in, and now that the apartment was filled with her own furniture, fittings and books, it was the perfect haven and she loved to spend time there.

By eleven o'clock, she had finished her chores and was relaxing in a huge, soft armchair by the balcony doors with a mug of freshly brewed Arabica, a feel-good glow about her. Her first big case was all but finished and it had gone fantastically well. She was re-reading Dante's Inferno in Italian for possibly the fiftieth time when her mobile rang.

"Jenni—"

"Cotton! Where are you?" Rob McPherson's sharp voice barked in her ear. There were no niceties.

"At home, gu—"

"Well, whatever you're doing, drop it. You need to come straight here, to the SCF. The big boss wants to talk to you. Imme-diately."

His tone was cold, full of suppressed anger.

"What's it abou—"

The phone went dead, leaving Jennifer staring at the display. She thought of calling Derek Thyme to see if he knew what was going on. But then it dawned: the big boss? She assumed by that McPherson meant either the Ice Queen or her boss, Detective Chief Superintendent Peter Hawkins. She'd only spoken to him once at length, on her first day. Rather overweight, and reluctantly balding, he seemed nice enough if rather distant. He had a reputa-tion for rigid adherence to the rules, rather like the Ice Queen, but his methods were less ruthless. No point in calling Derek; it was unlikely he'd know anything.

She looked at her clothes. Jeans and a sweatshirt. That wouldn't do, but she'd need to be quick.

When Jennifer walked into the main squad room, she immediately registered the silence: the usual buzz of conversation eerily absent. Heads turned towards her, eyes cautious, concerned looks on all the faces. She raised her eyebrows a fraction as she caught Derek Thyme's eyes, but the response was a tiny shake of the head. Clearly neither he nor anyone else knew what was going on.

"Cotton! This way!" commanded McPherson from the corner of the room.

He was standing by a door that opened onto a corridor leading to the inner sanctum of bosses' offices. Jennifer followed him to the corner of the building: the DCS's office. McPherson knocked on the door, opened it and stood aside to let Jennifer pass. Then he followed her in, closed the door and stood in front of it, as if to guard it and prevent her escape.

Jennifer was shocked to see not one but three of her senior officers in the room. They were all seated at the far end behind a long table, a set-up used for promotion board interviews. And for disciplinary hearings. In the centre, leafing through a file was the DCS. To his right was Mike Hurst who was quietly drumming his fingers on the table as he stared at a point in space beyond Jennifer's left shoulder, while on the DCS's left sat Olivia Freneton, her face thunderous as her eyes pierced into Jennifer's. The memory of a comment from Neil Bottomley about Darth Vader crossed Jennifer's mind.

"DC Cotton, come over here," ordered the DCS as he closed the file and looked up at Jennifer.

There were two chairs on Jennifer's side of the table, but there was no invitation to sit. She took a few steps forward, glancing back at McPherson as she did. His rough-hewn features registered little, except he looked ten years older.

Jennifer stopped three feet in front of the table and stood to attention, her eyes fixed on the wall behind the DCS's head. She knew she must have done something terribly wrong and was frantically racking her brains to consider all the possibilities. A report she'd forgotten to write? One she'd left important details out of? Perhaps one into which she'd put too much detail, making the CPS angry because the defence would have access. In the few milliseconds of deafening silence from her bosses as they all turned their attention to her, she trawled through many possibilities, but she was stumped. She couldn't think of anything.

Then the silence was shattered.

"DC Cotton," barked Hawkins. "I'd like you to tell me what the hell you think you're up to." His tone was more than threatening.

"I don't understand, sir. Is there a problem?"

"A problem!" he yelled. "Of course there's a problem. A huge bloody problem! You have more than likely compromised the whole case!"

Jennifer felt her knees buckle while her gut had developed a free-falling existence all of its own.

"I ... I don't know what you mean, sir."

Her eyes flickered towards Freneton and back. If it were possible, the superintendent's frown was even deeper, her whole demeanour darker and more threatening. The corners of her mouth dropped in a sneer.

"We'll give you one chance, Cotton," she snarled, interrupting Hawkins. "One chance to explain. But let me make it perfectly clear. Your career's on the line here; you might even be prosecuted for trying to pervert the course of justice."

Jennifer's mouth opened and closed like a fish on a rock, but no sound emerged.

"Well!" yelled Freneton, making Jennifer jump in fright. "Jesus, girl, what is wrong with you?"

Jennifer was fighting to remain standing to attention, her breathing heavy. She was reeling from the verbal barrage, the implied accusations that she knew nothing about.

Freneton continued, her words a series of stiletto thrusts.

"We have some more results. Lab results. DNA results. Your profile."

"My ... profile, ma'am? You mean you think I've contaminated the scene? That's impossible."

She turned to McPherson whose face now looked as if root canal would be preferable to being there.

"Guv, you saw me do the preliminary examination of the X-Trail. I gloved up and touched nothing inside the car. I know I didn't wear a mask, but I didn't speak or sneeze or anything while I was looking in the car. I couldn't have contaminated it. And even with the gloves, I touched nothing except the door handle, and the shoe when I bagged it. At the scene in the woods, I was fully gowned, masked and everything, so it can't even be saliva—"

"Shut up, Cotton! Stop babbling!" yelled Freneton.

"It's got nothing to do with scene contamination, DC Cotton," interrupted Hurst, his voice insistent but deliberately softer. He was livid with her but that didn't dampen his dislike of Freneton. If she continued like that unchecked, she'd have Cotton a quivering wreck on the carpet.

"Like me, and everyone else on the team, your DNA is on record for elimination purposes for exactly the reasons you just described: in case anyone is sloppy enough to contaminate the scene. It's a serious matter when it happens, we know that, but we have to accept that it does happen."

Jennifer was nodding frantically. "I know that, sir, I know why it's done."

In her mind she was running through every occasion she had had anything to do with any of the physical evidence, and she could think of no time when she could have screwed up. She knew the rulebook backwards and sideways and could recite it chapter and verse, in Italian or French if need be. And she took pride in adhering to it.

Hurst continued. "One of the things the lab does is to run all the profiles, full and partial, and all the controls against each other — it's part of the protocol — and one of their more astute young scientists noticed your DNA."

Jennifer was shaking her head. "What do you mean, sir, noticed my DNA? What's so special about my DNA?"

Olivia Freneton was ready to pounce; she wanted to be the one to deliver the killer punch.

"It's very similar to Henry Silk's, DC Cotton, that's what's so special, as you put it," she snapped, her voice still hovering precariously on the controlled side of rage. "It contains what the scientist called several rare alleles, which are something of a research interest for the scientist. When she then found that Silk's DNA has the same rare alleles, our astute young scientist asked for our approval to carry out a paternity test. And her conclusion, confirmed by her seniors, is that Silk is your father. Ninety-nine point nine percent certain. He's not even an uncle, Cotton; he's your father!"

She banged on the table with her fist, taking everyone by surprise.

"Henry Silk is your father, Cotton!" she repeated, emphasizing every word.

She paused, taking satisfaction in watching Jennifer absorb what she'd said, that they'd discovered her secret. Then she continued to drag the blade around in the wound she'd opened up.

"And, DC Cotton, I don't and won't accept for a moment that you didn't know. We've spent the last hour going over conversations various of us have had with you in the last week or so and it would appear that you've tried hard to persuade more than one of your colleagues that Silk is innocent. Now we understand your motive."

Jennifer could almost feel McPherson cringing behind her as she remembered their conversation in the pub. Judas! she thought. But that thought was an aside. Jennifer was incensed and her anger cut through her shock.

"Ma'am, I can assure you, I can assure you all," — she glanced briefly at Hawkins and Hurst before focusing back on Freneton's malevolent gaze — "I had no idea that I was related to Henry Silk in any way. It's a total shock and in fact, I dispute it. I think there's been some sort of cock up. My father was a doctor who was killed in a car crash before I was born. Obviously I never met him but I know my mother loved him dearly. Like most people, I only know about Henry Silk from what I've read in the glossies; I'd never met him before last Monday."

She paused, panting, desperate to defend herself. Something else occurred to her.

"And anyway, if you've been reviewing my conversations with the team," — her tone was verging on sarcastic as her eyes flashed to Hurst who was now examining his fingernails, avoiding eye contact — "you'll know that *I* was the one who found the red shoe in Silk's car. And *I* was the one who noticed the scratches on his neck. Do you think I would have done that if I were trying to protect him? I think he's as guilty of the murder of Miruna Peptanariu as all of you do. It's the sheer stupidity of his actions I find difficult to fathom."

She was almost shouting.

"Watch your tongue, DC Cotton," snarled Freneton. "You can protest all you like. I, for one, do not believe you. You're off the case, young woman, and as your squad commander, I'm suspending you from duty until further notice. Your dishonesty has created a huge amount of extra work for everyone and will cost the SCF a fortune. You'll never work with this team again; they won't want you. When the defence finds out, and I doubt we can keep it under wraps, they'll be screaming 'foul'. And I can't even begin to imagine what the press will do when they get hold of it. They'll have a field day; make us look like complete idiots. All thanks to you, DC Cotton."

Her voice was rising as her rage started to get the better of her.

"Didn't you once stop to think of the waves you'd be creating, or that your secret wouldn't eventually be discovered? Thank God we found out now. If it had happened during trial, we'd never have recovered."

She stopped to take a slow and deliberate breath, and then continued in a more even voice.

"I'm also going to report this to the Internal Investigation Branch, and knowing them, they'll have your hide. I can't imagine anyone here will stand in their way. For the present, DC Cotton, I should warn you that you are not to breathe a word of any of this to anyone, inside or outside the team. If you do, I'll make it my personal business to ensure you are kicked out of the force in disgrace. Now, get out of my sight."


Jennifer was shaking. She lowered her head and shifted her eyes from Freneton to Hawkins, and then to Hurst. Benign, friendly Mike Hurst. He was her mentor, more than any of the others, and now he hated her for something that must be untrue, and if it wasn't, something that she had still had no knowledge of.

All she could perceive in their eyes now was hostility. She realised her chin was quivering more than the rest of her. They were not going to see her break down and cry. She turned swiftly on her heel and without even a glance at McPherson, who had to step smartly out of her way, she pulled open the office door and left.

She was hardly conscious of walking along the corridor and into the squad room. As the door slammed behind her, she became aware of every pair of eyes in the room watching her, but she couldn't look at any of them, not even Derek. She grabbed her bag from where she'd left it on her desk on the way through and rushed out of the door.

Derek Thyme watched her go. He was as alarmed and confused as the rest of them — they'd all been listening to the yelling, shouting and arguing from the inner sanctum all morning. He looked across at one of the other DCs, Joe Renton, one of the older ones. Not over bright, but steady and reliable. Renton caught his eye and nodded after Jennifer.

"What you waiting for, Justin? You're her mate; go after her, find out what the hell's up."

Derek shot out of the room and caught up with Jennifer on a half landing on the stairs. She heard him coming but ignored him.

He grabbed her arm. "Jennifer. Jen. What's happened? Are you OK? I've never seen any of them so angry. Not even the Ice Queen and she's always angry. McPherson was apoplectic; I thought he was going to have a heart attack."

Jennifer stopped and half-turned towards him.

"I can't tell you, Derek. They've forbidden me."

She had a sudden thought that if what she'd been told was true, they had no right to ban her from announcing who her father was. But then the thought of how that would be received hit her.

"All I can say is that I've been suspended. They want to prosecute me, Derek."

"What! Why? What've you done? That's rubbish; they can't do that. I don't believe it."

"Look, Derek, it's better we don't even skirt around it. I can't say anything, Nothing. No hints. They're bound to question you when you go back and even if they haven't seen you follow me, they will still question you as part of their investigation. You're a close colleague; they're bound to."

"Question me about what? I don't get it, Jennifer. Anyway, if they're going to question me, they'll tell me what it's about so you might as well tell me now. Won't make any difference."

"Yes, Derek, it will. Let them tell you if they want and then let them swear you to secrecy until the press gets hold of it. For my part, I can't and I don't want to even come close to opening up the possibility of you being in any way complicit."

Derek stared at her, trying to work his way through the complexity of her sentence. He gave up and took hold of her shoulders.

"Jennifer, whatever they're accusing you of, I don't, can't believe that you've done something wrong. You've got a brilliant mind — I'm in awe of you — and you're going to make a great detective. It gives me a buzz just working alongside you, even though I know I can never be as good as you are."

She touched his arm and sagged.

"Thank you, Derek, you're very sweet. It's good to know I've got one friend here."

"You've got more than one, Jennifer. The whole team feels the same."

Jennifer pulled open her bag and snatched out a tissue. She could feel tears welling up in her eyes.

She managed to stall them and wipe her nose.

"Look," she sniffed, "you've got to watch your back. You all have. Freneton will take no prisoners."

She stopped and looked at the ground, suddenly overwhelmed again.

Derek was still not taking no for an answer.

"Jennifer, you've got to tell me."

She looked up at him but hardly saw him, her mind working overtime. She suddenly let go of his arm and ran back up the stairs, leaving Derek staring after her with his mouth open.

She banged open the door to the squad room, strode through and into the corridor beyond. Hurst was back in his office talking to McPherson. Jennifer pushed open the door without knocking and marched up to Hurst while totally ignoring McPherson. She hadn't forgiven him.

"What the hell are you doing here, Cotton? You've been suspended." Hurst was shocked and distinctly uncomfortable. The Ice Queen might emerge from under her rock at any moment and accuse him of collaborating with the enemy.

"You've been ordered to leave. Any time you spend near this case is compromising it further."

Jennifer ignored his rant. "Boss, I want another DNA profile done on me. I think there's been some enormous screw-up. There's no other explanation. What they think is my DNA can't possibly be. There's no way that man can be my father."

Hurst took a deep breath as he thought about it. Finally he nodded. "That's a fair request, Jennifer, but I hope for your sake, for all our sakes, that you're right."

He looked at McPherson. "Rob, take her back to the squad room and get someone to take a buccal swab from her, witnessed. Then get the sample to the lab and get it fast-tracked. I need that result ASAP."

He turned back to Jennifer.

"After that's done, DC Cotton, get out of here and don't come back until you hear from me."

## Chapter Sixteen

Late the following afternoon, Jennifer was at home in her apartment unable to concentrate on anything, her mind still spinning around the meeting with her senior officers the day before. She had spent the past twenty-four hours racking her brains for any indication in her past that her being Henry Silk's daughter could possibly be true. If only she could ask her mother, but she couldn't.

A cardboard box on the coffee table in front of her was full of old family photographs she had selected from several much bigger boxes stored at the family house outside Milan when she moved to the apartment in Nottingham. There were many of her as a baby and a small child, either alone or with her mother and Pietro, joyful images from holidays in the sun and the snow, the house in Sardinia, various yachts, fashion shows, parties. There were also many Jennifer had selected of her mother as a child with her own parents. Jennifer had never known them; they died before she was born. She remembered thinking it slightly odd at the time that there were none of her mother from around her mid-teens until when she was twenty-three and holding the newborn baby Jennifer in her arms. Now she found it more than odd: there was a distinct gap.

She was idly flicking through the photos when her main gate

buzzer sounded through the intercom. Whoever it was had held their finger on the button for too long: it wasn't a casual caller.

She sighed, reached over to the handset and pressed a button. "Yes?"

"It's Rob McPherson. We need to talk."

Jennifer considered telling him to go away, that he was the last person she wanted to talk to. Instead, she pressed the gate release button.

"It's flat three," she said, pressing the door release for her apartment. "The door's on the left."

She heard the front door close and McPherson's footsteps as he came up the stairs.

"In here," she called through to the hallway at the top of the stairs. She wasn't going to get up and greet him.

McPherson appeared at the door, his eyes automatically scanning the room, the detective in him noting its important features.

Jennifer indicated an armchair opposite to where she was sitting and he sat down.

"Nice place," he said absently, although his eyes had now settled on the box of photographs.

"Thanks, but I doubt you've come here to view the property."

He looked up, his square jaw set, his eyes troubled.

"The lab has profiled the sample you gave yesterday, Jennifer, and it's the same result. Hurst also got them to repeat Silk's profiling. There's been no cockup: all the profiles match the previous ones. They are sticking by their opinion that Henry Silk is your father."

Jennifer leaned forward, putting her head in her hands, her eyes staring blankly. She was gutted. She'd pinned her hopes on a mix-up of samples.

McPherson waited until she looked in his direction.

"Hurst is spitting; he thought you were right. Freneton is giving him hell — they hate each other, as you are probably aware. Look, Jennifer, I need some background from you. Could you tell me something of your childhood, your family? Tell me about your mother, what she told you about your father. If you want us to believe your story, we've got to have something to go on."

Jennifer stood and walked over to the balcony doors. In Lincoln Circus below, she could see two children of about three and five playing with a ball, giggling, laughing, calling out to their parents who were laughing and waving back. An ordinary, normal family, a family whose lives hadn't just been shattered, people who would go home, enjoy their evening meal, watch TV, read to the kids.

She felt like screaming, tearing her hair, beating her fists on McPherson's head.

She turned to face him, leaning against the French doors. He was watching her carefully.

"Jennifer," he started, "about yesterday. You must have thought I was doing the dirty on you, telling tales."

"Weren't you?"

"She gave me no choice, the Ice Queen, I mean. She's like a Rottweiler. I've had some tough bosses in my time, but she takes the biscuit. But I wanted to say that I'm sorry. It was nothing personal. When she hit me with the DNA results, she made it sound like the end of the world. A huge conspiracy on your part."

Jennifer nodded vaguely and walked slowly to the sofa. She sat, pulling one leg up under her.

"What do you want to know?"

"Can someone talk to your mother? She's still alive, I take it?"

Her reply was a caustic snort. "Yes, she's very much alive and you're welcome to talk to her. But I don't think it will help you."

"Why?"

"She's in a care home in Milan, a psychiatric care home. She's suffering from a severe form of early onset dementia. She doesn't know what day it is, and most of the time she doesn't know who I am, let alone anyone else. So good luck."

She folded her arms and looked away.

"I'm sorry to hear that, Jennifer. That's terrible. How old is she?"

"Forty-eight."

"Jesus. Milan you say?"

"I told you the other day I was brought up in Italy, in fact, I was born there. But I went to quite a smart international school and in many ways I consider myself as British as you are. Not that being

Italian would be a problem for me. Once I'd decided that I wanted to be a police officer, a detective, in fact — much to my mother's horror, and my stepfather's — I thought seriously about joining the Italian police. But there are too many police forces there, mostly in competition with one another, and they're all extremely male oriented. I couldn't see a future, so I chose to come to England. I was at university here and it seemed the logical way to go."

"Yeah," said McPherson, "I can appreciate that, the male-oriented bit, I mean. I watch Montalbano on the telly, even though I have to read the subtitles. Not too many female detectives in that."

Jennifer smiled. "Once in a while I have to resort to the subtitles too, even though my Italian's fluent. It's set in Sicily, as you know, and they use the Sicilian dialect sometimes, which is difficult."

McPherson could sense she was relaxing slightly. "Tell me about your background."

"As I said, I was born in Milan some months after my mother moved there in 1988. She'd previously worked as a fashion designer in a small fashion house in London.

"She was engaged to a doctor, Simon Jefford. According to her, he was a real looker and wonderful with it, and he seemed to get more so in my mother's memory as the years went by. She had a difficult time at my birth; she nearly died and the doctors advised her to have no more children. But I'm jumping ahead.

"Before I was born, in November eighty-eight, back in the summer of that year, Simon Jefford, who had recently qualified, wanted to go on a drive around Europe with his mates, two of his closest friends. It was something they'd talked about and planned to do all the way through medical school. Just three blokes: girl friends and fiancées weren't invited.

"So off they went in a VW camper and trundled around Europe. But there was an accident in what was then still Yugoslavia. Somewhere in the middle of nowhere, outside Belgrade, there was a head-on collision with a huge truck driven by some drunk. It was nighttime and he veered across the road, wiping out the van and killing all three of them.

"Apparently my mother had a breakdown, nearly lost me a couple of times, blamed the whole thing on pretty much everyone and everything she could. She decided she hated England, London in particular — she's half Italian, did I mention that? She sold up, moved to Milan and got a job in what even then was quite a prestigious fashion house. That's where she met my stepfather, Pietro Fabrelli."

"*The* Pietro Fabrelli? Even a fashion caveman like me's heard of him."

"Yes."

"Blimey, you kept that quiet."

Jennifer shrugged. Her attitude was that it was no one else's business and anyway she hated name-dropping. She'd told HR; that was as far as it needed to go.

"He fell for her and they married. Of course, they couldn't have children, but he always treated me like his daughter. However, he didn't adopt me, so I kept my mother's name."

"Which is …"

"Cotton. She's Antonella Cotton. Her name was originally Italian, Cotone, but she changed it in England and never changed it back."

"So she's actually Antonella Fabrelli, then."

"No. Married women in Italy don't take their husband's family name, only the kids. In my case, as I said, I was a stepdaughter, so I kept the name Cotton."

McPherson sat back in his chair, feeling more at ease as the conversation progressed.

"You know, Jennifer, I'm inclined to believe you. It all sounds pretty convincing."

"Of course it's convincing; it's the bloody truth!" she snapped. "Do you think I'm making it all up?"

"No, sorry, that didn't come out right. But what I don't understand is how, if your mother was expecting you, Jefford would—"

Jennifer interrupted him. "Go off on a jolly?"

"Yes."

Jennifer's expression was wistful. "One of her great regrets in life was that he never even knew she was pregnant. She wanted to wait until he returned before she told him; reckoned he wouldn't have gone if she had, and she knew how much the trip meant to him."

"Yes, but he wasn't your father, clearly, so what was her relationship with Henry Silk?"

"I've no idea; I wish I had. Ever since the big revelation yesterday I've been trawling through every memory I can muster for something. I certainly never heard her mention his name, and living in Italy, we didn't watch British TV, so I'd never heard of him until I came here as a student and saw Runway."

She picked up some of the photos and flicked absently through them before tossing them back on the table.

"Listen, if you believe me—"

McPherson shook his head. "I said 'inclined to believe you' not that I did."

"Whatever. But if you were *inclined* to think that I genuinely didn't know, then if that's true, I can't possibly have compromised the case, can I? And what about Silk, I assume he has no idea that I'm his daughter. I mean, why should he?"

"Why indeed, and I doubt we'll be telling him. But regarding compromising the case, it's not that easy, as I think you realise. Even if you didn't know, the fact remains that you are Henry Silk's daughter, which places the whole investigation on difficult ground. And whatever we say, there will be plenty of people who don't believe us.

"As both Freneton and Hawkins explained, it's a loophole, a bloody embarrassing big one. Everyone will get egg on their faces. Imagine the headlines: 'TV Star Prostitute Killer Arrested By His Own Daughter Scandal/Farce/Fiasco — make that final word whatever you like. They'll have quotes from Human Rights Watch, Opposition MPs, anyone they can wheel out. Sky will feature it ad nauseam."

Jennifer shrugged. "There's nothing I can do about that; it's not my problem. And I should imagine that too many people know already for it to be kept quiet."

"Why? Have you told anybody?" snapped McPherson, his sharp response surprising her.

"No, of course not, not even Derek Thyme, though he badgered me hard enough. Believe me, I was within a whisker of telling him after the way Freneton spoke to me, but I didn't."

McPherson wasn't letting it go.

"The only people who know at the moment are you, me, Hurst, Freneton and Hawkins, together with a few people at the lab," he said sternly. "They've been told that it's classified, completely confidential, so they won't blab. The DCS will have to tell the assistant chief constable, who will, of course, go ballistic."

"What happens now?"

"I don't know. Do you think your stepfather knows the truth?"

Jennifer thought about it for a moment, then shook her head.

"No, I very much doubt it. He's always been completely open and considerate in talking about Simon Jefford; he knows how my mother felt about him. I think there would have been an edge if he'd known the truth. But what I meant was what happens now to me?"

As he leaned forward, McPherson's whole body language changed. They'd reached the difficult part. He wasn't now simply her guv; he was the messenger sent with bad news.

"Freneton wants you transferred out of SCF, probably back into uniform, somewhere out of the way."

Jennifer ground her teeth. "Like Newark, where I started?" she snarled.

"I've no idea; it's not my call. How come you started off there anyway, and not somewhere down south?"

"Why should I be down south? I was at Nottingham Uni, the original one, not Trent, and I applied to the Notts Force. I like the city and know it well. Seemed logical."

"Yes, but why Newark?"

"I'll admit that was a total surprise. There was a bit of a crisis there at the time — they were very short-handed. So I think I was posted by a computer.

"But guv, I really don't want to go back into uniform. I mean, they do a fantastic job and all that, a really difficult one at times and I have nothing but admiration for them, but it's not why I joined the force. My career is in CID. If I'm back in uniform, that's my career down the tubes through no fault of my own. You know how it will work. I'll be branded."

McPherson pulled a face. "I'm sorry, you have to believe me that we, the DCI and I, we argued for you, but the Ice Queen is adamant."

Jennifer pushed her mouth and chin into her hands.

"Since it's confidential, what excuse will she give?"

"Probably stress. She'll say you were finding the job too upsetting."

Jennifer banged her fist on the arm of her chair, jumped to her feet and started to pace the room.

"That's complete bollocks and she knows it!" she shouted, waving her arms. Her Italian background was coming to the fore. "If she does that, it'll follow me forever. I'll spend my career giving Highway Code instruction at schools. You surely don't think the team will swallow that, do you?"

McPherson started to look sheepish; Jennifer's future had clearly been discussed in detail.

"No, of course they won't. They'll be told that you've blotted your copybook big time. Viewed some confidential documents or something, documents that are way above your authority. I'm afraid it won't help your reputation with them."

"They won't believe a word of it."

"There are ways of making things sound very plausible, Jennifer."

Jennifer ran a hand through her hair. "Damn it!" she yelled. "I'm being completely stitched up. That's so unfair. Why is Freneton so against me?"

"Her reputation is formidable, I'm afraid. You're not the only one, believe me. When she takes a dislike to someone, they're history. Wherever she's been posted, there's a trail of ruined reputations."

"Bitch. What about Henry Silk?"

"What about him?"

"Doesn't he have a right to know about me? I am his daughter, after all. And isn't there a chance he'd find out?"

"How? We're certainly not going to tell him."

"Suppose his defence calls for all the forensic reports to be reviewed by their own experts. Wouldn't they spot it?"

McPherson rubbed his forehead as if it were suddenly paining him.

"Christ, Cotton, you have a way of ruining someone's day."

"And you don't? Anyway, it's better to anticipate problems and think of damage limitation in advance, wouldn't you say?"

"Now you sound like her. She's done nothing since she arrived except bend our ears about contingency planning, worst case scenarios, backups, lateral thinking, plan Bs, Cs, Ds, all the way to Z and back."

"Pity she's such a cow, we could get on," muttered Jennifer.

She stopped pacing and sat down again, her voice now quiet.

"Look, guv, I've been thinking a lot in the past twenty-four hours. I knew there was a possibility of my being sent back into uniform and if that's the decision, then I've made up my mind."

McPherson's eyes widened. He really didn't want to hear this.

"Jennifer, I—"

She held up a hand as she bit on the inside of her lip, trying to keep some control in her voice.

"I'll resign. If I can't be a detective, I'll leave. I'm not trying to blackmail you or give you an ultimatum; that's just the way it is. It'll break my heart because I've always wanted to be a detective ever since I was a kid and I know I'd be good at it. Shit, I am good at it. But I'm not going to be the victim of the whims of some vindictive bitch who's hell bent on buggering up my career. I'll do something else."

"Jennifer, that's ridiculous, such a waste. Let me talk to Mike Hurst. He's got Hawkins' ear, I'm sure they can do something."

She shook her head. "Sorry, but I don't believe you. I think their minds are made up too. I'm a problem, an embarrassment, and the best way to deal with it is to lose me in the system."

McPherson looked at his shoes.

"You realise that even if you do resign," he said quietly, "you won't be able to tell Silk, that it's privileged information."

"Only until after the trial, surely?"

"No, even after the trial, you'd be on sticky ground."

"I don't see why," she snapped petulantly. "There's nothing to stop me paying to have my own profile done, and nothing to stop him doing the same, and since I'd no longer be a police officer, there'd be nothing you could do to stop me visiting him in prison. I'm his daughter, after all; I'd have every right."

"Be careful, DC Cotton, you'll be treading an extremely dangerous line."

"I'll take that risk, guv."

She gave him a grim, mirthless smile.

"Know what, I'm only going to be calling you 'guv' for the next ten minutes, well, couple of days. After that, you'll have to call me 'ms' or 'madam' and I won't give a shit about any lines you or the big bosses care to draw, dangerous or otherwise. There's something about this case that stinks. You know that as well as I do."

McPherson stood. He'd had enough.

"No, Jennifer, I don't. Your being related to Henry Silk has no bearing on the case as far as I'm concerned. It's a side issue that doesn't detract in any way from the man's guilt or the strength and quality of evidence against him."

# Chapter Seventeen

## ONE MONTH LATER

Charles Keithley followed the unsmiling prison officer as he unlocked and relocked a succession of doors in the confusing maze of corridors that led from the visitors reception area in Skipshed High Security Prison, Derbyshire to the legal interview room. As always, Keithley had been required to leave everything except his file with the case papers in a locker at reception. No phone, no iPad. He'd even left his car keys rather than set off alarms.

As a visiting solicitor, he was allowed to see his client away from the prying ears of other prisoners. And the one guard sitting at the far end of the room was out of earshot if they kept their voices down.

Henry Silk was sitting at a table in the middle of the room, waiting for him. As Keithley approached, he stood and held out his hand.

"Good to see you, Charles."

Keithley noticed immediately that Henry's greeting wasn't accompanied by his normal half-smile, a creasing of the eyes.

"You too, Henry. Sorry that it's been nearly three weeks; there's been a lot of admin stuff with the case that needed going through before I came back to you."

He paused as they sat.

"You're looking rather sallow, Henry; you don't seem your usual self."

Henry looked up, the ghost of a rueful smile at the corners of his mouth.

"You should try being in one of these places, Charles. It's dehumanising. Everything is regimented, controlled. And among the inmates, there's an undercurrent of anger, violence. Many of the actual prisoners, as opposed to those on remand like me, don't see any reason why they shouldn't give in to their violent tendencies. It will make little difference. They're already locked up in a cell for many hours a day. What's going to change if they satisfy a blood lust?"

Keithley's face showed his concern. "Have you been threatened, Henry? I can probably get you moved. It's ridiculous that prisoners on remand are kept with convicts. It's not supposed to be like that."

Henry shrugged. "They always cite overcrowding and ignore any protest. But no, Charles, I haven't been threatened, and even if I had, moving wouldn't be likely to achieve much. One of these places is much like another. It would just be more inconvenient for you if they located me hundreds of miles away.

"As it happens, I'm passing the time playing mind games. I'm using my acting skills to keep the cons and the guards guessing as to what I'm really like. I change my character regularly. It's a diversion and I've found that it keeps them at arm's length. They seem to have decided that I'm nuts because my moods are so inconsistent. There's also a reputation that precedes me of being a tough guy. I suppose I've got something to thank that soap for."

"You heard that they killed you off, your character in Runway, I mean."

Henry snorted his disgust. "That bastard Jonty Peters couldn't wait. Jumped at the chance to offload me. So now, even if by some miracle my case is dropped or I'm found not guilty, I can't go back."

"There was quite an uproar in the glossies; it wasn't a popular move."

"It's done, Charles, and it will take an exceptional scriptwriter to undo it."

He paused and sat back wearily in his chair.

"I think what's probably wearing me down is that my head is still reeling with the whole case. It's well over a month since my arrest and I keep thinking that I'm suddenly going to wake up from this nightmare.

"I have no idea about anything that happened that night and it's driving me crazy. I can't get my head around it. The only thing that's really keeping me going at the moment is the thought that something will turn up, some clarity of thought will hit me, or something will happen to cast doubt on the evidence."

His eyes shifted to Keithley. That Henry hadn't been looking directly at him had worried the solicitor — Henry normally held the eyes of whomever he was talking to, and there would have been far more animation to whatever he said.

"To that end," continued Henry, "how are you getting on, Charles? Any breakthroughs?"

Keithley sighed as he shook his head.

"I'm still exploring a number of avenues, but it's not looking good. The prosecution has a strong case with all the forensic evidence and the CCTV footage. It looks sound and no doubt they are scrutinising it to close any possible loopholes."

"What about your forensic people?"

"They've come up with nothing. I'm afraid that after reviewing all the evidence, they agree with the conclusions. The procedures have all been followed to the letter and there's no indication that anyone has screwed anything up — contamination and so on.

"The thing is, Henry, we're not dealing with traces here, you know, one or two fibres, a partial DNA profile on a smear some-where. There's loads of good, solid material."

Henry nodded. "Did they have anything to say about that, given that my position is that it must have been planted?"

"Both our experts say that although there seems to be an abun-dance of forensic evidence, it's not so much that they would be suspicious. And since no one can come up with any explanation as to how or why it might have been planted, they are struggling to fault it."

"So the prosecution will have plenty of means, but no motive."

"Exactly, and that's going to have to be the thrust of our barrister's argument. The old car crash is bound to raise its head, but he'll be ready for that. Fortunately, you've never publicly taken a strong position on anything controversial, no daft right or left wing comments in the press, so character witnesses and lack of motive will be what we'll use."

Henry nodded his agreement. "I don't tend to mouth off privately either, so I doubt they'll dig up some old soak to pour boiling oil on me." He paused, sighing. "I should have tried hypnotherapy."

"What?"

"You know, get someone to release my unconscious mind. Find out what happened to me that night, because I've no bloody idea. But I doubt it's on offer from the counselling services here."

Keithley pulled a face. "I can make enquiries if you think it would help."

Henry shook his head, radiating his dejection. "No, it would be a waste of money."

Keithley glanced down at the file he'd brought with him.

"There is one thing that cropped up, bit strange, but I don't think it's really likely to help."

"What?"

"Well, we've known each other a long time, since the early nineties, in fact, and I don't recall you ever mentioning that you had a daughter."

"A daughter?" Henry snorted derisively. "I haven't mentioned it because I don't have one. Why, is someone claiming she's my daughter? It wouldn't be the first time, it kind of goes with the territory, although it's usually some star-struck loser claiming that I'm the father of her child. Easy to deny, of course, especially these days with DNA. I've already had a letter from some idiot who says she wants to marry me. Even suggested conjugal visits. Tell her to get lost, Charles."

"It's not quite as easy as that, Henry. You see the young lady in question came to my office and cut straight to the chase — quite a forthright young woman. She told me that I should have your DNA profiled independently of the police lab profile."

Henry frowned. "I thought that had been done."

"It has, which rather surprised her. So she asked if our DNA expert could have a look at something and comment. Then she handed me a file containing several sheets of the scientific mumbo jumbo that the DNA people put out. I asked her what it was and she said it was her and her mother's DNA profiles that she'd paid a private lab to produce."

Henry raised his eyebrows. "And she wanted them compared with mine?"

"Exactly. She seemed perfectly sensible, if rather ardent, but clearly not playing a game to waste my time and your money."

"You mean you didn't think she was some gutter journalist trying to set me up for a sleazy headline."

"Oh, she's certainly not that. You see, I recognised her as soon as she came through the door, and you will too."

"Really? Who the hell is this mystery woman, Charles?"

"DC Jennifer Cotton."

"What! You're kidding me. You're saying that DC Cotton is claiming to be my daughter? She's off her head."

"I can't comment on the state of her mind, Henry, but I've had the profiles all checked by our expert, Dr Merriton, and she says that Jennifer Cotton's claim is correct. She is your daughter."

Henry sat back in his chair, his face fixed in shock. Then, as his mind started processing the information, a smile slowly formed at the corners of his mouth. For the first time that morning he became animated, his introspection gone.

"That, Charles ... that ..." He stopped and let out a bark of amazement. "That is the most bizarre thing I've ever heard!"

He paused as another point hit him.

"But she was in on the interviews, came with those other plods to pick me up. Christ, she was the one who found the shoe in my car *and* she spotted the scratches on my neck. Are you saying that all along she knew she was my daughter?"

Keithley smiled, encouraged by seeing the real Henry back in the room.

"That's exactly what her bosses thought as they unceremoniously dumped her from the case. No, she had no idea at the time. One of the lab scientists noticed the similarity of your profile to hers, carried out a paternity test and blew the whistle."

"Wow! I'll bet that ruffled some feathers."

Henry's eyes were roaming the room, piecing together events.

"You know, I wondered why she disappeared. I mean, she seemed to be the girl of choice and then suddenly she wasn't in on the interviews any more. Her replacement wasn't nearly as good looking or as bright."

"Yes," agreed Keithley, "they played it very subtly, if you recall. They basically repeated all the interviews that she'd been involved in, and a few more so as not to make me smell a rat. They asked the same questions but in a different way using a different officer alongside Inspector McPherson. They made an excuse about the recordings being damaged, said the sound was distorted and that they needed to redo them. I'm sorry, Henry, I fell for it; I should have questioned it more."

"It wouldn't have made any difference," said Henry, "they would have kept plugging away. But I'll bet they were sweating."

He sat forward, now drumming his fingers on the table.

"I wonder who her mother is? I've never met anyone called Cotton, not that I can remember. Is she married, this girl? What was her maiden name?"

"No, she's single."

"How old is she?"

"Twenty-five."

Henry did the sums. "So, she was born in 1989. I—"

"No," interrupted Keithley. "Nineteen eighty-eight. November 1988."

Henry frowned through more sums.

"That means she was conceived in, what, February or March of that year. I was still married to Antonia at the time. Just. Our marriage was well on the rocks and she'd told me she wanted out. But she never let that sort of detail get in the way of her basic urges. Any port in a storm with our Antonia. Of course, it wasn't long before the accident. Well, a couple of months."

The memories of that time came flooding back. He and Dirk Sanderley had been best mates. Dirk was round at their apartment so much that he almost lived with them. Antonia revelled in it all, encouraging Dirk to stay, encouraging everyone to stay. Henry had complained occasionally that Victoria Station had fewer people passing through it. Actors, directors, people from Antonia's fashion world; it was never ending. He and Dirk would take off from time to time; sometimes Antonia would come, sometimes not, more not towards the end. He remembered that Antonia had been unwell during the month leading up to the accident. Now he knew why: she had been pregnant. Why hadn't she told him? Yes, of course, she didn't think it was his and anyway, they were going their separate ways. That was the reason she hadn't gone to France with them, to the film festival. He shook his head. More drug festival than film. Dirk was well into everything by then, and starting to get argumentative and aggressive whenever Henry tried to steer him back on course.

He snapped back to the present.

"Did she tell you anything else about herself?"

"No," replied Keithley, "She refused. Said she'd been forbidden to reveal the information about the DNA profiles that were produced as part of the police investigation, so she arranged for her own."

Henry smiled. "Sounds like a chip off the old block. I like this girl already."

"She wants to see you. She said she'll discuss things with you, but no one else, for the present."

"Well, I can hardly pop over to her place for a cup of tea and a chat, so she'll have to come here. And if she's my daughter, the authorities can't object."

"I can arrange it, Henry. But, you know, you don't seem over-surprised to find you have a daughter."

Henry laughed. "Hey, I'm surprised all right. It hasn't quite sunk in, that's all. Antonia must be her mother, mustn't she?"

"I don't know, Henry. That was all before I knew you, and Miss Cotton wouldn't say more."

Henry was only half listening.

"I thought there was something about her, that day back in Luton," he enthused. "Never occurred to me that she might be my daughter, though."

He took a deep breath, his eyes on Keithley's file on the table.

"When Dirk was killed, I got the blame, as you know. But Antonia's reaction was ten times, a hundred times worse than everyone else's. She was like a mad dog, raging. Completely refused to speak to me. Cut me off. The divorce whistled through in double quick time and that was that. I never saw her again. I didn't really mind; I'd had more than enough of her and I had my own problems. I thought I'd never work again. But I did think it rather strange that she seemed to disappear off the face of the earth."

He looked up at Keithley.

"Is any of this going to help the trial, Charles? I mean, the police must be extremely embarrassed that my daughter was one of the investigating officers."

"They're embarrassed, you can guarantee it, but it seems they've covered their tracks well. They've more or less fixed it so that they won't have to call her as a witness. I could get our barrister to, of course, but I doubt in the long run it would help, given that when she was on the case her behaviour was exemplary."

Henry smiled again at his old friend.

"OK, Charles, if you can arrange it, I'd be delighted to meet DC Jennifer Cotton."

"Actually, Henry, she's now just plain Ms Jennifer Cotton. She has resigned from the police."

## Chapter Eighteen

It took ten days for Charles Keithley to work his way through the red tape. He found it frustrating until he was reminded that if Henry had been a convict rather than a remand prisoner, it would have taken far longer. The system didn't make it easy for anyone.

Unlike the visit with Keithley, Jennifer's was in the main interview room, a dreary space of twenty small tables and twenty pairs of chairs. There was no privacy, so the norm was a surreal set of hushed conversations, like people talking in a church.

The procedure for visits was that the visitor was escorted in first and told to sit at one of the tables. After that, the prisoner was fetched.

As she saw Henry being led through the door from the main prison, Jennifer stood up, feeling awkward. She was shocked; he looked gaunt, he'd lost weight, but there was a sparkle in his eyes, unlike other prisoners she'd glanced at around the room.

"Hello, Jennifer," he said as he reached the table. "What should we do? Shake hands? Hug?"

"Let's just sit and talk," she said, and sat down.

Henry followed suit and there followed an awkward silence with each of them studying the other's face.

Finally, Henry broke the ice. "This is a bit of a turn up. I still haven't quite hauled it on board. I don't mean to jump straight in, well, I suppose I do really, but may I ask who your mother is?"

Jennifer was immediately defensive. "Why? Are you trying to place me as the possible offspring of one of a long line of conquests?"

Henry smiled, wanting to ease the tension. "Now, now, there's no need to be hostile. I'm not like that. I know that many actors have quite a reputation for being ladies' men, but sadly my reputation is altogether different."

Jennifer was still stern faced.

"I know. I'd read about you in the glossies even before the case."

"Then you'll know that I lead … led … a quiet, almost reclusive life trying to make a living in an industry that was forever trying to marginalise me."

Jennifer suddenly relaxed.

"Yes, sorry, I didn't mean to sound like some aggressive police officer. I wasn't that sort of police officer, anyway."

It was now Henry's turn to be serious.

"Charles Keithley told me that you'd resigned from the police. To be honest, I was stunned. I can't imagine why you would do that. Remember, I've seen you in action and you were streets ahead of the rest of those clowns who interviewed me, the senior ones included."

He saw Jennifer's chin quiver; clearly her decision was still a raw wound.

"When they found out that you were my father, they didn't, wouldn't believe that I didn't know. There was one in particular, — the detective superintendent — who was relentless. She would have had me hung, drawn and quartered. They were rightly embarrassed by it all, so even though I think I persuaded some of the bosses that I was totally innocent, the damage was done. I had to be taken off the case and if I'd stayed, I would have been sent back into uniform. I couldn't accept that; it's not the career I wanted. So I chucked it in."

"That sounds appallingly vindictive. Does this superintendent person think you fiddled the results of the case, tampered with the evidence? You were the one who found the shoe! At the time I wondered if you'd planted it by some clever sleight of hand."

For the first time, a smile flickered at the corners of Jennifer's mouth, softening her whole face. Henry felt his heart melting.

"No, it wasn't the evidence," she said. "They were worried about the fallout, especially the senior types. It all gets absurdly political in the elevated ranks — the chief super, assistant chief constable and above are all paranoid about the press. I think their idea of hell would be a never-ending phone call from a tabloid editor with dirt to dig and a direct link to Whitehall."

Henry's eyes creased; he liked his daughter more each second. He took a deep breath.

"Anyway, Jennifer, your mother? And, of course, your father. Who were you told was your father?"

"My mother's name is Antonella Cotton, She is, or rather was, a fashion designer, not a particularly special one, but as it turned out, that didn't matter. She worked in Milan, which is where she still is, and where I was born and brought up."

"Why didn't it matter?"

"She married Pietro Fabrelli, the boss of the fashion house she worked for. You've probably heard of him, most people have. He's my stepfather, and a generous one too."

"Pietro Fabrelli! Wow! I'm impressed. Have you always known he was your stepfather, rather than your father, I mean?"

"Yes, I have. My mother never tried to hide it from me that my real father was a newly qualified doctor, a brilliant man with a stellar future ahead of him, she said, who was killed in a car crash in Europe along with two friends."

"Did she say where?"

"Somewhere in the former Yugoslavia. His name was Simon Jefford."

Henry shook his head. "That name doesn't mean anything to me, I'm afraid. Have you checked, about him and the crash, I mean. You were a police officer, it should have been easy enough."

"No, I had no reason to, and anyway there are strict procedural protocols these days for searching the police databases. You can't just dive in and check up on someone or something if it's not part

of an ongoing investigation. All access is logged and it's taken very
seriously if someone takes a wander around the files."

"Interesting. So it's not like they show it in films or on TV?"

"You must be joking. In movies they get information so quickly
that it's there almost before the crime has been committed."

"You have to take short cuts if you want to squeeze all the
action in to an hour or so," said Henry, smiling.

He paused, his eyes roaming over Jennifer's face, taking in her
features, her hair, the set of her jaw.

"Could you tell me more about your mother? What's she like?
Have you told her about me?"

Jennifer frowned briefly, making a decision. She reached into
her pocket, brought out a photo and catching the eye of the nearest
guard, raised her eyebrows in question. The guard sauntered over,
taking his time.

"May I show this to him, please?" asked Jennifer.

"Who is it?" said the guard.

"My mother."

"OK, this once, but you shouldn't bring anything in with you,
and Silk, you can only look; you're not to touch it."

"Yes, sir," said Henry automatically, his jaw clenching.

Jennifer dropped her eyes, realising it had been a difficult
moment for him.

"Sorry, I didn't mean to embarrass you."

She held up the photo for Henry to study.

"Antonia," he said, nodding. "It had to be, really."

"Antonia?"

"Antonia Caldmore. At one time, Mrs Antonia Silk, although
she always preferred to use her maiden name."

"She was your wife? When?"

Henry looked back at the photo that was now lying on
the table.

"Mid to late eighties. Ours was not a marriage made in heaven.
It only lasted three years and even then there were dalliances on
both sides. We were too young and both in crazy industries.
Antonia was twenty and I was twenty-two. She was very impres-
sionable, thought she was going to make it big in the fashion world,

especially once she had made connections in the acting profession. To be honest, I'm not actually sure why we got married; I suppose we thought we loved each other.

"I was doing OK, beginning to get known, but, as for many, the parties and the liberal life were huge distractions. My best mate was Dirk Sanderley, who was really going places. Some people thought I was following in his wake, but that wasn't actually the case. He was a good actor, but without wishing to brag, I think I was every bit as good. What he did have was the charm and the extra special good looks. Looks are like fashion, you know, they have their time, and Dirk's were perfect for that time."

"I've seen photos of him," said Jennifer, "and a couple of the things he was in. He was a bit too moody for my taste."

Henry was amused. "Prefer them softer, do you, Jennifer? But you're right, if he were starting out today, he might not cut it quite as easily."

He sat back, relaxing a little, realising that he was enjoying her company.

"Anyway, I knew Antonia was attracted to him, but he was my best mate and he respected the fact that she was my wife. Or I thought he did.

"At the time, Antonia and I were well on the way to divorcing. There was yet another party, this time in France at a film festival. I had been drowning my sorrows for a while and people were used to seeing me the worse for wear. Ironically, at that party, I had almost nothing to drink and I smoked only one reefer. Nothing else, although the lies put out in the press at the time told a totally different story. Dirk, on the other hand, was out of it. He was high and plastered. And when he was like that, he became aggressive. I stepped in to prevent him having a punch-up with a weedy and obnoxiously whiney American film director — Dirk would have flattened him and probably spent the rest of his life paying off the damages. As it turned out, the rest of his life amounted to about an hour, so perhaps I should have left them to it.

"I decided we should go home. We argued but we ended up in the car with me driving. He was impossible, kept on grabbing the wheel, insisting he should drive. I fended him off a few times, but then on a tight corner, he did it again. I was going a bit fast and we drove straight into a tree. I woke up two days later to find that Dirk was dead and I was a pariah. According to the press, who were all over it, I'd killed Britain's biggest box office talent since Olivier. They crucified me with lie after lie. I didn't get any work in the UK or the US for several years.

"I only saw Antonia a couple of times after the crash. Initially, I thought she'd come to support me, but she was foul. I was stupid to think otherwise since the divorce was now through. She blamed me completely, really over the top. Now I think about it, she would have known by then that she was pregnant and maybe she thought someone else was the father. I later heard whispers about an affair with Dirk, but I dismissed them as gossip. Perhaps they weren't, perhaps they were true and she thought he was the father of her unborn child.

"The last time I saw her, she behaved in the same vitriolic way. She still didn't look pregnant so I had no notion. She informed me that she never wanted to see me again, that she was going to disappear out of my life forever. I thought she was being typically melodramatic, but she was right. It was like she was lifted up and transported to somewhere I had no knowledge of. From that day to this, there hasn't been a single word. Not that I'm blaming her; I didn't try either. I had my own problems and it took all my time getting round them. By the time I started to get a bit of work, I'd pretty much forgotten about her."

Jennifer sat in silence, staring at him, trying to come to terms with the truth.

Finally she took a deep breath. "If that's all true, then everything my mother told me about my father was made up. There was no Simon Jefford; she invented him as part of the story to exclude you. I don't know what to say."

Henry pursed his lips. "I'm sorry to have broken it like that; I had no idea."

Jennifer was only half listening. "It never really dawned on me before, I must be stupid, but there's only one photo that I was shown of the person she called Simon Jefford. Now I realise it could have been anyone, an old boyfriend, anyone. It's strange though, the person you described doesn't sound a lot like my mother. She was devoted to Pietro and I don't think there were others. It's true that she was a party animal and she liked being the centre of attention, but it never occurred to me that her behaviour was more than mild flirting." She shrugged. "Who knows? Perhaps I'm being naïve. I'd certainly agree that she has a temper, especially when she can't get her own way."

Henry leaned forward, elbows on the desk, chin on his hands.

"From what you say, she's clearly never mentioned me to you. She's going to be pretty surprised, angry I should think, if you choose to tell her. I wouldn't blame you if you didn't."

Jennifer shook her head, a wistful smile on her lips. "I have — told her, I mean. She was neither surprised nor angry. As I expected, she just smiled and talked about the weather. It's a coping mechanism."

Henry frowned. "I don't understand."


For the next few minutes, Jennifer explained the details of her mother's rapid decline into dementia and the stage it had now reached.

"Three weeks ago when I flew over to get a buccal swab for her DNA profile, she thought I was a nurse."

Henry was genuinely shocked. He reached out his hand to touch Jennifer's arm, a move that surprised her, but she didn't pull away.

"How terribly sad, Jennifer. I'm so sorry."

"Yes," she said, "it is. She's so lucky to have Pietro; he's utterly devoted to her, and as I said, before she started to lose it, I think she was to him. He's put her in the best possible hands; the home she's in is top notch and super-expensive.

"He's always been more than generous to me too. Paid for my university education here in England and supported me when I said I wanted to be a police officer. He even set me up with a smart apartment in Nottingham when I got my first posting in Newark. I didn't want to live there and it's not a bad drive. That's why I was able to chuck in the job without having anything else. I've got no mortgage to pay and I've got income from stocks that Pietro bought in my name years ago, so I'm under no pressure to rush into something else."

"Lucky girl. Do you think he knows about me?"

"I really don't know, but I somehow doubt it. My mother never talked about her early life. She always dismissed my questions as too tiresome when I was growing up. For her, it was as if life started once she moved to Milan. Anything before that wasn't talked about. She's led an entirely Italian life for twenty-five years, hardly ever speaking English. With her dementia, she might not even understand it any more."

Henry looked down. His hand was still on Jennifer's arm. He smiled slightly in embarrassment as he withdrew it.

"That's a sad tale, for her and for you. I'm sorry. And I'm amazed that she's managed to keep everything from you for all these years. She must have really hated me and blamed me for being responsible for the death of the man she thought was your father. Tell me, did she ever mention her own parents?"

"Only that they were killed in a train crash in Turin some years before I was born. Her father was Italian, hence her original surname, Cotone. Her mother was English."

When Henry didn't react, Jennifer picked up the significance immediately.

"You're now going to tell me that's not true, aren't you?"

"I don't want to upset you, Jennifer."

"You might as well come out with it. I'm quickly getting used to the idea that my mother lied about her life."

Henry slowly brought his hands together in front of him.

"To my knowledge, Edward and Pauline Caldmore never left these shores. He was a bank manager in St. Albans, she a teaching assistant in a nursery school. They were nice, ordinary people whose only child, Antonia, was pretty wild. She wasn't lying about them being dead, and it was a train crash. But in the north of England when Antonia was nineteen, a year before we were married."

"So I'm not in any way Italian?"

"I'm not so sure about that, after all, you were born there. Do you have an Italian passport?"

"I do, as well as a British one. Pietro organised the Italian one when I was very young, probably through the system known as 'clientelismo'. He's powerful enough to gain favours when he wants them in exchange for certain bureaucrats' wives being dressed in the latest fashions. It's how much of Italy works, but I don't question it too closely."

"And you a police officer! But it means legally you are Italian even if your parents were not. And you're fluent in the language—"

"Native speaker."

"—Exactly. And you love the country, like I do. Italy's been good to me too. I've had plenty of work in Rome, thanks to my speaking Italian. I won't be as good as you, but I get by."

"You're one big surprise after another."

He grinned at her and held out his palms in a typically Italian gesture.

She laughed, which thrilled him.

"Look, Henry — you don't mind if I call you Henry, do you? I mean, I don't think I can call you daddy, or even babbo."

"Henry is perfect, Jennifer, and I promise not to call you sweetheart or darling."

She laughed again. "People will just think you're a dirty old man if you do. But what I was going to say was, do you mind if I continue to work with Charles Keithley? I like him and he's pulling out all the stops for you. I want to help, to explore every avenue for you. I don't think the police did a particularly thorough job. We were all guilty of accepting what was there in front of us without really questioning it."

"Jennifer, I'd be delighted. That's the best news I've had since I was arrested. But please be careful. Don't go sticking your neck out. I don't want you getting into trouble."

"I'm no longer a police officer, so they can't stop me as long as I don't use anything I found out before, and I don't start trying to persuade any of them to help me."

She looked around the room. "This place worries me. And you do too. You've lost weight and frankly, your complexion is grey."

Henry shrugged. "The food's terrible. I'm a fussy eater in that I avoid a lot of things that are staple here. It makes it difficult. And the sheer monotony of the place is relentless. You couldn't begin to imagine how much cons look forward to visits like this. I've only been here a month and it's such a special occasion. The thought of twenty-five years is too horrible to contemplate, especially when you're innocent."

He paused and fixed his eyes on hers. "You do believe I'm innocent, don't you? You're not just doing this out of some misguided sense of loyalty to your long-lost father?"

Jennifer took a deep breath. "My conviction of your innocence gets stronger every day, and this visit has certainly helped. But I still don't know you well enough to work out whether you're a bloody good actor spinning me and everyone else a clever line, or whether it's the truth."

Henry nodded in appreciation. "Well, that's forthright enough. All I can say is, yes, I am a bloody good actor, but I can assure you that I haven't been acting today. It's all me."

## Chapter Nineteen

Sally Fisher picked up her phone and glanced at the screen. The caller's number wasn't one she recognised.

"Hello?"

"Hello, my name's Jennifer Cotton. I was given this number by Petra Moorfield. Is that Sally Fisher?"

"Yes, it is. Are you a friend of Petra's?"

"Er, no, not exactly. I'm a friend of Morag, her younger sister; she was a flatmate of mine when I was at uni."

Always suspicious of cold callers or people trying to get a back-door to her art-forgery-expert husband Ced, Sally kept up the questions.

"I remember the name. Morag, I mean. She was at Leicester, wasn't she?"

She knew she hadn't been: her response was another test for the caller to pass.

"Leicester? No, I don't think she ever went there. She was at Nottingham with me. Well, we didn't read the same subjects, but we shared a flat with a couple of other girls. Her subject was maths, while mine was English and Italian literature."

"And why did Petra give you my name?" continued Sally, although she was relaxing now. The voice on the other end sounded genuine enough.

"I remembered Morag saying that her sister was a brilliant biochemist with an interest in forensic science, won some prizes when she was with you at Manchester. When I spoke to her, Petra, that is, she said that she'd moved on to other biochemical studies and suggested I call you. You see, I have a few forensic questions that need someone experienced in the field to answer. I was hoping you might be able to help me. You are a forensic scientist, aren't you?"

Sally was now happy to continue.

"I was. I'm now a full-time mother of one little girl and expectant mother of another child, sex as yet unknown. My husband is desperate for a boy; he's already planning lots of male-bonding ironman stuff, but Claudia-Jane and I reckon we'll be more than a match for them."

"Claudia-Jane?"

"My daughter. What's it about? I'm about to go out to a toddler thing."

"It's all rather complicated to discuss over the phone. I was wondering if I could pay you a visit. But I don't want to be a nuisance."

"You're a sort of friend of Petra who I'm still vaguely in touch with, so it's no problem, as long as you don't mind having Claudia-Jane crawling all over you."

"Sounds fun. How old is she?"

"Two-and-a-half going on twelve."

Jennifer laughed. "Would the day after tomorrow be OK? Late morning?"

"Fine. Give me your email and I'll send the address and directions."


Two days later, shortly after eleven thirty in the morning, Jennifer drew up outside the Fishers' town house on a quiet estate on the outskirts of Knutsford in Cheshire. Her assessment of the street was automatic, her policing skills still finely tuned. Well maintained gardens, newish cars, a few casually but stylishly dressed mothers with pushchairs, some joggers. Everyone looking comfortable and relaxed. No sign of any disaffected, out-of-work youth.

She rang the bell and the door opened immediately.

"Hi," said Sally. "I saw you pull up outside. You are Jennifer, aren't you?"

"Yes," replied Jennifer, reaching into her pocket for her warrant card, then stopping herself. That was in the past.

She held out her hand. "Pleased to meet you, Sally. Thanks so much for agreeing to see me."

"Come in, come in. Excuse the mess. Claudia-Jane has taken over almost every room downstairs this morning. There are toys all over the place."

On cue, her daughter appeared at the living room door dragging a huge cardboard box.

"Mumma?"

"No, sweetheart, you don't really want that one as well, do you?"

"Mumma?" persisted Claudia-Jane.

Sally stooped to pick up her daughter with one arm as she grabbed the box with the other. Jennifer was impressed by her physique. At nearly six foot one, Sally's well-toned body showed that her mention of iron man wasn't idle talk: she was seriously fit.

Sally was steering her daughter's interest back to the living room.

"Let's bring it in here, sweetheart. Mummy wants to talk to Jennifer."

Claudia-Jane's brows furrowed as she looked back at Jennifer, who in turn smiled at her.


"May I get you something to drink? Coffee? Tea? Have you come far?"

Jennifer was sitting on a sofa holding a large fabric dinosaur that Claudia-Jane had presented to her with the word, 'Dino'.

"Coffee would be great, thanks. Black, no sugar."

She took a stegosaurus that was now being offered in addition.

"He's lovely, what's his name?"

"Steg-gy."

Jennifer looked up. "Not too far. Nottingham."

"It's far enough," said Sally, surprised. "I could have saved you a journey. I know some of the people in the new lab there."

"Forefront Forensics?"

"Yes, I used to work for them in the main lab here in Knutsford."

Jennifer was hesitant. "I didn't really want to go there."

"Really? What is it you want to know about? They haven't screwed up, have they?"

"No, not at all," said Jennifer, opening a notebook she'd taken from her bag. "What I wanted to ask is—"

"What did you say you did?" interrupted Sally.

"I didn't, actually. Why?"

"It's just that you have the air of a police officer."

Jennifer laughed. "Oh dear, how transparent. Let me explain."

Sally put up her hand. "Continue with your prehistory lesson for a moment. I'll fetch the coffee. Claudia-Jane, show Jennifer the tyrannosaurus."

"Got big teeth!" roared Claudia-Jane.


Jennifer gave Sally a summary of the case and the evidence against Henry. She had also explained the discovery of her relationship with Henry and what had happened as a result.

Sally moved a camper van from the coffee table to make room for her cup. The camper had a fabric shark crammed into it looking uncomfortable.

"They gave you a pretty rough deal. Isn't there some sort of appeal process?"

"They didn't sack me. I resigned because I knew that even the best-case scenario would see me ending up somewhere I didn't want to be, probably forever. It's done and dusted now and I've come to terms with it."

It was immediately clear to Sally from Jennifer's body language and general tone of voice that she had anything but come to terms with it; that her decision was still an open wound.

Jennifer looked up from her notebook.

"What I was really hoping to discuss with you was that given the ton of forensic evidence implicating Henry as the culprit, how likely is it that he's been set up? I suppose what I'm really asking is whether that is too ridiculous a notion."

Sally scratched her head. In her time as one of the smartest forensic scientists with Forefront Forensics, and previously at the now-disbanded Forensic Science Service's laboratory at Chorley near Manchester, she had seen several cases where evidence had been planted. A couple had involved corrupt police officers while others involved colleagues or relatives of the person originally arrested for whatever crime was being investigated. Only one of the cases had been a murder, but the principles were the same: the aim of the actual guilty party was to divert attention away from himself by associating someone else with the crime.

"First question," she said, "is how certain are you that Henry Silk is innocent? Because the evidence is stacked against him all right."

"Obviously I'm not a hundred percent sure since I've only met him a few times," replied Jennifer. "But the more I think about it and about him and what he's like, the more convinced I become of his innocence. And it's not only because I've now discovered that he's my father; I had my doubts before. I must admit I haven't much experience with murderers, but all along Henry struck me as a very genuine man. He doesn't come across as some psycho spinning me a tale while really plotting the slaying of his next victim; he's truly confused and bewildered by the whole thing. I suppose what I'm asking for is a fresh but experienced and impartial mind to look at the alternatives."

Sally nodded. She loved this sort of challenge and missed it.

"OK, I should say that it's possible, certainly, but extremely difficult. It would take a lot of planning and a detailed knowledge of what the lab was looking for and how we go about our work. Obviously there have been cases in the past where people have been set up, but whoever it is doing the framing, the normal mistake they make with trace evidence is overkill, mainly because they want to be sure that the evidence is found."

She paused to break up an imaginary fight between two prehistoric creatures that Claudia-Jane was orchestrating and getting quite heated about.

"You can imagine, as an ex-police officer, how it might go," she continued. "If, for example, they want glass fragments from a broken window to be valuable evidence, rather than content themselves with planting a few shards like you'd normally find, they'll scatter half a broken window over a significant piece of clothing and for good measure shove a large glass fragment from the window in one of the pockets. That amount of evidence would always raise flags in the lab and there would be discussions about how to proceed, since the case officer himself might be the person who's planted the stuff. It can be tricky, a minefield of diplomacy, which isn't normally a scientist's strong point."

"Do you think that could be true in this case?" asked Jennifer. "After all, there is a lot of evidence."

"Well, you know the police officers; I don't. Is there anyone involved, directly or indirectly, who strikes you as someone who could do it?"

Jennifer took a sip of her coffee as she thought about it.

"No, no one," she said, shaking her head. "I mean I don't know many of them well, but they are a cohesive and competent team, both the police officers and the civilians. They're impressive. And it's not as if Henry's a local. He comes to Nottingham from time to time in plays, but that's all, I think. I was on the ground from the start with the evidence; I certainly don't think there's been any tampering, and no one behaved oddly, drawing attention to evidence." She winced. "Except me, of course."

Sally smiled. "I'm confident we can rule you out. But I think the answer to your main question is yes and no. There's a good variety of evidence — fibre transfers, hair, fingerprints from the victim, positive DNA matches, the shoe in the car, a tyre print and so on. But for each of those, apart from perhaps the fibre evidence, the amount found is within the normal range you'd expect. And for the fibres, the rather large quantity can be explained by the fact that the culprit almost definitely carried the victim some distance while he was wearing a pullover and scarf that would both shed good amounts with such strong physical contact."

"But surely," said Jennifer, "given that Henry isn't an idiot, he would have been aware of all that. Why would he be so stupid as to leave all that evidence just waiting to be found?"

Sally absently straightened out the stegosaurus's spines.

"I agree, it does kind of beggar belief. But, you know, most criminals are not brain of Britain. They're driven by lust, greed, hatred, passion, malice and spur of the moment loss of control. Seldom do you see the cold-hearted assassins that feature in so many crime shows."

She paused, her brow furrowed. "You know, the one thing that really bothers me is the scratches on Henry's neck and the corresponding debris of blood and skin under the victim's nails that are a match with Henry."

"Yes," said Jennifer morosely, "and I was the one who noticed them."

"Planting them would really take some planning and execution," continued Sally. "I'm struggling with that one. And then there's the CCTV. You say it tracked him more or less from his room, through the hotel to his car, then to the pick up, out of the city, and then back into the city, the hotel car park and then back inside the hotel?"

"Exactly."

"How good was the ID from the CCTV?"

"It gave the car registration number, which is what led us to Henry so quickly."

"No, I meant the images of his face. How good were they?"

"There aren't any. His face isn't visible once in any of the footage."

Sally pursed her lips in thought. "Now that is interesting. You'd think that someone as careless as Henry appears to have been would have been almost jumping up and down waving at the cameras. But that's not the case. If fact it's the only time that precautions seem to have been taken."

"Yes," said Jennifer, "the visor was pulled down to mask his face, which is an odd thing to do at night."

"Very odd and very deliberate. You know, Jennifer," said Sally, sitting back and smiling, "I find that extremely suspicious."

"Why, exactly?"

"Well, you're thinking that the killer wasn't Henry but someone setting him up. Let's imagine the scenario. The killer would have to have dressed up in Henry's clothes and deliberately got himself videoed on the CCTV, but he couldn't risk his face showing. So he'd keep his back to the camera, or if he couldn't do that, keep his head down. In the car, in order to avoid any CCTV shots that could show the driver's face, he would pull down the visor — traffic cameras are almost always way above car level so that precaution would be most effective. Was he wearing anything on his head in the videos?"

"A baseball cap."

"Was that normal?"

"Yes, he wears it all the time to reduce the chances of being recognised in the street."

"OK, the killer probably knows that. Now, the killer also wants to make sure there's good forensic evidence and of course he would want to use Henry's car, whereas if Henry is guilty, you'd think he wouldn't have used his own car."

"No," disagreed Jennifer, "he'd only not use his car if the whole thing was premeditated. If he'd only gone out to pick up a prostitute, there'd be no problem with using his car."

Sally tapped a brontosaurus against her lips. "Yes, but in that scenario, you're saying that there must have been a fight that got out of hand, he killed her, panicked and drove back to the hotel." She shook her head. "No, makes no sense, not even if he panicked. I mean, what would you do?"

Jennifer was with her. "I'd drive back towards the city, perhaps, and then dump the car somewhere quiet and claim it was stolen. I wouldn't need to clean up the car in that case."

"No, but you'd dump your clothing, surely?"

"Beyond question. And I definitely wouldn't return to the hotel with the car and be able to act calm and collected, perform in a play and go merrily on my way."

Sally smiled. "Good. OK, back to the framing scenario. If the killer is impersonating Henry, he must have access to Henry's hotel room to get his clothes. And Henry would have to be absent — no, that doesn't make sense because we know Henry was wearing them earlier. And there are still the scratches. How would the killer do that?"

"Remember," said Jennifer, "that he claims total memory loss after returning to the hotel until he woke up the next day feeling wasted."

"So he might have been drugged. You need to get him to think harder; it could be crucial."

"Don't think he doesn't know that; he's done little else since he was arrested."

"Listen, Jennifer, let me think it all over and I'll give you a call. Ced will be interested; he's got a brilliant mind, and if I get a chance, I'll talk to Claudia-Jane's parent guardian — we don't do godparents — she's red hot."

Jennifer stood. "Of course. Thank you. And thanks so much for listening; it's really helped. I'm more than ever convinced now of Henry's innocence. You've given me more hope than I've felt in this case so far."

Sally nodded. "My pleasure. Unfortunately, none of what we've floated around would mean much in court, not without something else. But perhaps it'll help in the long run, who knows?"

## Chapter Twenty

Early the following Monday morning, Jennifer was on her regular run around The Park. In the six weeks since she'd resigned, one advantage of not working all hours was that she had sharpened her fitness. Her eating habits had also improved — three nourishing meals a day instead of snatched sandwiches, pub snacks and filthy coffee from the machine in the corridor. However, she still had no idea of how in the long term she was going to fill the aching hole in her life. Never having contemplated another career, she was floundering emotionally.

But for now, at least, she had the all-consuming challenge of Henry. She had visited Charles Keithley in his offices in Hampstead, talked at length to Dr Pauline Merriton, the retained DNA and forensic expert, reviewed and reread copies of everything the defence had so far from the CPS. She'd been back to the crime scene in Harlow Wood, now no longer screened off, she had driven the route Henry's car had taken, both in the daytime and at night, and she had sat in the bar of the Old Nottingham Hotel, walked its corridors and stairways, and examined the car park. None of it had taken her much farther forward.

It had now been five days since her visit to Sally Fisher and she was itching to talk to her again but reluctant to call. She had felt a resonance with Sally; she'd immediately liked her, been impressed by her clarity of thought, and hoped that she would become a friend. She imagined that Ced, Sally's husband, would likely be the same as his wife — world renowned in his field of art forgery detection and the author of a groundbreaking computer program for comparing paintings from the analysis of their brush strokes, he had to be pretty special. She'd seen a photo of the Fishers in their living room and been taken by Ced's open, friendly face, his loose-limbed athleticism obvious in the easy way he stood holding his beloved daughter, his other arm looped around his wife.

Jennifer pounded up Park Drive towards Newcastle Circus, turned right and was intending to sprint the final hundred yards along Duke William Mount to her apartment when her phone rang. It was strapped to her arm, monitoring her performance and she ignored it until it occurred to her that it might be Sally.

It was still ringing when she ground to a halt on a path in the middle of Lincoln Circus and grabbed it from its pouch.

"Derek!" she panted, after hitting the accept button. "You caught me … in a sprint. What … do you want … at this hour?"

She heard a laugh from her ex-colleague. "Chasing bad guys, Jennifer?"

"Those days are over. What can I do for you?"

"Make me a cup of coffee?"

"Really? I didn't think you'd be allowed to even talk to me."

"No law against it. And I think you might be interested in what I've got to tell you."

"OK. Have you had breakfast?"

"I've heard about those. Remind me."

"It's a meal taken in the morning after you wake up. Sets you up for the day."

"Interesting concept. I don't think it'll catch on in the nick."

"Time you tried it. Get your backside round here. The gate code is eight nine four five; I'll leave my front door on the latch. Help yourself to coffee if I'm still in the shower."

Derek looked wide eyed at the plate of bacon and fried eggs

Jennifer presented to him at her breakfast bar in the kitchen, her own plate equally large.

"Do you eat this every morning, Jen?"

"Yup. Being a lady of leisure has some advantages."

"What about all that fat? Isn't it bad for you? And no toast to soak it up?"

"You know, you shouldn't believe all the rubbish the government puts out about diet, Derek, it'll send you to an early grave. This is paleo, what our genes and bodies are programmed for, and it's magic."

"Where d'you get these eggs? They're huge, and what a colour."

"Organic farm out near Southwell. They have this novel notion that chickens are meant to run free, peck at things in the ground, be the little omnivores they're supposed to be."

"Wow!"

"Now, enough of Cotton's Nutritional Tips, what have you got for me? You sounded enthusiastic on the phone, or was that just the blood coursing through my ears?"

Derek put down his knife and fork, and wiped his mouth on a paper napkin.

"I was down in Bristol at the weekend seeing a mate from training school, Norrie Frampton. He joined CID down there early last year, about the same time I did here in Nottingham. We like to get together for a few beers from time to time, compare notes. We've got a sort of ongoing competition about who's going to make sarge first."

Jennifer pretended to choke on a piece of bacon. "Is there much money involved?" she spluttered.

"Don't be like that, Jen, there's no harm in having ambition."

"Only kidding, Derek, just don't live up to your reputation and be an hour late for your sergeant's exams."

"Very funny. Now, do you want to hear this or not?"

"I'm all ears," she said, giving him her best Cheshire cat grin.

"Right. Well, of course, Norrie wanted to know all about the Henry Silk case since it's been big news in the press. Still is."

"Tell me about it."

"Yeah, they don't seem to want to let it go. Every day there's a fresh story from a hack who's dug some has-been out of the woodwork for another Silk quote."

"Yes, and everyone of them a slanderous lie. Henry's thoroughly pissed off. He knew he didn't have many friends; the list is even shorter now."

"I'll bet. Anyway, Norrie seemed to be taking more than a passing interest in the case, even for someone in CID, so I asked why. He told me that he was involved in the investigation of a similar case last year in Bristol, soon after he joined CID."

Jennifer was suddenly serious.

"Similar in what way?" she said quietly.

"It was the murder of a prostitute working the old port area in Bristol. Her body was found in a wooded area not too far from the Clifton Suspension Bridge."

"Should you be discussing this with me, Derek?"

"The case is all over, Jen, it's not a problem. Now, what was interesting was that the girl wasn't sexually assaulted and nor had there been any consensual sex, as far as they could tell. Nothing on the swabs, vaginal, anal or oral."

"I was enjoying my bacon and eggs, Derek," said Jennifer, putting her knife and fork down.

"Don't be daft. You've heard and seen far worse and carried on munching on a sandwich. I've seen you."

"Hmm."

"Also," he continued, "she was clobbered over the head, but only once, and then she was strangled, not suffocated with a poly bag like Miruna."

"So that bit's different, then."

"I said it was similar, not identical. But she was found in a wood."

"Did they find what she was hit with?"

"A side-handle baton."

"Interesting choice. I take it the weapon in Henry's case hasn't been found yet?"

"No, it hasn't, but don't quote me; it's confidential, as you know."

"Was there a shoe missing?"

"No, I don't think so."

Jennifer shrugged her shoulders as she stood to clear the plates.

"I don't see that it's that similar. There have been plenty of prostitutes and other women whose bodies have been dumped in woods."

"I know, but it gets stranger. It was nearly forty-eight hours until the body was found, but the morning after the murder — although, of course, no one knew there'd been a murder at that point — the body of a prominent councillor from Cardiff was found dead a hotel room in the centre of Bristol. When CCTV footage from the area where the girl operated was looked at, the vehicle that picked her up was linked to the councillor. That was traced on other CCTV to the woods and then back to the councillor's hotel. They also linked him eventually, rather like Silk, with lots of forensic — fibres, DNA, hair, although there wasn't as much as in Silk's case, as well as the CCTV."

"How did he die?"

"Overdose of sleeping pills."

"Suicide?"

Derek shook his head. "Very unlikely, apparently. They reckoned he might have accidentally taken one or two too many and the strain of the pills on top of his night's activities caused his heart to give out. He was in pretty ropey condition, according to the pathologist."

"What were the pills?"

"They didn't release that for a while, although some slime bag of a reporter wheedled the info out of someone. Actually, it might have been a controlled leak since the dead man was distinctly unpopular with the police both in Bristol and in Cardiff. Threw his substantial weight around a lot."

"Are you going to tell me what the pills were or do I have to guess?"

"Oh, sorry. It was Rohypnol."

"Roofies. That's the date rape drug. Not easy to get now, even on prescription."

"Norrie reckons it's not that difficult and the man often went to Eastern Europe where they're readily available."

"Did the councillor have any connection with the girl?"

"No, and despite being an obnoxious bastard, he wasn't known to have used prostitutes."

Jennifer got up to get some more coffee capsules from a jar.

"Another cup, Derek?"

"Thanks, but I'd better get into the SCF; Freneton's on the warpath this week about punctuality. She never fails to find new and innovative ways to break our spirit."

"Tell her you were with me. She'll have you posted to the Shetland Isles and then she'll be out of your life forever. You could be the first black detective up there. That would be novel."

"I wish."

Jennifer pressed the button on the coffee machine and reached for a mug, but then changed her mind. Her bike ride would come first.

"Listen, Derek, thanks for that; it's food for thought. And it's given me an idea for some research."

Her bike ride completed, Jennifer was taking her second shower of the morning when she heard her phone ringing. She hoped the caller would leave a message since there was no way she could reach it in time.

There was no message but Jennifer recognised Sally Fisher's number in the call register and called straight back.

"Sally, hi, it's Jennifer Cotton. Sorry I missed your call, I was in the shower."

"Lucky you. I've been up since five."

Jennifer laughed. "Actually, I've been pounding the streets and then putting my bike through its paces."

"Ah, a girl after my own heart; I thought we had something in common. I'm about to do the same once Ced gets back from his run. Look, I'm sorry I didn't get back to you sooner. The day you came over, Ced was called away to Italy on an urgent case; he only got back yesterday afternoon."

"Italy? Whereabouts?"

"Milan."

"My old stamping ground."

"Really? You're not Italian, are you?"

"No, but I was born there, a stone's throw from the Last Supper. I'll tell you all about it sometime."

"Love to hear it. Ced's often over there. As you'll know, you can't move in most towns for Renaissance paintings."

"Too right. We had a few fifteenth-century frescos adorning the walls in the house where I lived."

"Now I do want to chat, and so will Ced. You must come back soon."

"Can't wait. I studied art history as a subsidiary. Loved it, so it'd be great to talk to him."

"Gets better all the time. Now listen; your stuff. I talked it over with Ced last night once Claudia-Jane had gone down. He loves a good puzzle and it really whetted his appetite. He immediately picked up on something that I think bothered me when you were here, but then we moved on to something else and I forgot about it."

Jennifer stopped rubbing her hair with a towel and waited.

"Did you say that there were some long blond hairs found, possibly from a wig?" continued Sally.

"Yes, there were. Two. One was on the girl's outer clothing, the jacket, and one on Henry's pullover. The lab couldn't be certain they were from a wig. Apparently there was some residue of glue on them, but one that is found occasionally in hairsprays. Why? Do you think they are important?"

"Did the girl own a long blond wig?"

"No, I'm pretty sure she didn't." Jennifer was rubbing her hair again as she wandered over to the coffee machine.

"So where did they come from?" asked Sally.

"No idea. I think they were more or less ignored since there was nothing to compare them with. It was assumed that they were on the girl's clothing from some earlier appointment or from a wig she'd used, and got transferred to Henry's clothing."

"But you said that she didn't own one."

"No, but these girls swap things around, you know."

"Sure. But suppose for one minute that they are significant. I mean connected to the case."

"How?"

"How possible is it that a woman is involved?"

"A woman?" Jennifer shrugged. "I suppose it's possible."

Sally was now warming to her theme, the enthusiasm clear in her voice.

"It would go a long way to explaining how Henry was rendered unconscious in his room. Assuming he's not gay—"

"No, he's definitely not."

"Right, well, supposing he met someone, I don't know, in the hotel bar, say, and it was a set-up. She could have slipped him something—"

"Roofies?" interrupted Jennifer.

"Yes, that would be good. Why did you suggest those?"

Jennifer gave her a brief outline of the Bristol case.

"Interesting," said Sally. "I'll definitely muse on that."

"So, do you think that we're looking at two people," said Jennifer. "A woman to spring the honeytrap and get the target unconscious, and a man to dress up in the target's clothing, pick up the girl, kill her, and then return to the hotel?"

"Mmm," muttered Sally. "Possibly, but I don't like it."

"Why?"

"Exactly. Why? The motive for a team of two or more people committing a crime is normally completely different from that for one person. For two or more, it almost always hinges around money. But for one perpetrator, all sorts of motives can be possible."

"Yes, but either way, it would still be very calculated and the question of why is still there. Why Henry, in fact?"

"Perhaps you should put it to him."

"I shall."

"OK. That's great. Look, I've had another thought and the possibility of it being a woman makes this an interesting one. When you were involved in the investigation of the case, were the hotel guests checked?"

"Their names taken, you mean? Yes, the list for the night of the murder was gone through; it's routine practice. As I remember, there was no one with a criminal record, not even drunk driving, which is unusual. Just the regular sort of bunch you'd expect: businessmen and women, conference-goers, tourists. You know."

"Yes. But now that you've heard about the Bristol case, I was wondering if it might be worth looking at the guest list from the hotel in Bristol to see if there's any overlap with the Old Nottingham list."

"Mmm. Not sure how I can get hold of them. I can't ask Derek. If someone found out, he'd be in all kinds of trouble."

"You're the detective; you'll think of something."

"Ex-detective."

"I wonder."

# Chapter Twenty-One

Jennifer had no sooner rung off from talking to Sally than she was pressing the call button for Charles Keithley. His secretary put her straight through.

"Hello, Jennifer. Any news from your forensic friend?"

Jennifer had decided she would keep Charles in the loop on everything she was pursuing in the case. He had been more than open with her, giving her access to everything he had; it seemed only fair to be the same.

"Actually, Charles, yes, I have. She called a few minutes ago."

She outlined Sally's thoughts about the implications of the long blond hairs.

"That's an interesting idea," commented Keithley once she'd finished. "I hadn't really thought along those lines. I'm seeing Henry this afternoon. Is it all right to talk to him about it?"

"Certainly it is," enthused Jennifer. "You never know, it might trigger a memory from that night. Listen, Charles, there's something else. I also had a visit this morning from Derek Thyme, my ex-colleague at SCF."

"He likes living dangerously, does he?"

"He should be in the clear unless the Ice Queen has spies hiding behind the trees outside. He mentioned what I think is a possibly connected case in Bristol."

Keithley listened in silence as she told him the details, although Jennifer could hear the rustling of paper as he made notes.

"Interesting similarities," he said, after a pause as he checked his notes. "But the case is closed. They have the culprit, albeit a dead one, so surely it's more academic than anything?"

"On the contrary, Charles, it raises an interesting alternative. Let's suppose for a moment that for both crimes, the same culprit was involved, framing the councillor in the first and Henry in the second. After all, a similar MO was used in both."

"Similar but not the same," countered the solicitor. "Criminals are creatures of habit, as you well know."

Jennifer sighed. Keithley's conservative attitude was not what she wanted to hear.

"You could be right, of course," she said. "You probably are, but I think it's worth following up. I'm also thinking of trawling the newspaper archives for prostitute murders around the country where someone has been convicted, but protested his innocence throughout the trial and is still protesting it from the confines of his cell."

"That'll keep you busy."

"Yes. It's a pity I don't have access to the police computers, but online newspapers and one or two other archives should be a start. You see, I've been thinking. If I'm right about these two cases, and if perhaps there are more, if they're spaced out over a long enough period of time and in different parts of the country, they probably wouldn't have been connected during any of the investigations since in all cases there will have been a culprit offered up on a plate. None of them would be outstanding crimes, cold cases or anything like that. They would hit the plus side of the police statistics and be forgotten about. They'd never be flagged for anything."

"Still a long shot, Jennifer, but worth a try. I don't know if I can offer any resources to help you; I'm up to my eyes at the moment."

"Don't worry, Charles, I'm happy to do it. However, there is one thing that's connected you might be able to help me with."

"I'll do my best."

"In the bundle of papers you have from Henry's case, do you

happen to have the guest list from the Old Nottingham for the night of the murder? I know we, the police, that is, got it. It's routine to do so."

"Mmm, I don't remember seeing it. I doubt it would be included since it would be of no relevance in the trial. I'll check, but I don't think so. Can't your friend Thyme get it for you?"

"Too risky. No, I've had an idea about a story I could spin; I'll see if I can use my feminine charm on the barman at the hotel. Could you remind me which room Henry stayed in?"

She heard the rustle of papers again.

"Let me see," muttered Keithley to himself. "Yes, here it is. Room two zero two."

"Thanks, Charles. Please give my love to Henry."


Jennifer thought through the story she'd concocted and decided she needed to give herself more credibility, and since hotels are always more sympathetic to their guests than strangers walking in off the street, that's what she would be: she would reserve a room for the night.

She looked at her watch: eleven thirty. Rather early to be checking in, but not too early to book. She went online and made a reservation for that night. In the box for special requests, she asked for a room on the second floor.

With some hours to kill, she opened up her laptop and began the long process of searching through online versions of national and local newspapers for prostitute murders.


By seven that evening, she'd had enough of trawling the Internet. She was finding her initial broadbrush approach to the search quite difficult to refine, given the variety of parameters. Tomorrow she'd try something different: major city by major city. With an average of about seven hundred and fifty murders a year in the UK, it was going to take a while, even if many of them were not murders of prostitutes.

She picked up the overnight bag she'd packed, tossed in her

laptop and set out on the ten-minute walk to the hotel, hoping that the receptionist would be both male and cooperative. However, as she walked through the main door into the lobby, her heart sank. The receptionist sitting behind the desk was Sheryl, the girl she'd questioned two days after Miruna Peptanariu's murder. She'd forgotten all about her.

She quickly sat in one of the armchairs in the lobby, her back to the desk, and picked up a magazine. Fortunately, Sheryl was busy with a guest seeking directions to the Broadmarsh Bus Station and hadn't noticed her. She tried to tune in on the conversation and had almost decided she should get up and leave when the main door banged open and a flustered young man she didn't recognise burst in clutching a cycling helmet.

"Michael!" hissed Sheryl. "You're twenty minutes late. I'm meeting me boyfriend at half past; he'll be wild if I'm late."

"Sorry, Sheryl, I had a puncture. Thanks for covering, I owe you."

"I won't forget it, either," promised Sheryl as she grabbed her bag and headed for the door, leaving her guest still wondering how to get to the bus station.

Jennifer sat back in relief. She decided she'd wait ten minutes for Michael to calm down before checking in.

At ten o'clock she came down from her room and made for the bar. She was within Michael's age-noticing parameters so he immediately followed her from reception.

"What can I get you?" he asked, with a smile that told Jennifer he would appreciate a drink himself.

"A red wine, thank you."

Michael poured and hovered. Jennifer let him suffer for a minute before telling him she was looking for some information about a conference centre near the river Trent. Oh, and would he like a drink?

"Used to work there," he said, beaming. He turned to pour himself a vodka and spent the next ten minutes giving her a mountain of useless information.

She smiled encouragement as she moved the conversation round to his present job, which he told her he'd had since January.

"Do you like it here?" she asked. "It's certainly my favourite whenever I'm in town. I think this is my fourth stay."

"Your face does look a bit familiar," he said. "When was the last time?"

Jennifer was suddenly cautious. She hadn't been the one to interview him, but he might have seen her with Derek.

She pretended to check the calendar on her phone.

"Quite recently," she said. "May the twenty-ninth."

She watched his eyes, wondering if he'd make the connection, but clearly he didn't.

"Actually," she continued, "I was wondering if you can help me. I need a receipt from that stay to claim my expenses and I've lost the original. My boss is a real skinflint and will take any opportunity not to pay. You couldn't print out another copy for me, could you?"

"No probs," he shrugged in his coolest style. "Wait there and I'll get it. What was the name?"

"Cotton. Jennifer Cotton."

"Be right back."

Jennifer casually followed him to the desk where he was punching keys rather slowly and looking puzzled.

"Won't be a minute," he said. "Not a routine I've done before and this system isn't exactly user friendly."

"Want a hand?" offered Jennifer. "I'm good with computers."

He pursed his lips and glanced around. "I shouldn't really, but there's no one around and it would probably be quicker. Thanks."

Jennifer made her way around the desk and leaned over the keyboard.

"Let's see. Arrival date: twenty-ninth of May. There. Name of guest: Cotton. Enter. Oh, it says there's no record. That's weird, I wonder if there's a glitch in the software. Perhaps I could try the guest list for that day; maybe the receptionist misspelt my name. OK?"

"Sure," he said, still trying to look casual.

She hit a couple of keys and the guest list appeared. She

scanned the menu, hit another key and the list refreshed with room numbers alongside. The first one she noticed was Henry Silk in two zero two.

"That's really odd, I can't see my name anywhere."

She looked up, involving him. "You'd think a single woman would stand out on the list that's nearly all men."

She turned her attention back to the screen. There were only four women listed as single-occupant guests. Indhira Chandraya, who stayed three nights; Emily Chan, four nights; Amelia Taverner, one night; and Sharon Peterson, one night. Both Taverner and Peterson had occupied rooms on the second floor.

"Very strange," she continued as she hit another button. "Oh whoops, that was stupid. I've hit print by mistake. Where's your printer? You don't want to leave any incriminating evidence."

"It's in the back office," said Michael, suddenly looking worried. "Glad you thought of that. The day girl would give me hell. I'll pop through and fetch it."

As he turned away, Jennifer lifted her phone and photographed the screen. Then she hit another button and Amelia Taverner's credit card details appeared. After snapping that, she repeated the process for Sharon Peterson.

By the time Michael returned, the screen was once again showing the overall guest list.

"Any luck?" he asked.

"No," said Jennifer, frowning at the screen. "You know, I'm sure it was May the twenty-ninth."

"We could try other days?" suggested Michael.

"Let me check my diary. It's in my bag by the bar."

A moment later, she was back, flicking through a diary. She suddenly hit the heel of her hand against her forehead.

"God! I'm stupid. I remember now, I didn't stay here at all in May; it was in April. The night I was in Nottingham in May, my secretary booked me in to the Riverview by mistake. I gave her hell. I much prefer this place; it's so convenient. I'll pop down to the Riverview in the morning and ask them."

She put on her best guileless grin. "Sorry to cause you so much trouble."

## Chapter Twenty-Two

By eight the following morning, Jennifer was back at her apartment. She didn't fancy the hotel's breakfast and having had one close encounter with Sheryl, she didn't want to push her luck by checking out once the girl's shift had started.

As she sipped her coffee, she opened her laptop and called up the Google searches from the previous day. She knew she should be methodical and continue checking through all relevant murders in the country over the last ten years or so. If the killer had used the same MO, there would be a hotel associated with each case. Once she'd made a shortlist of likely cases, she could visit each hotel and spin a line in the hope that she could get sight of the relevant guest list.

But was she wasting her time? Suppose the killer hadn't used the same MO, or worse, used different names?

There was one way to find out: the Bristol case. It had a similar pattern. She closed her laptop's lid. Bugger being methodical; she was itching to check out the Bristol hotel.

She was already tapping on Google maps on her phone before she realised that she'd made no notes on Derek's visit, and worse, he hadn't mentioned the name of the hotel where the councillor was found. Some detective I am, she thought as she hit Derek's name on her favourites list.

The call was answered in two rings.

"Derek, hi, it's Jennifer."

"Hi, Jen, how's it going?"

"Good. Look, this isn't a difficult time, is it? You're not about to go to a meeting with the boss?"

"Hang on a moment."

His voice became more distant as he held the phone away from his mouth. Jennifer heard him cough and say, "Sorry, Olivia, you'll just have to wait a minute, this is an important call. No, no 'buts', it's Jennifer. Learn some patience."

"OK, Jen," he continued, the phone now back to his mouth. "I've put my meeting on hold and Freneton has gone off in a huff."

"Idiot!" laughed Jennifer. "Where are you?"

"About to drive into work."

"No time for a detour?"

"Very tempting; Cotton's Cuisine and Coffee was brilliant, but I only made it in by the skin of my teeth the other day. What about tomorrow morning?"

"You're welcome to pop in, but the info I'm after I need today. Now, in fact."

"Shoot."

"I've been thinking about the Bristol case and there's something I want to check. What was the name of the hotel where the councillor — what was his name?

"Gordon Dewi Rees."

"OK," she said, scribbling in her notebook. "What was the name of the hotel where Councillor Rees was found dead?"

"The Bristol View. Why do you need that?"

"I want the guest list for the night he died there."

"You're going to march in and demand to see the guest list? You're joking; you have no authority."

"I'm not going to demand anything. I'm intending to use some feminine guile. It worked last night at the Old Nottingham with Michael, the night receptionist. I came up with two names from the twenty-ninth of May that look interesting. I want to see if there's any overlap at the Bristol hotel."

"Why did you do that? We already have the guest list for the Old Nottingham; I remember getting it."

"Yes, but you haven't committed it to memory any more than I have, and if you start leafing through the case file, someone might get suspicious."

"Good point, but I think you might be pushing your luck with the feminine guile thing. From what Norrie told me, the Bristol View is pretty smart. The receptionists will likely be on the ball, not naïve like that twit Michael. And the trouble is that you can only try your approach once."

"Not quite true, Derek. If I fail, I could wait until there's a change of shift and ask a different receptionist."

"And hope that she hasn't been told anything by the first one."

"You're all encouragement, Thyme."

"Just being realistic. When are you planning to go?"

"Right now. I was walking out the door when I realised I didn't have the name of the hotel."

When Jennifer pulled into the car park of the Bristol View Hotel, her heart sank. Derek had been right: this hotel was completely different from the Old Nottingham. From its elegant entrance to its huge sash windows and granite stonework, the late Victorian design put her in mind of somewhere Hercule Poirot might have stayed in the 1930s. It even had a doorman in full morning suit and top hat.

She checked her hair in the sun visor's mirror and replaced her slip-on casual shoes with a pair of high heels she'd stowed in the footwell of the passenger seat. She was pleased that she taken heed of Derek's comment about the hotel and changed into a business suit before leaving. At least she wouldn't look out of place. Grabbing her briefcase and handbag, she climbed out of her car and locked it.

She looked up at the hotel and wondered if she should have made a reservation, tried her story on the night staff again. Perhaps she should, but at least she'd check out the reception area and if it all looked too daunting, she'd make a reservation on her phone and then while away a few hours on her laptop in a coffee shop before she checked in.

As she walked towards the entrance, she cursed her lack of forethought. She didn't even have an overnight bag. If she did decide to spend the night, she'd have to buy one.

"Good morning, miss," said the doorman as he pulled open one of the large, brass-edged double doors.

"Thank you," said Jennifer, smiling at him. She took a deep breath, walked into the lobby and once again felt her confidence draining. Every one of the hotel staff seemed to be in uniform: bell boys, receptionists — three of them — and a concierge.

She took a few steps forward and stopped to survey the scene, trying to decide on her strategy. Right now, making a reservation looked the most promising idea: there was no way she would be given sight of one of the computers by any of the staff presently on duty.

To her left were several sofas for guests or visitors. As she took a step towards them, she heard a man's voice from close behind her.

"Jennifer Cotton?"

She spun round to see a racially mixed but predominantly Indian-looking man of about her age, dressed smartly but casually in a pair of beige trousers and a lightweight, designer rain jacket over a mid-blue Polo shirt. His dark eyes pierced into hers, his mouth set.

"Y…yes," she said. "Can I help you?"

The man pulled a leather document holder from his pocket and flashed a warrant card.

"I'm with the Bristol City police," he said, pocketing the card before she'd had a chance to read his name. "I'd like a word, if I may."

He indicated the sofas; there was clearly no 'may' about it.

Jennifer was worried. The last thing she wanted was for the police to be involved.

"What's it about?" she asked, not moving.

"If we could just sit down over there, Ms Cotton."

She sighed and sat on one of the sofas, her briefcase placed protectively on her lap.

The police officer sat in a chair at right angles to Jennifer's, took out a standard police notebook and opened it. He flicked through the pages until he found the one he wanted.

"It's come to our notice that you're interested in the councillor Rees case that occurred here about a year ago. We'd like to know why, Ms Cotton."

Jennifer didn't reply. She couldn't; she was in shock. She attempted to maintain a look of calm while she frantically tried to work out what was going on. The only people she'd told about the case were Derek — who'd told her about the possible Bristol connection — Charles Keithley and Sally Fisher. One of them must have informed the Bristol police. It couldn't have been Charles, he was working for Henry and could be trusted implicitly, and it couldn't have been Sally, surely, so it had to be Derek. Then she remembered that only Derek knew she was coming to Bristol that morning. He must have set her up, be working for the DCI, or worse, directly for Freneton. God, she'd trusted him, told him all about what she'd found out at the Old Nottingham and the ruse she'd used to get it. She was well and truly screwed.

She tried to compose herself, but the tension remained. When she spoke, she could feel her throat constricting.

"What did you say your name was?"

The police officer frowned. "Frampton. DC Norman Frampton."

It was Jennifer's turn to frown.

"I know that name. Where have I heard—"

She stopped as she saw Frampton's frown dissolve into a wide grin.

"Derek said you'd shit yourself."

"What!"

"Derek. Derek Thyme. Me mate. He called me, said you were coming to Bristol to stick your neck out. He was worried about you, asked me to help out, but thought I should wind you up a bit first."

"You bugger," cried Jennifer, sagging back into the sofa. "Derek … Thyme. I'll kill him!"

Frampton was still grinning as he held a finger to his mouth to shush her. Several people nearby had turned their heads at Jennifer's outburst.

"Had you going, though, didn't I?" he chortled.

"Jesus!" snarled Jennifer as she tried to contain her anger.

She sat up and took a deep breath. "Did he tell you what it was about?" she said, glaring at him.

Frampton leaned forward, suddenly businesslike, his voice quiet.

"Only that you're interested in the Natasha Pircu case, the prostitute who was murdered here last year. It was the first big case I was involved with once I joined the CID. When Derek told me the details of the recent case in Nottingham, it kind of rang a bell. Lots of similarities. Not that my bosses would be interested. The Pircu murder is all sorted as far as they're concerned. Rees was the man. Their only regret was that he dropped dead on them. They would like to have seen him put away; he wasn't exactly popular. But they certainly wouldn't want anything affecting their statistics, the bosses."

Jennifer was still on edge. She looked at Frampton's clothing.

"You're rather casual for a DC; it's all suits in Nottingham."

He laughed. "'Tis here too, but it's me day off. I'm on me way to visit me folks; they don't like jeans and T-shirts, so I compromise with this lot. Me dad's not so bad, but me mum's Indian, and a bit formal with it. Derek called me this morning and told me when you'd be arriving. He gave me your car number, so I hung around in the car park waiting for you. He also told me what you were thinking of trying at reception. Don't think you'd have got too far; they're a pretty professional lot here and they would likely have made a connection with the date you were going to ask about and called the nick."

Jennifer's face fell. "Yes, that was my worry. Once I saw the place, I decided to book a room and try my luck with the night staff."

Frampton pursed his lips and shook his head.

"The night receptionist's a difficult sod. Don't reckon it would have made any difference."

Jennifer sighed, "I must've struck lucky at the Old Nottingham."

"Yeah," nodded Frampton, "I reckon you did."

He paused, a glint of amusement in his eyes. "It was the guest list for the night of the murder that you were after, wasn't it?"

Jennifer missed the look; she was staring at the floor. "Yes," she whispered, the dejection clear in her voice.

Frampton reached inside his jacket, pulled out his phone and swiped the screen a few times.

"This one?"

Jennifer's mouth opened in surprise. "Is that the list? How did you get it? I don't want to get you into any trouble."

"No problem," grinned Frampton. "I was the exhibits officer on the case and I'm also exhibits officer on a big case we're working on at the moment, so accessing the exhibits store isn't an issue. I popped in on the pretext of needing something else, found the Rees case documents and snapped the list on my phone. It's all deniable, of course, no record. I can't let you keep it but you can have a look. Then I'll delete it."

He handed the phone to Jennifer.

"I don't know what to say," she said, as she scrolled eagerly through the list.

"Nothing to say," shrugged Frampton. "Like I said, this isn't happening."

Jennifer used her fingers to enlarge the image as she scrolled down.

Frampton leaned towards her, pointing at the phone. "If you swipe from right to left, there're four more images. I got the whole list."

As Jennifer carried on scrolling, the frown on her forehead deepened.

Finally she looked up. "Are you sure this is from the night of the murder?"

Frampton nodded and pointed again at the screen. "Of course. Look, there's the name of the councillor. He was only checked in for the one night."

"Yes," said Jennifer absently as she checked through the entire list once again. "I can see Rees' name, but the names I'm looking for aren't there. I was expecting one or the other of them."

Frampton sat back. "Not there? Really?"

"Yes. There are, what, eight women registered as staying on their own, five of whom are listed as being registered for several nights. I'm discounting those. Of the other three, two of the names are foreign — one's French and the other possibly Russian. The only English name is Catherine Doughthey. There's no Amelia Taverner and no Sharon Peterson."

She pulled a face. "Shit, I was convinced that one of them would be on the list."

"That's bad luck," said Frampton, taking the phone from her. "Does that screw up what you're doing?"

Jennifer nodded. "Well, it's certainly a bit of a setback. Listen — Norrie, isn't it?"

"Yeah."

"Norrie, despite the big wind-up, I'm really grateful to you. I think without your intervention I might well have blown it here, jumped in with both feet. I'll need to think through my strategy some more before I try anywhere else."


Back in her car, Jennifer sat and stared through the window as she thought through the implications of the names she'd seen on Norrie Frampton's phone, or rather the absence of the ones she was expecting to see. Her despondency only increased as she realised that if there was nothing apart from tenuous similarities to link the two cases, the chances of proving Henry's innocence would become slim at best. She needed to talk to someone about it. Someone sensible.

She grabbed her phone and pressed a couple of buttons.

"Sally. Hi, it's Jennifer. Look, are you busy? Oh, sorry, that's a daft question to someone with a two-year-old."

"Hi Jennifer. It's fine, Ced's taken Claudia-Jane for a bike ride."

"She can ride a bike?"

Sally laughed. "How much do you know about children, Jennifer? Ced's put a totally secure seat on the back of one of his bikes; he straps her into that. She sits there like the Queen of Sheba telling him what to do. She loves the helmet he's bought her; wanted to wear it to bed the night he brought it home. He'll be dressing her in Lycra next. Now, what can I do for you? You sound rather flat."

Jennifer sighed and launched into an account of events that morning, leaving out Norrie Frampton's wind-up.

"So you see," she said, as she finished, "my investigation has gone down the tubes. I was banking on either Amelia Taverner or Sharon Peterson being at the Bristol View on the night of the Natasha Pircu murder. Convinced, in fact, that one of the names would be there."

Sally didn't agree. "I don't think it's the end of the trail, you know. Think about it. Assuming that we're right about the murderer being a woman, she's demonstrated that she's pretty clever, really thought things through. Suppose the name she registered at the Old Nottingham is false, not her real name, which is extremely likely. If she's a serial killer with a mission, would she really use the same false name at the hotels where she's set people up? It would be a flaw in her strategy, something that if noticed would make someone like you want to investigate further."

"So you think she might be using more than one name?" Jennifer's lack of conviction sounded in her voice. "But both Amelia Taverner and Sharon Peterson used credit cards, which means that if she's not one of them, she's somehow got hold of the real Taverner's or the real Peterson's cards. I know that credit card theft is common, but it would be pretty risky to use a stolen card in these circumstances. It might have been blocked, which would flag if she tried to use it."

Sally was nodding as she listened to Jennifer's objections.

"So perhaps she got the card some other way. Have you checked up on these two women?"

"As far as I can, yes. It turns out that Amelia Taverner is an extremely unusual name. In fact, I could only find one person with that name in the whole of the UK, using Google and the White Pages for my search. Unfortunately, Sharon Peterson is more common; there are quite a few scattered around the country."

"OK," said Sally, "let's start with Amelia Taverner. Where does she live?"

"In North Yorkshire, a place called Pateley Bridge."

"I know it," replied Sally. "It's in the Dales, really pretty area. How old is she?"

"I don't know. I checked the electoral register, but that doesn't always give ages or even approximate ages, and for her, it didn't."

"What about the other name you turned up down there?"

"Catherine Doughthey?"

"Yes. You said that was the only name on the list that was a likely candidate, didn't you?"

Jennifer sighed. "Yes, I think so. I doubt that the killer would spend more time than necessary in the hotel. She wouldn't want to draw attention to herself. Of course, she could have been using one of the foreign names."

"How do you spell Doughthey?" asked Sally.

Jennifer spelt it for her and immediately heard Sally tapping on her keyboard as she muttered to herself.

"Let's see if we can find where … Wow!"

"What?"

"I've looked her up. Like Amelia Taverner, it's a pretty rare name. According to Google, there're only three in the UK, but guess where one of them lives?"

There was silence on the other end of the phone; Jennifer didn't dare guess.

"Pateley Bridge!" declared Sally triumphantly. "Now that's got to be more than a coincidence. What about the credit cards? Are they the same issuing bank?"

"I hadn't considered that," said Jennifer as she leafed through some papers in her bag. "Here are the numbers. Yes, they start with the same digits."

"Could be significant," said Sally. "I've called up the coding list. Sing them out."

Jennifer quoted the first six digits, the bank identifiers, and waited.

"Visa cards from the North Western Bank," announced Sally

after a few seconds. "Right area, so it could mean something. What about Sharon Peterson?"

Jennifer found the number. "It's different," she said. "It's a MasterCard from NatWest. I know that because I have one. It starts with the same digits."

As she was speaking, she was busy tapping on her phone.

"I wonder if there's anything more about Doughthey. Here's the electoral register. Bugger! Her address is there, but again no age. It's a different address, by the way, so they are not living under the same roof, assuming they are in fact really two people."

She paused, thinking through the information. Then she added, "Sally, that's brilliant. You always buck me up; I was really floundering. Now, I think I really need to continue my search for other cases around the country. If there are some, I'll try to think of some way of checking out guest lists at whatever hotels are involved. If either Amelia Taverner's name or Catherine Doughthey's pops up, we'll really be onto something."

"Or," added Sally, "perhaps there's a third name, or even a fourth, and they all live in Pateley Bridge."

She gave her voice a mysterious air. "The Pateley Bridge Murder Club."

Jennifer laughed, but was unconvinced. "This isn't the telly, Mrs Fisher, it's the real world."

## Chapter Twenty-Three

It was five days before Jennifer called Sally again, five days of progress. Jennifer's excitement echoed down the phone.

"Sally, hi, it's Jennifer."

"Jennifer, I thought you'd be calling soon. You sound far more buoyant than the last time we spoke. Where are you?"

"I'm on the A1 driving back from Newcastle. I couldn't wait to tell you the latest developments, but I've also got to get back to Nottingham. I'm seeing Henry this afternoon. Are you free to talk?"

"Actually, Claudia-Jane and I are at a toddler group, but right now the kids are all involved in an activity, so the mums are standing back. I'm outside the room, but I've got her ladyship in sight in case there's a meltdown. So, tell me all."

"Well, first, after we spoke the other day, I went home and really hit the searches. It took ages but it was worth every minute. I found a total of three other prostitute murders in the last seven years where there has been strong forensic evidence to implicate the killer, but where the killer has completely denied any involvement. In each case, the culprit was traced back to a hotel in the city where the prostitute was working. Three cases, three easy convictions and three men languishing in prisons around the country wondering what's hit them and, as far as I know, still protesting their innocence."

"Where were the murders?"

"The first was in Leeds in 2007, the next in Newcastle in 2009, and the other one in Manchester in 2012."

"And you've got details from each?"

"Yes, once I'd identified them, I searched through all the newspaper reports, pulled out all the relevant info from them, and everything else I could find online. Then I hit the road to visit the hotels."

"You didn't try the Old Nottingham approach, did you?"

"No, I decided that would be too risky. The Michaels of this world only work in small hotels and each of the hotels in the three cases I was following up was more like the Bristol View than the Old Nottingham."

"But you got what you were after."

"Oh yes, although the receptionist in Manchester was so difficult to start with that I really thought she wasn't going to play ball. In fact, I thought she'd made the connection between the dates I was giving her and the murder that occurred at that time. But I then realised that difficult was her default position. I won her over by switching on the tears, quivering my chin, the lot. I was proud of myself; I reckon I've inherited Henry's acting talents."

"That's my girl. What was your spin?"

"I told them I was trying to trace my sister Abigail, that she was the rebel in the family, five years older than me, who'd disappeared in 2005. I said that a rich relative had died leaving the bulk of her fortune to the two of us, and that it seemed only fair to try to trace her. I then got a bit weepy again and said that I'd dreamed of finding her after all these years, that we'd been so close as kids even though she was much older than me. Sniffle, sniffle, snuffle. I said that we, the family, had used a private detective to try to trace her and he'd discovered that my sister had been using three pseudonyms over the years — Amelia Taverner, Sharon Peterson and Catherine Doughthey — and that she'd moved around the country quite a bit. I realised, of course, that if our killer has used other names, I might get nothing, but I thought it worth the risk. I told each of the receptionists that my sister often stayed in hotels and posed as an antiques dealer."

"Antiques dealer?"

"Yes. She had to do something and so I had her going to antiques fairs which happened to coincide with the dates of the murders. I was trusting my luck that the receptionists I was talking to wouldn't remember whether there were antiques fairs on those dates or not. So, for the Manchester case, I told the receptionist that my sister was known to have been living somewhere outside Manchester in 2012 and that she had stayed in a hotel or hotels in the city centre in August of that year when there was a big antiques fair on. The murder was on the fourteenth of August."

"Did she swallow that?"

"After the tears, yes. In fact, she told me she remembered the fair. But, as I said, I've no idea whether there was really one at that time or not."

Sally laughed. "Funny what people remember when they're trying to help. It shows you how unreliable eyewitnesses can be."

"Yes, after her initial resistance, she became my new best friend; couldn't help enough. I was really stretching out the story by the time I left, promising to let her know if I found my sister. Anyway, what I discovered was that an Amelia Taverner stayed at the hotel on the fourteenth of August 2012, the night a young Scottish woman who had been working as a prostitute in Manchester for the previous six months was murdered. A man called Timothy Norton Backhouse, who had been also staying in the hotel that night, was quickly arrested on suspicion of killing her and subsequently tried and found guilty. Of course, all the receptionist told me was Amelia's name; fortunately she didn't make the connection about the date."

"Wow! That's fantastic! What about the others?"

"The Newcastle murder, which was in June 2009, involved a Polish prostitute who'd come to the UK from Holland three months previously. I've just come from the hotel there. I was passed on to the manager once I'd spun my tale, which worried me a bit — I thought the shutters might come down — but he seemed keen to impress me so it was easy enough. In fact, he was so helpful that

I thought for a moment he was going to show me the computer screen with the guest list, but he backed off. Anyway, for that case, Catherine Doughthey's name was there for the night of the murder, and the fall guy was a Gregory Jonah Walters."

"Better and better," enthused Sally. "You know, that name rings a bell. Let me think; in 2009 I was working in the Forefront Forensics lab here in Knutsford. We did cases from all over the country; perhaps we did that one. I'll have to look back at my casebook; I kept a note of all the major cases I was involved in for when I write my memoirs, you know."

"Bound to be a bestseller," laughed Jennifer.

"You bet, as long as there's plenty of blood and gore, and I can wax eloquently for hours on that. So, what was the third case? Two thousand and seven, did you say?"

"Yes, in Leeds. I used the same approach and it worked a treat. If anyone with the name Abigail Cotton ever registers as a guest in any of those hotels, they'll be straight on the phone to me, except they won't get through 'cause I gave them a fake number."

"Which name was used there, in Leeds? Amelia Taverner or Catherine Doughthey?"

"Amelia Taverner. It looks as if our killer alternates the name she uses. Amelia Taverner in Leeds 2007, Manchester 2012 and Nottingham 2014, and Catherine Doughthey in Newcastle 2009 and Bristol 2013."

"That's brilliant, Jennifer. Actually, there's an interesting trend there. Have you noticed the time between the murders is getting shorter? There have now been three in three years. Our killer is getting more ambitious."

"Yes, if in fact they are all connected."

"You're doubting it?"

"Well, suppose there are two women out there called Amelia Taverner and Catherine Doughthey who have nothing to do with each other and who happen to travel the country for whatever reason. One happens to have stayed in three hotels in the past seven years where there happen to have been murders of local prostitutes on the same nights—"

"By men who happen to have also been staying in the hotels," interrupted Sally. "Come on, Jennifer, don't try and talk yourself out of the positive aspects of what you've found. For there to be no connection between the cases and these two women would involve ridiculous coincidences."

"Maybe, but they might also have stayed in a hundred other hotels where there were no incidents. If that were the case and the whole thing is no more than a series of coincidences, then it would completely pull the rug out from under my investigation and wreck the chances of proving Henry is innocent."

"You can't get cold feet now, Jennifer. What does Charles Keithley say about it?"

"He wants to go to the CPS with it. But I've told him that we don't have enough, that we've got to get more. We don't want to screw up the chances of getting Henry's case dropped. Charles has somehow arranged to get me a visit to see Henry late this afternoon. Normally it takes a couple of weeks, but he's managed to swing it. I'm going to tell Henry everything I've found out and try to persuade him to tell Charles to hang fire."

"What else are you going to do? Check back before 2007?"

"I went back as far as 2005. I could go farther, but if we are dealing with a serial killer, she has to have started sometime. Oh, God, I've just had a thought."

"What?"

"Well, I've been concentrating on the murders of prostitutes, that was the key to my searches. Suppose she's been murdering other women who aren't prostitutes?"

"It's possible, but if there were too many cases happening around the country that were apparently clear cut, each with an obvious culprit based on amazing forensics, and yet with culprits protesting their innocence, someone would notice and start making connections like you have, but for different reasons."

"I hope you're right, but it underscores what I've got to do next, which isn't going farther back in time."

"So, what is it?"

"I'm going to visit Amelia Taverner and Catherine Doughthey."

"What! That could be extremely dangerous if one or both of them is behind these cases."

Jennifer's laugh betrayed her nervousness. "Don't worry, I can look after myself. The police give you good personal defence training. I went way beyond the required basic stuff; I took every course there was and passed. I left a good number of bruises behind me, you know, although I picked up a few too. Anyway, I'll spin a tale to them, tell them I'm lost, looking for someone."

"I'm not sure about this, Jennifer. I don't think you should go on your own. Ced could go with you. He's strong and knows a lot about self-defence. He's put it to the test too."

"Really?"

"Long story. But I know he'd be more than willing to go with you."

"Thanks, Sally, but I think it would be less threatening if I were to arrive on my own. I'll perhaps dress down; look a bit old-fashioned. That should relax them."

"OK, but at least tell me when you're going so when you disappear, I can tell the police where to look for your body."

"Very reassuring," laughed Jennifer.

She took a deep breath. "Let me think. It's Friday today and I'm seeing Henry later. I could go over the weekend, but it would probably be better to wait until Monday, do a bit more searching online. Turning up on a weekday will give me a broader range of options for a story."

## Chapter Twenty-Four

Jennifer didn't enjoy driving in England. Although it was more ordered compared to Italy, where cars would routinely follow at a distance of around six feet at speeds of eighty mph or more and overtake in the most suicidal of situations, the sheer density of traffic on British motorways and main roads never failed to frustrate her. She wondered if so many cars and trucks could actually have a purpose or if people were on the roads solely because they enjoyed traffic jams.

The drive from Nottingham to Pateley Bridge was a little over a hundred miles. Mostly motorway, apart from the road through the Dales from Harrogate, the journey would probably take her a couple of hours, given the heavy Monday morning traffic. As she made her way north along the M1 motorway, she thought about her visit to Skipshed prison the previous Friday.

Sitting in the visitors hall waiting for Henry to be brought from his cell, Jennifer realised she had been itching to see him again. She had missed him and suddenly felt guilty that it had been over three weeks since her last visit. There had been a couple of brief phone calls, but they weren't the same. He had been guarded in his conversation, acutely aware of possible eavesdroppers.

When Henry was escorted in, his smile at seeing her told her he felt the same. She stood. She was allowed physical contact and this time she didn't hold back as she hugged him.

"Henry, how are you? I'm so sorry that it's been so long."

She continued to hold his hands as they sat down, her smile warm as she scrutinised him.

"You've lost more weight. That's not good. Is there no way I can get food to you to supplement your diet?"

Henry's eyes creased as he smiled back at her.

"You don't have to worry, Jennifer, I'm fine, really. I've been passing the time doing a lot of exercises in my … cell. I'm fitter than I've been for a while."

He paused, squeezing her hands.

"You know, it's so good to see you. I can't tell you how much I appreciate what you're doing on my behalf. I can't believe it. You should be concentrating on sorting out your own life, your future, your career."

Jennifer was shaking her head. "None of that matters until we've sorted out yours, Henry. The more I look into your case and the others I've discovered, the more I realise that you've been the victim of a huge set-up. God knows why, but you have. I'm determined to get to the bottom of it and I'm equally determined not to let it go to trial. That would result in a huge miscarriage of justice."

Henry swallowed hard as he felt his emotions taking hold. "You're an angel, Jennifer," he said, shaking his head slowly. He paused, taking a deep breath before continuing. "Charles has kept me up to date with what you've discovered. He's champing at the bit, you know. He wants to take it all to the Crown Prosecution Service. Insist they drop the case."

"No," replied Jennifer, "there's still not enough. And even if they did drop it, your name would continue to be dragged through the mud. The press would act like you'd got off on a technicality. You'd still be guilty in the court of public opinion. We've got to find out who the real killer is, show that you were entirely a victim."

"Do you think we'll be able to do that?" he said, then he chuckled. "Listen to me, I'm saying 'we' when all I'm doing is sitting in this place watching as events unfold, contributing nothing. What I meant was, do you think you'll be able to do that?"

"You hardly have much choice over your location," said Jennifer, "but yes, I get more confident every day. With the four other cases that are so similar, I think we can crack it."

"Four?"

"Yes, I completed my tour of hotels this morning in Newcastle. Someone calling herself Catherine Doughthey stayed in the High-gate Hotel about half a mile south of the city centre on the night of the seventeenth of September, 2009, which was the night of the murder of a prostitute called Inka Cropfen. The man arrested and later charged and convicted of her murder, Gregory Jonah Walters, also stayed in the Highgate that night."

"Gregory Walters," repeated Henry, his eyes roaming the room for inspiration. "No, the name means nothing."

"Did you expect it to?" asked Jennifer.

"I'm not sure. It's occurred to me that whoever has set me up might be on a vendetta against a number of men who have crossed her in some way. So perhaps we are all connected. I've thought long and hard over the other three names — Rees, Backhouse and Edgerton, and I can't think of any connection. And neither can I now with Walters."

Jennifer nodded. "Pity, but it's a good point. Perhaps there could still be something that is significant in the background of all five of you, even if you don't know each other. I'll check further."

"Probably a long shot," said Henry, shrugging his shoulders. "But getting back to what you found at the hotel in Newcastle, isn't Catherine Doughthey the name of the woman who—"

"Stayed at the Bristol View hotel on the night of the murder there last year? Yes. I've told Charles about it. I called him from my car on the drive back to Nottingham, but he obviously hasn't had the opportunity to call you."

"That's brilliant, Jennifer. Do you think these two people, Amelia Taverner and Catherine Doughthey, are the same person?"

"I don't know. But there are people with those names living in the same village, Pateley Bridge, in North Yorkshire. Whether they are one and the same remains to be seen. I hope to find out on Monday."

"Monday? How?"

"I'm driving up to Pateley Bridge and I'm going to knock on their doors."

Henry's face clouded over.

"Jennifer. You can't do that, not on your own. We're dealing with a cold-blooded serial killer here, someone who wouldn't hesitate to kill you to escape or to silence you. Tell me you're not intending to go on your own. Can't your policeman friend, Derek Thyme, the Olympic runner, can't he go with you?"

Jennifer smiled. "That's not going to happen for two reasons. Firstly, he is, as you say, a police officer and he'd be for the high jump rather than the one hundred metres if he was found to be moonlighting on a case with me, and secondly, I think more than one person might make whoever Amelia Taverner or Catherine Doughthey really is or are disinclined to speak. Especially a six-foot-two West Indian, even if he has got the most amazing set of white teeth and a huge smile."

Henry's eyes crinkled. "Sounds like you're attracted to him."

"Attracted to him! I'm going to kill him when I next see him. You should see how he set me up with his detective constable mate in Bristol. I was shredded for a few moments and I intend to exact my revenge."

"Actually, it sounds like he's watching out for you. But seriously, can't you have a backup plan when you go to Pateley Bridge?"

Jennifer smiled to herself when she thought of Sally's comment about telling the police where to look for her body. She was still smiling as she drove through Glasshouses and descended the steep hill into Pateley Bridge.

She had decided to try the address for Amelia Taverner first. Her satnav guided her through the village and out onto a quiet road that followed a meandering stream. After about half a mile, when the soft-spoken male voice announced that she had reached her destination, she stopped the car and looked up to see three detached cottages set back from the road. They were on rising ground that would give them plenty of protection from flooding if the nearby stream developed ambitions of becoming a river, and

well separated from each other by substantial and picturesque
gardens. Number seventeen, Amelia Taverner's home according to
Jennifer's searches, was the middle cottage of the three.

She had decided against knocking on the door and asking for
directions. That seemed a bit lame when there was a perfectly good
visitors centre back in the village, although if Amelia Taverner
turned out to look like a serial killer, she could always revert to that
story. The problem was she didn't have any clue as to what a serial
killer might look like, especially a female one. Piercing blue mani-
acal eyes? A bloodthirsty leer? Jennifer shuddered and put on the
plain-glass, black-rimmed spectacles she'd decided to wear to help
with the navy-blue suit that she hoped made her look like the bank
employee she was going to claim to be. She was carrying a soft
briefcase slung over her head and shoulders with a long strap —
she wanted to keep both hands free, just in case.

The entrance to number seventeen was straight out of every
painting of an English country cottage and garden. A metal trellis
covered in large pink and red roses formed an archway that led
onto a paving stone path bordered by more rose bushes, the blooms
spectacularly large, the soft yellows and creams alternating with
vivid, crisp whites. Their perfume hung in the air as the morning
sun, filtered through the abundant foliage of nearby trees, painted
a dancing light across them. Jennifer gazed at the scene in disbelief,
doubts about the accuracy of her online research increasing by the
second. This setting was totally incompatible with a cold-blooded
killer, so despite what the search engines had told her, there must be
another Amelia Taverner somewhere else in the country. However,
now she was here, she might as well rule this one out.

She was about to knock on the cottage's powder blue front door
when it opened and an old lady appeared, a wicker basket over her
left arm and a pair of pruning secateurs in her right hand. Jennifer
eyed the secateurs with some alarm.

The old lady stopped abruptly and looked up at her.

"Oh, my dear, you gave me a fright; I didn't hear the gate. I
told Martin not to oil it; the squeak was quite useful, you know,
announced any visitors I might have, not that there are many. May
I help you? You look rather puzzled."

Jennifer stared at the woman in surprise. She was slightly built and appeared to be well into her eighties. At no more than five foot tall, she was nothing like what Jennifer had been expecting.

"Um, yes, I hope you can," stuttered Jennifer. "I'm looking for a Mrs Taverner, Mrs Amelia Taverner."

The old lady smiled and cocked her head. "Well, dear, you've found her, although no one calls me Amelia. I always thought it was too grand, a daft notion of my mother's. I'm known as Grace. It's my second name, but I always preferred it. My late husband did too."

"I'm sorry," started Jennifer, "did he …"

"Oh no, dear, he passed away thirty-five years ago. Heart attack. So young, really. Always smoked, that was the trouble. We didn't know then, did we?"

Jennifer took a breath and gave what she hoped was a reassuring smile.

"I'm sorry, Mrs Taverner, I didn't introduce myself. My name is Jennifer Cotton. I'm, er, I'm with the North Western Bank. We're conducting surveys with some of our long-standing customers with a view to enhancing our service quality. As you probably know, we pride ourselves on the personal touch, so, well, here I am. I was hoping you could spare a few minutes."

A flicker of confusion passed over Grace Taverner's face, but it quickly passed.

"Of course, dear, if that's what you want, but I can't imagine how I can offer much of value to you. Certainly not enough to warrant your driving all the way out here. I take it you're not from the local branch?"

"Eh, no, I'm not. I work at the Harrogate office."

"Exactly. Well, dear, ask away, but would you mind if we talked in the garden? It's a lovely day and I really need to carry on with my dead-heading."

She waved the secateurs in an alarmingly wide circle, causing Jennifer to take a nervous step backwards.

Jennifer opened her bag and retrieved a notepad.

"Um, the first thing I wanted to ask you, Mrs Taverner, is

whether you are satisfied with our credit card services. Obviously we're always concerned about fraudulent use and we—"

"Well, you needn't worry on that score," Grace interrupted. "I don't have a credit card. Never saw the need. I like to pay my bills on time, not run up a huge amount owing to the bank. It doesn't seem right."

Jennifer frowned. "Really?"

She fished into her bag and retrieved a sheaf of papers she had prepared. They were her own bank statements retrieved from a box file dating back to the days before online banking, but she had no intention of letting Grace Taverner look too closely at them.

"According to our records, there's a credit card issued in the name of Amelia Grace Taverner that is active, and indeed used from time to time."

She pretended to study the top sheet before adding, "Oh, dear, I hope there hasn't been a mix-up. Do you perhaps have a daughter with the same name as you?"

The old woman's eyes became suddenly wary.

"No, I don't," she replied quietly. "I was never blessed with children."

Jennifer pressed on. "Do you get any letters from the bank relating to a credit card?"

"No, dear, I don't." The old lady's voice was little more than a whisper. She glanced nervously at Jennifer before looking down at her hands. "Not any more, anyway. I used to, but they stopped, more or less. I still get the occasional one. It's all to do with this Internet thing that I really don't understand at all."

Jennifer realised that she was onto something, but also that she must be gentle.

"So, you had a credit card but don't any more?"

The old lady was beginning to look flustered.

"No, well, that is, yes, I think so. Look, why don't you come indoors? We'll have a cup of tea and I can explain. I don't think it will do any harm."

"Thank you," said Jennifer. "A cup of tea would be lovely."

The picture-postcard imagery of the cottage continued inside. Jennifer was led through a small, carpeted hall, hung with a series of signed prints of Peter Scott watercolours. She stopped to admire the paintings.

"These are beautiful. So precise and so full of movement."

Grace smiled. "Yes, they're lovely. I knew him, you know. Peter Scott. He used to come up here to sketch along the rivers and streams, and up at the reservoir. The third one along is an original, not a print like the others. He gave it to me. Delightful man. It must be worth something these days, but I couldn't bear to part with it. Not with any of them."

She ushered Jennifer into the sitting room and pointed towards a small, floral-patterned armchair with a white, embroidered cushion.

"Make yourself comfortable, dear, I'll pop along to the kitchen and make some tea. Let me introduce you to Languid."

"Languid?"

Grace gestured towards a large, long-haired white cat stretched out on a small sofa facing the fireplace.

"Languid, this is Miss Cotton. It is 'Miss', isn't it, dear?"

Jennifer smiled. "Yes, it is. What a lovely cat."

"I think of him as more than a cat. He's my constant companion, aren't you, Languid?"

Languid looked up sleepily to assess the newcomer before slowly closing his eyes as he settled his chin back on his paws.

"He has a beautiful coat," said Jennifer.

"He does, but it takes a lot of brushing. Fortunately, he loves it. In fact, he loves nothing more than listening to the radio with me while I untangle his fur."

Jennifer looked around the room. "You don't have a television?"

"No, dear, I got rid of it. It used to be quite good, but these days there's so much swearing and yobbish behaviour. And the news! The pictures were too awful. I didn't want Languid to see them. We much prefer the radio. It's far more civilised, don't you think?"

Jennifer smiled and reached out to stroke Languid. He responded with a contented purr as he stretched luxuriously.

"I'll fetch the tea," said Grace. "I think he likes you."

When Grace Taverner returned, she was carrying a tray loaded with a teapot covered with a white linen tea cosy, two porcelain cups and saucers, and a matching milk jug and sugar bowl.

"Oh, he really does like you! He doesn't often do that to people he doesn't know."

Languid had vacated his spot on the sofa and taken up residence on Jennifer's lap, a substantial amount of him flowing over the edge.

Grace sat down, a look of glee on her face. "It's not often I get to sit on the sofa, not unless I'm brushing his royal highness."

Languid ignored her as he gently extended his claws into Jennifer's thighs, purring loudly.

Jennifer was keen to continue her conversation. She took a cup and saucer from Grace, a somewhat awkward manoeuvre with a large cat now hooked on to her lap, and smiled.

"You were telling me about the bank's letters, Mrs Taverner."

Grace stirred her tea with a small silver spoon, an uncertain look on her face.

She sighed. "As I said, I do get them, now and again; every two or three years, I should say. But I don't open them."

Jennifer adjusted her position; Languid was heavy.

"Really? Why is that?"

Grace continued stirring. "Well, they're for Diana, you see, not me. They might be addressed to my name, but they're for her."

"Diana?"

"Yes, she lived here with me some years ago after her father died. Long before Languid's time. It's funny though, when he came along, he never really liked her. I've never known him reject anyone the way he did her. As soon as he met her, he started to growl and hiss. Most unlike him."

"She lived with you?"

"Yes, while she finished school and then when she was a student. She'd come back in the holidays, or whatever the university calls them."

"Vacations?"

"Yes, that's it. She was very hard working, you know."

Jennifer took her notebook from her bag.

"Why would letters from the bank addressed to you be for her?"

Grace looked uncomfortable.

"Well, it all goes back to when she was a student. It's probably different now, the banks have all changed, but then, in the early nineties, it wasn't so easy, was it?"

"I'm sorry, Mrs Taverner, I don't follow. What wasn't so easy?"

"Getting a credit card, dear. For a student. Diana always said that the banks didn't like giving students credit cards because they ran up huge bills they couldn't pay. She could only get an ordinary bank account with a chequebook. So she asked if I could apply for a credit card that she could use. She knew I had no use for one. I don't like owing money, as I said, so I agreed. She promised that she would always pay the bills, and she has. Always. She helped me to open an account at your bank that she would also use — I didn't actually have an account with your bank, you see. I still don't, not the one I use, that is, which is why I was a bit confused earlier."

Jennifer nodded her encouragement, excited by Grace Taverner's tale but not wanting to show it. She casually stroked Languid behind the ears and was rewarded with another ecstatic crampon-like assault on her thighs. She smiled at Grace through clenched teeth.

Grace continued to explain.

"Diana told me that there needed to be an ordinary bank account to pay money into so she could pay the credit card bill. It all sounded so complicated, but once we'd opened the account, I had nothing more to do with it, and as I say, she's certainly stuck to her word about payment. She must have done because there have never been any problems.

"For a long time, there were letters from your bank, which I left for her, but they stopped. She told me that was because she now does everything online, whatever that means. But I do still get occasional letters, as I said, every three years or so. Apparently they contain a new credit card when the old one expires. I've told her she should change the address, but she said that would be difficult, and anyway, she likes to have the chance to come and see me."

Jennifer picked at a thread in her skirt and wondered about the state of her tights after Languid's incisions.

"Why would it be difficult?"

"Because she lives in Australia and apparently can't have a British bank account."

Jennifer's heart sank. If this person Diana, with Grace Taverner's credit card, lived in Australia, how could she be committing murders in the UK? She needed some more background, hoping her questions wouldn't sound too pushy for someone who was supposed to be from a bank.

"Mmm," she muttered. "That's not entirely correct, but never mind. It's good that she visits you. How did she come to live with you, Mrs Taverner?"

"Diana's mother was an old friend of mine from when we were young. Like me, she married quite late. I never understood her choice. Neville, her husband, was a brute of a man. I could never stand him. He was so rude and certainly not shy about using his fists on her.

"Anyway, she fell pregnant; she must have been about thirty-nine, if I remember correctly. She had a difficult pregnancy and she died when Diana was born. I kept in touch with Neville, well, my husband did until he died; I wanted as little as possible to do with the man. We felt obliged, you see, for Gladys' sake — that was Diana's mother's name. We were concerned about how he might treat Diana. I don't think it was easy for the girl, but then when Diana was fifteen, Neville was killed in a car accident. His brakes failed. The police blamed him; he tinkered a lot with cars, taught Diana to do so as well. It was about the only thing they had in common. She didn't have anyone else, you see, no brothers, sisters, aunts, uncles, no one."

Jennifer nodded. "So she came to live with you."

"Yes, I suggested it at the funeral. My husband had been dead for some years by then. I thought the company would be nice and I'd be doing my duty by Gladys. I never had any children, you see, as I said."

Jennifer glanced at her notebook, but decided that taking notes might stop the flow of information. She looked up at Grace, who was lost in her memories.

"So, she finished school around here, and then, what, went to university?"

"Yes, to Leeds. She studied criminology." Grace shuddered. "It sounded horrible, learning all about those nasty types."

"Did she go to Australia soon after she graduated?"

"Yes, she was offered a really good job at a university there, in Sydney. She comes back every two or three years and makes sure her visits coincide with the issue of a new credit card. She says it's really useful having an account here; something to do with saving on exchange rates. I don't understand all that myself. I've never been abroad; I don't really see the point."

Jennifer carefully adjusted her position in the armchair again while hoping that Languid wouldn't do the same.

"So, she must be, what, in her late thirties?"

"Yes, she was born in 1974, late, so she's coming up forty. Gosh, I must remember to send her a card."

"You have an address for her in Australia?"

"Yes, dear, of course."

"Is she married? Children?"

"No, dear. She's always been something of a lone wolf. I don't remember her ever having a boyfriend. She certainly never talked about anyone or brought anybody home. And when she was younger, still at school, if any of the young hopefuls from around here came calling, they were given short shrift. She sent them all packing."

Jennifer smiled her encouragement again. "She sounds like an interesting person. Almost like a daughter to you. Do you have a photo of her?"

"Yes, dear, I do. There's one in my bedroom. I'll fetch it. Why don't you help yourself to some more tea?"

Jennifer took the opportunity to liberate her tortured thighs from Languid's caresses. Having carefully extricated his claws, she lifted him gently back onto the sofa, stroking him so he relaxed before she turned to pour herself some more tea.

When Grace came back into the room, Jennifer smiled up at her, her cup and saucer balanced on her knee as a barrier in case Languid was considering another sortie.

"Here we are," said Grace as she sat down in the other armchair — Languid was now once again completely occupying the sofa. "This is a nice one taken in the garden. Martin, my odd job man was here and he took it. Well, it's nice of Diana, not of me."

She laughed self-deprecatingly. "I don't make much of a subject, especially these days."

She handed the photo to Jennifer who glanced at it and nearly knocked the cup and saucer from her lap in surprise. She hurriedly put the porcelain back on the tray and sat up to examine the photo, gripping it tightly in disbelief, her heart suddenly pounding. It showed two women. Amelia Taverner, or Grace, as she was now thinking of her, smiling sweetly at the camera, and a woman in her late thirties who was anything but smiling. As far as Jennifer knew, she almost never smiled. Staring back at Jennifer with that critical, accusing eye she knew so well was her ex-boss, Olivia Freneton.

## Chapter Twenty-Five

As Jennifer stared at the face in the photograph gripped in her hand, the world around her seemed to grind into slow motion, everything apart from that face blurring, distorting. She struggled to comprehend what her eyes were telling her. Olivia Freneton was a serial killer? How could that be possible?

She looked up at Grace Taverner, who was now registering Jennifer's reaction and beginning to worry. Had she told her visitor too much?

"Are you … are you sure this is a photograph of Diana, Mrs Taverner?" stuttered Jennifer as she fought to control her breathing.

"Of course, dear. I may be old but I haven't completely lost my marbles."

She hesitated and then held out her hand. "But let me have another look, just to be sure."

Jennifer handed her the photo and waited.

"Yes, that's her all right," said the old lady after a few seconds. "So serious. I wish she'd lighten up, as people say these days. She has a lovely smile when she chooses to show it."

"Do you … do you have any other photos of her?"

"Yes, I do. I can fetch them if you like."

As she stood and tottered off to her bedroom across the hallway, Jennifer quickly pulled her phone from her bag and copied the photo.

"There are only three," said Grace Taverner as she came back into the room. She handed the photos to Jennifer. One was a well-taken portrait that showed more detail, enough to leave absolutely no doubt about who the subject was, even if the Olivia Freneton it showed was several years younger. The other two were similar to the first one she had produced, but less clearly defined.

"Mrs Taverner," said Jennifer once she finished examining all the photos. "Does Diana have a sister? Oh no, you said she was an only child. Does she have another name? Another first name, I mean. And, of course, what's her surname?"

The old lady was suddenly suspicious. "Why are you so interested, dear? You're not thinking of getting her into trouble with the bank, are you? Or me, for that matter? After all, I don't think we're doing any harm with our little arrangement."

"Absolutely none at all. Mrs Taverner. It's ... well ... Diana reminds me of someone I once knew. It's uncanny how alike she is, but it can't be her, of course, because the person I'm thinking of is married and lives in America. She hasn't been back to England for years. It was rather startling, that's all."

"What's your friend's name?" Grace's question sounded like a challenge, making Jennifer think the old lady didn't believe her.

"Deborah," she replied, thinking of one of the girls in the typing pool at the SCF. "Deborah Thyme. Like the herb," she added, hoping the addition of a surname would add some authenticity to her spur-of-the-moment story.

Apparently it did since Grace Taverner nodded absently. "What an unusual name. I don't think I've ever heard of it before."

She paused as she leaned forward to stroke Languid's head.

"Diana's name is unusual too," she said. "Now that I think of it, I've never heard of anyone else with her name either."

Jennifer waited but Grace just continued to stroke her cat. Come on, Mrs T, she thought, I want the name.

Finally, Grace looked up. "Interesting, dear, don't you think?"

Jennifer smiled at her. "I don't know, you haven't told me her name."

Grace put her hand to her mouth. "Oh dear, I get so easily distracted these days. Her surname is Freneton. What do you think?"

"Think?"

"About her name. Have you heard it before? I think it's very unusual."

"I couldn't agree more, Mrs Taverner. It is. And does Diana have a middle name?"

"Yes, dear, she does. Olivia. She's Diana Olivia Freneton."

Jennifer was having a hard time controlling her reactions.

"Does she … I mean, are you … have you seen her recently?"

"No, dear, I told you, she lives in Australia. I haven't seen her for, let me see, almost two years."

Jennifer was still confused. "So, she's back in Australia?"

Grace nodded. "That's where she said she was going, yes."

"You don't have a phone number as well as an address, do you?"

"I do, dear, yes. But it doesn't seem to work. I tried to call her last Christmas. I thought it would be nice; I was quite excited about it. But the call didn't connect."

She sighed, reliving the disappointment. Then shrugging, she added, "But I imagine she'll be back sometime next year to collect her card when it's issued."

Jennifer glanced at her notebook where she had scribbled some points that morning. She was desperate to leave, to sit in her car somewhere and process the bombshell that Grace Taverner had delivered, but first there was something else she needed to know.

"Mrs Taverner. I'm really grateful to you for being so helpful. As I said at the beginning, the bank is committed to improving its services and I think what you've told me today will be extremely valuable in helping us achieve our goal. Before I leave you to your wonderful garden, may I ask you one more question?"

"Of course, dear, I'm only too pleased to help, although I really can't see how anything I've said is of much use to the bank."

Jennifer smiled. "I was wondering if you know a lady called Catherine Doughthey. She's another customer in Pateley Bridge

I'm hoping to visit who has been with the bank for many years and, as I have with you, I want to reach out to her."

Grace chuckled softly. "I hope you've got a long reach, dear. She died two months ago. If you want to reach out, it will rather depend on what you do or don't believe in."

"She's dead?"

"Yes, I'm surprised you weren't informed. Her son is normally so diligent about these matters."

"How strange," said Jennifer, making a pretence of flicking through the bank papers. "Did you know her well?"

"Yes, we were good friends. We'd pop along to each other's houses all the time. Her house is only about half a mile farther along the road."

"Was she living here in Pateley Bridge when Diana lived here?"

Grace nodded. "Lived here all her life. She and Diana got on extremely well."

"Really?"

"Yes, Catherine had a couple of operations when Diana was at university. Hip and knee replacements, so she was laid up for a while. They coincided with Diana's summer holiday and she used to go round every day to help her. Rose wasn't really capable of helping, you see."

"Rose?"

"Catherine's daughter. She was about the same age as Diana, but she was — what do they call it these days? Special needs. Very. In my day she would just have been called simple. And to make matters worse, she was almost blind. It was about then that she went into a care home. She's still there. It's in Harrogate. I used to visit her with Catherine from time to time. Catherine's son never did. Heartless, is Geoffrey. But Diana, gosh, it brought out another side of her. She couldn't have been more helpful to Catherine."

I'll bet she was, thought Jennifer. Persuasive too, enough for the woman to let her use a credit card in her name. The scale of Olivia Freneton's long term planning was beginning to amaze her.

"And did she continue her visits the times she came back from Australia to see you and collect her new card?"

"She most certainly did, dear. As I said, they got on well."

She put a hand to her mouth as something occurred to her.

"Oh dear, I'll bet Diana doesn't know about Catherine. As I told you, the last time Diana was here was nearly two years ago."

"You mentioned a son. Is he now living in Catherine's house?"

"No, he lives in Manchester. He was up here long enough to clear out Catherine's things and prepare the cottage for sale, not a moment longer. He had no interest in it apart from what it was worth. But that reminds me, he did give me a box of photos that he said were of Catherine and me. Would you like to see them? There might be one of Diana; Catherine was always snapping away with her camera. The box is in my wardrobe; I'll fetch it."

While Jennifer leafed through the box of loose photos, Grace Taverner made some more tea. The photos were mainly of flowers from Catherine Doughthey's garden, but in the box beneath them was an album. She opened it and struck gold. Two photos of Catherine Doughthey with Olivia Freneton — who was as unsmiling as ever — and a letter addressed to Catherine with the North Western Bank's logo in the top left corner. The envelope was still sealed, but rather than open it, Jennifer slipped it into her bag. Grace was still fussing in the kitchen so Jennifer also had time to copy the two photos of Olivia onto her phone.

Jennifer was now even keener to get on her way, but she managed to sit through another cup of tea and some local gossip before she left Grace Taverner to her beloved Languid.

"I can't tell you how helpful you have been, Mrs Taverner. Would you mind if I please leave my number and ask that you call me if you hear from Diana? I'd be only too pleased to help her make a less complex arrangement for using a UK-based credit card."

"Sally, hi, it's Jennifer. I hope I haven't caught you at a bad time."

"Of course not. I'm relieved to know that Mrs Taverner hasn't tied you up so tightly that you can't reach your phone. Where are you? How are you? Still in one piece?"

Jennifer laughed. "I'm fine. I'm in a car park at Pateley Bridge. I've spent the last hour with Mrs Taverner and I couldn't wait to call you. Would it be all right if I popped in? I've got to discuss what I've discovered with someone; the whole case has blown wide open."

"Really? So who is this Amelia Taverner?"

"She's a sweet eighty-four-year-old lady who grows roses and lives in a picture postcard cottage—"

"Except when she's prowling around the country killing prostitutes and framing innocent men," interrupted Sally, and was relieved to hear a chuckle from Jennifer.

"Hard to imagine," said Jennifer. "But the credit card was hers, and she knows that someone else has been using it. In fact she agreed to that arrangement, even though she has no idea what it's used for and when. But I now know who the someone is and how she got hold of it."

She paused as she realised the importance of what she was about to say.

"Well," she heard Sally say, "don't keep me in suspense."

"Sally, you're never going to believe this, but she's my ex-boss, Detective Superintendent Olivia Freneton, aka the Ice Queen."

"Holy shit, Jennifer. Are you sure?"

"Absolutely. There's no doubt about it."

"So what happens now?"

"That's what I want to talk to you about."

# Chapter Twenty-Six

"You've been notching up the miles lately, Ms Cotton," called Sally as she walked down her drive, Claudia-Jane in her arms. "You must be knackered."

Jennifer climbed out of her car and stretched, working her neck muscles back and forth to remove the stiffness of another long stint behind the wheel.

"You can say that again," she said. Then she grinned and held out her arms. "But I'm never too tired to have a cuddle with Claudia-Jane."

"Jen-fer," squealed the two-year-old in delight.

"Wow! Flavour of the month or what!" exclaimed Sally. "You should consider yourself very privileged."

"Soulmates," said Jennifer, swinging Claudia-Jane around and skipping up the drive with her to giggles and gurgles of delight.

"Seriously," continued Sally as she closed the front door, "you can stay the night if you want."

"Thanks, Sally. Let's see how it goes. I should really get back to Nottingham."

Sally pulled a face. "Not the best of roads through Maccles-field, and the rush hour traffic can get busy. Anyhow, it's up to you. The offer's there and I don't see how you can pass up on an opportunity to bath Claudia-Jane, and of course enjoy some relaxing red stuff once she's gone to bed."

Jennifer shook her head. "I can't drink on my own; I'd feel guilty."

"You wouldn't be," laughed Sally. "I haven't made Ced give up just because I can't drink."

"What time does Ced get back?" said Jennifer as she put Claudia-Jane down on the sitting room carpet. "I'm warming to the idea already."

"He's not been out, except to pound the tarmac; he's upstairs in his office. He does much of his work from home."

"Of course he does. How brilliant."

"Tea? Coffee?" asked Sally.

"Coffee would be lovely, thanks," said Jennifer as she shifted several members of Claudia-Jane's prehistoric menagerie from the sofa so she could sit. "I'm awash with tea after my visit to Mrs Taverner. I had to make two loo stops on the drive down here."

"I've been thinking through your investigation," said Sally as she stirred her lemon and ginger tea. "It's one of the great things about having a two-year-old: you can use about five per cent of your brain power on them and they think you're giving everything, while quietly you can use the other ninety-five per cent thinking about other stuff, and junior doesn't even notice."

"Ced must find that useful too," said Jennifer, "with all the forensics floating around his brain."

"You must be joking," spluttered Sally through her tea. "Multitasking and man might begin with the same letter but that's about as close as they get."

She put down her mug and leaned forward.

"Anyway, what I was thinking is that while you've got some difficult-to-explain circumstantial stuff — difficult from your ex-boss's point of view, I mean — it's still only circumstantial. OK, you have five hotels over the years where she appears to have stayed under one of two assumed names on the nights when there were murders linked to someone staying in the same hotels, which is weird, sure. But if your boss is clever, and there's every indication that she is—"

"She's clever," agreed Jennifer.

"Exactly. Well, she would have seen the risks and covered herself."

"How do you think she'd do that?"

Sally shrugged. "One way would be to throw in a lot of white noise. What's she like? Presumably she's not a people person."

Jennifer's derisory snort summed up her feelings. "That's the understatement of all time. She's positively antisocial. She almost never joins in anything with her squads — ok, she's a detective superintendent and meant to keep a certain distance, but she's also meant to give out pats on the back from time to time, roll up the sleeves and lead by example. She does almost none of that. And she's a ruthless taskmaster. One slip and you're mincemeat publicly; two or three and you're on a transfer to nowhere."

"She sounds delightful," said Sally, with a sneer. "Actually, she sounds insecure. But she's not alone. I've met several senior officers, both in the police and the lab, who were like that. Far more common in the police though. With the police, most of the more difficult ones were in the funny-handshake brigade, which didn't help since they always look after their own to the exclusion of others. It's interesting; there are still a lot in the police. Obviously they don't advertise their membership, but I get the impression that women aren't over welcome. Not that most female police officers would want to be part of their weird rituals. So if she's something of a loner anyway, she's probably even more so amongst her peers."

She interlaced her fingers and cracked her knuckles, stretching her arms above her head.

"Let's think about it. For whatever reason, she's made a plan to kill prostitutes and frame men. Which is the more important to her, do you think? Killing the girls or creating abject misery for the men?"

Jennifer took a sip of her coffee.

"I think it's the men. Killing the girls is no more than a means to an end. She might have chosen prostitutes because they are easy targets and the mud of apparently using them will stick harder to the men she's framing."

"OK," said Sally, chewing a sliver of lemon peel she'd tossed into the brew in her mug, "let's not worry about the whys at the moment. She must be psychopathic so the whys are always harder to fathom. If she's got these two credit cards that she has renewed every two or three years, she must have been planning this lifestyle for ages, probably long before she put the plan into action."

"It could be, of course," mused Jennifer, "that there are many other murders where her MO was different, meaning I would have missed them. The thing that occurred to me was that her aim is to get her targets found guilty and sent down. The evidence would be strong, albeit circumstantial, and the trial short and sharp. The target will have been imprisoned on remand upon arrest and almost before he knows what's hit him, he'll be serving a long prison sentence. His head will be reeling. I certainly think that's where Henry still is, even though his case hasn't yet gone to trial. Despite trying to maintain an outward appearance of cool, his head must be in turmoil."

Sally was watching Claudia-Jane engrossed in a dinosaur turf war, but her mind was completely focussed on Jennifer's conversation.

"What a cold-hearted bitch. Do you think she knows her targets or picks them at random?"

"I don't think she knows them personally. I'm sure that she's never had anything to do with Henry. The apparent culprits in the other four cases I've found out about were something of a mixed bunch. I suspect she's read about them and chosen them as targets for some reason. But I'm also pretty certain that there's nothing to link them together other than the fact that they are men."

Sally scratched her head. "Right, let's think about her and the MO we know about. She's got these two credit cards that she seems to alternate using, cards that she probably never uses for anything else."

She paused as a thought occurred. "No, perhaps she does. Makes a few purchases to muddy the waters. And presumably she uses them in the hotels because that's what everyone does these days. People don't use cash in hotels any more. If she did, it might stand out in a receptionist's memory, which is something she doesn't want. However, she has to consider the possibility of some bright cookie like you rumbling her. She would need to explain herself."

Jennifer was nodding, working it out. "Yes, I can see where you're going. You're thinking she might develop a pattern of use in hotels for a night or two, hotels that are nothing to do with any murders. That would make the five we know about seem far less significant; they'd just be five in a large number of hotel visits."

Sally smiled. "Exactly. Makes sense, don't you think?"

"Actually, Sally, I'm not sure it does. You see, even if she could come up with some reason to use those cards rather than her own for hotel visits, anonymity or something, we mustn't forget she's a senior police officer. If she happened to be staying somewhere there was a murder, even if the murder weren't discovered until later, she'd be duty bound to report her stay, whatever name it was under. And for that to happen five times … No, if it were ever discovered, she'd be in all sorts of trouble."

"Good point," agreed Sally. "The police officer thing didn't occur to me. Nevertheless it would be good to link her more definitely with those cards. At the moment her using them is deniable. It's a pity you can't get access to the credit card statements."

Jennifer's eyes lit up as she remembered her visit to Grace Taverner.

"I wonder if I already have, for one at least," she said, reaching for her bag and retrieving the envelope she'd found earlier amongst Catherine Doughthey's photographs. "Have you got a knife? I'd like to open this with the minimum of damage."

Sally fetched a kitchen knife and Jennifer explained about the letter's origin.

"Bingo!" cried Jennifer as she read the contents. "This is a credit card statement for the card in Catherine Doughthey's name covering six months of last year. We were right; there's a pattern of spending here that now we're suspicious looks totally calculated."

She looked up excitedly as she slapped a hand on the statement.

"And it includes the stay at the Bristol View. Wow! This is great."

"Or not," said Sally. "I don't want to pour cold water, but firstly, there's the chain of evidence. You're sitting there holding the letter and there's only your word to say where you found it, and secondly, if she's hit with the suggestion that she stayed in the hotels on the nights of the murders using those names, she'll deny it."

"Shit!" mouthed Jennifer without saying the word. She was aware that Claudia-Jane was reaching the age where she would be repeating at random many words she heard, and emphatic expletives were a prime source of material. "We're really going to need something else."

Sally sighed. "Yes, you've got to remember that she's one of theirs, a senior officer, and they're going to find it hard to get their heads around the idea of her being a psychopathic killer."

Jennifer finished her coffee and put the mug on the tray. "There has to be something else or no one will listen. Is there nothing else on the forensic side that could be done?"

Sally took a deep breath and exhaled slowly, her lips put-puttering. They both laughed as Claudia-Jane tried and failed to copy her.

"I can't think of anything," said Sally, running over the lab tests in her mind. "Everything's been covered, as far as I can see."

As Jennifer exhaled her frustration, she glanced down at her business suit, and then across at Sally's leggings and long, loose top. She tapped her lips with a finger and thumb as an idea focussed in her mind.

"Could you talk me through the procedure for fibre evidence again?" she asked. "When you have a piece of clothing like, say, Miruna Peptanariu's jacket or Henry's pullover, what exactly do you do?"

"It's pretty straightforward," said Sally, dropping to her knees to wipe Claudia-Jane's nose and mouth. "You have a garment on which you think there might be foreign fibres — fibres that aren't from the garment itself or from anything else worn by the garment's owner. These fibres would be there from contact with something that someone else is wearing, contact that is normally fairly firm, like when we think that Henry Silk, or rather someone wearing his clothing, carried Miruna's body into the woods. There would have been strong physical contact and an abrasive action as she was carried, her clothes rubbing against his. So fibres would be, indeed were, transferred.

"What we do is lay out the garment on a large examination table in a room dedicated to the purpose of searching for this kind of evidence. The room will have been previously cleaned — clearly there must be no chance of contamination from any other source or recovery of any foreign fibres would be meaningless.

"In a modern lab, the examination would be in one of a suite of search rooms. These can be designated. For example, there will be one for the examination of victim's clothing and one for suspect's. Garments like Henry's pullover would be laid out on a clean sheet of card or non-shedding paper and any fibres on the surface lifted using adhesive tape. We call it taping the garment. It's a bit like removing fibres with one of those lint rollers, only the adhesive isn't as sticky — we don't want the tape to be full of fibres from the garment itself.

"We literally tape the outside of the garment, then stick the tape to a pre-cut piece of PVA sheet. The tapings are therefore effectively sealed and protected from any further contamination. They can now be stacked and stored for examination under a microscope without worry."

"Sounds like a time-consuming process."

"It is," agreed Sally. "In fact it's bloody laborious, especially the part where you're staring down a microscope for hours on end, but experienced people develop an eye for it and can search tapings pretty fast and efficiently."

Jennifer put her chin into her steepled hands. "Would you only tape the outside of the clothing?"

"Yes, of course," said Sally. "The contact will only have occurred on the outside. What's the point of looking on the inside?"

Jennifer wasn't satisfied. "Supposing someone dressed up in the alleged culprit's clothing. Wouldn't any fibres from the real culprit's clothes or underclothes that were on his or her body then be transferred to the inside of the garment rather than the outside?"

"Good point," conceded Sally. "Some would, yes. Not all, obviously. What you're describing is what's called a secondary transfer — when a fibre is transferred first to one surface and then another. Given that it's all a numbers' game, the amount transferred in a secondary transfer is always going to be less than in a primary transfer. And of course, you need to have something to compare the fibres with. We don't have controls from whatever Olivia Freneton was wearing, either under or outer clothes."

"OK," said Jennifer. "Suppose Freneton was wearing a wig, which we think she was — remember, there were two long blond hairs found. She was probably wearing it in the bar when she picked up Henry and the chances are that she was wearing it when she changed into Henry's clothes — she wouldn't want the possibility of her own hair getting on them. Obviously she'd be careful pulling his pullover over her head, but even so, there could have been hairs transferred to the inside of the pullover as she put it on, don't you think?"

Sally nodded as she thought it through.

"Yes, in that case, there would be wig hairs transferred to both the inside and outside. And the ones on the inside would remain there at least until the pullover was taken off, even, perhaps, until it was next washed. And since it was only a couple of days between the murder and Henry being arrested, and also since he's a man, it's extremely unlikely that the pullover would have been washed in that time. It would be a year for Ced if I didn't intervene."

Jennifer felt that they might have something. "Do you agree that it's worth following up?"

"Yes," said Sally, "I do, because it would add support to the suggestion that someone was dressing up in Henry's clothing. But how are you going to get it done?"

"I think I'll explain it all to Charles and he could demand a further examination by his own expert. He'll go for it, I'm sure. I want to talk to him anyway. I want to ask if I can view the CCTV recordings again, the stuff that's supposed to be footage of Henry. Previously it was assumed to be him since that's the way it was set up — we were guided into believing it was him. But if I were to look at it once again taking the view that it might be someone impersonating him, maybe I'll see it differently."

Sally pursed her lips in doubt. "Could be. However, while I don't want to dampen your enthusiasm, unless you see something startling, your opinion is still going to be very subjective."

## Chapter Twenty-Seven

Despite the lure of a relaxing evening with her new friends that would probably have included talking to Ced about Renaissance art — something she was itching to do — Jennifer reluctantly decided against staying the night. She needed to return home to change and she didn't want to do that and drive to London all in the same day: it would take too much time. She called Charles Keithley while on the way back to Nottingham and more or less insisted he make time to see her the following morning.

With an early start the next day, she was in Keithley's office in Hampstead by ten o'clock.

"Luckily for you, Jennifer," said Charles as he handed her a coffee, "the case I'm working on was adjourned yesterday for a week. Otherwise, we'd be snatching opportunities to talk outside the courtroom. And, you know, you could have saved yourself a lot of driving by explaining what you've found over the phone."

"There's too much for that, Charles, and anyway, with your agreement, there's something I'd like to do that I can only do by being here."

Charles was immediately suspicious. "Really? And what might that something be?"

"The CCTV footage from both the hotel and the street cameras. I was rather hoping that I could look through it. Would that be possible?"

Charles shook his head. "Not in theory, no. As I'm sure you are aware, it's sub judice. It's evidence that will be produced in the trial and must, therefore, remain confidential. You may be Henry's daughter, but that doesn't give you any right of access to the evidence."

Jennifer pulled a face. "But you can watch the tapes, or whatever they are."

Charles nodded. "Of course I can, I'm Henry's solicitor. I can review them with Henry or by myself — and by the way, they're discs; the CCTV footage from the hotel is digital like the traffic recordings, but an older system. The Nottingham traffic recordings are far better, although because it was nighttime, the definition still leaves plenty to be desired."

"Yes, I remember," said Jennifer, her face still a frown. "I saw most of them when I was still a police officer; I just wish I'd taken more notice. So it's ridiculous that I can't see them now."

She paused. She'd thought Keithley would be more forthcoming. Then she had an idea.

"Would you like to offer me a job?"

Charles was mildly amused. "What sort of job? You're not trained as a lawyer, by any chance, are you? I could do with another junior."

"No, I'm afraid there wasn't much law in my English and Italian literature studies. But I was a detective, albeit only for three months, and since my career with the police has gone south, I'm now considering setting up as a private detective. I fancy the challenge of the work. And surely you have a need for someone like that to help with certain aspects of the case."

Her smile was full of encouragement, but Charles' head was shaking. "I'm not sure how ethical that would be. It would be a pretty transparent attempt of trying to get around the law. I'll need time to think about it."

Jennifer gave him about three seconds to think about it before continuing with her argument.

"Supposing you decided to view the discs as part of your preparation, which you must need to do, and I happened to be in the room. Better still, suppose you were looking at them when I turned up and then you were suddenly called out of the room. If I were to take a peek, you'd never even know."

"You certainly don't take no for an answer, Jennifer, do you? No, that would be sloppy practice on my part, possibly actionable."

He paused and sighed. "However, you're not going to be a witness in the case, the prosecution will make sure of that, and of course you couldn't be a jury member … so, as long as we keep the matter to ourselves, no one else would be the wiser. OK, but your viewing the CCTV recordings here, in my offices, must remain absolutely confidential."

Jennifer beamed at him. "Fine by me."

But Charles still wasn't totally convinced. "Supposing you were to notice something significant, I don't know, a mannerism that isn't Henry's, or a way of walking? What can we do about it, apart from tell Henry?"

"Easy," replied Jennifer. "You could quite legitimately employ an expert to comment on the footage and hope they come up with the same observations. Perhaps it's something you should do anyway."

"OK," said Charles, "let's see what you can find. But whatever it is, I'm not sure how strong it might be as evidence."

"We won't know until we try," said Jennifer with a dismissive shrug of her shoulders. "Anyway, Charles, there's another reason why I wanted to speak to you in person rather than talk over the phone. You see, I know who's trying to frame Henry."

"You what! Why didn't you say straight away? Who is it? I take it you were right and it's a woman?"

Jennifer smiled at Charles' astonishment. "It was important to talk through the CCTV stuff before you got totally distracted. I knew that once I told you, you wouldn't have ears for anything else."

"You're probably right, but don't keep me in suspense any longer, tell me everything."

For the next ten minutes, Jennifer walked Charles through the events of the previous day and the discovery of photographs of Olivia Freneton with both Grace Taverner and Catherine Doughthey. Charles was motionless as he listened, his eyes fixed on hers, but she knew that his lawyer's mind would be racing with various possibilities that now presented themselves.

Once she'd finished, Charles stood and walked over to his office window, deep in thought. When he turned, his face registered a look of hope that in all their previous meetings had been absent.

"That certainly throws a whole new complexion on the case, Jennifer. Well done. For the first time since this whole nightmare started, I think there might be a chance we can get Henry off. But we'll have to tread carefully; there are still gaps in the evidence and before I present it to anyone, those gaps have got to be filled."

"You're right," agreed Jennifer. "Do you think it would be an idea to call the solicitors who dealt with the Leeds, Manchester and Newcastle cases? According to the news reports, there was CCTV in the Newcastle and Manchester cases, the ones that occurred in 2012 and 2009, but there was no mention of it for the Leeds case in 2007. I suppose it's possible that there were fewer cameras then, although it's not that long ago. Maybe the reporter was sloppy in his account. And anyway, the trials are over and the evidence a matter of public record, so releasing the CCTV recordings shouldn't be a problem, should it?"

Charles didn't share her confidence. "Not in theory, no. But we solicitors are a cagey lot; it might take more than a casual phone call. However, it's worth a try; the more video footage we get, the better. I'll get onto it now, but of course I won't disclose more than absolutely necessary."

"Brilliant," enthused Jennifer. "Would it be OK if we put aside your worries with the CCTV and I get straight on with viewing it?"

"How could I refuse?" said Charles, with a chortle of laughter. "But then again, you knew the answer to that question all along; you were just playing me. I'm still staggered that you didn't burst through the door shouting the news."

He walked over to his office door and opened it.

"There's an empty office down the hall. I'll get someone to set up a computer there. You know, perhaps I should offer you a job."

Jennifer was so engrossed in endless poorly lit images from the street cameras and low definition shots from the Old Nottingham hotel that an hour later she hardly heard Charles come into the small office he'd arranged for her. She certainly didn't notice the tension in his voice as he said her name. If she'd looked up, she would have seen the ashen look on his face, but as it was, she continued to focus her attention on the computer monitor.

"This is far more difficult than I thought it would be, Charles. The quality isn't good in most of the footage. But even so, the more I look at these recordings, the more I'm convinced that the person shown isn't Henry Silk. There's something about the walk as he goes through the hotel corridor, as well as the hand and arm movements. And then there's the hand when the lift button is pressed and the way the person gets into the car. It's really not masculine enough. Of course, I haven't made a study of Henry getting into a car, which is something of a problem. Has Henry seen all these?"

In the silence that followed, Jennifer suddenly realised that Charles hadn't said a word. She turned to him and finally saw the haunted look in his eyes.

"Whatever is it?" she said. "What's happened?"

Charles sat down in a chair near to Jennifer's.

"Listen, Jennifer, there's a problem."

"What? With the CCTV? I won't say anything, honestly, you can trust me."

Charles shook his head. "I know I can trust you; it's not the CCTV. It's the three other cases you unearthed, the ones where we now know that Olivia Freneton was staying in the same hotel as the alleged culprits on the same nights as the murders. I contacted all three solicitors and they were surprisingly forthcoming, far more than I would have been to a telephone call from a complete stranger. But then I discovered the reason for their candour."

Jennifer felt a cold shiver pass through her. "What reason?"

"They're dead. The culprits in all three cases. They're all dead.

Two committed suicide while the third was killed in a fight, a fracas really, in prison."

"A fight?"

"Yes. They're not unusual in prisons; the tension amongst the convicts often reaches bursting point. Of course, some like fighting for the sake of it or as a demonstration of control, a warning to the other prisoners. But the fights are seldom so severe that someone dies. Apparently the convict involved in the fight was a proper thug, a man with a shocking record of viciously violent behaviour."

"And the dead man in the fight, the one whose name I turned up?"

"Timothy Backhouse. The man convicted of the 2012 murder in Manchester. Apparently he was a quiet, rather timid man; the last person you'd expect to be involved in a fight, especially with a known hard man."

Jennifer could feel the cold shiver still gnawing at her spine.

"Which … which prison was it, the fight?"

"Maudslake, outside Leeds."

"Not Skipshed?"

"No, definitely not."

"Well, at least that's something." Jennifer's voice was barely more than a whisper; the sense of alarm she felt still palpable.

"What about the suicides?" she added.

"Do you mean where were they?"

"No. I mean were they a surprise? To the prison authorities or the families?"

"I don't have the details yet. The solicitors are sending the files by courier; they'll arrive first thing in the morning. It was the quickest way since not all the documents are scanned. They each reckoned it would be easier to photocopy the lot and put them in an envelope."

"Excellent," said Jennifer. "I'll stay down here overnight. I have the key to Henry's house; he told me to use it whenever I want."

She shifted her gaze to the now-frozen image on the monitor, but she saw nothing as she bit on her lip in thought.

"Do you think it's possible that Freneton could have some influence on which prisons the convicts are kept in?"

"I have no idea, Jennifer. I shouldn't have thought so, but who knows? She's clearly a devious woman whose planning skills are excellent. She seems to cover so much of the minutiae that I shouldn't rule it out. Who knows, she might have befriended someone in the prison service in order to gain access to the system, or to influence it in some way? Perhaps it was part of her long-term planning, the same way that she set things up with Amelia Taverner and Catherine Doughthey to let her have credit cards in their names."

Jennifer's hand suddenly shot to her mouth. "Oh, God, Charles, you realise what this means. With the Bristol suspect dead as well, Henry is the only one of the alleged culprits in the five cases we know about who is still alive. Don't you find that strange? Do you think that is Freneton's plan, her end game for her victims? She shows them what she considers to be mercy in that she has them killed, or somehow persuades them to take their own lives. It would be the ultimate control over someone. You set them up, destroy their reputation, make them suffer the ignominy that goes with that, you ensure that they are found guilty of a horrible crime and then kill them. She's playing God."

Charles wasn't so sure. "You could be right Jennifer," he said, his tone reflecting his lack of conviction. "But surely it would take a lot to persuade someone to commit suicide."

"Suppose they weren't suicides," argued Jennifer. "Suppose they were murdered and the deaths made to look like suicides."

"I don't know, I'll need to see the files. But running with your conspiracy theory for a moment, if Freneton is somehow involved, a more cynical interpretation might be that she is hedging her bets after the convictions. Think about it. When an innocent man is locked up for many years, if he has anything about him, he will endeavour to demonstrate his innocence. If he writes to enough people and his case is convincing, someone might pick up his cause and run with it. They're less likely to do that if the man is dead, especially if the manner of his death is suicide or some violent behaviour. There'd be nothing left in his credibility bank."

"Do you know how long it was between the convictions of these men and their deaths?" asked Jennifer.

"Yes, the times are quite similar. It was a little under two years for each of them. The shortest was for Edgerton, the one who committed suicide in 2007. He died a year and eight months after his conviction. It was a couple of months longer for Walker, who killed himself in Sunshore prison in Northumbria in 2009."

"Perhaps that's her preferred method of getting rid of them," suggested Jennifer. "Suicide. After all, it's more or less an admission of their guilt. If it doesn't work, then someone gives them a helping hand."

"If that's the case," said Charles, "we might at least have some time to play with. What I mean is that Henry's case hasn't even gone to trial yet, so he's probably not in any immediate danger."

"That's some reassurance," agreed Jennifer, "but we must warn him. He needs to be vigilant, careful who he mixes with. Listen, Charles, I think in the light of this, the only way to move forward is for me to report everything I've found to the police, to my ex-colleagues, in fact. It might not be easy to get them to listen, but I can tell them I've discussed it with you, that it's not just some daft notion I've dreamed up."

Charles nodded his agreement. "Yes, I think you're right. My first instinct was to start rattling cages at the CPS, but I also realise that this needs to be handled carefully. If the police do sit up and listen, it will be imperative that Freneton is kept well out of the loop. That will mean having only a few trusted people in the know, people with clout, until they are ready to sling the book at her. So all things considered, I think it would be prudent for you to take the first initiative."

"Thanks, Charles, I appreciate that. I just wish I had a plan."

She stood and walked over to the window that looked out onto the tree-lined north-London street, but the view hardly registered as she considered her next steps.

"There are three people that I think, no, that I know I can trust with this," she said, turning back to Keithley. "The DCI, Mike Hurst; the DI, Rob McPherson; and DC Derek Thyme. Hurst and McPherson certainly both have some clout and I'm sure they'll listen if I approach it correctly."

"I thought Hurst was part of the gang of three that accused you of lying about not knowing Henry was your father."

"He was, but I don't think he had much say in the matter. The other two in that gang were senior to him: Freneton and the DCS, who I'm pretty sure does what Freneton tells him. She was certainly in charge the day they hauled me in. She's probably got something on him; you know how it works."

"If you're sure, Jennifer. I have to leave it to your judgement."

"I think the first person I'll talk to is Derek. Once we've reviewed the three case files in the morning, I'll drive back to Nottingham and go through everything with him. I don't think it will be difficult to persuade him to see the DI or the DCI, or both together. I don't know; he and I will have to discuss it."

"It sounds as if he's a good colleague," said Keithley.

"More than a colleague," replied Jennifer, "he's a good friend, and he's far smarter than he gives himself credit for." She smiled. "Even if he is a shocking timekeeper. He's been nothing but supportive so far. He stuck his neck out for me with the Bristol case and persuaded his mate down there to do the same. No, if I have to rely on someone, he's the one."


Curled up in a leather armchair in Henry Silk's comfortable study later that evening, Jennifer balanced her laptop on her knee as she trawled the Internet for one more piece of the puzzle: information on Olivia Freneton's career progression in the police force. It was a task that would have taken her ten minutes on one of the internal police computers, but no longer having access to them, she had to go backwards through the years using newspaper reports that either mentioned Freneton's name as a case officer, or as a newly appointed officer in a region or city.

Finally, satisfied she had what she wanted, she closed her computer, and sat back to drink in the titles of the dozens of leather-bound books on the shelves around her. With many first editions among them, Jennifer could have easily spent the night browsing; dipping into one and reacquainting herself with a chapter from another. But the exertions of the last few days were catching up. Another time, she thought, preferably with Henry.

She closed the study door and went to the kitchen where she threw together a salad with leaves she'd bought in a nearby organic deli along with a selection of cheeses. A raid on Henry's substantial wine cellar provided an excellent Merlot.

After finishing the salad and two glasses of wine, she realised it was time to give in to her tiredness. She headed for the guest room where within two minutes of her head hitting the pillow, she was sound asleep.

# Chapter Twenty-Eight

As she took the Nottingham turnoff from the M1 motorway at two o'clock the following afternoon, Jennifer called Derek Thyme's mobile.

"Derek, hi, it's Jennifer."

"Hi, kid, what's up?"

"*Kid!*" exploded Jennifer, but then she realised that if Derek didn't want to address her by name, he must be in the SCF office.

"OK," continued Jennifer, grinding her teeth, "forget my reaction; I've worked it out. Listen, I need to see you very urgently and very confidentially. How quickly can you get round to my place?"

"Intrigued as I am, Mata Hari, I don't think I can make it before seven, I—"

"Seven!"

"Sorry, I don't have any choice. The Ice Queen has dumped a load of stuff on me that she wants the answers for by yesterday. I've got to make inroads with it today before I leave the office or I'll be toast. She keeps on giving me these strange looks. I reckon she doesn't trust me an inch; thinks I'm in telepathic communication with you or something."

"P'raps she fancies you."

"Yeah, right."

"OK, I'll have to make do with seven. But don't be any later.

This is far more important than anything dear Olivia might have for you."


Shortly after eight o'clock, Jennifer heard a car pull up outside the house. She ran over to the window and saw Derek letting himself in through the main gate. She had buzzed the front door before he reached it.

"Sorry, Jen," called Derek as he pounded up the stairs. "The papers got more and more complicated. I was worried that I was going to have to pull an all-nighter when Hurst looked in to say that Freneton was in London tomorrow for a meeting, so I had an extra twenty-four hours. She hadn't told me, the cow. She'd've quite happily had me slaving away through the small hours and then looking like an idiot tomorrow."

"Never mind, you're here now. Sit down there, on the sofa, while I get you a glass of red. Unless you'd prefer a beer?"

"I'm supposed to be in training …"

He paused as his eyes fell suspiciously on a large box file on the coffee table in front of the sofa. More paperwork.

"Red'll be great, thanks. I hope you've got a few bottles."

"Limitless supply. Italian connections, remember?"

She put two almost full glasses on the coffee table and sat in an armchair next to the sofa.

Derek raised his eyebrows. "Wow! You do mean business."

Jennifer grinned at him. "Derek, my friend, what I'm going to tell you will knock your socks off."

She raised her glass in a toast. "Here's to a life-changing moment."

Derek narrowed his eyes in suspicion. "Have you had a few of these already?"

Jennifer put down her glass and opened the box file. "Shut up and listen. I hope you're ready for this."

She took several folders from the box file and lay them side by side on the table in front of Derek.

"OK. These are the details of the murders of five different prostitutes in five different cities around the country during the last seven years. One is, of course, the murder of Miruna Peptanariu for which Henry Silk has been charged and is remanded in prison while awaiting trial. And you know about the rather weird circumstances of the Bristol case last year. For each of the other three, a man was arrested, charged and found guilty at trial, and convicted for life."

She paused to take a sip from her glass.

"Right, amazing fact number one. Of the five apparent culprits for these cases, only Henry Silk is still alive."

"What!" Derek put down his wine glass and leaned forward to pick up one of the files.

Jennifer reached out to touch his arm. "No, wait. Let me tell you all about it first, then you can read the details."

She pointed to the files.

"Each of these cases was supported by strong forensics — DNA and fibres — as well as CCTV evidence for four of them. But if you discount the forensic and CCTV evidence, there's nothing else. And there are no motives, no eyewitnesses, no known relationship between the dead girls and their apparent killers. The MOs for the murders weren't entirely the same, in fact the first two involved semen found in the girls, which is interesting in itself given what I'm going to tell you in a moment. For those two cases, the DNA profiles matched profiles on the DNA database from previous offences, which in both cases were drink-driving convictions. As you know, that sort of comparison is no longer possible since the Protection of Freedom Act forced the police to throw away all the profiles they'd taken from people arrested for minor offences."

She sat back in her chair, hardly able to contain the excitement in her eyes and voice as her story unfolded.

"But," she continued, "there is one factor connecting all the cases."

"Which is?" said Derek as he took a gulp from his glass. "Hey, this wine's good."

Jennifer smiled. "Straight from the extensive Fabrelli vineyards."

"I could get used to it. Now, what's that one factor?"

"One woman, two names?"

"Sorry?"

"Amelia Taverner and Catherine Doughthey."

"Never heard of them."

"One of them, Amelia Taverner, was on the guest list for the Old Nottingham on the night of Miruna Peptanariu's murder, which of course was the night Henry stayed there too. She was also staying at hotels in Leeds in 2007 and Manchester in 2012 on the nights of prostitute murders in those cities, the hotels being the ones where the culprits who were subsequently found guilty of the murders also stayed on the same nights."

Derek pulled a face. "Interesting coincidence?"

"Oh, it's more than that. The other person, Catherine Doughthey, was staying at the Bristol View on the night of the murder down there last year, which is the hotel where the councillor died after apparently murdering a prostitute, and she was also staying in Newcastle in the same hotel as another culprit on the night of a similar murder there in 2009. The details are all there."

She pointed again at the files.

"OK," said Derek, still not sounding convinced. "Are these two women connected in some way?"

Jennifer grinned at him. "You betcha. I traced them both to the same village in Yorkshire, Pateley Bridge, and I went to see them. Well, I saw Amelia Taverner; Catherine Doughthey is dead."

"Dead?"

"Yes, she died two months ago, aged eighty-six."

"What?"

"You heard me right. And guess what? Amelia Taverner, who is very much alive, is a sweet eighty-four year old who wouldn't hurt a fly who's living in a picture-postcard cottage cultivating roses. But it was her credit card used in the three hotels I mentioned and Catherine Doughthey's in the other two."

"So the credit cards were stolen? No, hang on, that doesn't make much sense."

"Of course it doesn't, the time frame is too long. Both ladies knew their cards were being used by someone else and they were in full agreement, although they didn't know what they were being used for. As long as the bills were paid, which they were, they were in no way affected."

Derek rubbed his chin thoughtfully, trying to absorb the story.

"That's pretty weird. Who were they trusting with their credit cards?"

Jennifer opened the box file and retrieved another folder. She opened it and took out two photographs and held them up.

"One of these — this one," she said, waving the photo in her left hand, "is of Amelia Taverner, although she herself uses her middle name, Grace, and the person she entrusted with her credit card. And this one," — she waved the second photograph — "is of Catherine Doughthey with the same woman."

She handed the photographs to Derek and sat back to watch his reaction.

Derek's eyes widened as he studied the two images.

"Christ on a bike, Jennifer, that's … Are you kidding me? Come on, you're having me on. You've photoshopped these to get your own back for me getting Norrie to wind you up in Bristol."

"Look at them carefully, Derek. They've not been doctored in any way. They're the genuine article. I haven't forgiven you for Bristol and I'm still planning my retribution, but this isn't it. This is the real thing."

Derek picked up his glass and took another large gulp.

"Right, Cotton, explain!"


Jennifer spent the next fifteen minutes telling Derek the tale that Grace Taverner had related a few days previously. Having covered that, she added detail from her Internet searches the previous evening.

"I've checked through Freneton's postings in recent years. There's quite a correlation. In 2007, she was in Leeds, but at a different station from the one that handled the prostitute murder in the file; in 2009 she was posted to Sunderland, a short way down the coast from Newcastle; while in 2012, she was stationed in Liverpool, which is not too far from Manchester. From there, she came here to Nottingham. The only place among the five cases I've unearthed she wasn't posted anywhere near to when the relevant murder occurred was Bristol. But guess what? She was on a temporary attachment in Cardiff for two months last year that coincided with the Bristol murder."

Derek was still finding it difficult to accept what he was being told.

"Jen, are you trying to tell me that the Ice Queen is behind these five murders, that she's set all these blokes up? Why? What's her motive?"

"I've no idea. But she must be psychopathic and a psychopath doesn't necessarily need to know his or her victims, all they need is an ongoing motive that's probably nothing to do with the victims. Hatred perhaps, some sort of vengeance. Maybe she was mistreated as a child. We know that her mother died when she was born and that she lived with her father. Perhaps he abused her and she now hates men."

Derek picked up one of the files in front of him and flicked through it.

"You said that Freneton went to live with this Grace Taverner around the age of fifteen when her father died. How did he die?"

"In a car accident. His brakes failed and the car plunged off the road in the Yorkshire Dales. I've checked the newspaper reports from the time. They lived in Harrogate. There was some suspicion that the brakes might have been tampered with, but the accident damage was too severe for the investigators to come to a firm conclusion."

She stopped, her brow furrowed. "I wonder what time Grace Taverner goes to bed."

She checked her watch: eight fifty-five. She pursed her lips and stared at Derek while she made a decision. Then she picked up her phone and called up the contact list, pressed a number and waited.

"Hello, Mrs Taverner, it's Jennifer Cotton from the North Western Bank. I called at your cottage the other day, do you remember? I'm sorry it's rather late. You weren't in bed, were you?"

"Hello, dear, no, I'm a bit of a night owl. Languid likes to listen to the ten o'clock news with me, so we never go to bed before that. But it's late for you to be working. Are you still in your office?"

"No, I do quite a lot of my work from home. I was finishing off a report about my interviews in your area when I remembered something I meant to ask you?"

"What was that, dear? Oh, hold on a moment, Languid wants to pop out and use the garden. He's so good, you know, always asks. Yes, Languid, it's that nice Miss Cotton."

Jennifer smiled to herself as she heard a door open and close in the cottage. Then Grace's voice came back on the line.

"There we are. Now, you were saying?"

"I was wondering if you drove a car, Mrs Taverner."

"Oh no, dear, not any more. I used to, but my eyesight's not what it was. I had perfect vision for years; I didn't need glasses until I was over sixty. But then I got cataracts and although they were treated, it wasn't the same. I still miss my car though. She was a lovely old thing. A Morris Minor, one of those with the wood on the side."

"A Traveller," said Jennifer. "What a coincidence! My boyfriend had one until quite recently; he loves old cars."

She pulled a face at Derek and held up her crossed fingers. Derek smiled, took another gulp of wine and went looking for the bottle. Jennifer snapped her fingers and waved her arm at a credenza by the living room door to show him where the bottles were kept.

"Unfortunately," continued Jennifer into the phone, "my boyfriend's car wasn't in the best of condition. How was yours? I have a feeling it was immaculate."

She heard a chortle down the line.

"Yes, dear, it was. I was fortunate to have Diana around. She used to tinker with it whenever there was a problem. She was a wiz with cars; did I tell you? About the only thing she had in common with her father. It was quite ironic, really, that he was killed in one. A car, I mean."

A silence hung in the air for a few seconds before Grace asked, "Why did you want to know if I drove a car, dear?"

Jennifer had anticipated the question.

"The bank has a discount arrangement with one of the big insurance companies which benefits many of our customers. I know you don't actually bank with us yourself, but I thought it might be useful for you to know. However, if you no longer drive, it doesn't really matter. I apologise; I've disturbed you for nothing."

"Not at all, dear. It's nice to talk to you again."

After a further exchange of niceties, Grace said she could hear Languid scratching at the door. Jennifer thanked her for her time and rang off.

"That was a tall tale," laughed Derek. "Why did you call her?"

"She'd told me that Diana, as she knows Freneton, had learned about car maintenance from her father. I wanted to confirm it was true rather than a line with no substance that Freneton was spinning to her. Now I know not only that it's true, but also that she will have had the knowledge to bump off her father."

Derek shrugged. "Do you want me to arrest her on suspicion of murdering him?"

"No, of course not, but it all fits, don't you see?"

Another shrug from Derek. "S'pose so. I mean, she could've. When was that?"

"Nineteen ninety-one."

"And when did she join the force?"

"In ninety-eight, at the age of twenty-three. Graduate entry, like me, but she was fast-tracked, unlike me. She was smart, determined, physically capable, good at all the unarmed combat stuff."

"Did you check up on anything prior to 2007?"

"I checked for similar cases to those five back as far as 1999 and found nothing. Mind you, the farther back you go, the harder it is without access to the police computers."

Derek smiled knowingly. "So is that what you want me to do?"

Jennifer shook her head sharply. "Absolutely not. You mustn't start accessing the files; all sorts of sirens might go off. No, as I told you, Henry is the only one of the five alleged culprits we know of who is still alive. I'm wondering if Freneton had a hand in that. If she did, then Henry is in real danger."

"But I can't go to McPherson and tell him that you think Henry's life's at risk," protested Derek. "He'll throw me out of his office. And even with the credit card thing and this Taverner person, and the other one — Doughthey — there's all the forensic evidence and the CCTV."

"I've been looking at the CCTV again," said Jennifer. "Henry's solicitor has copies, obviously, although I swore I wouldn't say that I'd seen them, their being sub judice. Anyway, the thing is, I don't reckon it's Henry on the CCTV; it's someone trying to copy him. I don't know, it's the way the person is walking."

Derek laughed. "Sounds like wishful thinking to me."

"Just as identifying him was from what we, the police, wanted to see," countered Jennifer.

"Whatever, Jennifer, it still isn't strong."

"I know, we need something else and I might have come up with it. I spoke to a friendly forensic scientist who reckons there could be some mileage in examining the inside of Henry's clothing, the pullover in particular. The trouble is that the request should, ideally, come from the police."

Derek wasn't so sure. "Ideally, perhaps, but not necessarily. The defence can request for it to be done either by or in the presence of their own expert, so long as they are willing to pay."

Jennifer picked up her wine, took a sip and put it down.

"Yes, but it would still be better coming from the police. Look, I've told Charles Keithley everything and he's agreed not to proceed until he knows whether anyone in the police is going to take it seriously. If they don't, he'll blow the whistle. The problem with that is that Freneton will almost inevitably get to hear about it and start covering her tracks. I'm already worried that she might have some contact with Grace Taverner, even though that's not actually due for several months. Who currently are Freneton's least favourite people in the SCF?"

"Ha! Take your pick!" snorted Derek. "Nobody actually likes her but she gets results. And, as you know, her organisational skills are impressive. She's clearly on her way to the top. But having said that, I've also heard that even the ACC avoids her."

Jennifer sighed, suddenly feeling the enormity of the problem.

"In order for this to be taken seriously, Derek, we do need the support of someone in authority, and therefore someone who ideally is senior to Freneton."

Derek was shocked. "You mean the DCS! I'm not sure I'd trust him."

"No, nor am I. And I certainly couldn't go to him directly. In fact, I don't think he'd even agree to see me."

"Of course you couldn't, but neither could I."

"But would you be willing to break the ice with one of the others? Try to sell it to McPherson or Hurst; get them on board?"

Derek grinned at her. "Fell into that, didn't I? But yes, I could give it a whirl. McPherson likes you, as does Hurst. We could all see he was hopping when your resignation was more or less forced."

Jennifer reached out and touched Derek's arm. "Thanks, Derek. You're a true friend. But what I am concerned about is that they understand that although you are telling them, it's on my behalf and you are in the clear, that you've not helped me or broken any rules. They must know that I've done everything off my own bat, all with info that is already available or that I got from Henry's solicitor. It's all legit and not come from police sources via you or anyone else."

Derek was still smiling. "You worry too much, Jen. But, hey, what about the bit on the phone just now where you were pretending to work for a bank. Slightly bending the truth, eh?"

Jennifer tossed her head. "I'm no longer a police officer. I can pretend to be anyone I want. And anyway, I don't know what you mean. Grace Taverner's an old lady; she must have misheard me."

"Yeah," grinned Derek, "exactly like I did. But seriously, Jen, thinking about it all and with what you've told me this evening, you don't have to ask me to jump on board and talk to the DI. I have a duty to report it to my senior officers."

## Chapter Twenty-Nine

Derek Thyme was sprinting to Olympic stardom in the final of the two hundred metres when the runner immediately behind him grabbed him by the shoulder and started shaking it.

"Derek. Derek! Wake up, for Christ's sake! You've got to get to the office, remember?"

He was having a hard time registering anything, let alone actually remembering. He stretched and realised he must be on a sofa. He turned his head in the direction of the voice and instantly regretted it as a succession of mortar bombs exploded in his brain. He groaned, turned his face into the sofa and tried to blank out the pain. He wanted to go back to the race.

"Derek!"

With a great deal of effort, he swung his legs round and sat up, his head spinning.

"God, that was a mistake," he grunted. He looked up and saw Jennifer's face beginning to focus in front of him.

Memories of the previous evening slowly started to crystallise as she thrust a glass of water into his hands.

"Drink this, you soak. Do you know how much wine you got through last night?"

"I don't remember you holding back either," he spluttered as he gulped down the water.

What was filtering unbidden into his memory now was an image of Jennifer insisting that he'd had too much to drink, that he couldn't drive, that he must stay the night. He'd looked hopefully into her eyes but the wrong light was on. All she'd done was toss him a duvet and point to the sofa.

"What time is it?"

"Seven. I've been up for half an hour making you copies of everything in the files."

"Seven! I never get up this early. Why—"

"P'raps that's why you're known as Justin. I reckoned you wouldn't want to go to work in those clothes, given you slept in them. So you need to go home, shower and change."

"Are you my mother?"

"Just looking after your best interests. And mine. You've got an important meeting to set up this morning. You need to look as if you're on the same planet as everyone else. Do you want some more water? Coffee?"

Derek winced again as he shook his head. "I'd best be getting home. Don't want to be late."

He pointed to the second box file that had materialised on the coffee table. "That mine?"

"Yes," said Jennifer as she picked it up and thrust it into his arms.

"I'll call you," he said, heading for the door.

She heard his feet thumping down the stairs and the front door being yanked open. Then a yell a moment before the door slammed shut.

"Thanks, Mum!"


Jennifer paced the floor impatiently for an hour, and then when she was sick of that, she went for a run and a bike ride followed by another hour of pacing. But Derek didn't ring. By lunchtime she was checking her watch every ten minutes, by three o'clock, every five. She read and re-read everything in the files, knowing that was the material Derek would be showing to … whom? The DI? The DCI? Maybe he'd got as far as the DCS. Christ, why didn't he ring? Had Freneton intercepted him? Read the files? Jesus, she was stupid to have let him go with all that information. If Freneton got hold of it, she'd be round to see Jennifer, wanting to destroy everything, wanting to kill her. She checked and re-checked the front door, making sure the three bolts were in place. The only weapons she had were kitchen knives. She should buy a baseball bat. Bit late now. What was she thinking? She was trained in unarmed combat. Christ, so was Freneton! And she had a reputation for not holding back.

At six she turned on the television to watch the news. Had the body of a black policeman been found in the Nottingham area? Glued to the set, she didn't hear the car draw up outside and so when the buzzer sounded, she jumped about two feet in the air. She grabbed the entry phone set, dropped it, and, as she grabbed at it again, pressed the door release by mistake. Shit!

"Who is it?" she yelled.

"It's me, Jen. The door won't open. What's happening?"

"Are you alone?"

"What? Of course I'm alone."

"Go back to your car; let me see you."

"Are you on the red wine again, Jen?"

"Do it!"

She ran to the balcony doors, pulled one open and darted to the railing. Down in the road she could see Derek leaning against the bonnet of his car, waving one arm casually at her and grinning.

Jennifer slid back the bolts and pulled open the front door, then she leaned back against the wall, her arms folded protectively across her chest as Derek walked in and closed the door behind him.

"Why so spooked, Jen?" he said, still grinning his idiot grin.

She dropped her eyes and shook her head. "You didn't call."

"Come here."

She looked up and saw his outstretched arms.

"You need a hug, Cotton."

"I do," she whispered as she pressed her head against his chest.

"Sorry," she said as they sat on the sofa. "I don't know what came over me. I was imagining all sorts of things."

"You were right to," he said, his voice suddenly menacing. He half closed his eyes and pinched the skin below his jaw with the thumb and index finger of both hands, as if he were about to peel off his face.

"Derek is dead in a ditch. I'm really Olivia Freneton in disguise."

"Idiot!" she said, punching him on the arm.

"Ouch! I'm arresting you for assaulting a police officer."

"Shut up and tell me what happened."

He shrugged. "I can't do both."

"Derek!"

He sat back and took a deep breath, suddenly serious.

"I'll tell you what, Cotton, have you created some waves. Shit hitting the fan would be the understatement of the year. It was more like an entire sewage treatment plant venting its load."

"Skip the scatological prose and cut to the chase, Thyme."

"OK. I got in soon after nine; all smart, clean and shipshape, although the head was still giving me trouble. McPherson was in his office looking grumpy as usual, so I knocked on the door and asked if I could see him, said it was confidential. He gave me one of his looks and pointed to a chair. I closed his door and started to explain, but it came out a bit garbled. However, he must have picked up on how serious it was because after about a minute he told me to shut up and wait. Then he walked out of the room. I was shitting myself; I thought he'd gone to get Freneton even though at that stage I hadn't even mentioned her name.

"But he hadn't. He came straight back and told me to go with him. We marched into Hurst's office and McPherson closed the door behind us. You can see through the glass partition, as you know, but Freneton was nowhere around, which was a relief. Didn't want her barging in.

"Anyway I explained what you'd found in more or less the order you told me. I said you'd found four other cases, found the names on the guest lists and emphasised, 'cause you'd told me to, that you'd done it all. I told them I'd wanted to help but you wouldn't let me."

"You shouldn't have said that, Derek; they could hold it against you."

"I think they took it the right way," he said, shrugging. "Anyway, when I got to the bit with the photographs of the Ice Queen, they both nearly had coronaries. Then Hurst went white while McPherson grabbed the files and started to read them all. Hurst picked up on that and wanted them too. They were like kids, almost snatching things out of each other's hands. I had to intervene to make sure they had covered all the info. I told them it would be better if I summarised it all before they read over it, so that they had a broad picture. You would have been proud of me, Jen, they just sat back and took it. 'You're right, Thyme,' Hurst said to me. 'Bullet point the lot.' So I did."

Jennifer touched Derek's arm and grinned. "Well done, partner, I wish I'd been there."

"Yeah, well, I'd expect them to take it from you, you seem to be able to wind them round your little finger, but it was a new experience for me. Felt good.

"Anyway, once I'd gone through everything, you know, the credit card thing, Freneton's history with Amelia Grace Taverner, her postings, and of course, the point about all the other blokes convicted of the murders being dead — that stopped them in their tracks too—"

"So it should."

"Yeah. Anyway, once I'd covered it all, Hurst said they'd need to discuss it and that I wasn't to say anything to anyone. I think that was the hardest part 'cause when I went back into the squad room, everyone wanted to know the score. They'd seen me go into McPherson's office and then Hurst's, and now they could see Hurst and McPherson tossing the papers around and waving their arms. They were at it for ages. Twice a WPC knocked on Hurst's door for something, first one and then another ten minutes later. He bawled at them both to get out and stay out."

"So how long did this go on for?" asked Jennifer.

"Like I said. Ages. I reckon it was nearly lunchtime. I was

getting worried because the lads wouldn't let it go. One after the other they kept dropping by my desk for a chat. I've never been so popular. Then someone had the bright idea of a pub lunch with a couple of those young civi research girls, the pretty ones. I reckon they thought they'd distract me into saying something. Fortunately, McPherson appeared at the right moment and called me back into Hurst's office. We were there for another half an hour while they asked me more about various bits you'd told me. Some of it I could help with but most of it will need your input."

"When do they want that?"

"I'll tell you in a mo. They booted me out again and they both went off to the DCS's office where there was a repeat performance of the whole morning's dramatics, only even noisier — you know what Hawkins is like when he gets wound up. I couldn't actually hear what they were saying, of course, because the office door was closed, and I couldn't see anything 'cause Hawkins' office has walls, not glass, but there was certainly a lot of ranting and raving. It was funny, when the lads got back from the pub, one or other of them would keep finding excuses to pop along the corridor to see if they could pick anything up. The DCS's secretary was getting totally pissed off, since she's the barrier between him and the human race. Her mood got even worse when she also tried to go into his office and got a bawling out for interrupting him in a meeting."

"What about Freneton?" asked Jennifer. "Where was she when all these high dramatics were going on?"

"Fortunately, she was out for the day. Over at county headquarters, I think. But she'll be back tomorrow, so that will be interesting."

"Do you know if they're running with it? I'll need to know so that I can brief Charles Keithley. Although he's trying to remain calm, I know he can't wait to get something moving. Every day Henry is inside is a day too many for Charles, not to say Henry, of course."

"Yeah, I can sympathise. You must feel the same, Jen."

She smiled at him. "I do, but at least now I think there's some hope."

When Derek didn't smile back, Jennifer registered it immediately.

"Don't you agree?"

"Up to a point, yes, but there's still a way to go. However, the outcome of today is that Hawkins has set up a confidential team comprising the three of them: him, Hurst and McPherson, and me, although Hawkins said that he will probably bring in a couple of outsiders to help me. I'm really just their gofer at the moment."

"It's going to be difficult keeping Freneton out of the loop," said Jennifer. "Her antennae are hypersensitive."

"Yes, they know that. McPherson told me that the DCS is hoping that they can get something quickly to either implicate her more strongly, or exonerate her, in which case it would all go away."

Jennifer shook her head. "Don't you believe it. Charles won't let this drop and neither will I. We want Henry off the hook."

"I didn't mean that," said Derek. "I don't think there's much doubt in their minds that Henry has been set up. The biggest thing for them is getting their heads round the fact that Freneton's involved. It's a big deal, Jen, as you know. The fallout will be horrendous. I'm sure the DCS can already feel a noose of blame tightening round his neck."

"What do they need from me?"

"Obviously they want to see you, but most definitely not in the nick. The DCS and Hurst were adamant about that; they don't want you anywhere near the place. You bumping into Freneton could be a disaster. She's not stupid and if she gets to thinking that you're onto something, she might start taking matters into her own hands."

"Why do you think I was so spooked today? I was running exactly that sort of scenario through my head."

Derek's eyes found hers. He shrugged, trying to look nonchalant.

"I … I can stay, if you like. If you're worried."

Jennifer took his hand. "Thanks, that's sweet, but I'd feel guilty if you spent another night on that sofa."

"Doesn't have to be the sofa," he said, his voice little more than a whisper.

She put a hand on his cheek. "I don't think I'd be … I mean, I'm extremely preoccupied. Look, it's a tempting idea, but … I'm not quite ready."

She reached forward and kissed his cheek, then she picked up his arm and pulled it around her. "But I'd like another hug."

Derek stroked Jennifer's hair with his free hand. "This is nice."

She snuggled further into his arms. "It's the calmest I've felt all day."

After a few moments, she raised her head. "So when and where do they want to meet?"

"Tomorrow morning, eight o'clock at Trowell services on the M1. Southbound side car park. Go on at junction twenty-six."

"Yes, I know it. It can't be soon enough. I'm really worried about Henry's safety. What exactly did they say about that?"

"The DCS is going to pull the reports from the Leeds, Manchester and Newcastle cases for the details. They particularly want to know about the two suicides. So yeah, they were concerned. But as we've said, all three happened after the trials, so Henry's probably safe enough at the moment."

Jennifer sighed. "Would you like a drink?"

"Thanks, but no. Like I said last night, I'm supposed to be in training. My coach'd kill me. And the way I felt this morning … Actually, Jen, I'd better go."

She said nothing for a few seconds, and then whispered a reluctant-sounding 'OK.'

They stood and she reached up and kissed him lightly on the lips.

"Thanks, Derek. I feel much better now."

He took her hands. "You've got my number on your speed dial, haven't you?"

She smiled. "As speedy as it gets on an iPhone, yes."

"Right. Well, make sure to call me if you feel spooked. I'm only about ten minutes away."

"I didn't know your mum lived so close."

Derek snorted. "I don't live with my mum any more! I've got a flat in a new development in Beeston."

"Sounds nice."

"It is. You'll have to drop by and see it sometime."

"I will, now I know your mum's not going to answer the door."

"See you in the morning, Cotton."

"Trowell services."

# Chapter Thirty

Jennifer arrived half an hour early at Trowell Services, positioning her car so that she could see all vehicles pulling into the car park.

She had slept badly until around three thirty, after which she had fallen into a deep but troubled sleep, only to shoot out of bed in panic when the alarm woke her at six. Between then and her leaving home at seven, every point in her case against Olivia Freneton had raised its head, extended sharp, mocking claws and tortured her with self-doubt. Freneton may be a bitch to work for, but a murderer? Spectres of civil actions and defamation of character mingled with her mental images of the photographs of Amelia Taverner and Catherine Doughthey smiling sweetly at her, while the memories of Freneton in those same photographs now showed her with a victorious, sneering smile.

And now she was going to get the third degree from Hawkins, not known for either his patience or tolerance of over-assertive junior officers. God only knew what his attitude would be to a young detective who'd resigned under a cloud of suspicion.

As she switched off the engine, Jennifer checked her watch. Seven twenty-nine. They wouldn't be this early; there was time for a visit to the loo. She had no idea how long the meeting would take, but she didn't want to be wriggling for need of a pee, or worse still, have to interrupt matters for one.

Returning to her car, she took a sip from the insulated mug of coffee she'd brought with her, but with further thoughts of loo breaks, left it at that, despite a yearning for more caffeine.


At three minutes to eight, DCS Peter Hawkins' Range Rover pulled into the car park followed by Rob McPherson's ageing Sierra. Hawkins parked his car well away from any others; McPherson pulled up next to him. They clearly hadn't spotted Jennifer's car fifty yards away so she got out, locked it and made her way towards them. As she did, the front passenger door of the Range Rover opened and Mike Hurst got out, gesticulating to McPherson to move his car farther away, presumably, thought Jennifer, so they could keep a better eye on any other cars that came close. Were they expecting Olivia Freneton's car to appear out of the blue?

While McPherson repositioned his car, Hurst looked around and saw Jennifer. He waved and pulled open the front passenger door, indicating to her to get in. He would sit in the back. As she paused by the Range Rover, Jennifer glanced at McPherson's Sierra and noticed Derek sitting in the front passenger seat. At least there was one amongst them who would be on her side.


Jennifer positioned her briefcase on her lap and turned to see Hawkins staring through the windscreen, his pasty face set with an expression that clearly said he was only there under sufferance. He wasn't a tall man and too many formal dinners had seen any waistline he once had disappear under the unhealthy bulge that was now his gut. His podgy fingers still gripped the steering wheel while his small, bulbous eyes roamed the car park. As Jennifer looked across at him, she noticed his comb-over for the first time. Somehow it had been less obvious when face-to-face in his office; now it looked like a ridiculous attempt to hide the inevitable, the remnants of his once wavy locks rather lonely survivors on a desert island of pink crown.

"Mr Hawkins, I'd like to thank you for agreeing to meet me. I—"

"I didn't agree to meet you, Cotton, I demanded it."

His strong East Midlands accent sliced through the car.

"And you can cut the civi crap. The last time we met you called me 'sir'. Let's keep it simple and stick to that shall we?"

Jennifer could feel her hackles rising. She took a deep, controlling breath.

"Th…that was a few weeks ago. I'm now just a member of the public. I—"

"Do you have any back pay still to come?"

"Er, yes, I do. But—"

"Then you're still a police officer in my book. Now let's get on. I haven't got all day to sit here listening to your thoughts on etiquette."

He turned his face to her for the first time and glowered.

Jennifer flicked her eyes towards Hurst, who had positioned himself in the rear seat immediately behind Hawkins. She saw the slightest shake of his head telling her to swallow her pride.

"Yes, sir," she mumbled.

Satisfied with his victory, Hawkins returned his gaze to the car park, every movement of every car being noted. He took a breath and Jennifer saw his jacket button strain against the extra pressure.

"Now, Cotton, you and your terrier-like resistance to letting go of anything have caused me a major headache."

It's not about you, you stupid shit, thought Jennifer.

"Yes, sir," she repeated.

Hawkins grunted. "It's as well that Detective Superintendent Freneton was away from the SCF yesterday because she'd have been bound to get wind of something. However, she's back today and it's going to be all but impossible for her not to smell a rat. And if she gets even a shred, a sniff of something, she'll be banging on the doors of every senior commander from here to London. And she's got some heavy contacts, friends in high places. Believe me, Cotton, you have no idea."

He stopped, his fingers working at the steering wheel while the words he didn't want to say lined themselves up in his head. He breathed in deeply and pulled sharply on the wheel, as if to help the words escape.

"However," he snarled, his jaw set, "despite all that and the fact that you've got me sticking my neck out so far I look like a bloody giraffe, having read carefully through your notes and having discussed them at length with both the DCI here, and DI McPherson, I've come to the conclusion that you may have something. *May* have. It's all circumstantial and therefore there could be a logical and legitimate reason or reasons behind all of it. I know Silk's solicitor has given you what he's found about the circumstances of the three other deaths in custody, but I suspect the police files will have more. We're still looking into that. I've told Thyme to get the files toot sweet. I've also ordered a re-examination of Silk's clothing to include searching the inside surfaces, like you suggested."

Jennifer was still trying to imagine how a man with no neck could look like a giraffe. She coughed, interrupting Hawkins' flow.

"May I ask one thing here, sir? I know that Charles Keithley, Henry Silk's solicitor, would much prefer it if his own expert could be present at any further examination of the clothing. Would that be OK?"

Hawkins dropped the corners of his mouth in disapproval. "Doesn't he trust the lab, Cotton? It's not regular practice to have the defence expert at what will effectively be an initial examination, this part of the clothing not having been examined previously."

He paused but Jennifer held her tongue. She was beginning to get used to his style of denial and negativity followed by agreement. All that was required was the patience to let him work his way through his pomposity.

Finally he sat back and folded his arms over his belly.

"But, I suppose, in the circumstances …"

He glanced in the mirror. "Mike, make a note."

"Yes, sir," replied Hurst. He hadn't told the DCS, but he'd already briefed the lab not to start until the defence expert was on site.

Hawkins flicked his eyes briefly at Jennifer before continuing his survey of the car park.

"Of course, Cotton, even if they find wig hair, like you think they will, it's still going to be hard to pin anything on Detective Superintendent Freneton, or anyone else, for that matter."

Jennifer nodded. "I know, sir, but every little helps, and there may be something else to connect her."

"What are you expecting, her business card stuffed down his pullover? We've no grounds to seize any of her clothing for comparison, you know. Not at this stage, probably not at any stage. You realise, Cotton, that if nothing comes of any of this, and if the deaths are shown not to be suspicious or connected to each other or to Detective Superintendent Freneton, and eventually there's a legitimate reason for her to have been in the hotels, this investigation will stop. There'll be nothing, and God help you if that's the case and she finds out."

Jennifer gripped her briefcase. The DCS's confidence was coming and going in waves.

"I know all that, sir, but it must be worth the risk. I'm prepared to be the fall guy on this. At least I can't be sacked since I've already resigned."

"It's gone much further than you, Cotton," snapped Hawkins. "Simply by entertaining the idea of these further investigations, the responsibility is firmly with me. Although, of course, Freneton would doubtless explore all avenues for retribution, and suing you for defamation of character would be high on her list, sure as eggs are eggs."

Jennifer wasn't fazed. "Good luck to her, sir. For me, it's essential that all avenues are explored for Henry Silk's sake, since I am totally convinced of his innocence, as is Charles Keithley."

"That's his job, Cotton."

"No, sir, his job is to prepare the defence, whether he believes Henry's innocent or not."

Hawkins bristled. "Careful, Cotton."

"Sorry, sir, but the point is he has to explore every angle for the barrister to present at trial. And if doubt can be raised, the jury might find in favour of Henry. But I don't want it to go that far. I'm hoping that the charges will be dropped. You see, that was my initial aim when I started looking at everything. I had no idea that Detective Superintendent Freneton might be involved, and even if it can't be shown that she's the guilty party, I think you'd agree that there's now huge doubt about Henry's involvement. And if it's not her, then there's someone else out there framing Henry."

Hawkins pursed his lips. "I understand you think the CCTV might show more. I know you've watched it again. Not in the station, I hope."

The suggestion was so ridiculous that Jennifer wanted to spit it back at him, but she stifled the urge.

"No, sir, of course not. I managed to trick Charles Keithley into letting me see it. But I still haven't had time to see all of it, and of course there's the CCTV from three of the other cases, which I also haven't seen."

Hawkins nodded. "Yes, that's on the way."

"What I'd really like, sir," continued Jennifer, trying not to make her tone sound too desperate, "is for you to watch the footage from the present case again and then the others. All of you. Please. I don't want to say what I think, having watched some of it, since I don't want to influence you. I—"

"We're quite capable of making up our own minds, Cotton, regardless of what you think."

"I know, sir, I wasn't trying to imply you weren't. But when you view all the footage, I'd really like you to consider that it might be someone other than Henry Silk. Obviously in the footage from the other murders, it can't be him. But could the person shown be the same person in all of them? Are there any similarities, gestures, mannerisms? You've known Detective Superintendent Freneton for more or less a year now—"

"Considerably longer than that," he growled, not trying to hide his distaste at the thought. "But so what?"

"Well, sir, you know how she walks, holds herself. Perhaps there's something. An expert in posture and gait might be able to help."

Hawkins shook his head. "Some ivory-tower academic with his head up his arse. No, Cotton, for every one of them, there'll always be another with a contrary opinion. Totally unreliable, in my book."

God, thought Jennifer, this man is so old school he's hardly in the twentieth century, let alone the twenty-first.

Hawkins paused, and Jennifer waited. He was doing it again. Finally, he sighed. "But we can have a look at what can be done. Now, I know that you've put everything into your notes, and they're impressive, if clearly biased."

He held up his hand as Jennifer started to object.

"No, Cotton, don't interrupt. They're bound to be; the man's your father. What I was saying was that I'd like you to tell us, as briefly as you can, since we haven't got all day, what your initial thoughts were as you started all this. How you progressed. I want to get it clear in my head that this isn't some vendetta against Detective Superintendent Freneton for basically forcing you to resign, your principles being what they are."

Hawkins' change of tack surprised Jennifer, but she was pleased: he was thinking positively.

"I can assure you, sir, that angry as I was at the stance taken against me, and not only by Detective Superintendent Freneton …"

She paused to let that sink in, but Hawkins stonewalled the remark, his pudgy skin even thicker than it looked.

"I can assure you," she continued, "that my intentions were to look at what I could of the evidence. Like everyone else, I initially thought Henry Silk was guilty, but the more I searched the more I became convinced otherwise, and not only because he's my father. As I said, I had no idea of any possible involvement of Detective Superintendent Freneton. I was completely gobsmacked when I saw her in the photographs."

Hawkins held up his hand again.

"OK, Cotton, take me through all that again, the discovery of the names and your visit to this Amelia Grace Taverner. Concisely, if you will."

Jennifer took a breath and gave what she hoped was a clear summary of the events leading up to the discovery of Olivia Freneton's history with Grace Taverner.

When she reached the part about finding a credit card statement hidden among Catherine Doughthey's photographs, she remembered something else.

"There's another point that needs following up, sir, that obviously I couldn't pursue. The credit cards and bank accounts in both Amelia Grace Taverner's and Catherine Doughthey's names. They would give us a pattern of spending and dates that might correlate with a suspect's movements."

She didn't want to keep on saying Freneton's name.

"Ahead of you, Cotton," said Hawkins, with a self-satisfied smirk. "We should have something later today."

He checked his watch. "Talking of which, it's time at least one of the squad I've set up was in the office. We don't want Detective Superintendent Freneton sashaying around, as she's prone to do, making note of what's on our desks. Nor do we want her answering any phone calls on our behalf. From the lab, for example."

He turned to Hurst. "Mike, pop over to McPherson and tell him we're almost done here and to get his arse into the office."

As Hurst got out and walked to the DI's car, both Jennifer and Hawkins sat watching him.

"One other point, Cotton. Who's this forensic scientist you've been hobnobbing with, the one who's given you insight into further examinations? I hope she's not from the new lab we're using on the ring road, 'cause that could put a spanner in the works as well."

"No, sir, she's not. She's the friend of the sister of an old uni friend of mine. She doesn't live around here. She knew nothing about the case until I briefed her on it. Everything she came up with was based on what I told her."

Hawkins grunted in reluctant acceptance as he shifted in his seat. He reached forward to start the engine.

"You know, Cotton, this case is a bugger. However it turns out with Detective Superintendent Freneton, it's looking increasingly as if your Henry Silk has been set up by someone. So sooner or later, the force is going to have a shitstorm on its hands. I can see the headlines now and all the smart-arsed journalists asking how she could possibly have got away with it for so long and how we could have got it so wrong."

Jennifer smiled to herself. In spite of all the hot air and bluster,

Hawkins was starting to sound convinced. She couldn't wait to relay progress to Henry, and to Charles Keithley.

"Right, Cotton, bugger off home and keep your head down. As soon as we've got anything, positive or negative, I'll let you know. Got it?"

"Yes, sir."

## Chapter Thirty-One

Returning to the SCF at nine twenty, Peter Hawkins was surprised to be told by Mike Hurst that contrary to expectations, Olivia Freneton had not shown up for work that morning.

"Have you called her house, Mike?"

"Yes, sir, first number I tried. There's no answer; the phone goes to a brief answer message."

"And you've asked around the squad room in case some clown took a message and forgot to pass it on?"

"Yes, sir. She hasn't called in."

"Bloody odd, particularly from a stickler for the rules like Freneton. What about her mobile?"

"Left voice messages on that too, sir. And a text."

"Get onto county HQ, will you? Talk to Doug Watson. He will have been the lucky man coordinating her team yesterday. Check she was there and if she appeared to be ill or anything."

Hurst was back in Hawkins' office within minutes.

"Still no answer, sir. But I contacted Doug Watson who said she was there all day yesterday; left at five p.m."

"How did she seem?"

"According to Doug, she was her usual steely self in the

morning sessions. 'Had forgotten to take her happy pill, as usual,' is how he put it."

Hawkins grunted.

"But after lunch," Hurst continued, "she was different, distracted. Not really at the party, Doug said. They wondered if she'd had a few over the break, but I assured him that she seldom touches a drop."

"Send someone round to her house, see if anything's amiss. No, better still, go yourself. She'll only bawl out a PC if he knocks on her door. If there's no answer, have a look through the windows. If she's lying on the floor, we can go back in three days' time and see if she needs help."

Hurst stared at his boss. Had he just cracked a joke? Perhaps he was serious. Either way, he wasn't pleased to have been sent on an errand, but from the tone of the instruction, he was hardly in a position to delegate it further.

"I'll go now, sir," was all he said.

On his way out, he bumped into McPherson.

"Busy Rob?"

"Nothing too urgent."

"Good. Come with me, if you will."

"Where are we going?"

Hurst could sense several pairs of ears tuning in his direction from the squad room.

"I'll tell you in the car."


Doug Watson from Nottingham City and County HQ had been right: the Olivia Freneton who faced the management group the previous afternoon had been uncharacteristically different from the usual brusque, no-nonsense detective superintendent they were used to. Distracted to the point of occasionally stumbling over her script, no more than about twenty-five per cent of her mind was focussed on the discussion she was supposed to be leading. The rest of her attention was many miles away as the potential implications of what she'd discovered swirled around her brain.

It had started during the lunch break with a routine purchase of petrol at a garage three miles down the road from the HQ complex. She hadn't wanted to eat lunch with the group; being with them through a long and tedious morning had been enough — were these really the crème de la crème from the various forces who were destined to be tomorrow's leaders in law enforcement?

Olivia kept a list in her phone diary of certain chores that needed her attention on a regular basis. Among these were reminders that purchases were to be made every three months using Amelia Taverner's and Catherine Doughthey's credit cards to keep the accounts ticking along. A note that today was scheduled for using the cards had appeared on her screen earlier that morning. It was a simple enough task she'd carry out over lunch: she'd buy petrol with one card and a snack somewhere with the other.

But then Catherine Doughthey's card was refused.

"Sorry, love," said the round, middle-aged women at the cashier's desk in the petrol station. "The message says the card account's closed. Sure you've given me the right one?"

"Absolutely sure," said the scowling Olivia. "I only carry one. Could you try it again?"

The woman sighed, cancelled the transaction and pulled the card from the reader. She glanced at it disapprovingly, rubbed the magnetic strip on her sleeve and then reinserted it.

There was a silence as they both waited. When the reader pinged, the woman turned the display in Olivia's direction.

"Same," she said. "See? It says 'Card account closed. Contact your bank for details'."

Olivia took the card, opened her purse and paid in cash.

"I'll give the bank a call," she muttered. "There must be gremlins in the system since I certainly haven't closed it."

What concerned Olivia was that in all the years she'd had both accounts, none of the cards had ever failed. She wondered if Grace Taverner's card would be the same. If it was, she had a problem.

She jumped into her car and drove to a nearby village where instead of going to the pub as she'd planned, she headed for a bakery to buy some filled rolls for her lunch. She offered Grace's card and to her relief the transaction went through perfectly.

However, whatever the glitch was with Catherine's card, it needed addressing. She took out an ageing Motorola with an even older SIM card, one of several phones she used for anonymous calls.

Five minutes later, having pressed a number of buttons in response to the automatic answering service and been treated to worn-out extracts of over-played classical music, a real person came on the line, a woman with a sing-song accent, her consonants clicking. As Olivia explained her predicament, she wondered where in the world the call centre was located.

"My name is Rose Doughthey. I'm phoning on behalf of my mother Catherine Doughthey who has an account with you that includes a credit card. I was shopping with my mother this morning when she tried to pay for something with that credit card. The payment was refused with a message that the account had been closed. Since that isn't, in fact, the case, I'd be grateful if you could check it on your system."

She read out the card number along with its expiry date.

"Is your mother there now?" said the woman. "You'll understand that it's her I have to speak to regarding her card."

"I'm sorry, but she's taking her afternoon nap. She's eighty-six, you see. I'm not asking you to reactivate the card; all I want to know is what the problem is so that I can explain it to her. She was very unsettled by it; she felt as if she'd been accused of doing something illegal. You know what old people can be like."

"Yes, of course," said the woman, her tone now softened with some sympathy. "Let me see, according to the data I have here, the account associated with that card was closed, er, yes, six weeks ago."

There was a pause during which Olivia could hear the tapping of some keys.

"I think there must have been some mistake," said the woman after a few seconds.

"Mistake?"

"Yes. I'm sorry, Ms Doughthey, but according to this, we were told that your mother had died."

"Died? That's ridiculous," ad-libbed Olivia. "Look, I think I know what's happened. My brother has been given power of attorney and he has probably closed the account. His high-handed dealing with my mother's affairs has been extremely upsetting, especially when she's quite capable of looking after herself."

"I'm afraid that there's nothing I can do at this end," said the woman.

"I know," said Olivia. "It's my damn brother!" She let her voice level rise to keep the woman onside. "He really pushes too far at times. I'll take my mother to the local branch and deal with it."

Olivia sat back in the driver's seat of her car and stared through the window. Damn, that was one half of her safety net gone. She knew it would have to happen one day; after all, Catherine was eighty-six.

Knowing she'd be hard pushed to mimic an old lady, even over the phone, she'd given Catherine's daughter Rose's name to the bank's call centre. She'd better check that Rose was still in this world too — it was essential to Olivia's contingency plans that she didn't shuffle off just yet.

And what about Grace, that sweet little old lady she had used for so many years? She was now eighty-four; she'd better still be alive.

Checking the time, she realised that she needed to get back to the afternoon's grind. First thing in the morning she'd drive over to Pateley Bridge to find out exactly what had happened to Catherine. She could make some excuse to Hawkins later.

All through the afternoon, Olivia tried to reassure herself that if Catherine really had died it was a minor inconvenience, nothing that couldn't be solved. It was time she made some more up-to-date arrangements anyway. Why was it then that she had a hollow feeling in her gut, a sensation of the thread she had so carefully spun beginning to fray as it unravelled?

The following morning, Olivia left her house in the Nottingham suburb of Wollaton at seven. Little did she realise that as she approached the M1 junction 26 slip road at seven fifteen to head north, Jennifer Cotton was three cars ahead of her, about to head south to Trowell Services for her meeting with Peter Hawkins.

The first thing she noticed when she pulled up outside the cottage that until recently had belonged to Catherine Doughthey was the North Yorkshire Properties 'For Sale' sign by the gate, together with a garden returning to nature. A quick glance through the windows removed any final doubts: the house was empty; Catherine Doughthey must be dead. Nevertheless, Olivia wanted to hear it from the horse's mouth, the most convenient horse being in the estate agent's local office near the bridge over the river Nidd at Pateley Bridge.

"Serenity Cottage, madam? Lovely property and in top condition for its age," said the keen young salesman whose name badge identified him as Mervyn. He stood to reply to Olivia's enquiry, his smile all encouragement as he held out his hand, delighted to have a customer so early in the day.

Indifferent to his enthusiasm, Olivia ignored the hand.

"The garden seems rather overgrown," she replied. "How long has it been empty?"

"Let me see," said the salesman as he tapped on his keyboard, an action that immediately lost him many points in Olivia's inflexible book. Having details of all his properties at his fingertips shouldn't mean having to use those fingertips to tap on a keyboard; they should be in his head. What else had he got to do?

"Two months," beamed the young man, oblivious to Olivia's unspoken criticism and dark looks. "The previous owner died and her son inherited the cottage. But he had no use for it so it's up for sale. Between you and me, I think he'd accept well below the asking price," he added with a knowing wink.

Not from what I remember of Geoffrey Doughthey, thought Olivia.

Grace Taverner was sitting in an armchair with her second cup of tea of the morning listening to Radio Two, Languid's preferred station. She frowned when the sharp knock sounded on her front door.

"I don't think we're expecting anyone, are we Languid?" she said as she put down her cup and saucer. The pampered feline's self-satisfied purring didn't miss a beat.

Grace stood and tottered into the hallway.

"Hello, Grace," said Olivia as the front door opened.

"Diana! What a surprise! Oh, how lovely. Come in, come in. Why didn't you call? Languid, look who it is."

Languid looked up and immediately pulled his lips back in a snarl, the fur on his head rising. All his animal instincts told him this human was not to be trusted, never had been.

"Languid!" chastised Grace, "That's no way to behave."

Olivia gave a mirthless laugh. "I shouldn't worry, Grace, for some reason your cat has never liked me. His predecessor didn't either."

"Sit yourself down, dear, I'll put Languid in the kitchen. He's very naughty. Would you like some tea?"

"Thanks, Grace, that would be perfect."

"When did you arrive? In England, I mean," called Grace from the kitchen.

"A week ago," Olivia called back. "I couldn't get up here before. Quite a lot to do in London."

"Oh, I hope you haven't gone to any trouble," said Grace putting a cup and saucer on the coffee table. "But, you know, it's so nice to see you, dear. Would you like a biscuit? Or perhaps some lemon cake? I made it yesterday, my special recipe."

"Not at the moment, Grace, I'm still full from breakfast. Sit down and tell me all the news."

Grace's face fell as she remembered the most important news.

"Oh, dear, I've such sad news, I'm afraid. It's about Catherine. I'm sorry to say that she passed away two months ago. It was very peaceful. The doctor said it was in her sleep. Best way, don't you think? Just nod off and not wake up. I hope I go like that, when my time comes. Although I don't know what Languid would do."

Starve to death, for all I care, thought Olivia.

"Grace, that's so sad. You two were such close friends. What's happened to the house?"

"Geoffrey couldn't put it on the market fast enough, horrible man. He sold everything in it he could, and what he couldn't sell, he threw away. He has no soul, that one."

"What about Rose?"

"I don't think she really understood any of it. According to Geoffrey, she didn't seem to register her mother's death."

"But she's OK otherwise?"

"Oh, yes. Happy in her own little world, poor thing."

Grace spent the next ten minutes chatting inconsequentialities while she bustled in and out of the kitchen fetching more tea and the lemon cake. Languid hovered by the door scowling at Olivia. Not only was her very presence an affront but also she was sitting on his sofa.

Olivia was beginning to feel reassured that nothing worse than the inconvenience of losing Catherine Doughthey's credit card had happened when Grace gasped and looked up from her tea.

"Oh, Diana, I nearly forgot, what with all our chitchat. A most interesting thing happened a few days ago."

Olivia frowned, wondering what 'interesting' meant.

"I had a visit from a bank official, a young woman. She wasn't from my bank but the one that we went to for that credit card you use in my name."

"The North Western Bank?" Olivia felt herself tense as she asked the question.

"Yes."

"What did she want?"

"She said she was conducting a customer survey and started asking me about credit cards. I was a little confused because as you know, I don't have a credit card and I don't bank with the North Western Bank. Anyway, she produced some papers she said were my account statements and I'm afraid that I told her that although the card was in my name, it was for you. When I told her why we'd made the arrangement, she seemed quite happy; assured me it wasn't a problem. I hope you don't mind, Diana."

She did mind, she minded very much. She wanted to reach out and wring Grace Taverner's withered neck.

"No harm done, Grace, I'm sure," said Olivia, measuring her tone with care. She didn't want to alarm the old woman. "What else did she say?"

"I told her about the problems you'd encountered here because you live in Australia. She understood the thing about exchange rates, which is just as well because I don't, and she said that she could arrange something if you contacted her. She was very interested in you; she said she'd always wanted to go to Australia. I told her a few things about you, not much, naturally; it wasn't her business."

Grace had decided that the lie was only a small one.

"No harm done, Grace, I'm sure."

"Of course not. She wanted to see your picture."

"Picture?"

"Photograph, I mean. I showed her one of you and me that Martin took in the garden. Do you remember?"

Olivia remembered but she could hardly speak. Her life was getting more difficult by the minute. With effort, she managed the slightest of nods.

Oblivious to the electricity she was generating, Grace blithely continued.

"I thought you would, dear. Of course, we got talking about Catherine too; she thought it was wonderful that you were so kind to her. I showed her a photo of you with Catherine as well."

"Where did you get that?"

"Geoffrey gave me a box with a lot of photos in. It was among those."

"Seems a bit nosey to me, Grace, for a bank official. Did she want anything else?"

"Oh no, dear, she was a sweet girl. Languid really took to her. Although I did think it a bit strange when she called me on the telephone a couple of nights ago. Quite late it was."

"What did she want?"

"Said she was writing her report and thought of me. She asked me about car insurance."

"But you don't drive any more, do you?"

"No, of course not. I told her about my old Morris Minor Traveller and how you used to look after it for me, kept it running long after its time. I told her you were brilliant with cars. She said that she used to have one too, a Traveller, but that mine sounded far better than hers."

Alarm bells were now clanging in Olivia's ears. This was ancient, forgotten information that should remain buried.

"Sounds like this lady and I should talk," said Olivia through clenched teeth. "What was her name? Did she leave a number?"

"Yes, dear, I've got her card over here."

Grace stood and walked over to a desk.

"Where is it? Ah, yes, here we are. She asked me to call her if you made contact; said she'd really like to meet you. I could call her now, if you like."

"That's fine Grace, I can do it." Olivia took out a pen and pad from her bag. "Let me write down the number."

Grace read it from the card. Olivia looked up, waiting.

"And her name?"

"Oh, yes, of course. It was Jennifer Cotton."

# Chapter Thirty-Two

Grace Taverner was still chatting away, oblivious to the bucket of ice-cold water she had flung over her visitor. But hardly a word registered with Olivia; her mind was fully focussed on working out what had happened.

Olivia didn't think like most people, didn't react emotionally to situations that would have most people running scared. Hers was the mind of a cold-blooded, calculating killer who took full advantage of her intelligence, never allowing personal feelings to interfere with the execution of her plans. And if something happened to the detriment of one plan, another would be pulled from the mental pile to replace it.

Confident in her ability to act and react, to adjust, fine tune, realign and move on, Olivia was impervious to worries about being caught. She was too good for that. She spent hours brainstorming, mind mapping, plotting outcomes, second guessing behaviour and formulating plans to cover as many eventualities as she could imagine. Her main reaction to any apparent setback was to collect and analyse all available data, formulate her response and implement a revised way forward. Her contingency planning had, of course, covered the possibility of her being discovered, and she had several avenues she could follow for an exit strategy. That wasn't the issue; she felt confident she could escape. The issue was the how and the why of her discovery, and who should pay the price for getting in her way.

She had to admit that she had underestimated Jennifer Cotton. It had been obvious from the day of the young officer's arrival several months previously that she had a good brain. That she was way above average in her detective skills, with a logical approach to problem solving, only served to enhance the pleasure derived from outwitting her. But what blindsided Olivia, as well as her colleagues, was discovering that Henry Silk, a man so carefully chosen, was Cotton's father. Given that neither Silk nor Cotton knew of their relationship, it wasn't surprising that Olivia hadn't included that scenario in her contingency plans.

If she was honest with herself, Olivia was cross that she had let Silk and Cotton's relationship get the better of her. While she'd taken perverse delight in destroying Cotton's career, she now knew that not having Cotton around to watch had been a mistake. The girl was tenacious and clearly she was going to make every effort to disprove the case against her father.

She sighed silently and looked across at Grace. Her persistent prattle was undermining Olivia's concentration. She needed to get away from this old fool who had inadvertently ruined everything. Her initial reaction was to kill her and her cat. It would be quick and easy; but was it wise? If Grace's body happened to be discovered before Olivia had a chance to cover her tracks, she could be creating trouble for herself. No, for now, there were far more urgent things. Once all the dust had settled, Grace Taverner and her cat's continued existence could be further considered.

With an excuse of a meeting in York that had slipped her mind, Olivia said her goodbyes and left. No sooner had she gone than Languid reclaimed his right to the sofa, but not before he had turned a large number of circles on its cushions to drive away any residual demons.


Olivia hit the road. She needed to get to her house to retrieve some essential things before anyone parked a police car outside it. She was a skilled driver — police driving courses had ensured that —

and if necessary, she had a blue light and siren she could attach to the roof to clear a path through any hold-ups.

As she sped back towards the motorway, she focussed her mind on events. What had put Cotton on to the credit cards? She would have seen the guest list for the Old Nottingham hotel, but that wouldn't have meant anything on its own — Amelia Taverner would have been just one more unknown name on the list. She must have somehow learned of one of the other murders, noticed a similarity, and checked the guest list of the hotel where Olivia's target had stayed. From there an obvious next step would be to search for reports of other prostitute murders with the type of irrefutable evidence that Olivia had provided, cases where the suspect had stayed in a hotel on the night of the murder. If she was good, Cotton would have found five cases, three where Amelia Taverner had stayed in the same hotel as the suspect on the night of the murder, and two where Catherine Doughthey had done the same. If she then traced both names to Pateley Bridge, a visit to dear Grace would almost certainly have confirmed Olivia's connection to both women.

Olivia ran a hand through her short hair and paused. Hair. Blond hair must have been found on Silk's clothing or in his car. The dead prostitute had dyed orange hair, so the blond hairs found might have given Cotton the idea that the real culprit was a woman. She gave a rueful smile; Cotton was a good adversary, there was no doubting that.

What Olivia needed to assess right now was the extent of the damage. Was what Cotton had unearthed enough to ruin her future with the police? Had Cotton already told her ex-colleagues, and more to the point, did they give her theories any credence? Even if she hadn't told the police, she would undoubtedly have discussed what she'd found with Silk and his lawyer. If it worked for the lawyer, he would not be likely to let it go.

But what actual evidence did Cotton have? There was the credit card use and the links to Grace and Catherine, which now meant Grace since Catherine was dead. Grace could also be removed, but killing her at this stage would serve no purpose, apart from the pleasure of wringing her neck, since there were plenty of people still living in Pateley Bridge who knew of Olivia's connection to both Grace and Catherine. And Cotton would almost definitely have made copies of the photos of Olivia with both women. The credit card use in the hotels would be damaging — what possible reason could Olivia give for having been in those hotels at those times and, as a police officer, not reported the fact? That on its own was probably enough to screw her. It didn't of course make her the murderer. What else did they have? — blond hairs they could link to nothing and CCTV footage. Was that a potential problem? Could she be one hundred per cent sure that nothing on any of that footage linked her with Henry in the current case or with the other culprits in the old cases? She'd been careful, very careful, but … However, assuming the CCTV got the police nowhere, she could think of nothing else. Her planning had seen to that.

So she was unlikely to be accused of murder, but her career was probably going down the tubes. Even if it didn't, her present MO was blown: if there was ever another similar killing, her colleagues would have her under the microscope, determined to find a connection between her and the crime.

The motorway traffic was light, enabling her to cruise at the eighty-five mph that was most people's interpretation of the seventy limit. Thank heavens she had checked the credit cards yesterday. If she hadn't, instead of now speeding back to Nottingham, she might be in an interview room in the SCF trying to explain herself to her boss, Peter pig-eyes Hawkins. She obviously couldn't honeytrap him, but that wouldn't prevent her from killing him sometime. The creep was everything she hated in men.

What was the next step? Clearly as recently as yesterday Hawkins knew nothing. Perhaps Cotton's information hadn't gone that far. Perhaps she'd only told McPherson or Hurst and they were sitting on it, trying to dig out more before they presented it to the high-ups. After all, it was dynamite: the idea of a senior female police officer being a potential serial killer would be hard to swallow without good evidence, especially when all the evidence pointed to other people.

Surely if Hawkins had known and was willing to run with it, he would have fabricated some excuse to call Olivia back to the SCF and then hit her with it. She needed to test the waters: call Hawkins on the pretext of apologising for not going into work and not phoning. He was hopelessly transparent most of the time, especially with women. She'd be able to tell immediately what he knew from his tone of voice.

She waited to call until she was almost home. Parking two streets away from her house on Linden Vale, Wollaton, she took her phone from her bag and turned it on. As soon as it powered up, it started pinging messages and 'missed call' texts. Whoops! They'd been trying to contact her all morning; Hawkins would be hopping. She brought up her contacts list and found his number. But before she could press the call button, the phone rang and Hawkins' name appeared on the screen. She decided to attack, to swamp him.

"Sir, I'm so terribly sorry. I'm covered in confusion. I have literally just remembered that my phone was turned off. When I turned it on and found all the missed calls, I had to sit down before I fell down. I don't know what to say except that I've been totally distracted by a family crisis."

"Where the hell are you, Detective Superintendent Freneton? Absence without permission is a serious matter, as you well know."

"I'm in Exeter, sir. I drove down here last night."

"What are you doing in Exeter?"

"It's my aunt, sir, my mother's sister. You probably don't know that my mother died when I was born and her sister brought me up. She's effectively been my mother all my life."

"Is she ill?"

"Yes, sir. Very. I got a call yesterday lunchtime when I was on a break from the meeting at HQ. It was from my cousin, her son. He's about the same age as I am. He told me she'd had a massive stroke and fallen down some stairs, and that she was in hospital in an ICU about to go in for an operation. I told him I'd get down as soon as I possibly could, but that I had important commitments for the afternoon. I left at five and drove straight down here. I didn't think to call; I was so preoccupied with worry. And as soon as I got to the hospital I was ordered to switch off my phone. I was up all night waiting for my aunt to come round from her operation. She did, finally, at six this morning and, amazingly," — Olivia let her voice break — "she recognised me."

She paused briefly to let her display of false emotion take effect on her boss, and then continued.

"The doctors think she's going to be ok, but apparently there's a distinct possibility of more strokes. I'm afraid that having spoken to her, I put my head down on a couch in the waiting area and I crashed out. I only woke up ten minutes ago and then remembered about my phone."

A deep sigh from Hawkins sounded in Olivia's ear. Had she been convincing?

"I'm very sorry to hear about your aunt, Olivia. But I must say I'm staggered that you overlooked calling in. Besides being against protocol, it's completely out of character."

"If you decide to discipline me, sir, I'd quite understand. I don't have a sensible excuse; I panicked. It's not a feeling I'm used to and it took me totally by surprise. I don't know what else to say."

"We can talk about that later. How long will you have to stay in Exeter?"

"Well, I need to check with the doctor on how she's been doing this morning, but if necessary, I can be back in the office late this afternoon. Is there something pressing that needs my attention apart from briefing DCI Hurst on the robbery operation we're planning next week?"

There was a pause that was slightly too long as Hawkins decided on the best strategy. He wanted her back, but not immediately, not while they were tying up the remaining evidence. But he didn't want to alert her and risk losing her.

"There's, er … no need to hurry back. It's a long way. You've been under a lot of pressure. The raids for the robbery investigation are late next week. Monday will be fine to get everything up to speed. Why don't you take your time, Olivia, make sure that your mother, sorry, aunt, is ok."

Another pause, this one definitely too long, followed by an over-cautiously voiced question.

"Which hospital did you say you were in?"

I didn't, thought Olivia, and there's only one reason you'd be interested. You know something, perhaps not everything, but enough to want to put a tail on me. A watershed moment, Peter Hawkins, thank you.

"It's the Royal Devon, sir," she said, pleased that she knew the name of Exeter's main hospital.


As soon as he put the phone back on its cradle, Hawkins yelled for his DCI. "Mike, in here. Now!"

Hurst bustled through the door while Rob McPherson, who had also heard the shout, hovered in the corridor.

"You too, Rob," beckoned Hawkins.

"What is it, sir?" asked Hurst.

"I've just spoken to Freneton."

"She called in?"

"No, I called her for about the tenth time this morning and she finally answered."

"Where is she?"

"Exeter."

"What in all that's wonderful is she doing there?"

"'S'what I said. She told me she was called away urgently yesterday because her aunt was in an ICU after a fall. Life-threatening, it would seem."

"And that prevented her from calling in?"

"Said she panicked, couldn't think straight. She had to turn off her phone in the ICU and forgot to turn it back on."

"Sounds like a load of bollocks, sir," grunted McPherson. "I can't imagine Freneton panicking about anything and I certainly can't imagine her forgetting about her phone."

"You could be right, Rob. It was an interesting call; she was unusually polite, calling me 'sir', which she seldom does unless she wants something. Let's check it out. Get onto the Royal Devon hospital ICU and check if there's an elderly female patient there who was admitted yesterday after a massive stroke and a fall. Mike, call personnel. Tell them you have my authority. I want to know if it's on record that Freneton's mother died when she was born and that she was brought up by an aunt."

Olivia tossed her phone onto the passenger seat. For thirty seconds she sat motionless as the details of what she now intended to do played out in her mind. This is what she loved about contingency planning: it was all there, pre-ordained. All she had to do was go through the checklist.

She started her car and drove towards her house. But when she reached the end of her road — one of many that led onto the main road through the featureless estate — she drove slowly past, her eyes scanning in all directions. There were no police cars and no stationary anonymous saloons with passengers trying to look casual. She continued her circuit around the block and entered her road from the far end. As she approached her house, she pressed a button on the dash and the garage door swung open. Within thirty seconds, the door was closed again, her car now hidden within the garage, and Olivia was entering the house through a side door.

If Hawkins is good, she thought, I've got about ten minutes before a squad car shows up. But he isn't good; he's fat and slow, so I've probably got at least an hour, maybe all day. But let's not push the luck.

She ran upstairs and pulled open a wardrobe door in her bedroom. Inside was a holdall containing all she required for setting up another male victim, and a rucksack with essential documents for her escape. Everything else in the house was expendable; she wouldn't be returning. The apartment in West Bridgford near Trent Bridge had all she needed for now, the apartment that wasn't rented in her name, the apartment that no one knew about.

She peeled off her clothes to her underwear while she glanced through the window to the street. Nothing. She reached into the wardrobe and pulled out a pair of leather motorcycling trousers and a snugly fitting leather jacket, both black. She quickly put them on, grabbed her bags and without a backward glance ran back to the garage where she dropped the bags into one of the boxes at the rear of her top-of-the-range BMW K1300 GT.

She sat astride the bike, pressed the starter and its powerful engine purred into life — Olivia hated motorbikes that needed to make a statement; this beauty never roared. Thirty seconds later, as the garage door closed onto its magnetic locks, she was gone.

## Chapter Thirty-Three

After her meeting in Trowell Services on Friday morning, Jennifer followed Peter Hawkins' instructions and went home to await events. She tried to contact Henry but was told that she had to make an appointment to call at a specific time and that there were no more slots until Monday. So she called Charles Keithley and briefed him.

"I think that as Henry's solicitor I'll have more luck getting through, Jennifer," Keithley informed her once he'd listened to her letting off steam. "But there's not a lot to say until the police have finished their latest enquiries."

Jennifer was frustrated. "I know that Charles, but I want Henry to know that we are making progress, that we're trying everything." She couldn't hide the desperation in her voice.

"He knows, Jennifer, he knows full well, and he's very upbeat about it. Look, why don't you call me later once you've heard from your contacts."

Keithley's attempt at reassurance didn't help. After two more hours of pacing the floor and getting aggressive with her vacuum cleaner, Jennifer had to get some air. With her mobile strapped to her arm and set up to receive calls from her house phone in addition to normal calls, she hit The Park's roads with an intensity that surprised even her. When an hour of sprints and jogs still left her tense, she moved to her bike. It was a damp day and the roads were slippery. Twice she hit her brakes too hard approaching a corner at a more than sensible speed, and twice she only just managed to stay upright as she slithered to a halt.

On the second occasion, her weak smile to a concerned dog walker radiated guilt — if she hadn't stopped in time, she might have flattened the small poodle that was now eyeing her suspiciously.

"Sorry," she said, her voice sounding pathetic to her ears.

Finally, shortly after five o'clock, her mobile rang.

"Jen, hi, it's me."

"Derek, I've been climbing the walls. Is there any progress?"

"Yeah, a bit. I've just been to see Hawkins with the records from Amelia Taverner's credit card statement, and Catherine Doughthey's. They're pretty much as expected. The current accounts are interesting. There are occasional injections of funds — presumably to cover the card bills — that are from an Isle of Man account in a name that doesn't mean anything. The bank reckons it'll be hard to trace."

"Same source for both accounts?" asked Jennifer.

"Yup."

"Good. Every little helps. And despite what they say, they might be traceable. Anything else?"

"Yeah, it seems that Hawkins spoke to Freneton."

"Why shouldn't he speak to her?"

"I mean he spoke on the phone. She didn't turn up this morning and according to McPherson, Hawkins was hopping. She'd had her phone switched off."

"Interesting."

"It gets better, Jen."

Derek relayed the information that Hawkins had given him about the call.

"Took them a while to check everything, but apparently personnel had nothing on record about an aunt, only info on Freneton living with her father until he was killed. And according to the hospital in Exeter, there were no cases yesterday that fitted the description Freneton gave. No old ladies who'd fallen down stairs following a stroke." He gave a dry laugh. "McPherson was wild. Apparently the hospital wouldn't tell him anything; he had to call the local nick and persuade them to go in person to the ICU. So it took a while to get the info."

"People are scared of their own shadows these days," snorted Jennifer scathingly. "Listen, how certain is Hawkins that she was actually calling from Exeter?"

"Good point, Jen. I think he took that info at face value. Maybe she was actually waving at him from across the street."

"It's checkable," replied Jennifer.

"Phone company?"

"Exactly."

"Right, Jen, I'm on it. Call you back."

Realising that it was unlikely that Derek would be calling back immediately with data from the telephone company — this was the real world, not the movies — Jennifer decided that distraction was the best option. She poured herself a glass of a particularly delicious cabernet from the Fabrelli vineyards and curled up in her armchair with Dante. Hours later, she awoke in total darkness. It was midnight; there was no way Derek would be calling tonight.

"Jesus, Derek, how long does a phone trace take?" was Jennifer's demanding response to Derek's call late the following morning.

"It's the weekend Jen. I had to call in a couple of favours not to have the request deferred until Monday. Anyway, listen, you were right, and when I told Hawkins he yelled at me for not thinking of it sooner."

"Gratitude or what?"

"Yeah, my reaction too. You'd think he'd be pleased to hear that Freneton was in Nottingham when she called him pretending she was in Exeter."

"Where in Nottingham?"

"Close to her house, but she's not there now, I've been round to do a spot of unauthorised snooping. Found the side door to the garage was unlocked. Her car's there but there's no one home."

"You knocked, of course."

"No, Jen, I stood in the road shouting her name. Of course I bloody knocked. And rang the bell. And called her house phone. I could hear it ringing from outside, but there was no answer. She's not there."

"But her car is; that's interesting. Have you called the DVLA to check if she has more than one vehicle licensed in her name?"

"You think she's done a runner?"

"Dunno; she might've. She's nothing if not anal when it comes to planning, and a vehicle unknown to us would give her a head start. If Hawkins is serious about her, it might be worth putting her on the stop list in case she tries to leave the country."

"Probably wouldn't use her own name, Jen."

"No, you're right. The stop list should perhaps include Amelia Taverner's name, and Catherine Doughthey's."

## Chapter Thirty-Four

While Jennifer Cotton had been curled up with Dante, a few miles away in her apartment in West Bridgford Olivia Freneton was planning her endgame.

She had reviewed once again everything she knew the police would have on her, and, having considered it all, she was satisfied that it still didn't amount to much. Certainly not enough for a prosecution, maybe not enough for her job to be at risk. However, she'd made her decision and she had grudgingly accepted it. There would be no going back. Literally. She wouldn't be gracing the offices of the SCF ever again.

But she certainly wasn't going to go without some payback. Hawkins and his team didn't have enough to pin the Henry Silk case on her, nor the others, and with what she was planning, there would soon be another case on their desks that wouldn't be attributable to her either. How frustrating for them. They'd know full well she was the culprit rather than the sucker all the evidence pointed to, the one who'd soon be sleeping through the night at the Fields View Hotel in West Bridgford while Olivia was out on his behalf disposing of another prostitute. Both Hawkins and Hurst were close to retirement; how sad for them to disappear to their respective gardens under clouds of incompetence.

She hadn't planned to carry out another disposal so soon after the Henry Silk one — any more than one a year would have risked connections being made. But now her scheme was blown she'd be hard pushed to use it again and have the blame fall on the target; the police would be wise to her technique. So this last disposal was purely for the intellectual satisfaction of carrying it out under their noses. It would take a couple of days of careful planning — it must be executed with the same level of skill and attention to detail as the others. She had a list of potential targets, well-known creeps that she'd love to destroy — a High Court judge, a clergyman and a squeaky-clean pop star among them. However, none was conveniently placed. She wanted a target in Nottingham and the easiest way would be to check in to the Fields View Hotel and wait in the bar in her long blond wig and business gear. There was bound to be some guileless, testosterone-driven hero looking to make a pick-up. It was all too easy.

She tossed her list of long-term targets back onto the desk where she was sitting and drummed her fingers on its surface. Despite her supreme self-control, she could feel an anger rising. Her brilliant scheme had been destroyed and along with the pleasure of ridding the world of more useless men, she would miss the pleasure of outwitting her colleagues time after time.

She thought back over how her personal vendetta against the male of the species had progressed. She had come a long way from her first blooding — the disposal of her foul, disgusting father, the man who had abused her repeatedly when she was too young to understand or resist, the man who had made her realise that all men were no better than animals. The attitude of most women didn't help either, taking daily mental abuse, if not physical, from their men, seldom knowing what their spouses were up to when not at home: she'd never met a man who couldn't be tempted to stray with a little persuasion. As for the women who died directly at Olivia's hand, they were utter filth, which was why she had chosen them as the victims of her schemes. Their deaths impacted on no one; they were nothing.

With many more victims under her belt than the five prostitutes, Olivia had honed her skills for many years, learning by her mistakes, polishing her technique, never compromising on quality, never allowing herself to be completely satisfied with her performance — although she had to admit it: she was pretty damn-near perfect, a master craftswoman, an expert in her specialist field.

She was proud of her achievements over the years, even in the early days. After disposing of her father and realising she had a taste for more, she had experimented with a couple of other disposals.

The first was a teacher at the school she was put in when she went to live in Pateley Bridge with the naïve Grace Taverner. He'd been easy. Something of a hunk, he fancied himself and was known to be screwing around, despite having a young wife and child. Bastard. It had been so easy. He was a runner who loved to roam the Dales. Plenty of places there, plenty of reservoirs and reservoir dam walls. All she had to do was find out his favourite route and wait. He knew her of course, so she had to be sure to kill him.

Pretending she was injured, that she'd twisted her ankle, she sat and waited by a reservoir wall until he came along. There was no one around. He'd stopped, checked her ankle — rather too far up her leg for her liking — chatted her up and even tried a grope as he helped her to her feet. She'd knocked him out with a rock, undone one of his shoelaces to make it look like he'd tripped, scuffed his bare knees on a rough stone, and tipped him over the edge, making sure his head would hit something on the way down to the water. Easy. Accidental death, said the coroner. No suspicious circumstances.

Then there were the two students she'd hitched a lift with when she was travelling around Europe in one of her university vacations. Thought they'd struck gold with her until their van plunged down a ravine in Greece with them in it, her father's skills put to good use again. She loved the power, the sense of supremacy, the total control over when and where a man's life would end.


Following her early experiments, she had soon developed a

yearning to catch bigger fish, and once the idea of adopting the identities that went with credit cards had occurred, she had the makings of a long term plan, so long as Grace Taverner and Catherine Doughthey were in agreement, and, of course, alive.

That the game she played was dangerous was part of the attraction. Killing someone was easy; pitting her wits against society in general and her colleagues in particular raised the thrill level immeasurably. This was why she had become a police officer. Her training had given her unparalleled insight into the system, specialist knowledge and training, and it was the perfect cover. She was hidden in plain view. Who would suspect a high-flying police officer, especially a woman, even if she was a bitch to work with?

Her police career had also taught her much about forensics. Of course she could always have read about it — she was clever and had a good scientific understanding, but the on-the-ground experience of courses in labs and talks by scientists was far better. She'd worked out how to plant the right amount of evidence, she'd learned about drugs and she was thrilled to discover that Rohypnol was perfect for her use. She'd acquired stock enough to last her for many years.

When she started with her plans for framing her targets, the UK's DNA database was like manna, a wonderful gift. Under the rules applying at that time, anyone arrested for a recordable offence — a crime you could potentially go to prison for, which was most of them — would have their DNA profile added to the national database forever, or so it seemed at the time. All she had to do was establish that a target had been arrested for something minor, normally drink driving, then get hold of his DNA and plant it.

The obvious choice for DNA was semen that she'd put into the vagina of the prostitute the man would be charged with killing — a messy business she didn't enjoy for one moment. Not so much putting it in the girls — that was easy using a syringe with no needle attached — but the getting hold of it. For that she'd had to have sex with the man using a condom, keep the condom without his knowledge and then plant the semen in the girl the same night while the target was out cold from Rohypnol. The first couple of attempts were disastrous. The sex was easy, although as always she hated it, but administering the drug hadn't worked as it should: one target had simply walked away. However, practice makes perfect.

Then the law changed. All the DNA for minor offences was thrown away meaning she could no longer rely on the initial link to the suspect coming from that sort of evidence. She'd actually been quite relieved since she increasingly hated the sexual side of her activities. She had started to take advantage of the CCTV systems that these days were everywhere, disguising herself in the clothes of her target and making sure she appeared on camera. Once the link had been made, there was the fibre and fingerprint evidence she'd plant and then, to gild the lily, some DNA. In the Henry Silk case, the use of a mannequin hand with false nails had been sheer brilliance. She'd fully intended to use that again, and she would, one last time. But that didn't allay her anger at being discovered, nor the need for the discoverer to pay. There was no doubting it: Jennifer Cotton was too clever by half.

While she was a formidable adversary against whom Olivia would enjoy pitting her wits, this sort of battle was all about winning, and you can only win once; the ultimate victory. Jennifer Cotton had to die and Olivia would delight in making her death painful, the end lasting long enough for the girl to appreciate fully that while brains were one thing, ruthless cunning was something else entirely.

She would make Jennifer Cotton the finale to her spree, call at her house in The Park after she'd dispatched the hapless prostitute and planted all the evidence on sucker from the bar at the hotel on Tuesday evening. She'd talk her way in, overcome the girl and spend a few hours watching her die slowly, enjoying every moment of her anguish.

But before killing Cotton, and before making her plans for the Fields View Hotel, there was the first part of her killing spree to organise. She had been tempted to leave it out, leave Henry Silk alive and let the joy of his now-inevitable release from prison be shattered when he learned of the death of his daughter.

However, her original plan for Henry was better. He had to die too, and he would be the first to go.

# Chapter Thirty-Five

At eleven o'clock the following Tuesday morning, Derek Thyme sat back from his computer screen to reread in disbelief the third of three emails that had arrived in rapid succession over the last two minutes.

"Christ on a bike!" he stammered. "I don't believe it."

He swivelled his chair towards Rob McPherson who was, as usual, at war with his own computer, his long-suffering keyboard bearing the brunt of his anger.

"Guv," said Derek, his voice taut with concern. "I think you should take a look at this."

"What is it, Thyme? Can't you see I'm busy?"

"With respect, guv, I think this takes precedence."

"It better be good, Thyme. If what's on my screen disappears into the black hole of cyberspace, I'll be sending you after it."

Ignoring the rant, Derek got out of his chair and indicated to the DI to sit.

McPherson sat while Derek used the mouse to scroll to the first email.

"Read that one, guv, then I'll pull up another."

McPherson grunted as he let his eyes absorb the text.

"Next," he ordered, as he finished reading it.

Derek called up the next one, let McPherson read it, and then clicked on the final one.

"Christ, Thyme, this is serious!" yelled McPherson, jumping from the chair and nearly colliding with Derek. "Have you forwarded it to Hawkins and Hurst?"

"Not yet, guv."

"Never mind. You can brief them directly; it'll be quicker. Come on, man, move it!"

He ran for the door and turned in the direction of the DCS's office, banging on the partition glass of Hurst's office as he ran past.

"Mike! You need to hear this."


Peter Hawkins looked up from his computer as his three officers burst into his office. "Where's the fire, gentlemen?"

McPherson turned to Derek. "Thyme?"

"Yes, guv," answered Derek. He took a step towards Hawkins' desk.

"Sir, a couple of minutes ago, I received the information on the deaths of the other three culprits we now think Detective Superintendent Freneton might have set up, the two who topped themselves and the one killed in a fight in prison."

Hawkins glared at him, but remained silent.

Derek hesitated, then ploughed on. "Well, sir, the thing is that the other party involved in each of them, that is the brawl in which he was deemed to be an innocent victim, and the two suicides, he was the same con."

Hawkins' glower deepened. He hadn't understood a word.

"Any chance you could stop talking in riddles, man?"

"Sorry, sir. The con, his name is Norman Bryan Edmunds, was the other party in the fight in which Timothy Backhouse was killed in Maudslake prison in 2012."

"Why is that important?"

"According to the info I've received this morning, he was known to have befriended Colin Edgerton in Maudslake prison in 2007 shortly before Edgerton hanged himself, and then he shared a cell with Gregory Walters in Sunshore prison in 2009. And Walters didn't hang himself, he OD'd with Rohypnol."

"The drug found in the Bristol case?"

"Yes, sir, and if Silk was set up, it could have been used on him; the symptoms he described would fit."

"How come this Edmunds was moved to Sunshore and then back to Maudslake?"

"He's a lifer, sir, and an extremely violent one. The prison authorities have been experimenting with moving his type around to prevent them from establishing their own fiefdom in a prison."

"You think Freneton had a hand in arranging it?"

"Not sure, sir, but she knows him. She was a detective sergeant in Leeds in 2006 when Edmunds was sent down for murdering two security guards in a warehouse robbery. They were particularly vicious killings. He's serving a minimum of twenty-five years, with no consideration of parole before 2031. Freneton was on the team that put him inside and apparently she conducted most of the interviews."

"With plenty of opportunity for off-the-record heart-to-heart chats," mused Hawkins to himself. "What else do we have on him, Thyme?"

"Not much, sir. He was married — his wife divorced him in 2008. They had one child, a daughter born in 2001 he's apparently very attached to."

Hawkins nodded. "Could be a lever — threaten to harm the daughter. Where is he now?"

"That's the thing, sir. After the fight in Maudslake in 2012, he was transferred to Skipshed."

"Skipshed! That's where Silk is."

"Yes, sir."

McPherson was starting to get agitated. He had seen the emails and needed no convincing of the urgency of their problem.

"Sir," he interrupted. "With respect, I really think we need to act on this. It's true that the deaths of these three cons happened after their trials, between one and a half and two years after, in fact, whereas Silk's case has yet to go to trial. But if Freneton is involved in all these cases and for some reason wants her victims dead, then Silk could be in danger."

"How so?"

"Freneton's disappeared, hasn't she? I mean, she hasn't turned up this morning or yesterday …"

He turned to Hurst whom he knew had been trying to contact her.

Hurst nodded. "That's right. She isn't answering her mobile, in fact, it seems to be turned off. One of the uniforms I sent round to her house earlier called me a few minutes ago to say there's no one there. I was about to contact the techies to see if there's any way of tracing a phone even when it's turned off."

Hawkins shook his head. "There isn't. Don't waste your time."

"The point is, sir," said McPherson, cutting in again, "it would appear that Freneton is aware that we're on to her. Don't know how, but she's nobody's fool, as we well know. If she knows then she'll also realise that the case against Silk will likely be dropped. He'll walk. So there's a chance, if she was planning to have him killed at some stage, either in a fight or by somehow persuading him to top himself, that she will want to do it soon."

"You're right, Rob," said Hawkins as he reached for his phone. "Obviously Edmunds is the danger here. If I get the prison to isolate him immediately, we can get over there and interview him. If he is behind some or all of the other killings, and he's somehow been told by Freneton to kill Silk, then with a bit of persuasion we'll not only prevent the killing, but we might also get something more concrete on Freneton."

He scowled at the phone dial, but changed his mind.

"Ann!" he yelled to his secretary. "Get me the governor of Skipshed prison. Tell him it's extremely urgent, a matter of life and death."

## Chapter Thirty-Six

Norman Edmunds was an uncompromisingly violent man whose very presence radiated aggression. At six foot four and two hundred and fifty pounds, his muscular frame looked as if it would burst through his drab prison garb. His huge head was shaven, what little neck he had rippled with rolls of thick flesh, while his face was that of a prizefighter — a nose that had lost all indication of its original form and heavy, misshapen brows knitted over dark, brooding eyes. His arms were sleeved with tattoos that extended to his neck, lower face and much of the top of his head.

Before Peter Hawkins' arrival, Edmunds was escorted from his cell by two of the biggest guards in Skipshed prison to the special security interview room where his chained wrists were attached to a ring bolted to the floor. The table in front of him was also bolted to the floor, as was the chair on which they sat him. He was never allowed to be with a visitor unmanacled.

Governor Harold Maskerton met Hawkins in the prison's guest car park. They had known each other for many years, serving on various Home Office committees covering law and order, and while they had a certain mutual respect for each other's jobs, they were anything but pals. About the same age, Maskerton was as thin as

Hawkins was fat and slightly shorter. He wore a carefully trimmed beard, grey now with the passing years.

"What do you want with Edmunds, Peter?" he asked as soon as Hawkins climbed out of his car, not bothering with any niceties. "Whatever it is, all you'll be likely to get is his usual barrage of verbal abuse."

"Confidential enquiry, Harold, I'm afraid. It's sensitive, horribly bloody sensitive."

He turned as Rob McPherson walked round from the passenger side of the car. "Do you know DI McPherson, Harold?"

"Don't think we've met," replied Maskerton with the briefest of glances towards McPherson. His eyes returned immediately to Hawkins.

McPherson let the rebuff ride over him, but nevertheless wished he had stayed in the SCF where Mike Hurst was continuing his attempts to contact Olivia Freneton while Derek Thyme was searching out more background on her connections to any other convicts with a violent reputation.

McPherson's reply, directed to the side of Maskerton's head, was voiced with a sharp edge of sarcasm. "No, not had the pleasure."

Maskerton ignored him. "He'll be shackled," he said to Hawkins. "It's the only way he's allowed to see anyone, including his daughter."

"How many guards?" asked Hawkins.

"Two. Why?"

"Do they hover or stand back?"

"Your choice, but I wouldn't have them stand too far back, if I were you. Edmunds can move like lightning for such a big man, even if he is shackled."

"I'll bear it in mind. What I want is to be able to talk to Edmunds in confidence. It might be the only way I can get through to him."

"I can't let the guards leave the room."

"Not asking, Harold. I only want them to keep their distance. I'm thinking of interviewing him on my own, leaving Rob here to enjoy the view of the Derbyshire hills. One police officer with

Edmunds is more than enough — I know how much he hates us."

"He hates any form of authority, Peter. Watch your step; he's a mean bastard."

Norman Edmunds frowned through his deeply furrowed brow as Hawkins entered the interview room and sat opposite him. One corner of his upper lip lifted in a snarl and his broad Birmingham accent cut through the room.

"Wha'd'ya want, copper? You're taking up me valuable exercise time. I gotta keep fit; it's the only way to survive in this shithole."

Hawkins had met plenty like Edmunds during the course of his long career and even though the man was probably the biggest he'd ever faced, he remained unfazed. He deliberately waited ten seconds before replying, his eyes fixed on the bridge of Edmunds' nose.

"Let me put what I want this way, Norman. You answer a few questions to my satisfaction and you can be back with the boys playing snakes and ladders in no time. Waste my time and the interview could drag out for hours. You might miss your playtime altogether."

He paused, waiting for any sign of a reaction, but Edmunds' face didn't flinch.

"It's come to my notice, Norman, that you and I have a mutual friend," he continued, this time speaking quietly so that the guards would find it hard to hear.

"No friends of yours is gonna be a friend of mine," growled Edmunds.

"Oh, you'd be surprised. This one's certainly very close to me, and I suspect she is to you. She works for me, and works hard. My kind of person: doesn't always follow the rule book too closely, if you follow me."

The blank stare in Edmunds' eyes gave no indication whether he'd even heard.

"She was telling me about your family, Norman. Pity about

your wife divorcing you like that. Not very nice for you to think of someone else shacked up with her, sharing her bed. Quite a looker, your wife, from the photos I've seen in your file."

Edmunds' scowl deepened farther and his chains rattled as he clenched his huge fists. The guards, clearly jumpy, edged a step closer, but Hawkins held up his hands, telling them with a sharp glance to stay put. He turned his eyes back to Edmunds.

"And how old would your little girl be now? Let's see. Thirteen, is it? Difficult age for a girl, especially one from your neck of the woods. She could get into all sorts of trouble, meet all the wrong people. Pity that. I've heard she's a bright little thing; pretty too, like her mother."

Edmunds' breathing had become rapid, rasping, the air taking a torturously unnatural path through his nasal passages as a result of all the pounding they'd taken over the years.

Hawkins could now see something else in the convict's eyes. Anger. He was trying to work out what Hawkins was about.

Edmonds suddenly sneered, his mouth coming about as close to smiling as it might. "She's got something on you, copper, ain't she?"

"Your daughter?"

"You know who I mean, copper. She must've sent you here to run her errands. What did the screw say you was? Chief Super? Bit senior to be an errand boy."

He waited to see if his ridicule was having any effect. When Hawkins didn't react, he continued. "Or maybe you've joined her little club. Dish out your own form of justice, do you? Wanting to get suckers like me to do your dirty work. Well, you can forget it, copper. I ain't doing nothing for you."

Hawkins sat back in the uncomfortable chair, shifting his position to accommodate his aching back.

"You were her snitch, weren't you, Norman? Back in Leeds, back before you let your pathetic temper get the better of you with those two security guards. They were Irish, weren't they? Got many paddies in here, have you? Bet they'd love to hear about how much you admire them."

Edmunds snorted. "Don't think a few Micks're gonna worry me, do yer?"

"No, but the Micks might worry your daughter, Norman. Want to make sure that she's educated in the ways of the world, if you follow me."

This time the rattling of the chains was louder.

"You bastards are all the same, ain'tcha. You sound just like her."

Hawkins smiled and held out his arms. "She taught me well, Norman."

Edmunds was no longer listening; his short fuse had burned its length.

"Christ, I'd like to get her on her own in here for five minutes. She might be tall and fancy herself at karate and stuff, but I'd fucking flatten her. She'd be pulp. Her and her fancy name. Olivia Freneton. I'd fucking Olivia her. She'd be pleading for me to kill her."

Hawkins could hardly contain his delight. Edmunds had said her name.

But he needed more.

"Is that right, Norman? Well, you can imagine what would happen to your daughter if you did. Olivia has a long reach."

Hawkins waited again, but Edmunds' head of steam appeared to have fizzled out.

"Eight years, Norman. Eight slow, tedious years. That's a long time to have been doing someone's dirty work. And how much longer will it go on before she decides you're a liability, a danger to her, that you might say something? Like you just did, in fact. She wouldn't be very pleased to hear it, would she? But even if I decide not to tell her, she'll know that you're becoming a risk. You see, Norman, sooner or later, sooner probably, it'll be your name on the ticket. It'll be you someone is waiting for in the shadows, waiting with a sharp knife."

He paused again, letting the silence work for him before continuing more softly.

"I can stop it, you know. Get her off your back."

Edmunds grunted as he worked his mouth, baring his cracked

and broken teeth. "I'd like to see you try. She'd come after you in no time. You'd be easy meat for her."

Hawkins leaned forward, his voice quiet again, his tone conspiratorial.

"How does she get her messages to you, Norman? She wouldn't be seen dead in a place like this."

Hawkins' attempt to feed in the question failed. Edmunds saw through him immediately, his harsh cackle echoing round the room.

"That would be telling, copper. I don't think you know as much as you're pretending." He folded his arms dismissively.

Hawkins tried not to let his annoyance show.

"Maybe, maybe not. But I do know this. You can't say 'no' to her, can you? Otherwise your daughter will be hurt, really hurt. Like I said, Norman, I can stop that. Wouldn't you rather rot in this place knowing that your daughter was under no further threat? What was the threat, anyway? Kill her? Maim her? Have her raped? — passed around a gang until she was pulp? Olivia can do all of that; has done all of that, I can assure you," he lied. "So tell me, how do you get your instructions?"

Edmunds looked away for the first time, dropping his eyes and scratching at the folds of flesh that were his neck. He'd made a decision. This copper was obviously on to her so he might as well protect his back. It was now his turn to speak quietly, not wanting the guards to hear.

"Phone call, phone message actually for these wankers to give me." He nodded towards the guards. "Never speaks directly to me; they won't allow it. Tells them she's my sister. I've got one, yer know. A sister. But when she gives her name, she says the names in the wrong order. Right names, wrong order. The screws ain't rumbled it; they think me sister's a thicko. They're the thickos; stupid shits. Me sister's Maeve Carla Edmunds — always keeps our name even though she gets married from time to time. But when Freneton phones, she says it as Carla Maeve Edmunds. Works every time, not that there have been many times."

"And what about the name of the target? How does she give you that?"

"Target?"

"The con she wants hurt. How does she give you the name? How did she give you Henry Silk's name?"

Hawkins was surprised when Edmunds sat back and threw out another hacking laugh.

"Is that what this is all about, copper? You been pulling my plonker, ain'tcha. Getting me to give you her name. Well, the joke's on you, copper. Henry Fucking Silk? Sorry to tell you, but you're a bit late for that one."

"What do you mean?" demanded Hawkins, suddenly alarmed.

The hacking continued; this was becoming a huge joke for Edmunds.

"Your timing ain't too good, copper." He glanced at a clock over the door. "I should think that Silk's well out of it by now."

Hawkins felt a cold shiver of panic in his spine. "But I checked when I called the prison earlier. He was fine and the governor was told not to let you near him."

Edmunds let out a bellow of laughter as he wiped the saliva from his mouth onto his upper arm.

"How did you ever get so senior, copper? You ain't up to much. You don't think I do all Olivia's dirty work for her myself, do you? She might have something on me, but I got plenty on the cons in here too. And it ain't just these."

He snarled and lifted his arms, closing his fists to tighten his massive biceps.

Suddenly realising he'd said too much, Edmunds changed his tone.

"Anyway, I ain't had no message about Silk. I'm not the only one in here she's got stuff with. But I did hear something. Like I said," — he looked up at the clock again — "bit late now."

He leaned forward and tapped his nose.

Hawkins shot to his feet and yelled at the guard. "Get me out of here! We've got to get to the exercise yard. Move it!"

One of the guards spoke into a radio and the interview room door opened. Hawkins was through it in a flash, the sound of Edmunds' mocking laughter in his ears as he breathlessly forced his out-of-form legs to run along the corridor.

## Chapter Thirty-Seven

Henry Silk was feeling buoyant following a call over the weekend from Charles Keithley with the news from Jennifer. Keithley was convinced that the police would soon recommend that the CPS drop all charges. He had nevertheless had to counsel Henry to be patient, telling him the wheels would inevitably move slowly despite his frequent calls insisting on urgent consideration of Henry's case.

"Stay calm, Henry," he'd said before ringing off, his voice all encouragement and positivity. "I'm beginning to see light at the end of the tunnel."

As the row of prisoners shuffled into the exercise yard, Henry took a deep breath and smiled. A warm breeze was blowing from the nearby Pennine foothills as the sun broke through the ambling clouds. He thought he could even hear birdsong. Certainly not a day to be confined in a prison, but at least the afternoon exercise schedule would remind him a little of the freedom that would soon be his.

The forty prisoners broke from the line and, creatures of habit, headed for their preferred positions, some to natter in conspiratorial tones, some to swagger, some to cut deals, some to play basketball. Others, Henry included, preferred their own company, walking the perimeter of the fenced area like caged animals maximising their space.

Henry normally kept his distance. He didn't want to get close to either the convicts or the remand prisoners, most of whom would soon also be convicts. He refused to succumb to their mindset, their acceptance of their sentences and the inevitability of years of mind-numbing boredom. To do so would be to give up, to take the road to conformity and become institutionalised. Once on that road, life was a downward spiral, one that led inexorably to a world far removed from the world outside the fence. He'd spoken to cons who had been behind bars for ten or more years. To a man, they were dulled, their intellects scrambled, their comprehension of the ever-changing, vibrant and dynamic pace of life outside lessened with every passing year. It was no wonder that those who had served long sentences found reintegration with modern life bewilderingly difficult. He sympathised with them, but he was determined never to become one of them.

Now his head was full of the possibility of imminent and permanent freedom. He would get his life back and maybe some sympathy vote for a change. He might even get some decent parts. And the wonderfully positive thing to arise from his ordeal: the discovery that he had a daughter; the lovely, intelligent and tenacious Jennifer. Without her, he would be doomed to an unbearable life, knowing he was innocent but never able to prove it. He couldn't wait to get to know her properly, to be part of her world and she part of his.

A soft, apologetic voice jarred him from his reverie as he paced the compound.

"Henry."

It was Horace Turnbull, the unctuous, former bank manager with whom he shared his cell. Turnbull was serving seven years for defrauding his bank and a number of its customers of three hundred thousand pounds over several years.

Starstruck, he couldn't believe his luck in having been put in a cell with what he liked to describe as a major player in the entertainment world. He seemed to think that his crimes had almost been worth it just to rub shoulders with someone so famous. Henry had tried to put him straight, and when that hadn't worked, had scolded him for aiming his sights too low.

"Christ, Horace, if you're going to defraud, to steal, at least make it worth your while. How long do you think that a few paltry hundreds of thousands would have lasted? You should have been looking at millions. Many millions."

Horace had explained that it had all been for his demanding wife and high-maintenance daughter.

"A dear girl, Henry, and one who never misses an episode of 'Runway'. A constant and devoted fan."


"Henry," repeated Horace, his tone now more urgent.

Henry stopped and looked down at the little man. "What is it, Horace?"

Horace raised an arm and pointed to a group of large men standing near a basketball hoop.

"They want to talk to you."

Henry looked towards the group.

"What do they want?"

"They want you to join their game."

"The last time I joined them I ended up sprawled on the ground with a cut lip. Tell them … wait a minute, why are you their messenger boy?"

"They all had their heads together discussing something in hushed tones when I was walking past. Suddenly an arm reached out and grabbed me, yanked me in amongst them. That big one, the one at the front with the racist tattoos on his arms and hands, he told me they wanted you to play, told me to get my fat arse over here to tell you. Could you teach me to box, Henry? I'd like to flatten him."

Henry smiled grimly at the thought. "I've told you to keep your distance, Horace. They are not nice people."

He lifted his arms toward the group, mimed throwing a basketball and shook his head to tell them, no, he didn't want to join them.

"I should stay on this side of the compound, Horace, if I were you," said Henry as he turned his back on the group and walked away.

Within seconds, a huge hand grabbed his shoulder.

"Didn'tcha get me message, Silky boy?"

The con's other hand spun Horace around.

"What did you tell him, pansy?"

Henry looked at the hand on his shoulder. The words 'White Supremacy' were tattooed across the back against an array of burning crosses.

"Leave him alone," snarled Henry. "He gave me your message, but I don't want to play."

He pushed the man's hand away.

Tattooed Hand's eyes caught Horace's. "Hop it, creep."

Horace slunk away through a group of six heavily built men who had materialised to form a loose circle around Henry.

"Seen you playing, Silky boy," said Tattooed Hand. "You got a good eye. Want you on me team."

Two of the group started bouncing basketballs, the threat in their eyes compounded by the synchronisation of the bouncing.

Henry's eyes flitted back and forth between them, then he glanced at Tattooed Hand. As he did, one of the ball bouncers hurled his ball at him, catching him off guard and hitting him hard in the chest. The ball rolled away.

"Whoops!" said Tattooed Hand. "That wasn't so good; thought you was better than that. Looks like you need some practice."

Without any warning, the second bouncing basketball was hurled at Henry. Henry reached out an arm to deflect it, but the arm was yanked to one side. Again the ball thumped into Henry's chest.

He turned angrily to Tattooed Hand.

"Let me go and I'll catch it. Otherwise find someone else for your team."

The man sneered his reply. "Didn't quite get that, Silky boy. Still want some practice, did you say?"

Out of the corner of his eye, Henry saw yet another ball flying in his direction. His responses were good and he got both hands up, only to find them grabbed and pulled away. For the third time, a ball thumped into Henry's chest.

"For Christ's sake, man, what's your problem? Do you want me to play or not?"

The man's sneer immediately twisted into a black, threatening grimace.

"You accusing me of something, actor boy?"

Henry shook his head in disgust and turned away, only to find his shoulder grabbed again as the man's hand spun him round.

"I'm talking to you, actor boy. Show me some respect."

Henry had had enough. He turned and faced the man, his hands on his hips.

"What's the issue, Cuthbert?" He spat the man's name derisively.

A cloud of fury descended over Tattooed Hand's features. He poked a meaty index finger into Henry's chest.

"You don't never use that name, d'you hear me. Never! No one calls me by that name!"

Out of the corner of his eye, Henry noticed that the group of large men had now tightened the circle around him, blocking him and Tattooed Hand from the view of the guards. Tattooed Hand delivered a second vicious poke to Henry's chest, sending him staggering backwards. As he tried to regain his footing, another strong pair of hands pushed him forward so that he almost fell into Tattooed Hand.

"That wasn't very polite, actor boy. You picking a fight?"

Aware that he was being set up, Henry crouched slightly and raised his fists in defence.

"If that's what you want, Cuthbert, come and get it. But make it just you and me."

This time, Tattooed Hand ignored the forbidden use of his name. He threw his head back with a laugh. Suddenly, with a slight flick of his wrist, there was a knife in his hand.

Henry instinctively took a step backward, but a foot appeared in his path and he fell heavily onto his back.

He looked up from the ground to see Tattooed Hand nod to the circle of men. They immediately began jeering loudly as they closed the circle even more tightly. One kicked at Henry as Tattooed Hand casually knelt down over Henry and raised the knife.

A series of piercing electronic squawks suddenly filled the exercise yard followed moments later by a coarsely amplified voice screaming over a loudhailer.

"Stop! All of you! Boyston! Put down that knife!"

The group of men melted away, heads down, doing their best to blend in with the horrified group of prisoners in the exercise yard. They could all now see Henry lying on his back, his hands and arms held protectively in front of him as Tattooed Hand knelt with the knife still poised in the air above him.

"Drop it, Boyston! NOW!"

Tattooed Hand's eyes were fixed in hatred on Henry's as he calculated whether to carry out what would clearly be a fully witnessed murder, or to stop.

His hand wavered slightly, and then he slung the knife to the ground. Within moments, a group of guards had dragged him off Henry, thrown him face down on the ground and handcuffed his wrists behind his back.

"He started it," yelled Tattooed Hand. "The actor started it. Ask anyone."

His reward was to have his face jammed firmly into the concrete.

## Chapter Thirty-Eight

"He was what!" yelled Jennifer down the phone to Derek. She was close to tears after having listened to the account of the thwarted attempt on Henry's life.

"Tell me he's fine, Derek. Tell me! They should release him immediately. Every minute more spent in that place puts him at risk. Don't they realise that?"

"It's OK, Jen, he's not injured in any way. Like I told you, the guards got to him in time," said Derek, trying to reassure her for the third time. "He's been isolated and the boss is onto the CPS. He'll be out of there soon."

"Not soon enough," snapped Jennifer.

Derek waited. He heard her take several deep breaths, followed by a sigh.

"Sorry, Derek, you don't deserve my wrath; you deserve a medal. If you hadn't brought those emails to the high-ups' attention straight away, Henry would be dead by now."

"Yeah," mumbled Derek, now embarrassed by her praise, "it was a near thing. My opinion of Hawkins has gone up enormously. He's not just the fatty sitting on his arse in his office I thought he was."

"I'm sure your badgering helped," said Jennifer, still not totally convinced about the DCS.

"Actually it was Rob McPherson's badgering; he's the one that kicked the boss into gear."

"Perhaps you can give him a hug from me, then."

"I think he'd break my arms if I tried. Anyway, you can do it yourself. The other reason I called is to tell you they want another meeting."

"Really? Why? Surely they believe me after all that's happened?"

"I'm not sure, what the meeting's about, I mean. All I know is that about half an hour after Hawkins and McPherson got back, Hawkins yelled for Hurst. There was a bit of a barney, judging from the noise, then McPherson was called in. Ten minutes later McPherson comes to me and tells me that it's now OK to call you and tell you what's happened, and that they want to see you."

Jennifer ground her teeth. "I'll forget for the moment that I was left out of the loop when Henry, *my father*, was in danger—"

"They told me specifically not to call you, or to tell you if you called, Jen," interrupted Derek. "Anyway, there was nothing you could have done, and any delay …" He let the point hang in the air.

"Yes, you're right of course," said Jennifer, now all contrition. "Sorry." She took another deep breath. "OK, this meeting. Do they want to go to Trowell again? False moustache and dark glasses?"

"Actually, Jen, they're getting beyond that. They want to come round to your place."

"Who's they? And when?"

"All of them. Hawkins' confidential team. Hawkins, Hurst and McPherson. They want me to bring them round. Like, now."

"Who's manning the phone for your secret squad?" said Jennifer, ever covering bases.

"Bottomley's been brought on board. He didn't know whether to be angry that he'd been left out initially or happy to be in on getting Freneton. Anyway, he'll be holding the fort in the office."

"Bet he'll be telling everyone too. He's a bit of a blab."

"Hawkins threatened to wring his neck personally if he says a word."

Jennifer smiled at the thought.

"You haven't said why they want to see me, Derek. What's happened beyond the attempt on Henry's life?"

"Hawkins would only say that they wanted a powwow, pronto."

"Powwow? What is he, the Lone Ranger? I'll bet he has a secret stash of cowboy movies."

When Mike Hurst's car, driven by Derek, pulled up outside Lincoln View House. Jennifer buzzed the main gate and her front door and waited while the four men made their way up the stairs.

She sat them down in the living room and asked if they wanted coffee.

"If we can get started while you're making it, Cotton," said Hawkins as he took in the room and contents.

Derek winced. When would the DCS get it that Jennifer was no longer a police officer?

"Nice place," called Hawkins through to the kitchen where Jennifer was fetching a large jug of coffee she'd made once she knew they were on their way. "How can you afford this?"

Nosey bugger, thought Jennifer.

"I play the Asian stock markets in the hours of darkness, sir. It helps that I never sleep."

"What?" exclaimed Hawkins, to the others' amusement.

"Actually, sir, I have a very generous stepfather," said Jennifer with a smile as she walked back into the living room.

"Lucky girl," grunted Hawkins. "Right, coffee ready? I've got some results from the lab to tell you about."

He nodded to McPherson who passed him a beige folder he'd been clutching.

Hawkins opened it and removed a typewritten sheet of paper.

"These are the preliminary findings on the new examination of Silk's clothing."

"I heard that the lab had some results," said Jennifer, as she put a tray on the coffee table. "I was talking to Charles Keithley about them this morning. He called to moan that his expert hadn't been given all the findings."

Hawkins gave a dismissive shrug. "Just because his expert was at the lab witnessing the re-examination doesn't mean that he's entitled to all the results immediately. There are other considerations to be made."

Jennifer wasn't letting it go. "Hardly in the spirit of mutual cooperation, sir. And by the way, the he was a she. Dr Pauline Merriton."

Hawkins gave an exasperated sigh.

"If you'd keep quiet and listen for a minute, Cotton, you might learn something."

Jennifer smiled sweetly at him as she pulled her index finger and thumb across her lips.

"Now then," continued Hawkins, looking down at the report. "As you predicted, trace evidence was found on the inside of the pullover. They found three blond hairs that are the same as those found on the outside and in the car. They reckon, now they have several, that they are all from a wig. The irritating thing, of course, is that there is still nothing to compare them with, so they don't mean a lot on their own."

He stopped, his face serious.

Jennifer waited. She knew that Hawkins wouldn't have made a special trip to see her just to tell her about wig hairs that had no present value as evidence. There must be something else. She glanced across at Derek, but from the look on his face, she could see that he also hadn't been told anything. Hurst and McPherson were both staring into their coffee, their faces unreadable masks.

Hawkins pulled another sheet of results from the folder.

"There's something else, Cotton. Actually there are two things."

"Yes, sir?" Jennifer was suddenly in fear of what had been found. Was it going to implicate Henry after all?

Hawkins continued his scrutiny of the paper in front of him.

"This," he said, waving the paper at her, "would have been potentially damning for Silk if we'd had it a few weeks ago, but as it turns out, it now probably goes the other way."

"I don't understand, sir," said Jennifer.

"Of course you don't, Cotton. It's the results of the examination of the weapon that was used to knock Miruna Peptanariu unconscious."

"I didn't know that had been found," said Jennifer. She glanced at Derek, who raised his eyebrows and pulled a face to indicate that he too had no knowledge of it.

"We kept it under wraps," said Hawkins.

"Really?" harrumphed Jennifer, unimpressed. "What's the weapon?"

"A side-handle baton. A dog walker found it. His dog picked it up in some dense bushes and brought it to him. Fortunately, the dog's slobber didn't ruin the fingerprints."

"You recovered fingerprints?" said Jennifer, suddenly worried.

Hawkins nodded. "Two good sets, both of them matching Henry Silk's."

"Where on the baton were they?" asked Jennifer.

"The best were on the retractable part of the main handle, which was extended when the baton was found. There were also some smudged ones on the side handle that didn't show enough detail for comparison."

"Wasn't the same sort of weapon used in the Bristol case?" asked Jennifer, turning to Derek.

Hawkins answered for him. "It was. The baton design was identical. So given that, and the location of the matching fingerprints, it seems more than likely they were planted by Freneton once her target was out cold. She'd only have the handle out when she disposed of the baton, otherwise she'd keep it retracted to avoid smudging the fingerprints."

"Interesting that she dumped the baton in the woods," said Jennifer. "It didn't need to be found to clinch the case, since there's so much else. But if it were found, she'd assume you'd regard it as icing on the cake. Not something you'd expect from someone planting evidence. Tells you something about her capacity for planning, don't you think?"

Hawkins nodded. "I don't think any of us doubt Freneton's skill in that direction."

He placed the sheet back in the folder and extracted another.

"I said there were two more things; this is the second. The

scientist poked around the seams on the inside of Silk's pullover, near the neck, and found what she thought was a tiny spot of blood."

Jennifer felt a chasm opening in her gut as she remembered the scratches on Henry's neck. If the spot tested positive for blood and the DNA profile matched Henry's, then it would be further evidence against him, although she couldn't begin to imagine a scenario given what they now knew about Olivia Freneton's involvement.

"Charles Keithley didn't say anything about that, sir," she said, her voice little more than a whisper.

"Charles Keithley doesn't know yet, that's why," snapped Hawkins.

Jennifer felt her anger rising again. Keithley had every right to know; it wasn't fair that results were being kept back. She clenched her jaw, forcing herself not to react. As her fingers drummed quietly on her coffee mug, she looked up at Hawkins' face. He was totally relaxed, his eyes no longer stern.

"The blood's been profiled. It's not Henry Silk's and it's not the dead girl's."

Jennifer was shocked, unable to make sense of the information.

"Then … whose is it?" she said.

Hawkins closed the file, sat back and crossed his legs, picking at the crease in his trousers.

"As you know, for elimination purpose, the profiles of all police officers who could potentially contaminate a crime scene are kept on the Police Elimination Database. Although it was stretching a point, I had the profile of the blood from the inside of the pullover run against the PED."

He paused, enjoying the moment, before completing the account.

"The profile didn't match any of the officers who attended any of the scenes in this case. Not you, not anyone else—"

"But," interrupted Jennifer, "if the list of those profiled was limited to officers attending the scenes, it wouldn't have inclu—"

Hawkins cut her off by raising the palm of his left hand.

"Exactly, Cotton. I see we're on the same page."

He paused again, his eyes moving from Jennifer to Derek and back again before he continued.

"Right, I've discussed this with DCI Hurst and DI McPherson already. What I'm about to say does not go beyond these walls. OK?"

They both nodded.

"Say it," insisted Hawkins.

"Yes, sir," they said as one.

"Good," nodded Hawkins. "OK, I've checked the PED and it turns out Freneton isn't on it. She joined the force before it was compulsory to have your profile recorded and somehow she seems to have avoided getting included. Now, for obvious reasons I can't, at this stage, demand a sample from her so I've … taken an alternative route. We can't use this, but I snaffled a toothbrush from a drawer in Freneton's desk. She'd locked everything else, but one was open and the toothbrush was in it. I had the lab check it for saliva, which they found and then profiled the DNA. It matches the blood on Silk's pullover."

Jennifer's eyes widened as she felt her emotions rising. She bit down on her lip, trying to keep control.

"So it *was* her," she said, her voice hardly audible. "She did it. That blood must have got there when the prostitute tried to fight back as she was being suffocated."

Much to Derek's embarrassment, she took his hands in both of hers.

"This proves Henry's innocent," she said, squeezing his hands.

"Yes," agreed Hawkins, "but as I said, we can't use this as evidence because the profile was produced from an illegally obtained sample. Without her permission, it's useless, and if ever it got out that I'd done it, I'd be in more than deep shit, I'd probably lose my job."

"You must have been pretty convinced that she was guilty to have done that, sir," said Jennifer.

Hawkins nodded. "Yes, I was. You see, I've been looking into her background and her career progression on the force. I've got better access to such data than the rest of you. And putting it mildly, she's a vicious bitch who seems to have a real problem with men. She almost crippled a uniform sergeant who came onto her at a party a few years ago, when she was a detective sergeant. It was one of the rare parties she has attended. She didn't hold back in unarmed combat training either; seemed to take a delight in not stopping as short as she should with the odd punch."

Hawkins held up the file with both hands and tapped it on his knees.

"But that's not all, there's something else. DCI Hurst and I have spent hours poring over the CCTV recordings, as you suggested, Cotton. The upshot is that we're both pretty convinced that it's her. There are several things. They probably wouldn't stand up in court, especially since Silk's an actor and could probably have mimicked her."

Jennifer was shaking her head.

"Why, sir? Why would he do that? He doesn't know Freneton at all, as far as we know, and if for some reason he did and we don't know about it and he wanted to implicate her, then it's a pretty dodgy way to go about it. After all, he's more or less ignored the CCTV. When he saw it he just said it wasn't him. He didn't point any fingers; I was the one to do that."

"Good point, Cotton," Hawkins conceded.

"So what happens now?"

"What happens is that we need to find Freneton. She hasn't been seen or heard from since Friday when she claimed to be in Exeter but was in fact here in Nottingham. What's also going to happen is that once I go upstairs with this, the fan won't be able to cope with the shit that's hitting it. But that's the senior command's problem. I'm seeing the assistant chief constable in an hour's time. It's not going to be easy; he actually quite likes the woman and he'll be terrified of the fallout."

"Takes all sorts," muttered McPherson.

Hawkins grunted. "P'raps likes is too strong. Admires is more like it. He sees her as a role model for women in a force that's still very male-oriented."

Jennifer snorted her derision. "A role model on how not to behave, even without her penchant for murder."

As Hawkins put the sheet back in the file, Jennifer was thinking through their conversation.

"Sir, if she hasn't been seen since Friday, where has she been? Are we sure she hasn't returned to her house?"

"Pretty sure. I've had patrol cars checking it out regularly and a couple of uniforms have asked the neighbours. There's been no sign of her."

"So she must have somewhere else to go, if she's still around. Do you know where the call to Edmunds at Skipshed prison came from?"

It was Mike Hurst who answered.

"I had it traced. It was from a call box here in Nottingham, near the city centre, so yes, she's still around."

Jennifer was puzzled. "If she's still around, it must be for a reason. She knows without doubt now that she's been rumbled. You'd think she would have gone well away from here."

"Henry Silk?" suggested Hurst.

"What about Henry?" said Jennifer.

"She decided to kill him much earlier than she'd originally planned. She wanted to do it now, before he's released."

"But she didn't need to be in Nottingham for that," objected Jennifer. "She could have called from anywhere in the country. Has her house in Wollaton been searched yet?"

"Only Thyme's quiet look in her garage," said Hawkins. "That's what I want from the ACC. Given Freneton's seniority, I want his blessing for a search warrant. We should have that in a couple of hours. When we get it and go there, Cotton, I want you to come along. You'll have to stay in the car, I'm afraid, given you're a civilian, but I'd value your on-the-spot insight into anything we find."

"My pleasure, sir," said Jennifer.

"Retribution." The word rolled from McPherson's lips. They all turned to look at him.

"What's that, Rob?" asked Hurst.

"She's been rumbled and she must be pissed about it," growled McPherson. "She didn't want that fact to muck up her plans for

Silk, so she decides to have him topped earlier than originally intended."

He looked up from the spot on the carpet that seemed to have been providing him with insight.

"I've been thinking; she won't know that her plan failed, will she? Not unless she has other contacts in Skipshed who have a way of contacting her. There's been nothing released to the press and I think we should keep it that way for now. She might have a backup plan for the prison that she'd enact if the first one failed."

"Retribution makes sense," agreed Jennifer, "but it still doesn't explain her remaining in the city. It must make her more vulnerable."

"Perhaps we should all be watching our backs," said Hurst. "Looking into the shadows in case she's lurking."

"Who do you think she'd be most pissed at?" asked Jennifer. When there was no answer, she looked up to see all the men staring at her.

"Me?" She shook her head. "I'd like to see her try."

"I wouldn't," said Hawkins. "I think we should all be extra vigilant, but the notion of you being a target isn't daft. Now, we need to get back to the SCF; I've got my meeting with the ACC to go to. But Thyme, you stay here and check out the locks, go through the security with Cotton. I want to be sure that if Freneton calls by here, she can't just walk in without a bloody great alarm going off."

"Sir," objected Jennifer, "I think that—"

"Don't care what you think, Cotton. I want you back on my team, and I want you in one piece."


Jennifer spent much of the next hour briefing Derek on the sophisticated security system her stepfather had insisted on having installed when he bought her the apartment. He'd read articles in Italian glossies about Nottingham being the gun capital of the UK and he wanted to take no chances.

"Impressive stuff, Jen," said Derek after he had checked and rechecked every inch, "so long as you don't get conned into opening the front door."

"I'll be checking every caller on the monitor from now on, don't you worry."

"Actually, Jen, I do worry. I think maybe I should move in until Freneton is caught."

Jennifer laughed. "And if she's not caught? How many years are you planning to stay? That sofa could get awfully tedious after a while."

Derek pulled a face. "You think there's a chance she'd get away?"

"More than a chance. Olivia Freneton is a bright lady; psychopaths generally are. I think she'll have her exit strategy all worked out."

"P'raps," said Derek. "But it hasn't all gone her way. After all, you rumbled her, and then her bid to kill Henry failed."

"I'm not saying she's perfect; she makes mistakes like everyone else. Let's hope that whatever else she has planned, we can nip it in the bud. The problem is working out what the 'whatever else' is. So, DC Thyme, I think you should report back to DCS Hawkins that all in Fort Cotton is safe and secure. I'll let you out, triple bolt the door and not answer it to anyone I don't know."

## Chapter Thirty-Nine

Having dispatched Derek back to the SCF and probable wrath of Peter Hawkins for not staying longer, Jennifer carried out her own double-check of the bolts around the apartment. Most of the sash windows had been replaced during the building's renovation, the new ones the same design but far stronger than the originals. With substantial bolts, double glazing and individually alarmed — additions insisted on by Pietro Fabrelli's team — they were ready to announce the arrival of anyone who attempted to force them open.

Jennifer still didn't have a baseball bat, but she did have her truncheon, part of the police uniform she had yet to hand back. It was now sitting within reach on an armchair.

Reassured by the security, she put it to the back of her mind. Digging into a drawer, she pulled out an A3-size sketchbook and opened it on the breakfast bar alongside her various notebooks and loose-leaf files that contained all the information from the five cases and everything she had learned about Olivia Freneton. The answers had to be there and she was convinced that if she brainstormed for long enough, she'd find them.

Within half an hour, a single A3 sheet had become four. Spread across the worktop and taped together, they were covered in a densely packed network of boxes, lines, arrows, triple underlining, major points ringed in red, huge question marks and exclamation marks of frustration. As she sipped absently at her latest coffee, Jennifer's eyes scanned the sheets looking for the connection that would inspire her. But all she found was history: five cut-and-dried cases that she had connected but nothing to give her further insight into what was going to happen next.

What *had* emerged was the possibility of Freneton including Grace Taverner on her list of targets. Jennifer had immediately called Derek to tell him that the local force in Pateley Bridge should be asked to keep a check on her.

Jennifer knew all too well that she herself was a prime target, but it was unlikely that Freneton would walk up to her front door and knock. Much more likely was the probability that she would wait until Jennifer emerged from her apartment for a run or a bike ride. The Park was always quiet, the roads used only by the residents and delivery services. Someone running or cycling would be an easy target. Derek had worked this out as well and had made Jennifer promise that she wouldn't take a break for a spot of fresh air and a run. Jennifer had agreed at the time but after over two hours of intensive brainstorming, she was becoming frustrated. Right now, there was nothing she would rather do than pound the streets.

The hours slipped by without any further news from Hawkins' meeting with the assistant chief constable. What was taking so long? Jennifer was sure that a search of Freneton's house would reveal something, some insight into how she was thinking. It was an essential step if they wanted to move forward.

Finally, at nine thirty in the evening, Derek called to say that the search warrant had been issued. Hurst, McPherson and Bottomley were about to drive to Freneton's house in Wollaton, accompanied by a uniformed team in three patrol cars. Derek himself had been told to pick up Jennifer and take her directly to the house.

"Whatever took so long?" said Jennifer as she piled into Derek's Mini Cooper almost before he had stopped outside Lincoln View

House, her arms overflowing with her bag, the collection of A3 sheets and her two main notebooks.

Derek's foot hit the throttle and the car shot off along The Park's often-inadequate tarmac.

"The ACC proved to be a wimp. According to what Hawkins told Hurst, he was in total denial about Freneton, wouldn't accept anything Hawkins was telling him. Hurst said they had a row that will become the stuff of legend. It's as well that Hawkins isn't hoping for any more promotion because he didn't mince his words in telling the ACC what he thought of him once he realised the man didn't have a spine."

"What was his problem?" asked Jennifer, struggling to shuffle her papers into order as Derek threw his car around the network of tight corners that led from The Park.

"Didn't want to accept the responsibility of the possible fallout if Hawkins was wrong. It seems that Freneton had the man shaking in his shoes. He wanted to refer it all up to the chief constable."

"Why didn't he?"

"The chief constable's on holiday and the deputy chief, who's acting for him, was at some high-level meeting in London. Out of contact. Hawkins had to virtually beat the ACC about the head with all the evidence against Freneton before he finally capitulated. And even then, it took another half hour to get the warrant signed."

"Jeeze, what is it with these people?" snorted Jennifer. "They put all their officers on the front line while they sit at their desks being important, and yet when push comes to shove, if one of their own is implicated in something, they close ranks, refusing to believe what their detectives, whose judgement is totally trusted in other situations, are telling them. If Freneton gets away, or worse, completes all the tasks on her wish list, it'll be his fault."

Derek glanced at her and grinned. "You sound like Hawkins, Jen. He was breathing fire when he came back downstairs."

He nodded to the pile of papers on Jennifer's lap. "What's all that lot?"

"I've been doing a spot of brainstorming based on everything we have. I'm still trying, and so far failing, to predict what Freneton's up to, what she's planning, why she's still here in Nottingham when all her instincts must be telling her to leave."

"You mean apart from her burning desire to whack you?"

"Yes. And to that end, you are keeping an eye on traffic behind us, I hope."

Derek's eyes automatically darted to the mirror. "Thirty-two-ton truck bearing down on us, anti-tank gun mounted on the cab roof. You know where the seat ejector button is, don't you?"

"I'm serious, Derek."

"So am I, you muppet. We're not being followed. Trust me; I'm good at this."

"Sorry. Getting a bit twitched. I've only ever been threatened by football hooligans before and they always came off second best. This is a whole new game."

"D'you think there'll be something at her house?" asked Derek. "She can't have taken everything with her, surely."

Jennifer watched as another motorist lurched out of the way of Derek's blast on his siren, the blue light flashing. "You'd think so, but if she's got a second place somewhere, all the significant stuff could be there. The Wollaton house might be a smokescreen."

"Well, I guess we're about to find out," said Derek as the car screeched to a halt behind a patrol car outside Freneton's house.

Jennifer could see a group of uniformed police officers jogging up the path towards the figures of Hurst, McPherson and Bottomley who were standing in a huddle by the front door.

"Didn't Hawkins come?"

"No, he stayed at the SCF. I think he's dreaming that Freneton will pop in to pick up her handbag and he'll nab her."

"Good luck with that," said Jennifer, wincing as the battering ram carried by one of the uniformed officers removed the obstruction of the house's front door.

"How big is the garage, Derek?"

"Pretty standard. Why?"

"Not big enough for another vehicle?"

"Not a car, no."

"But space for a motorbike, perhaps?"

"Yes, I should say so, especially since Freneton's car isn't too big."

"You're right. It's an eminently forgettable white Honda Civic, as I recall. Millions of them around. There's even another one parked along the road. Look. She could come and go from here without anyone really registering it."

"What's your point, Jen?"

Derek had the driver's door half open. He was getting agitated, wanting to join in the search of Freneton's house.

"Only that if she left her car here, possibly never to return, she must have had some other form of transport. She wouldn't have called a cab; it would be too traceable."

"She could have got the bus. The stop's only five minutes walk away on the main road."

Jennifer shook her head. "Could've, but I doubt it. She'd prob-ably have been carrying something, a bag or two, and she would want to minimise the risk of being seen. She wouldn't have wanted to bump into a neighbour."

"I'll check for anything in the house. You know, insurance papers, service manuals. We already know that she has no other vehicles registered in her name or the other names we know she was using. Look, I really should get in there. Will you be OK here?"

Jennifer looked around. The street lighting wasn't good.

"I'll be fine; there are several uniforms around. But if you like, I'll go and sit in one of their cars."

"Good idea, Jen, I'll tell them to keep an eye on you."

As Jennifer hurried over to one of the patrol cars, a middle-aged uniformed constable she knew opened the door for her.

"All right, Jennifer, lass? Sit yourself down; we'll keep you out of any trouble."

She grinned at him. "Thanks, Ted. Nice to know I'm in safe hands."

Jennifer could see Hurst and the others moving around the house, all the rooms now ablaze with light. She was itching to join them, but for now it was forbidden territory.

After five long minutes, her mobile rang and Derek's voice boomed in her ear.

"She's not here, Jen, but she's been here recently. There's still fresh food in the fridge."

"Is there a computer?"

"No sign of one yet."

"Modem?"

"Er, no, I don't think so. Not one here in the hall and I haven't seen one in the living room."

She nodded. "She must be using a dongle. Less traceable. What about clothes?"

"Wardrobe's pretty full."

Jennifer drummed her fingers on the seat in frustration.

"Listen, Derek, could you ask Hurst if I can come in? He must agree that Hawkins' main worry was my safety and since there's obviously no danger, it should be fine. I'm going crazy out here."

"Hang on."

She heard footsteps and the mutter of voices. Then he came back on the line.

"Come on in, Jen. The boss says no problem."


"OK, Jennifer," greeted Hurst as she joined him in the kitchen. "This place is fairly minimalist, more of a hotel suite than a home. We've got some uniforms knocking on a few doors. I know it's late, but we need to know how often they see her. Maybe someone saw her last Friday when we know she must have been here. There're bound to be one or two around who spend their days snooping through the net curtains."

"Do we know if she rents it or if she's buying it?" asked Jennifer.

Hurst shook his head. "No idea. I suppose HR might know. But my guess would be renting, don't you think?"

"Yes," said Jennifer, nodding her agreement. "What about her car?"

"What about it?"

"Is it hers or is it rented? Is she paying in instalments?"

"Why? What's your point?"

"I'm trying to understand the way she thinks. If it's not hers, it's one less thing she has to consider. Stop the payments and walk away. The rental company will come knocking to reclaim it eventually, but she'll be long gone."

"Yes," growled Hurst. "Another indication of her meticulous planning. Thyme, go and have another look at the car. See if there's anything there to help us."

As Derek scuttled out of the kitchen, Jennifer turned to Hurst. "Boss, I'd really like to check out the wardrobe, see what clothes she's left here."

"I'll lead the way," said Hurst. "And Jennifer, I for one recognise that you are a civilian. It's Mike."

Jennifer smiled after him. "Actually, I have no problem with 'boss', especially now that I feel back in the thick of things."

As they walked into the bedroom, Jennifer immediately noticed the clothes Olivia had abandoned on the floor the previous Friday. Her visit had clearly been a brief one, she thought. She'd changed, picked up whatever she needed — which must have been packed and ready — and then left. No ties, no attachments.

She was surprised to find the wardrobe was full of clothes, a mixture of police uniforms, both regular and formal, a number of fashionable dresses, trousers, skirts, jumpers, cardigans and blouses, all neatly hung, and next to them a set of unfashionable items. From amongst these, she pulled out a full, pleated dark blue skirt, a worn navy blue jacket that looked like it came from a charity shop, and two cream cotton blouses in a style she would be generous in calling dowdy. Three pairs of spectacles sitting in a box on a shelf next to the hanging items were equally plain. Jennifer picked them up to look through them, doing a double take when one pair proved to be staggeringly thick, while the lenses in the other two pairs seemed to give no optical correction at all. She opened a large and shapeless handbag sitting next to the box. Inside was a copy of Christianity Digest.

"Boss," she called out to Hurst, who was searching a cabinet in the bathroom, "do you know if Freneton is religious at all?"

"Not to my knowledge, no," he called back. "Hardly fit in with what we know about her, would it?"

"Why?" he added, walking back into the bedroom.

She held up the magazine and pointed to the clothes.

"These must be her disguises from when she was staking out the hotels. I wonder if we looked carefully at the CCTV from the Old Nottingham lobby, we would see her there wearing this stuff in the days leading up to the murder."

"Certainly worth a look," agreed Hurst. He tugged at an ear. "Christ, she was nothing if not thorough. Left nothing to chance, did she?"

Jennifer wasn't into admiration. "Remind me, boss, she was at work in the days leading up to the murder, wasn't she? I mean, she wasn't taking time off?"

"No, she was there. Out and about a bit, as I recall — she was always claiming that she needed to get a feel for the city, being relatively new to the place. Why, where are your thoughts leading you now?"

She flashed a brief smile at him.

"Well, she could always have done the staking out in the evenings, I suppose. Come back here, change into this stuff, and go out again. But I reckon that for some things she needed to know, like watching Henry's movements for example, she would need to be there in the daytime, or late afternoon. She wouldn't really have had time to come all the way here. So, I'm wondering where she changed. I mean, the apartment or house we think she's using might be nearby, but I don't reckon that works since she's not likely to have used the Old Nottingham more than once. So, I'm thinking somewhere or something more useful, more versatile."

"Like a van?"

"Yes, exactly. A transit van would be perfect. She could leave it somewhere nearby, change in the back and pick it up whenever was convenient. A nice anonymous white van. There must be tens of thousands of them in this country, which makes them invisible."

Hurst was now with her.

"But of course, she wouldn't drive it here. It wouldn't fit in the garage and she wouldn't want to be seen in it. So wherever she's hiding out must have a large garage space, probably with an automatic door. This could be promising, Jennifer. I'll get some of the researchers onto it first thing. We'll get hold of all the CCTV tapes from street cameras in Nottingham from the time of the Silk case. See if we can spot Freneton near the Old Nottingham dressed in that gear. She might lead us to where the van is parked and if we're really lucky, we might see her driving it and get a plate number. With that, we could get an address."

"Not wishing to appear negative, boss, but that's a lot of lucky breaks. However, it does raise an interesting point. Freneton would think the same way. What I mean is she might anticipate us thinking along those lines eventually. After all, she is a police officer. She'd know that we'd probably locate wherever she's staying sooner or later, so this convinces me that once she's finished whatever it is she's planning here in Nottingham, she has no intention of returning."

Hurst took a deep breath and puffed out his cheeks.

"You're probably right, Jennifer, but as we've found, she's not perfect; she makes mistakes. If we can find this place, even if she's long gone, she might have left something behind. After all, she left that clothing."

He glanced at the wardrobe and the bag that Jennifer was still holding. "Anything else in those?"

"Nothing," she replied.

"You know," continued Hurst, "you have to hand it to her. When she set up the situation with Silk, and with the others in previous years in other cities, she ran the events like a script from a play. She had everything accounted for; she was leading us by our noses knowing what we'd find and how we'd interpret it. It wasn't only the sucker she put in prison that was duped, it was us too. She rubbed our noses in it every time."

He turned and saw that Jennifer was staring intently at him, a light on in her eyes that hadn't been there moments ago. She was looking at him but not seeing him. She suddenly put down the bag she'd been holding and rushed over to her own bag and papers that she'd put on the bed. She grabbed the sheets of A3 and spread them out, her eyes darting around the data. She ran her fingers over the boxes, arrows, highlights, following the information down to where she'd written 'Exit Strategy', 'Finale' and 'Swan Song'.

She looked up, a victorious gleam now in her eyes.

"What is all that stuf—" started Hurst, but she interrupted him.

"That's it, boss, you've hit the proverbial nail fairly and squarely," she said as she tapped the words that had thrown the switch in her head.

"I have?"

"Yes. God, it's so obvious! I can't believe I didn't think of it before. Don't you see, she wants to leave on a high, to embarrass us, or rather you, the force, since I'm no longer a part of it."

She paused, frowning. "She'll definitely have other plans for me. But what better way to collectively rub your noses in it, as you put it, could there be, while at the same time show her superiority, show how clever she is, and how daring."

She beamed at him.

Hurst had still not turned the page. "You're not making any sense, Jennifer."

Jennifer gathered up her bag and the papers.

"She's planning another murder, boss. She's going to honey trap some man, drug him, dress up in his clothes, pick up a prostitute, kill her, plant all the evidence and then disappear. You'll locate the man from the CCTV of his car, connect him to whatever hotel he's using and to the scene, but you'll know full well that he didn't do it. You'll have the usual ton of evidence but you won't be able to use any of it. You'll have to deny its value, say it's worthless. She'll still partly achieve her usual aims — she'll kill a prostitute, demonstrate what a shit the man is by letting himself be picked up, perhaps wreck a marriage into the bargain, and embarrass the hell out of you for letting the whole thing happen under your noses. Reputations ruined, egg on many faces from the chief constable downwards. Meanwhile, Freneton will have flown; probably left the country."

Hurst was now several shades paler than seconds before. He nodded as he absorbed everything she'd been saying.

"If you're right, presumably she'll be doing this soon."

"Sooner than soon, boss, I reckon she's doing it right now. Everything in one day: get Henry killed — she won't know yet that's failed — and set up some sucker in a total carbon copy of Henry's case."

"Christ!" exclaimed Hurst.

He yelled through the house for the others to go to the kitchen as he ran for the bedroom door. Then he stopped so suddenly that Jennifer almost ran into him.

"You've left one thing out, Jennifer."

"What?"

"You."

"Me?"

"Yes, this is all about retribution. She's been found out and she knows it; her game is over and she's got to make dramatic changes — new ID, new lifestyle, new place to live. I can't say she didn't expect it because her brilliant contingency planning will have allowed for it."

"But she probably didn't anticipate it happening yet," added Jennifer as she followed Hurst down the stairs.

"Probably not, but her motivation today is to get even. Kill whoever she can and dump shit on the rest. You, Jennifer, are on the kill list. I think she has every intention of paying you a visit. Tonight."

"Then we'll have her. But wait a minute, I'm not the only person she's planning to kill tonight. There's a prostitute some-where out there she'll have an appointment with."

They had reached the kitchen. Hurst quickly explained Jennifer's thoughts to the others before turning to her.

"Think, Jennifer, where will she be? How will it work?"

Jennifer was ahead of him.

"We need to call around all the hotels in Central Nottingham to see if they have an Amelia Taverner or a Catherine Doughthey registered for tonight."

Hurst nodded to Derek. "Thyme, get on your mobile and call up a list of all the hotels with their phone numbers. We'll divi it up and call them all."

"The brazen bitch," muttered Rob McPherson with a deep growl. His eyes left no doubt what he'd do to Freneton if he could get his hands on her.

Jennifer frowned, picking up on his words.

"Yes," she said. "Brazen is exactly right. I wonder if she's so brazen, so confident, that she'd use her real name. I think we should add the name Olivia Freneton to the phone enquiries."

"OK, boss," called Derek from where he'd retreated to concentrate on his screen. "I've got the list."

"Sing it out," said Hurst. "Jennifer, write them down with the numbers."

After a minute of rapid note-taking, Jennifer tore the sheet of paper she'd been writing on into five pieces and handed them out. Within seconds, Derek was calling the first number. As he walked out of the room, Jennifer heard him announce his rank, name and where he worked. She turned to Hurst.

"Um, boss, do I have your permission to impersonate a police officer?"

"You do, DC Cotton," grinned Hurst. "Go for it!"

The kitchen descended into a confusion of shouting as they all yelled down their phones, fingers in ears, urgency in their voices.

Five minutes later, a triumphant yell from Neil Bottomley silenced everyone mid-sentence.

"Got her! Christ, Jennifer, you were right. The bitch is using her real name. That was the Fields View Hotel, smart place near Trent Bridge. They have an Olivia Freneton on their guest list tonight."

As the others whooped their delight, Hurst checked his watch.

"OK, it's ten fifty. There's absolutely no time to lose. One of those squad cars can lead the way, but put up your blue lights anyway. We've got to get to the Fields View before she leaves."

## Chapter Forty

At nine thirty that evening, Olivia Freneton had been sitting in the bar of the Fields View Hotel dressed to kill, literally, in her pale grey business suit, the blond hair of her wig nestling gently on her shoulders. A ring binder of fictitious papers was open in front of her with several loose papers scattered across the table. Her black Cartier fountain pen sat alongside a pair of rimless Ray-Ban spectacles on one of the loose sheets. The condensation from a narrow tumbler of what looked like a gin or vodka and tonic with ice and lemon but in fact was only sparkling water was slowly soaking a flimsy tissue coaster by her right hand.

The hotel reminded her of the Bristol View, although it was much smaller. An air of quiet efficiency pervaded the art deco lobby and bar as the smartly dressed staff moved discreetly about their business. Olivia was pleased to note that while the coverage of the security cameras in the lobby was good, there were still blind spots she could use to her advantage. She did, after all, want to make her evening's activities as close to her previous predatory outings as possible, even if the overall outcome would be different.

What was particularly evident was the lack of coverage in the bar, the two cameras she had spotted both aimed at the bar counter itself. It seemed that like other hotels, the management limited trust in its barmen. This meant that her dealings away from the counter with whoever became her target for the evening would go unrecorded. A little guile would send him off to his room first with her following a minute or two behind. They need never be filmed in the same frame. Perfect.

The bar was slowly getting busier as groups of businessmen or conference-goers returned from their day's labours or early evening meals. The present occupants were a rather eclectic mixture of strutting, self-confident salesmen swapping tales from the trenches, a huddle of bewildered-looking Thai or Malaysian young men who appeared to be too young to be in the bar, and an intense foursome of sports-jacketed American academics, complete with leather elbow patches, who seemed to be playing a complicated-looking game of four-way chess on four iPads that required much grunting and intense scribbling in notebooks. Olivia studied each group and rejected them all. The only ones of slight interest were the salesmen. A few more rounds of drinks and they might start to notice her and attempt some alcohol-fuelled bravado. For now though, she was invisible to them, the way she wanted to be. It was still early; there would be others and one would stand out, she was sure.

The lack of a predetermined target excited her. It was new territory. Her targets to date had been carefully chosen, researched and then followed in order to learn how they walked and carried themselves. She had spent days fine-tuning the details, formulating plans, allowing for all eventualities. She'd noticed, however, that the operations had become easier each time as her experience grew. The Henry Silk set-up had been so automatic it had hardly been a challenge at all. She needed something else to keep the adrenaline flowing, something to keep her senses sharp. The unknown elements of tonight's outing would provide precisely that edge. She would have to make snap decisions, adjust her strategy on the run. It would be a fun way to play out her last foray before heading for pastures new. And what a scene of carnage she would be leaving behind. As she lifted her glass for a sip of water, the self-satisfied half-smile on her lips reflected the malevolence in her eyes.

Having categorised all the men in the room, she turned her attention to her papers, picking up her pen to make a fictitious note in the margin of one of the sheets. Almost immediately, she sensed a slight movement just beyond her field of vision, the presence of someone hovering. Without moving her head, she lifted her eyes. A slim, good-looking man of around forty had stopped by her table, a puzzled look on his boyish face.

"Natasha? It is you, isn't it? It has to be. God, I hardly recognised you, it's been so long. How are you?"

His voice was deep and slightly plummy, his vowels and confident delivery either public school or military, or both. Olivia kept her eyes on his while she tried to work out whether this was a genuine case of mistaken identity or a corny pick-up line. Whichever, the man immediately interested her. He was around her height, his clothes would fit her after some belt tightening and he wore a wedding ring on the third finger of his left hand. If his speech proved to be a pick-up line, he was a louse she'd enjoy making suffer.

She let her forehead pucker in a slight frown, a quizzical glint in her eyes. She tilted her head as if trying to place him.

"It's Peter," he enthused. "Peter Baines." He grinned. "Catcher."

"Catcher?"

"Yes. Nottingham University Rowing Society, twenty years ago now. Peter Catch-A-Crab Baines. Don't you remember? The first time they put me in a boat, I was all fingers and thumbs. Was for several outings. The coach despaired of me while people on the riverbanks took bets on how many of my strokes actually made proper contact. You probably laughed the loudest but then very kindly and very expertly you showed me what I was doing wrong."

His guffaw was rather forced, out of sync with the calculating look in his eyes. As he stopped and feigned a grimace of uncertainty, she knew he was lying: it was a pick-up.

Perfect, she thought, thinking fast.

"I'm sorry but I think you've got me confused with someone else," she said, her lips a thin smile. "I was never at Nottingham University; I was at Kings in London."

She paused and allowed her face to relax, her eyes to crinkle.

"But, you know, coincidences are amazing things. I did row, at Putney. Ladies eight. Same crew for two years. We did quite well."

It was partly true, she had rowed, but in a single scull. She couldn't stand the team effort, the camaraderie of fours and eights, not even doubles or pairs. Olivia was never a team player.

Peter Baines grinned at her. "Amazing indeed. But really, you're a dead ringer for Natasha. I can't believe it. Mind you, I haven't seen her for a long time."

He leaned towards her, his face all enthusiasm.

"And you rowed," he added, as if he'd only just processed the information. "Great. Listen, can I buy you a drink? Unless I'm interrupting your ..." He pointed at the papers on the table.

"Not at all," said Olivia, closing the file. "I've had more than enough of that lot for one day. My brain's scrambled with all these figures. Thank you. A drink would be very pleasant. Vodka and tonic, if that's OK," she said, pointing to her glass.

"Back in a jiffy," said Baines as he turned to almost bounce towards the bar. He couldn't believe his luck.

Olivia checked her watch. Nine forty. She had a feeling, a nagging nestling in her mind amongst all the contingency plans, telling her she needed to move things along fairly quickly, even though her old team were probably too distracted with the news of Henry Silk's brutal murder to have progressed far enough to make the right connections. But she couldn't be sure, and she wanted to get this part of her evening's entertainment sorted before she completed her fun with a few hours of watching Jennifer Cotton's slow and painful death.

This man Peter Baines was almost beside himself with eagerness. She'd be able to transfer the action from the bar to his room without any difficulty. A few well-chosen phrases of encouragement and seductive giggles in response to his inanities should have him salivating. Twenty minutes should do it, thirty tops.

She smiled at him as he brought the drinks back to the table, forcing her contempt for his pathetic male display to the back of her mind.

"So," he said, sitting down and stretching his neck from side to side. "Oh, that's better; been driving for hours. So, if it's not Natasha — you know, I still can't believe that — then who do I have the pleasure of drinking with?"

Whom, thought Olivia, groaning inwardly.

"Jane Brown," she said, holding out her hand. "Boring, isn't it? But there we are. Pleased to meet you, Peter. Tell me about your rowing. You know, I'll bet we met at a regatta somewhere."

Olivia's plan was soon well under way. After feigning a slight headache from all the noise suddenly echoing around the bar, Baines immediately suggested a quiet drink in his room. He too had a bottle of something special tucked away in his fridge, a fancy gin she'd never heard of.

"Sounds fascinating," she enthused. "I love the subtle nuances of flavour in a top gin, don't you? And that one is in its own stratosphere. You're a man of taste."

She was rummaging around in her bag as she was speaking. "Bugger! I can't believe it; I left my damn phone in my car. I've got to fetch it. My boss'll go ballistic if I don't reply to his messages. I've probably missed a few already. Listen, why don't you go on up to your room while I pop out to the car park. What's your room number?"

"Four twenty-one," he said, the puppy eagerness still in his voice.

"Perfect," she smiled, as she gathered up her papers.

By ten twenty, the gin was poured, Baines' glass now liberally spiked with Rohypnol following Olivia using her perhaps-I'll-have-some-ice-after-all routine. She hoped his heart was strong since the amount of the drug she'd dumped into his glass would knock out a horse.

At ten forty-five, Baines was unconscious on the bed, dressed only in his boxers, a series of scratches on his neck from the mannequin hand. Olivia had searched through his belongings and found a baseball cap embroidered with the name and badge of Bretherton Rowing Club. He was clearly as keen a rower as his chat-up line suggested. He'd think twice about using that routine again, assuming she let him live once she came back from dealing with the prostitute. She hadn't yet decided. After all, the whole evening's exercise was masterclass, a demonstration of her skill in outwitting her ex-colleagues. This fool on the bed was never going to be a serious suspect, so why should he live?

She gave herself a minute to find out more about him. He had slung his jacket onto a chair where his wallet was half hanging out of the inside pocket. Opening it, she found a family photograph of her rower with an attractive thirty-something woman, his wife presumably, and two children: a blond, curly-haired boy of about twelve and a pouting dark-haired girl of around eight. She tapped the photo against her other hand. Should daddy die? — the circumstances of his death indicating he had picked up a notorious killer that the police were too incompetent to find — or should he suffer the shame that the tabloid stories would bring regardless of whether he was written up as a victim or not? Either way, his sweet family life had changed irretrievably since he'd never again have the trust of his wife. She pursed her lips. She'd think about it over the next hour or so.

Dressed in Baines' clothing and wearing his baseball cap, Olivia returned to her room to leave the rest of the things she wasn't taking with her in the smaller bag, and to call the girl she'd contacted earlier. God, they were greedy. You'd think that the Henry Silk case would still be fresh in their minds, that they'd exercise some caution when contacted by a total stranger for sex in his car. But business was business for the girls on the street, life must go on, or, in the case of the one she was calling, be about to be abruptly snuffed out.

"It's Johnny," she said as the call connected on Baines' mobile. She dropped her voice an octave and fell into a lilting Birmingham accent. "Are you ready for me, love?"

"This different number," replied a concerned, young-sounding Chinese voice.

Another smarty, thought Olivia.

"Ran out of credit on the other one, love, sorry. This one's my spare, OK?"

"Don't know. Very busy."

Olivia sighed. Same old routine. "I'll pay you double, love. More if I like you."

There was a pause from the other end.

"Make up your mind, love, I ain't got all night." She was sterner now.

"OK. You flash light. I get in."

"I know the routine; I'll be there in fifteen minutes."


At ten fifty-five, Olivia hit the button on Baines' key fob as she walked purposefully through the hotel car park. A five-door VW Passat obligingly flashed its lights back at her. Moments later she was driving out of the car park and heading for Forest Road West.

# Chapter Forty-One

The convoy of the police car and two unmarked saloons took nine minutes to reach the Fields View Hotel. As they screeched into the car park, they were joined by two other police patrol cars. Hurst instructed the drivers to block the exits and check all cars wanting to leave.

Derek and Jennifer sprinted into reception, leaving Hurst, McPherson and Bottomley trailing in their wake. Derek was waving his warrant card and before he reached the counter, he was already instructing the two alarmed receptionists to call the duty manager. As Kevin, the male receptionist, lifted a phone, Derek turned to his frightened young female assistant. Two weeks into her job, eighteen-year-old Anju Patel was shaking in her turquoise sari as she dithered over processing an elderly couple, themselves flustered after a puncture on the motorway had delayed their arrival.

"Sorry, Anju," said Derek, glancing at the girl's name badge, "this takes priority. I need the room number of a guest called Olivia Freneton."

The girl hesitated.

"Now, Anju!"

The girl's fingers fumbled over the keyboard, only to be further put off by the arrival of McPherson's stormy features at the desk, his own warrant card thrust in her face.

"Get a move on, lass; it's an offence to obstruct a police officer in the execution of his duty."

Derek lifted his eyes to heaven as the girl glanced at her colleague.

"Do it!" Kevin mouthed, nodding furiously at the computer.

"It's room three zero seven," announced Anju, her large, deep brown eyes flitting from one police officer to the next.

"Thank you, Anju," said Jennifer, hoping her tone and accompanying smile would mollify the girl's terror.

"Get a pass key and come with us, please," said Derek to Kevin.

"Is there a problem, officers?" The manager was all concern as he rushed up to them.

"Neil, Rob, follow Thyme and Cotton," ordered Hurst. "And Rob, make sure Cotton keeps back, she's not jacketed; she's an observer. I'll brief Mr …"

"Underwood," said the manager.

As Derek and Jennifer disappeared through the door to the stairs, McPherson and Bottomley stopped by the two lifts.

"You stay here to watch that lift, Neil," said McPherson. "In case she's coming down while I'm on the way up."

Not wanting to miss out on any action, Bottomley pulled out a radio.

"I'll get a uniform in here to watch it, then I'll join you upstairs."

Looking along the third floor corridor as he hurried out of the lift, McPherson could see Derek Thyme about twenty yards away banging hard on a door. Jennifer was standing to one side of the door, making sure that the receptionist stayed behind her.

"Damn it!" spat McPherson as he sprinted along the corridor and grabbed Jennifer's arm, pulling her behind him.

"Guv—" she protested.

"You're not wearing a protective jacket," he snapped. "You shouldn't be here, so don't even think about moving until I say so. You can follow us in once we've checked it."

Having announced his presence at the top of his voice, Derek thrust the key card into the slot and as the green light showed, he pushed open the door. He stood to one side of the door frame as best he could, feeling extremely vulnerable in the bright corridor lighting as he peered into the darkness of the room.

"Superintendent Freneton, stay exactly where you are," he shouted. "The hotel is surrounded by police officers. I'm going to turn on the lights and enter the room."

He reached over to push the card into the lighting slot and the room instantly flooded with light.

He glanced at McPherson, who nodded at him. In one fluid movement, Derek scanned the room, the bathroom and pulled open the wardrobe doors.

"All clear, guv," he called. "She's not here."

Ignoring McPherson's order, Jennifer was physically right behind him, and mentally ahead of him in her assessment of the room. She quickly noted the pale grey business jacket and skirt laid out on the bed and the holdall on the floor nearby.

She knelt by the holdall and looked up at McPherson.

"May I, guv?" she asked, pulling a pair of disposable gloves from her pocket and slipping them on.

"Go ahead, Cotton," he nodded.

She unzipped the bag and pulled on the handles to expose the contents before carefully removing them, placing them one by one on the floor next to her. It was a gold mine, although no surprise to her.

McPherson and Derek watched as she laid out a number of polythene bags containing unused combs, a bag of surgical gloves, a syringe with its plunger pushed all the way down, a small bottle containing a clear liquid, and a medicine bottle labelled Rohypnol that rattled as she shook it. She peered into the bag and pulled out one further item. A white bra.

"Why'd she take that off, Jen?" asked Derek.

Jennifer hesitated as she scanned the items on the floor, unconsciously waving the bra in her hand. Then she nodded her head, puckering her lips in understanding.

"This is a carbon copy of the Henry Silk case, down to the last detail, although I doubt she expected us to find this stuff here: she's intending to return. But this bra would enhance her bust, and dressed as a man she wouldn't want that. I reckon she changed into a tighter one, a sports bra probably, to help flatten her chest."

"Not much to flatten, as I recall," muttered McPherson.

Jennifer ignored him as she jumped to her feet.

"Anyway," she said, her voice suddenly filled with urgency, "we've missed her. Somewhere in this hotel there's an unconscious man lying in his room. Freneton has left in his car dressed in his clothes. We have to find out who he is and get a trace on his car. She's clearly intending to kill another prostitute."

She turned to the receptionist hovering by the door, afraid to enter the room but spellbound by what he had seen.

"Kevin, come with us back to reception. We need a list of the men registered here tonight as single-occupancy guests, and we need it fast. Each one of them needs to be accounted for."

She ran from the room, hustling the receptionist to follow.

"How many rooms in this hotel?" she called as they ran along the corridor.

"A hundred and fifty-two."

"Jesus!" cried Jennifer. "How many of them occupied tonight?"

Kevin caught her eye as they barrelled onto the stairs, shrugging as he did. "Dunno exactly, but we're about three quarters full."

They ran across the lobby to the reception desk.

"Can this thing do any refined searching?" asked Jennifer, pointing at one of the computers.

Kevin looked at her, not understanding.

Jennifer sighed at his lack of wit. "I mean, can we ask it to list male guests having single occupancy?"

A light switched on in Kevin's eyes. "Oh yeah, it can do that."

"Good," said Jennifer, pushing him to the keyboard. "Get me the list."

As the screen changed, her heart fell. It seemed that the vast majority of the guests were in the category of male single occupancy.

"We'll have to refine the list," she said. "Let's assume that our man is British, white and aged around thirty-five to fifty, no sixty. We'll try those first. Here, let me."

She replaced Kevin in front of the screen.

"Right, Kevin, write these down as I call them out. Derek, you phone the first one on one of the house phones. If there's no answer, he's either out or he's our man, drugged and in a deep sleep. We'll make a shortlist and go banging on doors. Here's the first one, Derek, room one zero one, Robert Johnson, aged forty-three."

Derek dived for a phone as Jennifer moved to the next one on the list, which she called out to Hurst.

Over the next ten minutes, the desk was a jumble of four people making phone calls, Jennifer yelling out names and room numbers and Kevin scribbling furiously.

As McPherson slammed the receiver down on his last irate client — there had been much abuse by people not sharing his sense of urgency who were severely displeased at being woken by the police — Jennifer recalculated their tally of possibilities.

"We're down to twenty-three," she announced. "They're fairly evenly distributed among the five floors."

"Right," said Hurst, turning to the manager. "Pass keys. We need four. I'll go with you and take the first floor, Rob, you check the second floor with Kevin here, Neil, take one of the uniforms and do the third floor, and Thyme, you go with Cotton to the fourth floor. If we draw a total blank, we'll all meet up on the fifth floor."

"Boss—" Jennifer started to object.

"Don't argue, Cotton, you're not going alone. Now, let's move it!"

Derek and Jennifer ran to the stairs. "Quicker than the lift, Jen," he said, grinning, "if you can keep up."

"Stop jabbering and shift your arse, Thyme," she said, charging past him.

There were five rooms on their list. They knocked loudly on the doors of the first two and used the pass card to enter. The rooms were empty. As Derek pounded on the door of the third, it opened slightly and an overweight and balding middle-aged man wearing only a towel peered out nervously. Derek flashed his warrant card and announced loudly again that they were police.

"Is everything all right with you, sir?" he asked, craning his neck to see into the room. He was concerned that Freneton might have the man under threat.

"Yes, officer, really," stammered the man.

"I'm sorry, sir, but I have to check."

He pushed past the man, stopping where the short corridor opened up into the main part of the room. Sitting up in the bed, the sheets pulled up around her neck, was a surprisingly young and slim woman, a jumble of chestnut curls falling onto her bare shoulders. Her deep brown eyes caught Derek's and she smiled coyly.

"Timothy," she called to the man in the towel, her voice a husky purr. "What have you arranged this time?"

Jennifer had by now followed Derek into the room. She yanked on his arm.

"Sorry, miss," she said past him. "Our mistake."

"Are you sure?" said the woman as she let the sheet slip from her shoulders.

"What's this all about, officer?" demanded the man.

"Apologies, sir," said Jennifer, quickly pulling open the wardrobe door as she pushed Derek out of the room.

"The hotel will explain later," she called, glancing into the bathroom. "We need to go. Sorry to disturb you."

She slammed the door shut and caught Derek's eye.

"What?" he said.

She responded with a withering glance before looking down to check her list.

"Four two one," she said.

Derek was there first and once again banging on the door, announcing who he was.

Jennifer slipped the card into the lock, pushed open the door and activated the lights.

From the angle at which the man was lying, she knew they had found him. She ran over to the bed, instinctively taking the man's wrist.

"He's alive," she called to Derek, "but his pulse is weak and his breathing pretty shallow. Call an ambulance; he's going to need help."

As Derek punched the buttons on his phone, Jennifer looked Peter Baines up and down and gasped.

"Derek, look! His neck. He's got scratches exactly like the ones that Henry had on the left side of his neck."

"Ambulance on its way, Jen," he said, bending down to view the scratches. "Wow! You said she was doing everything the same. It's like a demo, a sort of masterclass."

"Arrogant bitch," snapped Jennifer. "I reckon she's really dosed this bloke up."

Derek was still inspecting the scratches.

"You should be calling Hurst, Derek," admonished Jennifer, as she scanned the room.

Derek punched his phone again.

"Boss, we've got him. Room four two one."

There was a pause as he listened to instructions.

"Yes, boss," he said. "I'll call them."

"His clothes are missing," said Jennifer, a note of triumph in her voice. "Unless he's super neat and folded everything away."

She pulled open the wardrobe and the drawers under the desktop.

"No," she said, shaking her head. "Just a normal man. The clothes are definitely missing. Freneton's wearing them."

Bottomley was the first to arrive, his uniformed officer in tow. Hurst blustered in immediately after.

"Sure this is the one, Jennifer?"

"No doubt, boss, and he looks in a bad way. We've called an ambulance."

"Good. D'you reckon she's taken his car?"

"I do, yes."

"Right, get down to reception and call up his check-in card. It should have his car number and maybe the make. Is his phone here?"

"Haven't seen it," said Jennifer as she glanced around the room again. "But I reckon Freneton will have it. If she's following the Silk scenario, she'll have called the prostitute from it."

"OK," said Hurst. "See if he gave the number to reception. If she's left it on, we might be able to trace it. Neil, get onto the tech people. Tell them to be on standby."

Bursting back into reception and rekindling Anju Patel's alarm, Jennifer didn't even ask as she took over the keyboard.

"Got them!" she called to Derek, who had followed her down the stairs. "There's the car reg and type. It's a Passat, and there's a mobile number."

"Sing out the car reg, Jen," said Derek, heading for the main door. "I'll check the car park."

Shaking his head as he ran back after about thirty seconds, he saw that Hurst, McPherson and Bottomley had joined Jennifer.

Hurst was checking his watch.

"Shit," he said, "it's eleven twenty. We're running out of time. How long will the techies take to trace the phone, Neil, assuming it's on?"

"I'll call them," replied Bottomley.

Hurst ran his hands through his hair in frustration.

"Where has the bitch gone?"

"I don't think we need to wait for the techies," said Jennifer.

They all turned to look at her.

"I've been thinking about it, about where Freneton would go. Everything we've found this evening has shown that she's copying her script for the Henry Silk case. Right down to changing her bra—"

"What?" interrupted Hurst.

"I'll explain later. But the point is, it's all for show. It's all to wave two fingers at us. She knows that Baines is never going to be a suspect. She'll have his phone, yes, but she will probably have turned it off. If she has, we won't find her that way."

She looked up at Hurst to see his features sag into weary submission.

"It doesn't matter," she continued, "we don't need to. Given what she's shown us so far, there's only one place she'd go. In her shoes, it would certainly be my choice."

Hurst was still frowning.

"Of course," said Derek. "Harlow Wood."

## Chapter Forty-Two

The girl, who called herself Mandy but whose real name was Gwo Li-fen, was nervous. Some of the other girls had warned her about taking on clients who wanted to pick her up in a car. Clients she didn't know. Miruna had gone to her death like that, even though she'd had options. Mandy had fewer options: she needed every client she could get. She wasn't attractive like Miruna, in fact Mandy wasn't attractive at all. Rail thin and flat-chested, with poor teeth, small eyes and plain, round features, her client list was short, comprising mostly Chinese and other Asian men, many of whom were brutal, scornful of her and tight-fisted. Some even refused to pay her at all. She had debts; she needed the cash, and whoever he was, Johnny had sounded like he had money he was willing to sling around. Mandy hadn't yet learned that if it sounds too good to be true, it probably is.

Waiting on the warm August night in the shadows of the dilapidated house on Forest Road West, she took note of every passing car. She had learned to judge their speed and their driving manner, learned to look for an air of studied nonchalance on the faces of the drivers. She had also learned to spot cars that passed more than once in ten minutes and cars she had seen passing on other nights, cars that didn't belong in the area. The police were a constant problem for her and the other girls. And she had to be especially careful because she was illegal. She had no genuine papers, and despite having paid a fortune for the fakes in her handbag — money she was still repaying at exorbitant interest rates — she knew they wouldn't stand scrutiny. The last thing she wanted was to be sent back to China.

She was nervous, pulling at the strap of her bag, playing too much with her hair. She envied the other girls. They had all learned to adopt that amazing air of looking busy without actually doing anything. Avoiding eye contact and gazing into the middle distance, they could pace a ten-yard patch for hours, mobile phones attached to their ears like floor walkers in a stock exchange, giving the impression that any interruption would seriously disrupt their day.

She checked her watch. The man had called over twenty minutes ago saying he'd be only fifteen and there was still no sign of the car. Unbeknown to her, she had missed the first pass of the Passat when she had rushed back into the house to fetch her mobile phone from its charger.

A car was coming down the road. Was that the one? Its headlights flashed; it had to be. She tottered from the shadows to the kerb on heels too high for her and bent to check. The window was down and a single word barked from the dark interior. "Johnny." She pulled open the front passenger door, got in and the car accelerated away.

"You're late," said the man. "Why weren't you ready? You know there are patrols."

"Sorry," muttered the girl. "Forget phone."

The man said nothing more as they drove along Forest Roads West and East, both of them keeping an eye out for any likely interception.

After stopping for the traffic lights, the car turned left onto the A60, heading north. Time for a question, thought Olivia.

On cue, the girl said, "Where we go?"

"Not far," was all the man said, but now that Mandy was settled and taking in the surroundings of the car, his voice didn't sound right. She needed to hear him say more.

"How much you pay?"

"I told you on the phone. A hundred. More if you're good."

It was enough for Mandy. As the car slowed near a junction behind two others, her hand was on the door handle, but Olivia anticipated the move. The locks clicked.

"Nervous, Mandy? No need to be."

"You woman." It was a statement.

"Is that a problem?"

"You police?" This time it was a question.

Olivia turned her head briefly to Mandy, her smile all reassurance as she dropped the Birmingham accent.

"No, Mandy, I'm not police, no way. I'm someone who likes a good time, but I need to be careful. I especially like Asian girls, Chinese girls like you." She brushed Mandy's cheek with the back of her hand. "And I can be very generous."

She paused, but Mandy was still looking straight ahead, both hands clasping her handbag.

"Surely going with a woman isn't a problem for someone with your experience?" purred Olivia gently.

Mandy chewed at a fingernail. She couldn't care less but she wasn't about to admit it. Reluctance might make this woman willing to pay more. On the few occasions she had had female clients, she'd found them far better than the men — they were more gentle, they always paid what she asked and they hadn't beaten her up.

The tired buildings of northern Nottingham began to thin out. Mandy was suddenly nervous again. She didn't know this area well and she didn't know the countryside at all. Miruna had been killed in the countryside.

"Where we go?"

"Somewhere nice and quiet where we can relax on this beautiful evening. Have some fun in the night air. It's not far."

Mandy was still far from sure and she certainly didn't want to be lying on the ground in some field. She was, however, reassured by the fact that this woman seemed to be in no hurry, her driving pace leisurely.

"What your real name?" she asked.

Olivia smiled, wondering what name she should use. But why did it matter? Within half an hour this girl would be dead.

"Olivia," she said.

"Pretty name," said Mandy. "I like Western name. That's why I Mandy. You give me money now?"

Olivia pointed to the glove box. "There's an envelope in there."

In a flash the girl had opened the glove box and was counting the five crisp twenty pound notes. She was wide-eyed, but it didn't prevent her wanting more.

"You say you pay more," she said, a hint of petulance in her tone.

"I might, Mandy." Olivia glanced at her and caught her eye. "If you're good."

"I good," said Mandy, tossing her head.

Half a mile from Harlow Wood, Olivia tensed as she heard the sound of a siren as a police car hurtled towards them from the opposite direction, blue flashes lighting up the fields in the distance. She braced herself for a confrontation. She didn't really want to kill young uniforms, but she would if she had to. The car appeared from round a bend but raced past them. Without slowing, Olivia watched it in the mirror until it disappeared.

She stopped the car by the barrier, the same one as before, which she knew from a check earlier wasn't locked. As with Miruna, she asked Mandy to get out and lift it, but unlike the Romanian girl, this one obliged without a hint of protest. Olivia was amused to watch as the girl stumbled along unsteadily on her high heels in the gravel and mud.

The barrier down once again, Olivia drove the car the three hundred yards along the unsurfaced lane to where she had stopped with Miruna.

She turned off the engine and, clicking on the interior light, she turned to study the girl's face properly. She was surprised by how unattractive she was, despite a heavy application of make-up. No wonder she was pleased to see the money; pity she'd never enjoy it.

She turned off the light again, plunging them into darkness.

Mandy felt her nervousness increasing. She didn't like the dark and she didn't like the woods. The trees, backlit by the almost-full moon, waved their branches in the slight breeze, beckoning to her. To Mandy's eyes, the movement was eerie and threatening; she knew that woods harboured ghosts. She wondered where Miruna had been killed. It was in a wood, she knew, but she didn't know where. The name would mean nothing to her anyway. Her eyes darted around the deep shadows as she gulped in panic when she thought that maybe it was this wood. Perhaps Miruna's tortured spirit was lurking here, looking for companionship.

"Not like woods," she pouted, both her hands clamped on her bag.

Olivia sighed. She needed the girl to relax, to get into position.

"Not a country girl, Mandy?" She reached out and touched her hand. "Don't worry about this place, I often come here to enjoy the peace and quiet, even at night. It's perfectly safe."

"Too dark," complained Mandy. "Turn on light."

"Why not?" said Olivia, reaching up for the switch. "There."

"Big light," said the girl, pointing towards the front of the car.

Olivia was less happy to do this, but it would only be for a few minutes. She rotated the headlight switch.

As Mandy visibly relaxed, Olivia explained that she wanted her to open the door briefly and give her room to climb into the passenger seat.

"Then you can kneel in front of me," she added as the girl put her feet down outside. "You're little; I like that. There's plenty of room, especially if you slip off those shoes, give yourself more room."

As the girl settled in front of her, Olivia reclined her seat.

"I can't wait to get out of these horrible clothes," she said, tugging on her belt. "Would you like to help me, Mandy?"

While Mandy took over, unzipping the trousers and pulling them and Olivia's underwear down together, Olivia casually reached her arms back over her head to check the position of the side-handle baton she'd stowed when she got in the car at the hotel. She grasped the handle, ready to strike, but then suddenly gasped. Mandy had moved faster than she'd expected and was already exploring her with her tongue, the thought of more crisp twenty pound notes pinging in her head like a cash register.

Enjoying the sensation more than she'd expected, Olivia relaxed her grip on the baton, stretching her arms and body to enjoy a few more moments of indulgence before she ended the girl's life.

Jennifer had been wrong about one thing in her predictions of Olivia Freneton's behaviour: whether it was oversight or deliberate, she hadn't turned off Baines' mobile. Its shrill ring, the tone set to that of an old-fashioned house phone, shattered the silence in the car. Olivia sat up with a jolt, instinctively hauling up her clothing and fastening her trousers. She grabbed the device from her jacket pocket, while Mandy sat back on her heels, wondering what was going on.

Olivia glanced at the screen to find that there was only a number displayed. She thought for a moment as the harsh ringing continued. It probably wasn't Baines' wife since a name and possibly a photo would display. But Baines was a louse — Olivia wouldn't be the first woman he'd picked up in a hotel bar. It could be a girlfriend or some previous conquest, and he'd be stupid to put a name against the number in case his wife saw the contact list. She smiled to herself. This was an opportunity to screw him a little further. She punched the answer button.

"Yes," she purred into the phone, her voice deep and seductive.

"Good evening, Olivia," said Mike Hurst. "Your car is surrounded and all the exits from this wood are blocked. Don't make matters worse for yourself by hurting the girl. Let her be and give yourself up."

## Chapter Forty-Three

Mike Hurst's car, driven by Neil Bottomley, had arrived minutes earlier at the barrier marking the entrance to the lane leading from the main road. The patrol car that had led the way had pulled up on the tarmac beyond the barrier, the driver having been instructed by Hurst through the radio to kill the siren and flashing lights about two miles down the road.

A uniformed constable ran from the patrol car to lift the barrier and Bottomley drove slowly through, followed immediately by Derek driving his Mini Cooper. Jennifer was in the front passenger seat.

On the way, Hurst had radioed for backup and had now received confirmation that patrol cars, six in all, were in position at strategic points in the square of roads beyond the boundaries of Harlow Wood. An armed response unit was still some minutes away.

As they rounded a bend about fifty yards along the lane, Hurst suddenly instructed Bottomley to stop.

"Rob," he said to McPherson, who was sitting in the back, "go and tell Thyme to leave his car there and join us here in mine. And tell Cotton that she's to remain in Thyme's car. Emphasise that until we've got Freneton in custody, she is not to move and under no circumstances to leave that car. She's not jacketed like us, and I don't want her involved in any action. Don't leave her in any doubt; threaten to handcuff her to the steering wheel if she objects."

He reached up to move the interior light switch so that the light wouldn't come on when the door opened.

"And, Rob, quietly does it," he added, his voice low.

McPherson ran back to the Mini Cooper, indicating to Derek that he should lower the window.

"First thing, Thyme," he said as he stuck his head into the car, "is move that switch on the interior light."

"Already done, guv. Jennifer—"

"Good," interrupted McPherson. "Next thing is that Hurst wants you to join us in his car. Only you, Thyme. Cotton, you're to stay here and not move a muscle."

"But guv—" started Jennifer.

"Hurst said that if you objected, I was to handcuff you to that," he said, pointing to steering wheel. "So shut it."

Jennifer narrowed her eyes at him, her lips pressed together in frustration, but said nothing further. Instead, she watched in steely silence as the two men ran over to the other car and got in. Its lights off, it disappeared into the darkness around the next bend.

As the lane straightened out, the four detectives saw the Passat about two hundred yards ahead of them, its interior lights burning and its headlights picking out the trees and lane ahead of it in stark relief.

"Stop here, Neil," said Hurst as he reached into the glove box for a pair of binoculars.

Bottomley had been inching along at a slow walking pace. Rather than touch the footbrake, which would send a red glow out behind them, he pulled on the handbrake.

Hurst passed the binoculars to McPherson while he radioed the patrol cars once again to ensure that one was in position at the far end of the lane. He didn't want a car chase should Freneton spot them and drive off.

"The doors are closed, Mike," said McPherson as he focussed

the binoculars on the Passat. "Freneton's still in there with the girl. They're in the passenger seat; the girl in front facing her."

"Christ!" said Hurst, through clenched teeth. "That's where she was when she clobbered Miruna. It can't be more than a few moments until she does the same to this girl."

He considered his options. His main concern was that if they charged the car, Freneton might still injure or even kill the girl out of spite. But if they waited for the armed response unit, the outcome would probably be the same: the girl could die as they waited.

He turned in his seat to look directly at Derek and McPherson. Speaking fast, he said, "We can't afford to wait, but she mustn't know we're coming. Slip out of the car and get along the lane to the Passat. Keep low. Thyme, go to the left, there's a slight clearing by the car. Stay in the dark. She won't see you approaching from the passenger seat. Rob, take the right side of the lane. When you're both close, I'm going to try Baines' number. If you hear it ring, give her time to answer it. She'll be distracted for a second or two, giving you time to dive for the doors. Thyme, try to extract the girl. Her life is a priority. Rob, the driver's seat is empty. Immobilise the car by grabbing the key from the ignition. As soon as I see you open the doors, Neil will hit the throttle and we'll be with you. If Baines' number doesn't work, we'll hit the lights which will be your cue to move."

Derek opened the rear passenger door next to him and slipped out. McPherson did the same on his side.

"Lads," called Hurst in an urgent whisper. "If you see Freneton raising the baton to strike the girl, don't wait, go for the doors."

Keeping one eye on the Passat's passenger seat for Freneton's arms, Hurst peered into the gloom immediately ahead of them. He could just make out the two men on either side of the lane as they ran in a crouch towards the car.

"Mike," said Bottomley, as he saw Freneton's arms reach behind her. His hand twitched on the gear stick, ready to move.

Hurst lifted the binoculars to his eyes and saw that Freneton's arms had stretched upwards, her hands still not holding anything. "Wait!" he hissed.

"They're in position," said Bottomley. "Thyme's moved to the left and Rob's hovering low by the boot."

"OK, I'm dialling the number," said Hurst.

A moment, then, "It's ringing."

Hands gripping the steering wheel, Bottomley heard his boss say, "Good evening, Olivia. Your car is surrounded and all the exits from this wood are blocked. Don't make matters worse for yourself by hurting the girl. Let her be and give yourself up."

Before Hurst had finished, he saw the two detectives spring forward from their respective positions. In one fluid movement, Derek opened the passenger door, grabbed the girl and pulled her out of the car. He used the momentum of the pull to swing her wide and send her rolling towards the nearby bushes.

Bottomley shifted into first and gunned the engine, headlights now on full beam.

No sooner had Jennifer watched Hurst's car disappear into the gloom than she realised that she was desperate for a pee. The adrenaline rush of the frantic race to the hotel from Freneton's house, followed by the locating first of Freneton's hotel room and then Peter Baines', and finally the high speed race through the mercifully quiet streets from Nottingham had all totally occupied her mind. But now, in the silence and darkness of the car, her bladder made its presence felt and she knew she had to obey, regardless of Hurst's instructions.

"Sorry, boss," she whispered, "but when a girl's got to go …"

She clicked open the door and slipped to the rear of the car. Then she remembered that round the bend immediately behind her were two uniformed officers who at any moment might come charging towards her in response to a call from Hurst. She didn't want to be squatting in the lane if that happened; she'd never hear the last of it. She thought of going instead to the front of the car, but the same argument applied.

There were dense trees to the left side of the lane, but mainly shoulder-height bushes to the right with a few scattered trees, the going far less dense. She walked quietly into the bushes, sufficiently

far that she couldn't be seen from the lane. She was about to squat
down when the moon broke from behind a cloud, its light reflecting
on something shiny a few yards ahead of her. She pushed away
some branches to reveal a pristine off-road motorcycle resting on its
stand under a tree. It was facing along a narrow path that led back
to the lane.

Her need to pee temporarily forgotten again, she turned on the
torch on her phone and reached down to touch the engine. It was
cold; the bike had been here some time. Her eyes roamed over the
motorcycle's sleek lines. A KTM, it appeared to be almost new, not a
mark on it. She ran a hand through her hair. No one would leave a
bike like this hidden here without a specific purpose. The nearest
houses were several hundred yards further along the road in a small
estate carved out of one part of Harlow Wood. She shone her torch
onto the ground around the stand. There was no sign that the bike
had been parked here before — it wasn't its regular spot. Then the
realisation dawned: it *had* been parked here before, just once. This
motorcycle was part of a contingency plan, a getaway vehicle if everything went pear-shaped. Once astride it and moving, the rider was
only yards from the lane and seconds from the main road. With a bike
like this, Freneton wouldn't even need to stick to the roads: she could
cut across fields if she was being pursued. She would have parked it
here at the time of the Miruna Peptanariu killing. When it hadn't been
needed, she had come along the next day, long before Miruna's body
had been found, and retrieved it. Today, she was following the same
script. And if the interception that was about to go down along the
lane went wrong and she escaped, she might well want to use it.

Jennifer's bladder was now pleading with her once again, one
step from taking matters into its own hands. She unzipped her
trousers and squatted down. As the sense of relief flowed through
her, she considered what she might do to immobilise the
motorcycle.


The surprise of two screaming policemen tearing open the Passat's
front doors and the petrified Chinese prostitute being ripped from

in front of her eyes delayed Olivia Freneton's response by a second at most. Derek Thyme was still swinging Mandy around and away from him when Olivia reached for the side-handle baton. She could see that McPherson's first priority was the key; his eyes were not on her. He had made the mistake of half climbing into the car as he lunged at the key dangling on the right side of the steering column.

Gripping both the baton's handles, Olivia executed a vicious swing that connected squarely with the bridge of McPherson's nose. Blood burst from the flattened tissue, spraying onto the windscreen as McPherson collapsed onto the seat. Olivia raised the baton again and whipped it down on his head with every ounce of her considerable strength. She didn't wait to see the effect: no one could be on the receiving end of such a blow and remain conscious. Instead, she focussed her attention on Derek Thyme, who was both bigger and stronger than she was. She jumped from the car in time to see him turn towards her as he recovered from the momentum of swinging the girl away from the car. At the same moment, she became aware of the roar from the engine of a fast-approaching car. A grim smile appeared briefly on her lips as she assessed her situation. Neither Bottomley nor the ageing Hurst would pose much of a problem individually — Olivia fought far dirtier than they'd ever imagine possible — but the combination of all three men together posed a problem. And maybe Jennifer Cotton was with them. Four to one were not good odds, and they would be even worse when uniformed officers arrived, which they undoubtedly would.

Derek's eyes were now fully focussed on Olivia. There was no time for her to circle and feint; she needed to attack. Gripping the baton with both hands and swirling it menacingly, she advanced, hoping Thyme would be distracted into watching it while she positioned her feet. Her eyes not leaving his, she waited until she saw him glance away for the briefest moment. Then she pounced. Stepping forward onto her left foot, she swung her right leg up, snapping it straight into a powerful kick as she did. She was aiming low, given his chest was protected by the reinforced jacket. Her foot buried itself in Derek's crotch and he tumbled backwards as if his feet had been torn from under him.

It wasn't a permanently crippling blow, she knew that, although he would be incapacitated for several seconds, at least. She wanted to finish him with the baton but she couldn't — she could hear Hurst's car screeching to a halt on the gravel and its doors opening. Any second, at least two overweight men would be throwing themselves at her and she didn't want to be distracted by killing Derek Thyme as they did.

As she sprinted the few steps necessary to reach the car, she saw Hurst was half out of the passenger door. She launched herself at it, spinning to hurl a kick at the handle. The door smashed back into place, slamming onto Hurst's right arm. There was a crunch of breaking bone as he yelled in pain. Olivia wanted to gloat, to enjoy the moment, but she couldn't afford that luxury. She started to raise the baton, ready to give Hurst the same treatment as McPherson when she heard the crunch of twigs underfoot followed by a piercing scream. Spinning around, she saw Mandy launching herself at her, the point of the knife clutched in her hand heading straight for Olivia's chest.

Olivia reacted fast. In a blur, her left hand whipped across the path of the blade to deflect it. The move worked, but instead of Olivia's hand connecting with the girl's wrist as intended, it found the razor-sharp edge of the knife. The blade cut deeply, blood spurting from the wound. Instinct took over as the pain seared through Olivia's left arm. She flicked her right wrist upwards and the baton, still clutched in her right hand, smashed into Mandy's chin like a prizefighter's uppercut. The blow lifted the girl from her feet, sending her tumbling backwards, but as Olivia stepped forward to finish her, a voice behind her said, "Give it up, Freneton, it's over. We've got you."

It was Bottomley, the fat detective sergeant. Olivia snarled, invigorated by the challenge — he hadn't even got a weapon; he was just standing there, slightly hunched. Out of the corner of her eye, she saw Thyme climbing groggily to his feet. This was getting out of control. As Bottomley took a step towards her, she flicked her liberally bleeding hand at him, spraying blood into his face. He faltered and she swung the baton at him, catching him in the mouth. There was a choking yell as he grabbed at his face and sank to his knees.

"Stop, you bitch!"

It was Hurst. He was stumbling towards her, his right arm dangling. He was clearly in great pain. She had to leave: there would be uniforms arriving in seconds and she'd be lost. Hurst was about eight feet away and advancing. She weighed the baton in her hand and then threw it hard at him. It was a clean shot, catching the side of his head and bouncing off into the bushes. As he too sank to his knees, Olivia took to her heels, tucking her bleeding hand under her right arm as she raced off along the track.


Standing about six feet to one side of the motorcycle's rear wheel and well shadowed by bushes, Jennifer was startled by the commotion along the lane that began with Derek and McPherson screaming as they wrenched open the Passat's doors, the noise intended to disorient and distract the occupants. She considered running to join the men but then she remembered Hurst's order. She pulled a face. Better get back to the Mini Cooper and wait; the four of them should have no trouble subduing Freneton. But as she turned away from the bike, she heard Hurst's voice yelling at Freneton to stop. She froze in her tracks. His voice had sounded different, strained. When Hurst's cry was followed by a dull thump and the crunch on gravel of pounding feet as someone raced down the lane in her direction, she realised that Freneton had not been stopped, that she was escaping. She crouched in the bushes and waited.

The pounding of feet was suddenly replaced by the sound of twigs and small branches snapping as Freneton broke from the lane into the bushes, ploughing her way through the undergrowth towards her bike. Jennifer pulled her body lower and waited.

The stillness surrounding the motorcycle was shattered as Freneton burst from the bushes. Jennifer had half-expected her to vault onto the machine, but instead she stopped on its right side, took hold of the grip with her right hand and eased herself on.

It was then that Jennifer saw Freneton's left hand tucked under her right armpit. She was injured! Jennifer waited as in one motion Freneton leaned forward on her feet to push the bike off its stand while she reached under the fuel tank to where she'd hidden the key. When she turned it in the ignition switch, Jennifer knew it wouldn't work: she'd cut the cable feeding it with a small pair of scissors she kept in the bag now slung round her neck.

This was the moment she should have pounced, while Olivia was still processing the fact that the bike was dead. But she didn't. Instead, she waited the extra second that was all Olivia needed to work out exactly what was going on. When Jennifer burst from her crouch and hurled herself at the figure on the motorcycle, her hands outstretched to grab her collar and pull her off, Olivia was ready. She ducked down, flattening her body onto the petrol tank, shifting the weight of the frame to her right foot as she leaned the bike in that direction. Jennifer saw her move but her arms were committed as they flailed forward. An instant before their bodies collided, Olivia brought her right elbow up sharply, burying it in Jennifer's diaphragm.

The impact lifted Jennifer's feet from the ground. Olivia pushed with her right foot, but the bike's rear wheel slipped on the loose stones and it slid away under her. Both women fell onto the motorcycle's frame, Jennifer on top but half paralysed by the blow to her body.

Olivia tried to push Jennifer's body up and away from her, but she didn't have the leverage and Jennifer sagged back. She needed to use both hands. Wincing with the pain of the cut, Olivia pushed Jennifer's torso upwards, her bleeding left hand now full in Jennifer's face. Then, bringing her right knee up to her chest, she shoved her hard with her foot, sending Jennifer rolling away.

Olivia sprang to her feet. She could hear people running along the lane, voices shouting in question. She glanced down at Jennifer, who was clasping her chest, but clearly regaining her strength. She wanted to finish her, this clever little bitch who had ruined her fun. Contingency plans were one thing — there were several outcomes to this mess already mapped out — but retribution was another. One voice in her head was screaming at her to finish the girl now

— it would only take seconds. But another voice told her that every second counted; that she had to leave. The first voice got the upper hand and she lashed a foot out at Jennifer's gut, burying it deeply, a gasp exploding from Jennifer's mouth. A second vicious kick, this time to the side of her head was rewarded with a loud grunt of pain.

She stood back. She didn't have time to kick Jennifer to death; she needed a weapon. Her eyes scanned the gloom around the fallen motorcycle searching for a branch, or better, a rock. Then she saw it, a large flat stone four feet beyond the bike's front wheel. She could hear the blood pumping through her head as the adrenaline filled her body with the strength for this final act before running into the darkness, before torches suddenly filled the scene with stark white light and strong hands grabbed and subdued her. Then above the rushing of her blood, she heard other sounds: the crashing and breaking of undergrowth, and the screaming of a voice getting louder and closer, a desperate, anguished plea for a response.

"Jennifer! Jennifer!"

She had bent over, her hand was on the stone, but it was too late. She stood and looked over to where Jennifer's now motionless body lay in a jumble of dishevelled clothing, hair, leaves and mud, her face covered in blood. Maybe the final kick to the head had been enough.

"Jennifer! Jen!"

Olivia turned, away from the direction of the lane, away from the shouting and running. She broke into a trot, her right hand pushing away the branches, her left back in the protection of her right armpit. Even this potential escape had been planned, a 'what if?' She knew where she was going and she had the edge. The discovery of Cotton's body would distract them, slow them. She didn't have far to go.

She was only twenty feet into her escape when she heard Derek Thyme crash through the bushes into the small clearing behind her.

"Jennifer! Oh, Christ. Jen!"

## Chapter Forty-Four

*Swirling grey mist and billowing smoke covered everything, making it impossible to see clearly. There were fires everywhere, fires lapping at her feet, fires singeing her shoes, fires still finding fuel in scrub already blackened to a crisp. But she was cold. So very cold.*

*She was following two men, one ancient and white-haired dressed in a ragged, stained toga, the other a younger man wearing doublet and hose, like someone out of the Renaissance pageants so popular in Italy. She couldn't see their faces or hear their voices, but from their animated gestures, they were clearly arguing.*

*Huge gates loomed into view through the mist and smoke, their tortured hinges creaking, metal tearing against metal. She didn't want to pass through the gates; she'd have given anything not to pass through them, but she had no choice: the two men ahead seemed to be drawing her on, controlling her feet.*

*On the other side, through clouds of ash, she could make out a sea of anguished people, terror in their faces as they tried to avoid clouds of hornets that stabbed at them incessantly.*

*As she drew level with the gates, she looked up at an engraved panel filled with writing. The last part was level with her eyes.*

Lasciate ogne speranza, voi ch'intrate
*Abandon all hope, ye who enter here.*

*"No!" she screamed. She pushed herself away, back into the mist and smoke behind her. The two men turned and beckoned.*

Jennifer. Jennifer.

*She was fighting her way through a forest, alone now, then wading through a river blazing with fire that in an instant became a sea of mud, clawing at her, clinging, pulling her down. Thunder crashed and her name echoed across the sky.*

Jennifer! Jennifer!

*The storm disappeared and the sky filled with a blinding light, dazzling her, torturing her eyes as the sound of the voice calling her name became louder and louder.*

Jennifer!

A hand was squeezing hers.

Her eyes opened and focussed slowly on Derek's face. He was smiling at her but his eyes were etched with fear.

"Jennifer," he whispered, "you're back."

She looked at his face in incomprehension.

"Where have I been?" she croaked.

"I don't know, Jen, but you're here now."

In spite of trying to inject encouragement into his voice, it was full of doubt.

*She drifted off again into a troubled sleep of demons. Tall identical female demons all with the same face. Olivia Freneton's face. One had a hand dripping blood, one was wielding a massive side-handle baton, far too large and heavy to lift but nevertheless she was lifting it. Another was holding a large fluffy white cat in her arms. The cat was terrified. That particular Olivia Freneton pulled her lips back in a snarl as the cat tried to wrest itself from her clutches. The others were all screeching with laughter at its terror.*

Jennifer's eyes shot open.

"Languid!" she screamed.

"Shh. It's OK, Jen," said a male voice close to her ear. "Hey, you're sweating."

A damp cloth dabbed at her face.

She turned her eyes to see who was holding the cloth.

"Derek?" she said, her voice the thinnest of whispers.

He beamed. "Yes, Jen, it's me, Derek. You know me?"

She frowned. "Of course I know you," she whispered. "Why shouldn't I? What am I doing here? Why does my head hurt?"

She shifted her body slightly and winced. "Ouch. And my chest. Why does that hurt?"

"Jen, they said it would be a while till you remember, they said …"

He stopped. Her eyes had closed again. She was asleep.

He bit his lip. He'd been lying to her. What they'd actually said was that there was a strong chance she'd never wake up, and if she did, she might never regain her memory. He remembered the doctor had patted him on the arm, thinking perhaps he'd over-stated it.

"Of course, she might wake up and be fine, Mr Thyme. It does happen."

Derek had glared at him. "You wouldn't put money on it though, Doc, would you?"

The operation had lasted nine hours. There were blood clots in her brain that if not reached and dispersed would cause permanent damage. And even with them dispersed, her survival was in the lap of the gods. That had been three weeks ago. Jennifer had remained comatose since. Vital signs good, brain functions better than expected, but still comatose.

*There was now just a nothing. No people, no spectres, no form, no sound, no colours. Nothing. Then, after about a century, distantly, she heard the faintest sound, the vaguest suggestion of air moving, the gentlest of onshore breezes barely strong enough to disturb a few hairs on her head. Zephyr breezes. And slowly, glacially, the nothing brightened as the breeze picked up. It was soothing, soft, cooling.*

She opened her eyes, looking straight up into the light.

"Derek?" she said.

When there was no answer, she moved her eyes to one side. There was someone there but outside her field of vision. She willed her muscles to turn her head. It wasn't Derek. This man was white. This man was …

"Henry," she said softly. "Oh, Henry."

A tear welled from the corner of her eye.

"Welcome back, Jennifer. I knew you'd make it," he said softly, fighting the emotion in his voice. "No daughter of mine would be beaten by a little bump on the head."

She stared at him for a long time. Finally she said, "I don't remember the bump on the head; I can't have seen it coming. But I do remember her elbow jabbing into my ribs like a spear. I don't think I've ever felt so much pain."

Henry's mouth was working, his eyes creased with pleasure.

"You remember that!" He was ecstatic. "How wonderful! Not the pain of course, but how wonderful that you remember. You're really back, Jennifer."

He stroked her forehead below the bandage covering her head.

"She broke three of your ribs," he said. "They were amazed that your diaphragm wasn't punctured."

"Did they catch her? Tell me they did."

When he didn't answer immediately, she knew.

"But they had the area surrounded," she protested, her forehead creasing as she strained to remember. "OK, Hurst knew it was a risk but there wasn't time. She was going to kill the girl. They couldn't wait for the armed response unit; it would have taken too long. Did they save the girl?"

"Yes," said Henry, his tone guarded. "They saved the girl."

"That's a relief," she sighed, momentarily missing the hesitancy in Henry's voice. "So my beating wasn't quite all for nothing."

Again, there was no response, only a look of sadness, regret.

"There's something you're not telling me. Derek! Is it Derek?"

He shook his head and squeezed her hand in reassurance.

"Derek's fine. He's been here for days, sitting by the bed, holding your hand, whispering your name. We all have, but Derek took the lion's share. I think he felt responsible."

"Idiot. It was my own fault."

She paused. "What do you mean, 'we all have'?"

"Derek, Pietro and I, we've sort of taken it in turns."

"Pietro? He's here?"

"Yes. He came straight over. He wanted you flown to some top clinic in Switzerland, but they said you couldn't be moved. Too dangerous."

"Typical Pietro."

He squeezed her hand some more.

"Jennifer, I've dreamed for the last three weeks of having this conversation, of hearing your voice, hearing you remember."

His voice faltered. "After what they said, when they operated on you ..."

"Three weeks? I've been out of it for three weeks?"

"And two days, yes."

She suddenly grinned. "When did they let you out?"

He laughed, the sound rich, resonant, full of joy. "The day after it all happened."

"The day after she tried to have you killed?"

"You remember?"

"Oh, yes, I remember."

She sighed. "And they let her get away? How in hell did that happen?"

"I don't know the details of it. Derek will tell you. I do know they were distracted by what had happened to you. You were obviously badly injured. Your heart stopped in the ambulance."

"Really?"

"Yes. It was close. Very close."

She nodded as her forehead puckered again in a frown. The fragments of what happened were only coming together slowly.

"I heard Hurst shout. He sounded odd."

"She'd hurt him. She hurt them all. Not Derek so much, he took a kick to the groin. Just winded really. But …"

"But what?"

"Jennifer. DI McPherson is dead. She killed him."

"She …" Jennifer thought she would choke as she felt her throat contract. Tears welled up in her eyes. "Rob McPherson?"

She sniffed and spluttered a sad laugh through a sob, her lips moving in all directions as she tried to speak.

"He threatened to handcuff me to the steering wheel."

"It's as well he didn't; you'd have been a sitting duck for Freneton."

"Henry? Can I sit up? Will they let me?"

"I think it's OK," he said, leaning forward to put an arm behind her back. "No sudden movement though."

"Henry, I want you to hold me. Put your arms round me. Oh, God. Poor Rob. He was a lovely man underneath that gruff exterior. Do anything for you."

She leaned her face into his chest and sobbed. He let her cry; let her pour out the pain.


Later, Derek filled in the rest of the details. Mike Hurst had blamed himself for everything, even though it was understood that any delay would have resulted in the death of the Chinese girl.

"As it was, she was probably only seconds from being whacked," said Derek. "The bosses reckon he should've tried more over the radio on the way. The armed response unit was only a few minutes behind. They claim he should have called them earlier. If he had, they would have been there with him."

"I don't agree," said Jennifer, shaking her head. "He called them as we were running from the hotel. I heard him. He was yelling down the phone as he got in the car. There was no reason to call them before. We just got there first — nineteen minutes, I think it was. Bat out of hell stuff, but it made a difference. And there was no reason to think it would get so violent. He made a tactical decision to go straight in."

"Which cost Rob McPherson his life," said Derek, his voice flat.

"Hurst saved yours though," she countered. "If he and Neil hadn't bombed down the lane, she'd have been beating you to death. Hurst shouldn't be taking the blame, he did what was right for the circumstances."

She paused. "How are Neil's teeth? Henry said he'd lost a few."

"Six," said Derek. "Took that baton right across his mouth. But he's OK. Resilient sort of bloke, Neil. He'll never forget it, but he'll be OK. I think he'll be going for early retirement though. Hurst too. He's put in his papers, but he's been told he'll have to wait until the official enquiry's over."

"I suppose my having been there isn't helping his case," said Jennifer.

"Big time, although Hawkins is claiming responsibility for that. What they do accept is that without you, there would definitely be one more dead prostitute, and who knows, she might have killed Baines. She certainly gave him a near death experience with the dose of Rohypnol she poured into him."

"Have they any idea where she went?"

"The sniffer dogs followed a blood scent to the car park in Thieves Wood, the part of the forest on the other side of the A60. She must have had a route planned and a vehicle parked there. No cameras there though, so there's nothing."

"White van," said Jennifer. "I'll bet it was a white van. I talked to Hurst about it when we were at Freneton's house. It would be big enough to drive the off-road bike into. She probably had ramps in it. The off-roader was for a quick getaway in an emergency, and it would evaporate into an innocent-looking white van. Bet she'll have had another place somewhere in Nottingham. Off the grid in another name. Somewhere with a garage big enough for the white van."

After three days, Jennifer was out of bed, sitting in a chair by the window dressed in jeans and a loose white top. She hated the hospital robes and had insisted that she be allowed to dress in her own clothes. Not wanting to stress her, her consultant agreed.

"Anything to keep you happy, young lady, I don't want you discharging yourself in a fit of pique. You have quite a bit of healing still to do and I want you where I can see you."

"I'm fine, Doctor, really. My head's not hurting nearly as much."

"Nevertheless, Jennifer, it's better you're here. At home, I've been told you might be tempted to run around the streets or jump on a bicycle. You will be able to do that, and soon, the way you're recovering, but for now, I want that temptation kept out of your way."

There was a knock at the open door and Peter Hawkins put his head into the room.

"I can provide handcuffs if that would help, Doc," he said. "It's probably the only way you'll guarantee keeping her here."

Jennifer gave him a disdainful look.

"I can pick handcuff locks," she lied.

The consultant smiled. "I'll leave you two together."


"Good to see you looking so well, Jennifer," said Hawkins as he sat in the armchair opposite her. "You gave us all quite a fright."

"I'm fine, sir, thanks."

She paused, her hands pulling at each other, her teeth biting on her lower lip.

"But I'm gutted about Rob. And I'm gutted I missed his funeral."

He nodded. "Yes, it was while you were still unconscious. Big turnout."

"I'll go and see his widow once I get out of here. And of course I'll visit his grave. I need some closure on that one. I still can't get my head around it."

"You all put your lives on the line that night, Jennifer. If Freneton had had her way, she'd have done for the lot of you. She's utterly ruthless and, thanks to the police force, highly proficient in unarmed combat. Put some sort of weapon in her hand and my money would be on her against almost anyone."

"What about the knife wound? Wouldn't it have needed treatment?"

Hawkins nodded. "Definitely. Mike Hurst saw it happen, saw the crazed look on the Chinese girl's face as she flew at Freneton, and he saw Freneton react. He said there was suddenly blood everywhere, so it must have been deep."

"Yes," agreed Jennifer. "Derek said when he first saw me he thought my face was smashed up, there was so much blood on it. But it turned out to be all hers from when she pushed me away."

She paused, looking at her hands, remembering her failed attempt to subdue Freneton. Everything had happened so fast.

"No indication of where she is, then?" she asked, looking up at him.

"We think she went abroad. Probably had a place ready and waiting. Her face is on all the Interpol stop lists, but you know how it is, faces can be changed. I doubt we'll see her back here."

"I wonder," said Jennifer, more to herself than to Hawkins.

He took a deep breath. "Anyway, Cotton, I've something to discuss with you."

She lifted her eyes to his, a quizzical smile at the corners of her mouth.

"Am I still Cotton, sir?"

"If you want to be, yes. I've been discussing things with the ACC who in his decisive way has run everything up to the chief constable."

She waited, amused by his jibe.

"The chief constable came back with an interesting suggestion. Basically, of course, I told him that I wanted you back, reinstated in SCF, if that's what you want. It won't be the same of course. Mike Hurst has gone, and Bottomley's almost definitely throwing in the towel. And Rob's …"

"Derek will be there though, won't he?"

Hawkins paused, looking down at the floor. "He's put in for a transfer."

"What! He didn't tell me."

"Only happened yesterday. He's going to need a lot of guaranteed time for his training. It seems his coach is very serious about him being in the next Olympic squad. Can't have him charging around Nottingham at all hours; he'll need his beauty sleep. So he's moving to a fraud unit based in the Met."

"The bugger, he might have said."

"I think he's probably a bit hesitant, and it really did only all happen in the last forty-eight hours. Don't be too hard on him."

"He'd better get gold," said Jennifer. "I'll be there screaming for him."

Hawkins smiled. "Anyway, Jennifer, in the light of all that, the chief constable has an alternative suggestion, if you're interested."

Jennifer frowned, wondering what was coming.

Hawkins sat back. "I told him I'm against it, that I don't want to lose you. But he's been looking into your background. The Italian stuff, and your studies at university."

"He has?"

"Impressed him. Especially the art history. There's an art forgery squad at the Met. Odd bunch, but they do some interesting work. Very international some of it. They're always on the look out for top class young officers with the right extra qualifications. Seems you tick all the boxes. And some."

He was watching her eyes and could tell she was hooked.

"There'll be a chap popping in for a chat tomorrow, if that's convenient."

"The Met," said Jennifer, her face lighting up. "I can go and live with Henry."

## Chapter Forty-Five

Ten days after Olivia Freneton's escape from Harlow Wood, Giacomo Riley walked into the sunshine from a café on the edge of Petit Han, a small village that nestled unobtrusively on a minor road twenty kilometres south of Liège in Belgium. He was carrying a tray of pastries and coffee.

"Here we go, Nore, these'll fill a gap till lunchtime."

Noreen Smart picked up a pastry packed with cream and sank her teeth into it.

"They'll certainly help, Jackie," she said, through a foamy white mouthful, "but me legs are still aching like mad."

"I've told you, Nore, you're working too hard. Leave the cycling to me; just let your legs go round."

"I do, Jackie, but they're still aching."

She eyed the gleaming tandem leaning against a wall by the table where they were sitting. Jackie cleaned it every evening after their day's cycling through the back roads of northern France and southern Belgium. It was relatively flat countryside he'd figured wouldn't be too much for Noreen to complain about on their first continental excursion. She was getting stronger, but he still had to do the lion's share of the work. He didn't care. At the end of every day, they'd find a campsite, unpack their tiny bell tent from the bike's panniers, cook dinner over a camping stove, drink some red wine and then crawl into their double sleeping bag. He was constantly having to remind Noreen not to squeal too loudly once they'd turned out their wind-up LED lamp.

After the trauma of finding the body of the murdered prostitute in Harlow Wood, it had been difficult to persuade Noreen to get back on the tandem. Her parents had been extremely understanding, not blaming Giacomo in any way. They'd believed the story about happening across the body as the couple had been strolling, stretching their legs after several hours in the saddle. Their main concern was that Noreen wasn't going to suffer any long-term psychological damage from the experience.

Giacomo had been his usual attentive self. He loved his girl and he wanted to see her right. And he wanted to get her out on the bike again. Woodland trysts were now out of the question, Noreen was adamant about that. But when her Jackie came up with the idea of camping in proper organised campsites, places with good facilities, security fences, other campers … and their own tent … she didn't take too much persuading.

He'd cycled around the area with his local club, done some racing, knew the terrain. He wanted to keep it simple for her.

He had and they were having a great time, although Noreen still liked to remind him about her tortured calves.

She was rubbing one as she finished a second pastry, her eyes looking at something on the far side of the tables behind Giacomo.

"That's what we want Jackie, one of them," she said, pointing with a creamy finger.

Giacomo turned to see what was interesting her so much.

"A motorbike?" he said. "You're joking. Noisy things."

"That one ain't, Jackie. I saw it pull up while you were inside. I could hardly hear it, it was so quiet. And it was a woman driving it. I was really surprised when she took off her helmet. Bit sour looking. But imagine; that'd be the way to travel. Looks very comfy."

Giacomo stood and walked over to the motorbike, taking in its sleek, no-nonsense design. He noted the badge on the side of the tank. BMW. Smart bike. His best mate's dad had an older, smaller model. This one looked in another league. He bent down to check out the engine.

"Can I help you?" said a voice from behind him.

He stood and turned round to see a woman dressed in black leathers eyeing him coldly. She'd just put down a tray on a table near the BMW, her helmet resting on a chair alongside.

"I was admiring the bike," he said, giving her a smile that wasn't returned. "Going far? Bet you could cover some ground on that."

"Touring," said Olivia.

"Camping, like us?" said Giacomo, nodding his enthusiasm.

"I prefer hotels," she replied.

"Right," he said. Then he noticed the bandage on her left hand.

"Come off the bike?" he asked.

She frowned as she followed his gaze.

"Oh, that. No, it's nothing. A cut that needs protecting."

---

The cut had worried her. It was deep and needed attention, stitches. A large number of stitches. But she couldn't go to an A&E, they would all have been notified. There was one person, but he was too far away that night; she'd have to go the following morning.

She had sprinted as quietly as she could, crossing the A60 a hundred yards away from where the police vehicles were parked near the barrier. She could hear sirens in the distance; the place would soon be swarming. And they'd bring dogs.

It was a few hundred yards through the wood to the car park and her van. Running with her hand tucked under her armpit was awkward, but she had to keep pressure on it in an attempt to staunch the bleeding.

She stopped at the edge of the car park. There was only one other vehicle there, an ageing Beetle whose springs were squeaking a quiet protest as the car bounced rhythmically. It was parked well away from her van.

Courting couple, she thought. They'll be getting a rude surprise before long as the police spread out their search.

She retrieved the key from where she'd hidden it on the ground behind the front offside wheel and climbed into the van. She had little time, but she needed to bind her hand. She grabbed some cotton waste and a relatively clean rag from behind the seat.

Within a minute she was away, her route taking her along a series of minor roads until she went under the M1 motorway at Pinxton where she turned south heading for Eastwood, Heanor and on to Ilkeston. There she went east, driving under the M1 again at Trowell, following the road through Wollaton close to her now-abandoned house. At the Nottingham ring road she turned right to drive anti-clockwise round the city.

Her sense of relief was palpable as she hit the remote to open the doors of the large garage in a back street of West Bridgford. It was the perfect anonymous haven, the flat over the top accessed directly by stairs from the garage.

The following morning, dosed up with painkillers, her hand cleaned and temporarily bound, she hit the road north to Manchester, hoping that the police weren't going to be stopping all white vans. They weren't and two hours later she pulled up outside a back-to-back terraced house in a street of mainly boarded up, abandoned dwellings.

The seedy, shuffling former doctor who lived there eyed her cautiously when he opened the door to her insistent knocking.

"Took your time, Norman," she said, pushing past him into the dingy slum. "I don't like being left standing on the street. Not in this neighbourhood."

She stuck her head into the front room where a tattooed youth was playing a computer game on an ageing television.

"Get him into the street to watch my van. I don't want any of your local boys touching it."

Norman barked an instruction to the youth as he picked up the remote to kill the TV. Then he followed Olivia into the kitchen.

She'd first met former Doctor Norman Swanson when she'd busted him for performing abortions on illegal immigrant girls in a surgery not fit for any form of human habitation, let alone medicine. He'd already been struck off for peddling prescription drugs, served time for it, and if she'd pressed it, he would have gone down for a long stretch. But Olivia had recognised an opportunity, told him his fortune, and thereafter he was hers for whenever she might need him. No questions asked. And she needed him now.

Having insisted he sterilise everything twice, Olivia had returned to her van neatly stitched and bandaged — Swanson was a competent physician, just an incompetent human being — and driven back to Nottingham. Dosed up with antibiotics, she'd waited a week, then another two days, after which she'd hit the road on her BMW. Her hand had healed enough for her to operate the clutch lever and she was going crazy holed up in the flat. She was also running short of fresh food, but there was no way she could risk going shopping, disguises notwithstanding. She figured that the SCF would have worked out that she had a place in the city, and they were probably checking CCTV tapes for white vans. It was exciting, but she didn't want to push her luck. It had been a near thing, thanks to the damn Cotton girl. She was gratified to hear on the local TV news that the girl was comatose and in a bad way. With McPherson dead and two of his team injured, it had not been a bad evening. As for the Chinese whore … one day she'd return the favour, drop by precious drop of blood.

But now she had to leave. Her panniers were packed with everything for her new life in rural Tuscany, a passport in Rose Doughthey's name in her bag. She would take the ferry rather than the tunnel, because they would expect her to take the tunnel, and then make her way slowly down through Europe using B-roads where there would be no cameras, no tolls, minimal police roadside checks, and, thanks to the EU, no border controls for the BMW with its new Italian plates.

Olivia finished her coffee and pastry, zipped up her jacket and buckled her helmet. She glanced across at the couple and their tandem and frowned — the couple in the Henry Silk case had been riding a tandem and this lad had a strong East Midlands accent. Coincidence? She wondered. Either way, with her bleached, spiky hair, heavy metallic earrings, dark, gothic lipstick and large fake tattoo on her neck, she bore little resemblance to the photos now distributed widely around Interpol offices.

She gunned the engine and drove off. Giacomo gave her a wave, but she ignored him.

"Cold fish, that one, Nore," he said, tucking into the last of the pastries.

# Afterword

I hope very much that you enjoyed reading this book as much as I enjoyed writing it. If you did, I should be extremely grateful if you could spend a few moments posting a review on Amazon or Goodreads (or both!). It needn't be long; one word will do — preferably a favourable one! Genuine reviews, however short, are worth a lot.

And equally as important, please recommend Irrefutable Evidence to your relatives, friends and colleagues. While word of mouth is very helpful to the cause of any author, it is particularly so for self-published authors for whom marketing is that much harder. If you tell a few people about this book or any of my other books, and they in turn tell others, the word will spread.

You can find more information about all my books and other book-related stuff on my website at davidgeorgeclarke.com. If you are on FaceBook, Instagram and/or Twitter, I'm there too:

*FB: David George Clarke - Author*
*Instagram: @davidgeorgeclarke*
*Twitter: @dgclarke_author*

# Acknowledgments

This novel could not have been completed without the brilliant help and encouragement of many people.

I had to delve back into my professional past far more in this book than in previous books, and for that I needed to dust off the grey cells to an alarming degree. My great friend Dr Bob Bramley, former custodian of the UK National DNA database and a man with a meticulous eye for forensic detail, painstakingly analysed the text and raised many, many points where I had strayed from the straight and narrow. I tried to pin the omissions on Olivia for being sloppy, but really I had no one to blame except myself.

Dr Sheilah Hamilton, a former forensic colleague in the Hong Kong Government Laboratory, also cast her critical eye over the text and brought up many points for reconsideration.

My heartfelt thanks go to both Bob and Sheilah for their input.

I should also like to thank Bob's wife Sian Bramley not only for her enthusiastic response to one of the early drafts, but also for her medical input. Jennifer is more than grateful to you as well, Sian.

As with my previous books, Anne Mensini, Sanford Foster and Luci de Norwall Cornish read early drafts, raising many salient points about the plot as well as helping to fine tune my grammar and style. I can't thank you all enough.

Thanks are also due to my son-in-law, Simon O'Reilly — the

fastest copy editor in the East! Brilliant Simon; we'll get to the bottom of the vagaries of the Kindle eventually.

I am also indebted to Susanna Capon, former TV producer and BBC commissioning editor for her invaluable comments and insight, especially with respect to the early chapters where she gently reminded me that less is more.

A number of others have also kindly read through the book in draft form and all were very positive and helpful in their comments. Thanks go to my sister Jill Pemberton, to my step-daughter Zoe O'Reilly, to Wendy Bearns and Eva Kolouchova, and of course to my wife Gail who has once again been a sounding board for ideas, a critical and constructive reviewer of drafts, and an enthusiastic supporter of the project.

I have designed my own cover once again, and there were, as ever, several versions on the way as it progressed from my original idea to its present form. Many thanks for comments and suggestions to Gail, Lea, Jonathan, Zoe and Daniel.

I am also very grateful to Susanna Moles for the loan of the wonderful red high-heel shoe that I used in the cover design, and to Rob Moles for suggestions on photographing it. That all came about at Casa Moles during a memorable summer's evening under a magical Tuscan moon.

Final thanks for brilliant proofreading and copy editing services go to Linda Davy in Hong Kong. Linda's remarkable eagle eye picked up many points that would otherwise have slipped through the net. I am indebted to you Linda; you're the best!

David George Clarke

## A Final Word

Do you have kids or grandchildren, a favourite godson or goddaughter, a class of kids you teach or support in some way? My wife Gail is an author and illustrator who has published seven beautifully illustrated children's books. They are written in rhyme that children from 4–9 years just love reading or having read to them.

*Patrick's Birthday Message*
*Searching for Skye — An Arctic Tern Adventure*
*Cosmos the Curious Whale*
*The Chameleon Who Couldn't Change Colour*
*Sharks — Our Ocean Guardians*
*Ndotto — An Elephant Rescue Story*
*Mischief at the Waterhole*

You can find more details at Gail's website:

www.gailclarkeauthor.com

31030659R00223

Printed in Poland
by Amazon Fulfillment
Poland Sp. z o.o., Wrocław